# THEATER OF SPIRITS

VICTORIAN GOTHIC SERIES

BOOK I

ROBIN TRENT

THEATER OF SPIRITS
VICTORIAN GOTHIC SERIES
BOOK ONE
ROBIN TRENT
DARK MUSE
PRESS

Victorian Gothic: Theater of Spirits by Robin Trent



ISBN: 978-1-7349238-7-2 (Paperback)



Front cover image by Robin Trent

Book design by Robin Trent using Canva.

Printed by Dark Muse Press LLC, in the United States of America.

First printing edition 2026.

Dark Muse Press

4030 Smeltzer Rd.

Marion, OH 43302

www.darkmusepress.org

# PROLOGUE

Dartford, Kent, England 1847

A violent peal of thunder tore the night in two, jolting the young boy from a fevered, uneasy sleep. The dream—that dream—had tormented him again. In it, his schoolmates ringed him like a pack of jeering wolves, their pointing fingers as sharp as knives, their laughter echoing with cruel delight. Thaddeus woke with a gasp, chest heaving as though the very air had been stolen from him. The nightmare lurked perilously close to truth; the boys at preparatory school tormented him so ruthlessly that he would have sooner faced the gallows than return. And yet, return he must, once the holiday reprieve came to its swift end.

He lay stiff and small in the vast expanse of the four-poster bed, its curtains billowing faintly with every draught. Outside, the storm raged with a savage hunger, but it was not thunder that next drew his attention. Something moved—soft, deliberate—in the shadowed corner near the door.

A sound followed. Heavy breathing. Slow. Wet. Uneven.

Thaddeus's gaze darted toward the wardrobe. Lightning ripped across the sky, and for a brief, terrible instant, the room was illuminated in stark white fire. In that flash, he saw the figure—tall, motionless, framed in the doorway as though carved from the darkness itself.

It wore a white nightgown, long and flowing, the lace at the collar fluttering with each ragged breath. For a terrified moment, Thaddeus wondered if his father had taken to sleepwalking again. But as the figure lurched forward, its steps hesitant, dragging, he knew—instinctively, irrevocably—that no living soul stood before him.

The spectre halted at the foot of his bed. The laboured breathing grew louder, heavier, until it thundered through the chamber as if part of the storm outside.

Thaddeus yanked the covers to his chin, then—with a tremor of desperate cowardice—hid entirely beneath the blankets. His heart hammered against his ribs like a frantic prisoner. When at last he mustered the smallest flicker of courage, he lifted the edge of the quilt and peered into the gloom.

The ghost remained.

It stood perfectly still, its bulging, lifeless eyes fixed upon him. The jaw hung slack as though unhinged, and its hair—wild, frizzled, haloed like a dandelion gone to seed—framed its ashen face with a dreadful absurdity. The storm clouds thinned for a moment, and pale moonlight spilled into the room, outlining the figure in a spectral glow. A cold unlike any earthly chill swept through the chamber. Thaddeus trembled uncontrollably as his breath left him in pale vapors.

The ghost leaned forward. Its hand, blue-white and trembling, reached out as if in supplication.

Thaddeus screamed. He kicked. He thrashed beneath the blankets like a trapped animal until—suddenly—a warm, familiar weight pressed onto the bed. His mother's scent, gentle and human, slipped through the terror like a balm. Her arms wrapped around him, and he clung to her neck, sobbing into the hollow of her shoulder.

A roar sounded from the hallway.

Horace Raynsford stormed toward the room, candle raised high, his figure grotesque in the flickering light. He looked every inch the wrathful patriarch.

"Judith! How many times must I tell you not to indulge the boy? He will never grow up if you continue coddling him!"

Judith did not release her son. She merely rolled her eyes—subtly, expertly—so her husband would not see. "I will check on my child whenever I deem it necessary, Horace. And you will not interfere. Go back to bed. Now."

Her voice carried a steel seldom heard in the household. Both father and son stared at her, equally startled.

Horace's jaw opened, then closed, then opened again like a fish gasping on dry land. Whatever words he sought refused to come. At last he turned, shoulders tight with restrained indignation, and strode from the room. His candlelight retreated down the corridor, shrinking until it vanished.

Judith returned her gaze to her son.

"Another bad dream?"

Thaddeus swallowed hard. "No, Mummy. It was a ghost," he whispered, fearful his father might reappear. Horace tolerated no talk of spirits. His mother, however, believed otherwise.

"They cannot harm you, darling," Judith murmured, brushing his damp hair from his forehead. "Ghosts are merely people who exist in another state. Nothing more. Nothing less."

It was a notion Thaddeus would carry with him for the rest of his life.

"I know... but they frighten me." His voice wavered. "I don't think I'll ever be brave like you."

"Oh, my little man," she said softly, cupping his cheek. "You already possess more strength than you imagine. One day, you'll find your courage—and when you do, you will be formidable indeed. Just you wait." She playfully tweaked his nose. "Never forget how dearly I love you."

She tucked the blankets securely around him and kissed his cheek.

"Good night, Mummy," he whispered.

"Good night, little man."

She left the room, and with her went the phantom shadows that haunted the corners. Thaddeus, warm beneath the covers, still felt the gentle imprint of her kiss. He cast one last wary glance toward the closet, assuring himself nothing stirred there.

He fought sleep valiantly.

But in the end, sleep won.

# CHAPTER ONE

Dartford, Kent, England Spring, 1862

"Are you prepared, young master?" Jackson's voice was soft, yet steady—an anchor in a household perpetually brimming with storms. The old butler's eyes, kind but weary, held a sympathy he dared not voice. He placed a gentle, reassuring hand upon Thaddeus's shoulder, the gesture both protective and resigned.

Thaddeus answered only with a nod.

Jackson drew a breath and opened the heavy oak door to Horace Raynsford's study. The hinges groaned like something waking unwillingly from slumber. Within, Horace sat enthroned behind an enormous mahogany desk—its carved lion heads glaring down as if to cow all who entered. The firelight caught the rim of his spectacles, giving his eyes the glint of polished steel.

"Sir, the young master is here," Jackson announced with a bow.

"Send him in," Horace said, peering over his lenses like a magistrate over a condemned man. "And close the door."

"Yes, Sir." The butler stepped aside, allowing Thaddeus to cross the threshold. The door shut behind him with the finality of a dungeon gate. Jackson remained outside, ears pricked despite himself. After decades in Raynsford Manor, he knew that listening was not merely habit—it was survival.

Inside, the study exhaled a suffocating heat. Heavy emerald curtains strangled the windows, allowing no breath of morning air to intrude. A thick green carpet smothered the floorboards, and the monstrous fireplace roared with an oppressive, unnecessary fury. Every choice had been orchestrated by Horace for one purpose: to unnerve and dominate.

"Sit down, Thaddeus. I must speak with you." The command cracked through the thick air.

Thaddeus chose a distant, oversized chair—deliberately far from both father and hearth. A small defiance. A tiny rebellion. One Horace would notice, and despise.

Horace inhaled, straightened, and adopted the strained civility he reserved for matters of legacy. "Thaddeus, you are aware that you will become Lord Raynsford upon my passing. Consequently, certain expectations must be impressed upon you. To begin—"

Thaddeus's mind drifted. He had heard this sermon countless times, its words etched into his memory like scars: duty, lineage, honour, decorum. While his father droned on—voice as dull as the crackling fire—Thaddeus envisioned anything else. A life unfettered. A path of his choosing. Not a future shackled to a title he never wanted.

"Thaddeus." His name lashed through the air.

Thaddeus blinked. Horace's face had drawn tight with irritation.

"Pay attention." The cane rapped sharply against the desk, the sound reverberating through the chamber like the toll of a judgment bell.

"Yes, Father." Thaddeus's voice was quiet, but it held an edge.

"It has been arranged," Horace said coldly, "and you will comply. I will brook no refusal."

Thaddeus stiffened. "What has been arranged?"

The question ignited Horace's temper. "When I speak, boy, you will give me the courtesy of listening!" He surged to his feet, pacing the room with stiff, furious strides, muttering into the pipe clenched between his teeth. He snatched a decanter from the cabinet, sloshed amber liquid into a glass, and swallowed it in a single burning gulp. "Always dreaming. Never grounded. Never reliable."

"I can hear you, Father," Thaddeus said evenly.

"As well you should." Horace jabbed his cane into the carpet. "You will marry Hortense Remington. Her dowry is considerable and will bolster our family's position. The arrangement has been settled. You will honour it."

The blood drained from Thaddeus's face. His hands clamped down on the carved armrests until his knuckles blanched. His breath thinned to a thread.

"No," he whispered.

Horace froze. He turned slowly, like a predator scenting defiance. In three strides he stood over his son, arm raised, cane poised to strike. For a terrible heartbeat Thaddeus thought he might actually bring it down.

But Horace hesitated. His fury trembled in his hand before he lowered it, step by step, as if wrestling down a beast within.

"You torment me," he hissed. "You force me to lose control. My own son—my disappointment." His voice grew soft, dangerously soft. "You will marry this girl. It is your duty and you will obey."

Thaddeus rose so abruptly that Horace stumbled back, startled.

"You dare confront me?" Horace spat.

"You dare demand that I trade away my life to mend your financial ruin?" Thaddeus snapped. His cheeks flushed with sudden heat, but he did not withdraw the accusation.

"You insolent wretch." Horace's voice quivered with venom. "Remember your place."

Thaddeus's reply was louder, more forceful than he intended—yet undeniably his. "I will not bind myself to a woman I do not love. I will not condemn myself to a lifetime of misery to salvage your reputation or your accounts."

Horace's rage ballooned monstrously. His face darkened to a shade bordering on apoplexy; spittle frothed at the corners of his mouth. "What?" he sputtered, nearly choking. "This—this is Judith's influence. Filling your head with nonsense! Marriage is a transaction, boy. A contract of commerce and consolidation. Love has no place in it." He slammed his cane to the floor. "You are a Raynsford. You will serve your lineage, or you will ruin it."

"You cannot dictate whom I marry." Thaddeus strode to the door and threw it open.

Jackson, caught eavesdropping, leapt back with a startled squeak.

"Come back here, you impudent fool!" Horace bellowed. "I will not tolerate this! I forbid it!" His collar snapped its button with the force of his fury, which sprang off and struck him across the cheek. He clutched his chest, breath wheezing as the fury drained into exhaustion.

"Summon my wife," he gasped, collapsing into his chair. "Tell Judith... to come at once. And shut the door."

Jackson bowed quickly—and closed the door with deliberate quiet.

A slow smile curled across the butler's face as he walked away.

At last, the young master had stood up to the tyrant of Raynsford Manor.

And what a magnificent row it had been.

Thaddeus tore down the corridor, his boot heals echoing like fleeing heartbeats through the cavernous halls of Raynsford Manor. The air itself seemed to constrict around him, thick with the weight of his father's fury. He needed escape—not merely from the room where Horace's voice still seemed to reverberate, but from the house, the estate and the suffocating lineage that sought to bind him like a chained spectre to its ancestral gloom.

He burst from the manor into the open air and made straight for the stables. He might have called for the stable boy, but impatience burned hot and wild in him; he could not bear a moment's delay.

His mind churned as violently as the storm clouds gathering on the horizon. His ears rang with the ghostly echo of his father's decree. It was always him who must sacrifice—never his gentle younger brother, never his bright and cherished sister. As eldest son, he was the offering laid upon the altar of Raynsford duty.

His hands shook as he tightened the saddle strap—a little too sharply.

Trotter cried out, shifting away with an indignant toss of the head.

Thaddeus exhaled, shame softening his frantic edges. "My apologies, old friend. I meant you no harm." The chestnut horse pressed his forehead to Thaddeus's, forgiving as only an animal can be. Thaddeus rested a hand against its warm cheek, grateful for the steadiness.

A slender hand, warm and delicate, curled around his forearm.

"Running from me so soon?" a familiar voice teased.

Thaddeus turned, and the tension eased from him as if unwound by her very presence. Athena stood in the dim light of the stable, her eyes—soft, almond-shaped, full of warmth—lifting to meet his. Her hair, long and silken, cascaded over her shoulders like a midnight waterfall.

"Athena," he breathed, drinking in her scent—jasmine, hearthsmoke, something undeniably her.

"What sorrow furrows your brow, my love?" she asked, stepping close enough that the shadows wrapped around them both. Her proximity melted him, as it always did. The thought of losing her carved a hollow ache beneath his ribs.

"I quarrelled with Father," he murmured, unwilling to voice the darker truth.

"Well," she said with a rueful little smile, "that is enough to sour anyone's day. Taking Trotter out, are you?" She tilted her head playfully, trying to coax him into meeting her gaze.

"I must clear my thoughts." He forced a small smile. "He knows how to needle me."

"Then ride until the world feels lighter," she whispered. She pressed a gentle kiss to his cheek before retreating with her parcels toward the warmth of the kitchen. But even as she walked away, a cloud of worry clung to her shoulders. She knew the cause of his unrest. She had long understood the unspoken truth: their stations in life ran parallel, never meant to intertwine.

Thaddeus turned back to his horse, murmuring reassurances as he checked the tack with meticulous care. His muscles coiled under his coat—readied for flight. Just as he swung himself into the saddle, the stable door creaked open.

Nathan, the stable boy, froze mid-step, eyes widening. "Forgive me, m'lord—I didn't know you were here. I was out with the muck." He darted aside as Trotter stamped impatiently, mirroring his master's agitation.

"It's all right, Nathan. Open the door."

The boy complied, leaping back as Thaddeus shot through the opening like a man pursued by demons. Nathan watched, wide-eyed, as horse and rider vanished down the path, swallowed by wind and dust.

Trotter's hooves thundered across the countryside, beating time with the frantic rhythm of Thaddeus's thoughts. The landscape blurred—trees smearing into dark strokes, fields dissolving into streaks of grey and green. It felt as though he rode not through England, but through the very marrow of his own despair.

All his life he had lived beneath Horace Raynsford's shadow—a looming, iron-wrought presence that dictated his clothes, his lessons, his bearing, his future. Every choice had been chosen for him. Every step measured. Every path predetermined. Now, even his heart was to be bartered away in a marriage forged in greed.

The reins creaked under Thaddeus's tightening grip.

Was this to be his fate? Bound in a gilded cage, husband to a woman he did not love, heir to a title that was more like a shroud than an honour?

The very notion suffocated him.

He slowed Trotter gradually, drawing a deep breath as the horse stamped and tossed its mane. A strange clarity washed over him—quiet, cold, resolute.

He could leave.

The idea rose in him like a lighthouse flame in storm-dark waters.

He could flee this suffocating estate. Escape to London. In that sprawling maze of soot and gaslight, where thousands swarmed like restless spirits, his father could never find him. London—with its crowded streets, its theatres, its secrets, its night-veiled freedoms. A place where Thaddeus Raynsford could shed his name and become a man of his own choosing.

Yes. Yes, it could be done.

A slow smile crept across his face—cautious at first, then blooming into something fierce and determined.

He would play the obedient son for a while longer. He would bow, and nod, and feign acquiescence until the moment was ripe.

And then he would vanish into the night.

His own life—his true life—awaited him.

And no Raynsford decree could bind what was already breaking free.

By the time Thaddeus returned to Raynsford Manor, dusk had swallowed the road. He guided his horse into the stables in a markedly lighter humour than when he had fled, his spirits buoyed—almost dangerously—by the boldness of his newfound resolve. Yet the moment his boots struck the straw-strewn floor and he relinquished Trotter's reins to the stable boy, a shadow seemed to fall across his path.

Jackson materialised at his elbow with the silent certainty of a spectre.

"Master Thaddeus," he intoned, bowing with mechanical precision, "your mother bids me deliver a message."

Upon the silver tray he extended lay a single linen-folded envelope, pristine and ominously formal.

A chill threaded its way along Thaddeus's spine. He knew—oh, too well—what such ceremonial neatness heralded. With wooden fingers, he broke the fold. His mother's elegant script stared back at him like a verdict:

*You are requested to attend dinner this evening and to make the acquaintance of your intended bride.*

*Mother*

The words constricted around his chest like tightening bands of iron. For one suspended moment he felt the fragile edifice of his plans tremble. *No*, he reminded himself fiercely. *This alters nothing. You must play the obedient son a little longer—only that.*

Thaddeus lifted his gaze, affixing the semblance of a smile onto his features—an expression so strained that even the ever-impassive Jackson did not appear deceived.

"Very well," he managed. "I reek of horse, so a bath must be prepared. See to it, will you, Jackson?"

"Yes, sir. At once, sir." Jackson bowed again and stepped aside, granting passage.

As Thaddeus strode toward the manor, the polished floors and shuttered windows seemed to watch him with mute, anticipatory judgement. Behind him, Jackson exchanged a conspiratorial wink with the stable boy, who grinned broadly while Trotter tossed his head and gave a restless, echoing neigh—as though sensing that the walls of Raynsford Manor were inching ever closer around its young master.

# CHAPTER TWO

The dining room had been transformed into a fragile illusion of grandeur. Fine china—too fine for their dwindling means—glimmered beneath the chandelier's wan light, while linen napkins, starched as if to defy reality, perched beside crystal flutes that had not seen wine of quality in years. Thaddeus paused upon the threshold, a faint grimace tightening his jaw. His parents were once more determined to play the part of genteel aristocrats, though the last vestiges of their wealth had thinned to a whisper.

"Well, do you not look dapper," Judith murmured, drifting toward him with a smile too light for her weary eyes.

"Good evening, Mother." He brushed a dutiful kiss upon her cheek. "I see all the preparations have been made."

"Tsk." She tapped his chest with her lace handkerchief, a gesture both playful and brittle. "Your father insists that everything be perfect this evening."

"Yes. It isn't every day one sells one's son for a dowry. One might imagine the money flowing in my direction, but alas..." Bitterness edged his voice like a blade.

Judith stepped back, studying him with a fleeting sorrow. "We all make sacrifices for the family, Thad. It is the way of the world." With a rustle of skirts, she turned and swept toward the kitchen, as though motion alone might keep her heart from breaking.

The Remingtons arrived in a wine-coloured Landau polished to a mirror's sheen. Mr. and Mrs. Remington descended first, stiff with importance, before their daughter emerged. Hortense was petite and fair, her golden hair piled high in glossy curls. Jewels trembled at her ears as she dipped her head, casting a shy, deliberate smile toward Thaddeus.

"My dear Miss Remington, I am honoured," he said, bowing low. When he rose, he offered his arm; she accepted it with a fluttering giggle, exactly as expected. Behind them, her parents exchanged approving glances, seeing nothing amiss—nothing of the turmoil seething beneath Thaddeus's polished exterior.

Dinner, orchestrated by Judith with obsessive care, unfolded like a play on a slowly tipping stage. Pheasant, vegetables, cherry pudding—each dish served with ceremonial precision. A French wine, suspect in provenance but elegant enough in bottle, completed the illusion.

Hortense, seated opposite Thaddeus, picked delicately at her food and confined her remarks to the weather and women's fashions, her voice soft as spun sugar. Another man might have found her charming. Thaddeus merely endured the rising irritation of a man trapped—her trivialities falling on him like the ticking of a clock marking the end of his freedom.

Athena entered then, carrying a tray. Her gaze lifted for the briefest moment—just long enough for despair to flicker across her features. Thaddeus's heart tightened. He caught her eyes, silently pleading for patience, for faith. It was his father's design—never his. But the moment did not escape Judith... nor, grievously, Horace.

Horace pivoted smoothly to Mr. Remington. "I was curious about your shipping ventures..."

Thaddeus drifted in and out of the conversation until Mr.

Remington declared with pride, "We transport everything—from spices and cotton to labor contracts. Black ivory, Mr. Raynsford. The colonies have an endless appetite for it."

Athena flinched as though struck. She retreated so quickly her skirts whispered like fleeing spirits.

Thaddeus's stomach twisted. Remington could call it labor, passage, brokerage, debt. Thaddeus knew better. Whatever name the law permitted him to write, the thing beneath it was servitude.

"Labor contracts," Thaddeus said coolly. "An elegant phrase. It almost conceals the chains."

Mr. Remington chuckled, a sound without warmth. "Yes, well, take the Americas, for instance. They trumpet freedom loudly enough, yet their ports, plantations, and brokers receive my cargo with even greater enthusiasm. Hypocrisy, plain and simple. Why should we be any different?"

The room seemed to press in around Thaddeus. He turned to Hortense. "And what say you, Miss Remington? Should we disdain a nation that binds men in chains while praising liberty?"

Hortense blanched, then lifted her chin. "I do not think it my place to have an opinion on such matters, Mr. Raynsford. I defer to those more learned." She raised her glass in a dainty salute to her father.

"Just so," Mr. Remington said proudly.

Thaddeus's irritation sharpened. "But suppose you were entitled to an opinion—what then?"

Her expression cooled. "If you insist: I believe every person has their place, and those born to servitude are suited to it. I see no contradiction in the Americans' stance. It is simply the natural order."

Mr. Remington beamed. "Spoken like a true Remington."

The pheasant turned to ash upon Thaddeus's tongue. "Well, the war in America may change all that. I hear Mr. Lincoln means to strike at slavery before the year is out."

"My son is sentimental," Horace interjected smoothly. "He does not yet grasp the ways of the world." He gave a sly wink to Remington.

Judith's eyes dropped to her lap, mortified. "Let us turn to brighter subjects. Hortense, my dear, your gown is exquisite. Is it not the latest French fashion?"

Relieved, Hortense preened. "Why yes—Father gifted it to me."

"Only the best for my little girl," Mr. Remington declared.

Judith glanced at her son then—saw the storm gathering behind his eyes. She gave him the smallest shake of her head, a plea more desperate than words. Thaddeus softened, barely. He raised his glass to her in a silent, bitter truce.

The remainder of the evening passed beneath a veneer of politeness, though the air grew tight with unspoken things. When the guests finally departed, Thaddeus accompanied Hortense to the Landau.

"Good evening, Miss Remington. I trust the dinner pleased you," he said with a distant politeness.

"Oh indeed," she said, radiant with self-satisfaction. "Until our next meeting, Thaddeus."

She glided into the carriage, pausing to cast him a coy look. He bowed deeply, his expression unreadable.

As the wheels rumbled away into the night, his mother appeared beside him.

He turned to her, face set in stone.

"No," he said simply—and strode up the stairs two at a time, vanishing into the shadows of the upper hall.

THE WEEKS that followed passed with disquieting swiftness, like pages torn hastily from a book. Within Raynsford Manor, the air itself seemed charged with a tense expectancy. Thaddeus moved through those days with the careful precision of an actor upon a stage —dutiful son, obedient heir—each gesture observed by the sharp and calculating eye of Judith Raynsford.

Horace, smug in his victory, assumed the subdued demeanour of his son to be the inevitable sulking of youth bending to paternal will. He had no imagination for rebellion; he could not conceive that Thaddeus's quiet had hardened into resolve.

Judith, however, watched him with a mother's instinct—the instinct that recognises secrets forming like storm clouds behind her child's eyes. She said nothing. She rarely did. But her silence betrayed her expectation: something was coming.

Thaddeus's plan had crystallised. He would not see Hortense Remington again—he would rather have red-hot irons plunged into his eyes. He had already told his mother no, and though she had not dared defy Horace openly, she had understood. The night of his departure crept ever nearer. The only bitterness that clung to him was the knowledge that he must leave without a word to her. She could not be implicated.

And Athena—dear Athena. A familiar sorrow settled over him at the thought of her. He reassured himself she would be safe at Raynsford Manor, far safer than where he intended to go. Once he carved a place for himself in the world, he would send for her. He would not abandon her to fate, nor would he ever treat her as Horace had treated Judith.

For Thaddeus remembered too well what life under Horace Raynsford's rule meant.

As a boy, he had once challenged his father to a duel—childish bravado born from righteous fury when Horace struck Judith. He remembered the humiliation that followed: the cruel beating his father delivered, and later the jeers exchanged among Horace's friends when the tale was retold as a jest. They admired Horace's "firm hand." They never cared what that hand had done.

Thaddeus had never challenged him again. Not openly.

It was on a bright, deceptively cheerful Saturday morning that Thaddeus received a welcome distraction. Palmerston Fitzgerald III —Fitz—arrived in front of the manor seated proudly upon his newest fascination — an experimental steam carriage, its brass boiler hissing like an impatient dragon.

Thaddeus stepped onto the drive just in time to behold the contraption.

"Fitz! Of course you would be the first to acquire such a marvel," he exclaimed, unable to suppress a grin.

"It's the pinnacle of modern ingenuity!" Fitz declared, hopping down from his seat with his usual exuberance. His bowler hat sat rakishly atop his head, his handlebar moustache twitching with pride.

A sharp, derisive snort sounded behind them. Both young men turned to see Horace looming in the doorway, his expression pinched with disdain.

"What is this infernal clamour?"

"Fitz's new steam carriage, Father," Thaddeus replied. "Is it not magnificent?"

"It is a mechanical folly bound to end in blood," Horace growled. "A ridiculous toy. Noisy. Unreliable. A boiler on wheels. One explosion and the road will be littered with fools." He dismissed the machine—and its owner—with a grunt and retreated into the house.

Thaddeus and Fitz exchanged solemn looks for scarcely a heartbeat before bursting into helpless laughter.

"Come along!" Fitz declared, slapping the side of the vehicle. "Let us take her out before your father has it burned."

Thaddeus climbed aboard, running his fingers along the leather and polished wood. "How fast will she go?"

"Four miles an hour in town," Fitz said. "But out here—ah! Here we may tempt fate itself." His grin widened, positively lupine. "Let us discover her true spirit."

They shot down the gravel drive, the motor-car shuddering like an excited hound straining at its leash. Out on the open road, Fitz shoved the lever forward until they reached the full, breathless speed of ten miles per hour. It was exhilarating—though Thaddeus privately noted that Trotter, his own horse, could outpace it handily.

Once Fitz slowed the vehicle, he cast Thaddeus a sideways glance. "You've been uncommonly quiet of late. Now that we're beyond your father's reach, will you tell me what shadows haunt you?"

Thaddeus hesitated, then sighed. "My parents... intend me to marry."

Fitz's moustache twitched. "Ah. And what monstrous deformity afflicts the poor girl? A wart? Buck teeth? A perfume that could fell a grown man?"

Thaddeus snorted despite himself. "Nothing of the sort. She is... suitable in every respectable way."

"Then why the long face?"

"It is her mind, Fitz. Her beliefs. They are as abhorrent as her father's—cruel, prejudiced, devoid of humanity. I cannot imagine spending a lifetime shackled to such coldness."

"Well," Fitz mused, "women do tend to adopt their husbands' views, once married."

"Not this one," Thaddeus said darkly. "Besides... I am not ready. I want a life of my own choosing. Adventures. Mistakes. Freedom. I will not let my father dictate my fate."

Fitz flicked a glance at him. "Then... what do you intend?"

"I'm leaving," Thaddeus said quietly.

The words hung between them like the toll of a funeral bell.

Fitz, usually the most unflappable of companions, faltered. "You? On your own? Thaddeus, have you any idea how to survive without your father's money?"

The truth struck him like a blow. His lungs tightened. His pulse quickened. But he met Fitz's gaze squarely.

"No," he admitted. "But terror will not keep me here. I am going to London."

Fitz stared at him a moment longer—then smiled, wide and proud. "Well, at least you are not fleeing to some far-flung empire. Write me once you find lodgings, and I shall come at once. Someone must ensure you do not starve or fall prey to footpads."

Thaddeus laughed, relief mingling with dread. "I shall write, Fitz. I promise."

"Good. Now let us abandon this mechanical tortoise and fetch the horses. I want to feel speed again."

Thaddeus followed, heart heavy yet strangely buoyed. Fitz's loyalty soothed the gnawing fear coiling in his stomach. He would leave. He would not be broken to Horace's will. And when Fitz visited him in London—perhaps even with the steam carriage in tow—Thaddeus hoped he would not be entirely alone in the vast new world ahead.

After Fitz's departure, Thaddeus resumed his quiet preparations for flight. In the dim hours of early morning or beneath the cloak of night, he packed his bags in secret, choosing only the essentials: garments that could pass for respectable in London, a few personal effects, and the small keepsakes he could not bear to leave behind. What had begun as a desperate dream had grown into a resolute plan. All he lacked now was opportunity—and that, fate would provide in its own unsettling manner.

For reasons he could not name, Thaddeus's newfound cheerfulness—his absent humming in the corridors, his lightened step—did not pass unnoticed. To Horace's mind, the boy's spirits were far too high. Thaddeus had never worn happiness well; it sat upon him like an ill-fitted coat. Sulking, brooding—that was expected, familiar. This blithe mood, however, roused an instinctive suspicion. True, he had brightened since Fitzgerald's visit, but Horace could not decide whether this reflected acceptance of his arranged future... or something else altogether.

He resolved to test the matter.

The summons came abruptly. Thaddeus was called to his father's office—an austere chamber whose very walls seemed steeped in old grievances. Unlike their previous encounter, there was no tempest brewing in Horace's voice.

"Sit down, boy," he said, gesturing curtly.

Thaddeus obeyed without hesitation. In truth, he no longer cared what command might come. Since resolving to leave, he found himself strangely unburdened, as though the chains long fitted to his spirit had grown thin and brittle.

Horace continued writing in a ledger as he spoke, his tone deceptively casual. "I require you to make yourself available in a fortnight. The Wilfreds are hosting a ball. Your betrothed will be in attendance —she is a particular friend of their eldest girl. You will escort her. It will do you good to be seen with the young lady, and will discourage any other sniffing dogs who may seek to lay claim to what is yours."

"I understand, Father," Thaddeus replied evenly.

Horace's pen froze mid-stroke. He lifted his gaze, studying his son's face as though it were an unfamiliar portrait. No defiance. No resentment. Not even resignation. Thaddeus appeared almost... tranquil. The sight unsettled him.

"Have you grown content with your future, my boy?" Horace asked, suspicion sharpening his tone.

Thaddeus returned his father's gaze unflinchingly. "Yes, Father. I am looking forward to my future."

A slow satisfaction spread across Horace's features. He nodded once and returned to his figures. "Good. I am pleased to hear it. That will be all. You may go."

Dismissed, Thaddeus withdrew from the room. Yet as soon as he was free of his father's sight, the corners of his mouth twitched upward. A quiet, breathless excitement filled him, lightening his stride as he made his way down the long, shadowed hallway.

Yes. The plan was nearly complete. His freedom—at last—was drawing near.

# CHAPTER THREE

The night of the Wilfreds' ball arrived with oppressive splendour. The great hall shimmered beneath a hundred gilded lamps, their reflections trembling like captive stars in the humid air. Beyond the tall windows, thunder muttered along the horizon—an answering growl to the storm coiling itself within Thaddeus's breast.

He escorted Hortense Remington as commanded, offering his arm with all the practised civility of a dutiful son. He smiled when expected, bowed with elegance, and murmured the requisite flatteries. He played his part to perfection, though each courtesy was another stitch fastening him into a life he had never chosen.

Hortense clung to him with unrelenting sweetness, her laughter high, and tinkling, her hand ever nestled in the crook of his arm as though she feared he might vanish should she release him. She allowed no other partner to approach him. She waltzed, she trilled through the Quadrille, and during the lively polka she clung so tightly that his breath constricted. Yet he never faltered. To the casual eye he appeared radiant—an eager suitor, a young lord delighted with his future bride.

Across the ballroom, Horace observed with smug satisfaction. Judith, however, harboured a subtle dread that coiled within her. She knew too well the bitterness in her son's heart and marvelled at the perfection of his performance.

During a pause in the dancing, Thaddeus inclined his head and murmured a polite excuse about stepping away for a moment. Hortense, half-encircled by a fluttering covey of young women, merely waved her fan at him—entirely confident he was ensnared.

Thaddeus slipped into a shadowed corridor, then through a side door into the rattling heat of the kitchen. When the servants' backs were turned, he slid out into the night. Circling the mansion's lantern-lit façade, he hailed one of the hired liveries waiting for guests. Fortune favoured him: Raynsford Manor lay only a short distance away, and the driver urged the horses into a brisk pace through the deepening storm.

The moment the carriage halted before his ancestral home, Thaddeus leapt to the steps, tossing the driver a hurried fare. The cab turned back toward the Wilfreds', leaving him alone with his racing heart.

He had nearly gained the stairs when Athena emerged from the dimness of the hall.

"You are leaving," she said—not in question, but in accusation.

"Athena," he breathed, and gathered her into his arms. He pressed his chin to her hair, inhaling the faint scent of jasmine and hearth-smoke that had always calmed him. "I must go. But when I have carved a place for myself in the world, I shall send for you. I swear it, my love."

She pushed back, searching his face with solemn eyes. Whatever she found there eased her trembling. "I understand," she whispered, though a solitary tear traced her cheek.

"I will write," he promised. "I shall send my letters to Jackson. He knows—he has always known. He will see they reach you."

He kissed her forehead, a vow pressed into her skin. Athena closed her eyes, believing because she loved him too fiercely not to.

He released her then, lest he lose all resolve, and strode toward the gallery. The portraits frozen in moonlight and encircled by heavy silence—he needed their cold company to steady him. Leaving Athena behind tore mercilessly at him; he feared that if she begged him to stay, he would break. He needed to shore up his courage against his father, against his ancestry, against the weight of the life he was defying.

Against his own trembling heart.

Lightning tore across the heavens, its brief, violent glare spilling through the arched windows of Raynsford Manor and illuminating the upper gallery in a wash of cold brilliance. Marble figures—saints, nymphs, and forgotten generals—loomed like judgemental sentinels. Among them stood Thaddeus, motionless enough to be mistaken for one of their number. He had hidden here often as a child, believing—foolishly—that if he remained perfectly still, his nurse would overlook him. She never had. The statues, however, remembered.

The manor itself, once a bastion of Raynsford pride, groaned under the weight of eleven generations. Its grandeur, like its fortune, had been eroding for decades. Damp crept through the walls with fungal persistence; a sour, mouldering scent haunted the corners where the fires had long gone cold. Too few servants remained to keep decay at bay. Portraits of grim-faced ancestors watched from their gilded frames, their eyes following him with an unyielding solemnity. Honour. Duty. Loyalty. Words that had been recited to him since infancy—worn thin now, hollow, brittle. His father's betrayal had stripped them of their nobility.

In the gallery's far corner, touched by the pale wash of moonlight, stood a figure dressed in Georgian finery—a red coat, black stockings, lace at the throat. Thaddeus regarded him with weary familiarity.

"*Remember who you are,*" the apparition murmured.

Thaddeus bristled. "Remember who I am? Have you lost your wits, Grandfather? Your son reminds me often enough."

The spectre only inclined its head. Ghosts seldom offered more than riddles and reproach.

"I will not sell my soul to pay my father's debts," Thaddeus hissed. "And you cannot make me."

The ghost bowed once more—an elegant, infuriating farewell—and dissolved into the dimness. Typical.

Was he to be abandoned by the dead as well as the living?

The thought hollowed him. His eyes burned with tears he would not permit to fall. After tonight, he would no longer have any claim to this place. He cast one last glance toward the stern faces of his lineage, then turned away, their silent judgments echoing through the dark behind him.

*Remember who you are.*

The words crawled along the walls, taunting him as he made his way to his chambers to retrieve his luggage.

He had waited weeks for this moment. Outside, the rain fell in relentless sheets. His parents would return from the Wilfreds' ball before long; time was slipping through his fingers. He must be gone before they crossed the threshold—before his father's voice, heavy as iron, could reach him.

Steeling himself, Thaddeus stepped into the storm. Lightning flared as he approached the waiting cab. He thrust his luggage toward the driver, who grumbled and heaved it onto the roof beneath a sodden tarp. The man cast Thaddeus a baleful look, as though the storm were his doing, then climbed to his dripping perch.

Thaddeus did not look back. He would not.

The carriage lurched forward, wheels cutting through mud, and London beckoned with all its unknown perils and freedoms. As the manor disappeared into darkness behind him, his body sagged with a deep exhale—the first true breath of liberty he had ever tasted.

The journey would last hours. Time enough to consider what came next. Time enough to question the wisdom of defying a Lord's decree—and to ignore those doubts with equal fervour.

He had lived too long beneath the suffocating shelter of Raynsford expectations. His father had already arranged his future, his marriage, his life—all to bind Thaddeus to the family's failing legacy. To be used as a pawn in society's endless games. The thought chilled him more than the storm.

Let them call him selfish. Let them name him a fool. Better a fool with freedom than a dutiful heir with a shattered spirit.

Deep within, another truth stirred—the one he had never dared speak aloud. He was called toward a different life, one not burdened by titles and obligations. Not the clergy, no; something far less respectable. A vagabond's life. A bohemian's existence. Adventure, discovery, unshackled days and unruly nights. Anything but the narrow, suffocating corridor of Lord Raynsford III's future.

He had always been different—marked. Since childhood, he had seen what others could not: shadows that whispered, spirits that lingered, the dead who reached for the living. His mother had nurtured the gift, calling it a blessing; his father had declared it evidence of indulgence. And so Thaddeus became the unwilling buffer between them, a fragile wall between two people who despised each other more than they loved him.

The George Inn awaited him in London. Tomorrow he would begin the search for a modest lodging-house, a life he could afford—at least until his money dwindled. After that... he would find work, or starve trying. What he would not do, under any circumstances, was crawl back to his father.

He would die first.

And as the carriage rattled into the storm-battered night, Thaddeus Raynsford almost welcomed that possibility.

# CHAPTER THREE

The George Inn glowed with a warmth almost otherworldly to Thaddeus, its low beams and amber firelight a tender contrast to the chill austerity of Raynsford Manor, with its marble floors and echoing halls. A muted hum of voices drifted from the tavern, softened by the thickness of the old stone walls. For the first time in his life, he had stepped into a place that welcomed rather than appraised him.

He approached the innkeeper and requested a room. The man, broad and ruddy, directed him toward a worn ledger resting upon a slanted desk.

Thaddeus signed his name with thoughtless habit.

The innkeeper leaned forward to inspect the signature, his eyes narrowing. "Thaddeus Raynsford... Are you Lord Raynsford's son?"

The very invocation of his father's name struck him like a blow. Fool—what a novice fugitive he made, leaving a trail with his own hand. If he could not sever himself from his lineage even in a ledger, how could he ever hope to escape it?

The innkeeper watched the young man's expression twist with dismay. "No offence meant, sir," he said softly. "We are a discreet house. There will be no further mention of your name." He hesitated before adding, "Enjoy your stay at the George... Mr. Priest."

It took Thaddeus a moment to grasp the offered alias, but once he did, relief washed over him. "Yes—Priest. Thank you, sir. Good evening."

A servant boy hurried forward to collect his trunk and lead him up the narrow stairs. Thaddeus followed, feeling the strange buoyancy of a man who has just sidestepped disaster.

In his chamber, he sat a moment upon the edge of the bed, studying the humble accommodations: a small hearth, its fire newly coaxed to life; a basin of cold water; a narrow window where rain pressed against the glass in silver sheets. He shed his damp coat and changed into dry clothes, grateful for the simple comfort. His bones ached from the long jarring ride, and his coat smelled of wet leather, rain, and the stale dampness of the carriage.

Downstairs, he took a modest supper with a cup of wine. The food was coarse compared to the fare at home, but he devoured it with a zeal born of liberty. His first meal as a free man. There would be countless adjustments ahead—strange beds, strange faces, a name not his own—but these were small prices for the promise of a life unshackled.

Across the room, a young woman watched him with unabashed interest. When he met her gaze, she smiled and fluttered her fingers. She had just begun to rise from her chair when the innkeeper's ample frame eclipsed her.

"Is everything to your liking, sir?"

"Yes, perfectly," Thaddeus replied, though he craned subtly to peer around the man.

The innkeeper followed his glance and frowned, though he said nothing. With a shrug, he moved off.

The young woman wasted no more time. She glided across the tavern, hips swaying, and slipped into the seat opposite him. "How are you this evenin', love?"

Her voice was sweet but carried the faintest rasp, as if worn thin by long nights. Thaddeus found himself staring at the back of her hand—its pale smooth skin, the light blue of veins beneath. She did not have the hands of someone used to hard labour.

"I am well," he said cautiously. "And you?"

"Oh, right as rain," she purred. "It's been so long since anyone looked my way. Makes a girl feel special."

"I find that difficult to believe," he murmured.

Her eyes flashed, ready to take offence, until he raised his hands gently. "I mean only that someone as lovely as you must attract many admirers."

She softened at once, smiling coyly. "Aren't you the charmer. Name's Annie."

"Pleased to meet you, Annie."

She lingered there, cooing and preening, watching each movement of his hands as he finished his bread. At last she leaned in, her voice dipping low. "Would you like some company tonight?"

"I'm afraid my heart is already promised," Thaddeus said.

She masked her disappointment with a brittle laugh. "Faithful lad, are you? Must be quite the lady."

He reached for his spoon—and dropped it. As he bent to retrieve it, Annie's hand darted to his cup. By the time he sat upright again, she lounged back in her chair, the picture of idle innocence.

"I suppose I am rather clumsy this evening," he said with a sheepish smile.

"Go on then," Annie urged softly. "Tell me about her."

He stared into his plate, swirling his food. "She is dark, mysterious... intelligent. Beautiful. I could not look away from her."

"And where is she now?" Annie asked. "Are you goin' to her?"

He took a long draught from his tankard, unaware of the watchful narrowing of her eyes. The drink burned strangely down his throat.

"My father forbids it," he muttered. "He wants me to wed someone respectable."

"Did he harm her?" Annie asked sharply.

The question sliced through him. He recoiled from it. "I... no, no he didn't."

Annie seemed to relax, the tension gone. "Tell me some more. Do you have a story about her?"

Thaddeus recovered, noticing Annie's mercurial temperament and wondering about her changeable nature. "Well, there was this one time when she let all the chickens out of the hen house. We had to chase them for hours."

He regaled Annie with stories from his boyhood, how he and Athena grew up together. It wasn't until he noticed that his stomach felt sore and he was extremely tired that he decided to beg off for the evening. "I'm sorry, I think I need to retire."

The innkeeper appeared again, no doubt summoned by the pallor draining Thaddeus's face. "Is everything well, sir?"

"Just... weary," Thaddeus murmured. "I think I should go up."

The innkeeper cleared away the dishes and withdrew. Thaddeus attempted to stand and swayed violently, gripping the chair rail to steady himself.

"I may have overindulged," he said breathlessly. "Annie... I should go."

"Let me help you, love," she offered—too eagerly.

He hesitated, distrust flickering across his features.

She smiled innocently. "I promise, I won't take a thing from you. Only help you to your room."

Still dizzy, Thaddeus relented. Annie looped herself beneath his arm and guided him with unsettling ease. His feet missed steps and the world tilted, the stairwell swam in shadow. She bore his weight as though she had done so many times before.

At his chamber door, his key slipped repeatedly from his fingers. Annie plucked it deftly from his grasp, turned the lock, and nudged the door open. The fire blazed, too hot for comfort, casting a feverish glow across the room.

"Here we are, love," she whispered.

She eased him onto the bed. He fell heavily across it, already lost to consciousness.

Annie grinned, baring slightly yellowed teeth. For a fleeting moment, she considered more carnal profits—he was handsome in a boyish way. She tugged off his boots with practised force, then reached for the buttons of his trousers. She paused. In sleep, his face looked impossibly young—almost innocent. With a shrug, she abandoned the idea.

His purse, however, she lifted without hesitation. It sagged heavy with silver. A fortune. Enough to buy her safety from the streets for months—perhaps longer.

Greed glinted in her eyes. Whatever pity she had dissolved instantly.

Thaddeus stirred, murmuring in his sleep.

A name slipped from his lips—a woman's name, laden with longing:

Athena.

ANNIE SLIPPED from Thaddeus's chamber and drifted down the dim corridor of the George Inn, her skirts whispering like silk over stone. Halfway to the stairs she paused, her expression souring. The innkeeper would demand his portion—as he always did. The privilege of hunting in his tavern came at a price, and a steep one.

With a muttered curse, she loosened the strings of Thaddeus's purse and dipped her fingers inside, fishing out a generous handful of silver. She tucked the coins deep into her bodice, tightened the laces, and adjusted her figure with brisk, practised movements until she looked both respectable and innocently unencumbered.

Her mood improved instantly. She glided toward the staircase, hips swaying with a triumphant rhythm, a wicked smile curling her lips.

The innkeeper stood waiting at the bottom, his bulk framed by the lantern light. His small, porcine eyes glittered upward at her. "Well now," he murmured, "don't you look like the cat that's swallowed the canary. A profitable evening, then?"

"Oh, indeed it was, love," Annie purred. She tossed the purse toward him. He caught it with surprising nimbleness for a man of his girth, and the metallic clink within made him let out a strangled, excited grunt.

"Oho... he's a wealthy one," the innkeeper breathed, already imagining the spoils.

"He *was* wealthy," Annie corrected with a sharp, crowing laugh.

"You emptied it?"

"He's got a grand old father to fill his pockets again," she said with a snarl. "Whereas I have no such blessing."

The innkeeper chuckled obscenely and spilled the contents of the purse across his palm, his fat fingers kneading through the silver with avid greed. Annie watched him count with a mixture of disgust and relief—grateful she had hidden her own portion before arriving.

At last he swept her diminished share back into the purse and handed it to her.

"Off to vanish again, are you?" he asked.

"You know I can't linger here," Annie replied, slipping the purse into her cloak. "Best to disappear into my rooms for a stretch—especially with a take like this."

The innkeeper's expression darkened.

"What's the matter, love?" she teased, leaning closer. "Will you miss me?"

"Awh, be off with you," he grunted, though a reluctant smile twitched beneath his moustache. "You'll sneak back soon enough. You always do."

# CHAPTER FOUR

Morning crept into the chamber with a pitiless brilliance, sunlight spilling through curtains some unseen maid had drawn wide. The harsh radiance stabbed at Thaddeus's eyes; he groaned and burrowed beneath his pillow like a wounded animal. His skull throbbed with every beat of his heart, his tongue lay thick and pasty in his mouth, and even the slightest movement sent sharp pangs of agony through his temples. It seemed safest —wisest—to remain utterly still.

Gradually, awareness pushed through the fog. He remembered the Inn. The tavern. The woman. Annie.

His eyes flew open—and he regretted it at once, a fresh spear of pain driving inward. He shut them again, forcing himself to conjure the fragments of memory: her laughter, her nearness, the glint in her eyes that promised something not pleasant. Why had he not noticed the way she stared at him?

The thought jolted him upright despite the torment in his head. "What possessed me to think the girl was decent?" he muttered, gripping the dresser until his knuckles whitened. What had seemed charged with sultry mystery the night before now warped itself into the shape of a nightmare.

But the truth pressed inward despite his wish to dismiss it. One draught of ale could not have felled him so completely. He had drunk stronger brews many times without consequence. No—this illness had come upon him in Annie's company. He remembered her guiding him up the stairs, her arm around his waist, her sweet, cloying voice urging him onward.

His stomach dropped. His hand flew to his belt. The purse was gone.

A cold wave of nausea washed over him. He staggered to his luggage, flung open the leather case, rifled through its contents. Clothes, boots, notebook—nothing amiss save the most important thing. His money had vanished.

He sank onto the edge of the bed, defeated. Fool. Simpleton. He pressed his palms to his throbbing temples.

New anxieties rose like spectres in the dim room. How would he pay his lodging? How long before the innkeeper demanded his due and tossed him bodily into the street? One single foolish evening had unravelled the delicate tapestry of his plans.

The simplest solution, of course, was to return home. A word to his father, and he would have funds again. But the moment he crossed Raynsford's threshold, his freedom would evaporate. Horace would lock him in a cage of duty until the wedding bells tolled. No—he would sooner walk penniless into the gutter.

He needed employment. Immediately.

Yet working with merchants or men of standing was impossible—his face too easily recognised, his lineage too loudly spoken in his features. Manual labour would scarcely pay his meals. He bit his lip, mind racing.

There was, however, one path. One he had contemplated before. London was awash in spiritualists, mediums, and purveyors of the unseen. And unlike the scholars and sceptics of high society, the poor—the simple folk—would not know him. They would welcome a man with his gifts. He could vanish into that world, take the alias Priest—yes, that suited him—and build a life hidden from his father's reach.

Once he was established, once his footing was secure, he could move on. Perhaps even rise.

It was a daring plan, a precarious one... but it was the only one left to him.

Detective Michael Barnes sat at his desk, the pale morning light drifting through the tall windows and settling upon the room like a gentle but unwanted guest. It lent the place more warmth than the season warranted. His morning had begun sluggishly; he sipped his strong, bitter coffee while gazing out at the sunlit courtyard below. Most detectives preferred tea, but Barnes had long been partial to the harsher stimulant.

He had served as a Bobby for many years before unravelling a murder that had thwarted every one of his colleagues. That solitary triumph propelled him upward. The promotion brought with it politics he detested, but the increased pay eased the sting, and so he bore it in silence.

He was only just preparing to rouse himself into the day's duties when his partner, Edgar Dickman, appeared at his shoulder as silently as a cat. "Contemplating the courtyard again, are we?"

Dickman, polished by money and upbringing, moved through the Yard's corridors of influence with enviable ease. Yet for all his refinements, he was a loyal friend, and together they made an unexpectedly effective pair.

"I am fortifying myself for whatever trials await," Barnes replied, eyeing the file in Dickman's hand. "What news from Head Office?"

"Oh, the usual sermon: keep it tidy, keep it quiet, we rely upon you," Dickman said with a dismissive flick of his fingers.

"In short, nothing of substance," Barnes said, offering his customary wry smile.

"No, nothing of substance at all. Still, it is quiet. Only the regular pickpockets and ladies of the night to trouble us. No true villains of note. One might almost call us fortunate."

"We ought not tempt Providence," Barnes murmured. "Better to savour a peaceful morning while it lasts."

"Not very like us, though, is it?" Dickman laughed softly.

"It would be a welcome change to investigate crimes rather than prevent them. If the citizens understood we were permitted to pursue criminals properly, perhaps they would conduct themselves with more restraint," said Barnes.

This was an old refrain between them—two men confined by the Yard's insistence that detectives must prevent wrongdoing rather than solve it. Among the upper ranks, an investigation was an admission of failure. Even with his title, Dickman often walked as though he still trod a common beat.

Barnes shifted the conversation. "And how fares your peculiar hobby these days?"

"Oh, well enough. I had some thoughts on blood spatter—curious patterns, really. I'm reading what the physicians have written. Not that any of it will be sanctioned for use." His disappointment hovered in the air.

"Fascinating," Barnes murmured, already engrossed in the file.

Their quiet exchange was cut short by a Bobby who entered, cap in hand. "Sirs, someone from the Home Office is here to speak with you." He offered a quick bow and withdrew.

Barnes and Dickman exchanged a startled glance.

"What the devil could they want?" Dickman muttered under his breath.

They proceeded to the chamber reserved for official visitors. The Chief Superintendent sat waiting behind a heavy desk, his fingers steepled like a man preparing to deliver a sermon.

"Gentlemen," he said, "pray be seated."

They obeyed, a ripple of unease passing between them like a shared shiver.

"You have been summoned," the Superintendent began, "because the department is under investigation for corruption. The Home Office has received... disquieting reports." He leaned back, the edge in his voice softening for only a moment. "You are not under suspicion—at present—and your records remain unblemished. Nevertheless, I require your assistance."

Barnes cast a brief look at his partner. "And in what manner would you have us assist, sir?"

"It is simple. I expect you to report anything you observe that might be deemed improper. Any irregularity, any breach of protocol —no matter how slight."

Dickman stiffened. Barnes studied the Superintendent with narrowed eyes. "Sir, we are no informers. To report on our fellows would compromise our standing and hinder our work. It would mark us for distrust."

"Perhaps you misunderstand," the Superintendent replied, his tone sharpening to a cold edge. "This is not a request. It is an order."

Silence settled heavily over the room. Both men inclined their heads in reluctant acknowledgment.

"That will be all, gentlemen."

THADDEUS PERFORMED his morning ablutions with mechanical precision, though his thoughts churned like a storm tide. How, in Heaven's name, was he to extricate himself from this wretched predicament? He might quit the Inn at once—feign an errand and promise to return later. Indeed, he might have to return until he secured new lodgings. He told himself that to flee entirely, abandoning every option, would be folly of the worst sort.

A sudden thought pierced the fog of his worry. He reached into the pockets of the trousers he had worn the night before. His fingers brushed metal. To his immense relief, a meagre scattering of coins lay in the right pocket. Pitiful though the sum was, it must suffice—for now.

Thaddeus donned his top hat, grasped his cane, and stepped from his room with all the deliberate composure of a gentleman embarking upon respectable business. He descended the corridor and staircase with steady stride. When he observed the Innkeeper's station unmanned, a breath of relief escaped him. Free from immediate scrutiny, he slipped out into the bustling street.

London's morning enveloped him at once—its cacophony of hooves, shouts, cart wheels, and vendors' cries; its mingled scents of coal, damp stone, and humanity. With each step, a little tension drained from his shoulders. For a few hours, he wandered in a sort of restless aimlessness, taking in the city while turning his problems over and over in his mind, never arriving at a solution.

He passed a succession of respectable offices—lawyers, esquires, merchantmen—men who might very well recognise him or, worse, report him. He pressed on. As he neared the heart of London, he found himself in a busy thoroughfare in Holborn. Several insurance companies had established their premises there, and he paused before one such building.

It struck him suddenly: he might take a position as a humble clerk in such a place. A dreary occupation, perhaps, but one that allowed a man to keep his head bowed and his name unremarked. Hidden in plain sight. It was a possibility—mundane, ignoble, yet strangely promising.

He turned from the building to the street beyond, where a row of fine houses lined the opposite side. One in particular snared his attention. A grand Georgian façade, stately and dignified, yet oddly animated by a steady stream of people entering its door. Curiosity tugged at him until he crossed the road to join the next small knot of visitors.

Only then did he see the placard affixed beside the door:

## CHAPTER FOUR

*Madam Baldry*
*Psychic ~ Spiritualist ~ Medium*

The words arrested him. Given his own peculiar gift, this was... intriguing.

Ahead of him, a young couple conversed in excited whispers.

"I have heard she is quite good—new to London, but promising," the woman said.

"Well, my dear," her companion replied, "one cannot know until one has seen for oneself. Such are the perils of being first. Still, I have cast my lot with yours now."

Thaddeus smiled to himself as he waited, along with the other members of the party, for the doors to open.

The house lay steeped in gloom, its heavy curtains choking what little daylight struggled to intrude. A dim, wavering glow from scattered lamps lent the entrance hall the air of a sepulchre. The guests were ushered down a narrow passage where shadows clung like cobwebs, then through a broad doorway into a cramped parlour that exhaled an air of disuse.

Red velvet draperies smothered the windows and hung over the entrance like funereal shrouds. A round table dominated the centre of the room, its surface polished to a dull gleam, while mismatched chairs and looming cabinets pressed against every wall as though crowding forward to listen. The place resembled some forgotten storeroom hastily converted for purpose, yet it was surprisingly clean, the air faintly tinged with lavender and newly opened shutters. Papers lay in precarious stacks upon every available surface—ledgers, sheets scrawled in hasty script, mysterious diagrams—more the workshop of a harried scholar than the lair of a mystic. One spark from a pipe would have reduced the whole enterprise to ash.

As though conjured from the air, a young woman appeared in the doorway, clutching a folded sheet. She approached the table with a stiff, business-like manner.

"As I call your names, kindly indicate your presence," she said, reading from the page. "Finnias Thompson? Margaret Murray?" Each name received a murmur of acknowledgment. Only one man remained unaddressed.

"And you, sir—your name?"

Thaddeus coloured faintly at the attention. "Thaddeus Priest, Madam. My apologies—I was under the impression this gathering was open to all."

The assistant shifted uneasily, her gaze flickering about the room as though seeking rescue. "I regret to inform you, Mr. Priest, that we cannot receive unexpected visitors. You will have to return another time."

"Nonsense," Mr. Thompson declared, bringing his cane down sharply upon the floorboards. "There is ample room. The lad may sit beside me. If a reference is required, I offer myself."

Thaddeus inclined his head gratefully. It was a rare comfort to encounter kindness in London, where his recent misfortunes had made him wary of every smiling face.

"So be it," the assistant sighed, bowing with thinly veiled disapproval. "Ladies and gentlemen—Madam Baldry."

The lamps dimmed at once, as though snuffed by an invisible hand, until only a solitary candle glowed upon the table. From a tall, curtained cabinet along the eastern wall stepped a woman—small in stature, with her auburn hair wound tightly back and her face pale as milk. Thaddeus suspected powder, applied with a heavy hand, to lend her an otherworldly pallor.

The assistant lit the candle at the table's centre and extinguished the remaining lights. Madam Baldry seated herself in the southernmost chair, composed her skirts, and lowered her head. A stream of muttered phrases—prayer or incantation, he could not tell—flowed from her lips. Her posture slackened like a puppet unstrung, then stiffened abruptly. When at last she raised her head, her eyes stared past them all, glassy and unfocused.

"The spirits of the Borderlands join us this night," she intoned, her voice a soft, wavering thing that occasionally squeaked like a hinge in need of oil. Several guests murmured in reverence.

Thaddeus observed her with a mixture of amusement and intrigue. What spirits? The room held nothing but credulous Londoners and a single candle.

"Place your hands upon the table, palms downward, fingers spread—thus." Madam Baldry demonstrated. "Bow your heads and meditate upon the Lord's Prayer."

All complied—except Thaddeus, whose religious inclinations were negligible at best. With his head half-bent in feigned devotion, he caught sight of the assistant slipping stealthily behind the cabinet from which Madam Baldry had emerged. His lips twitched in anticipation. So that was the trick.

When the prayer concluded, Thaddeus raised his head with appropriate solemnity.

"I call to any spirit willing to draw near. Is there one among you who bears a message for the living?" Madam Baldry asked.

Silence.

"I ask again—does any soul of the departed wish to speak?"

A loud, deliberate rap echoed from within the cabinet.

Thaddeus nearly laughed aloud.

"I hear you, O Spirit. Tell us—are you Martha?"

Silence.

"Mary, perhaps?" A sharp rap answered.

Mr. Landry gasped, clutching his breast. "Mary—my wife!"

Madam Baldry offered a faint, knowing smile. Thaddeus's amusement shifted into discomfort as he watched the man tremble with hope, mistaking trickery for communion with his departed beloved. One by one, the séance continued—names offered, raps returned, guests weeping or exclaiming, the air thick with longing and deceit. Some names were common, others oddly specific; Thaddeus suspected the assistant had more than passing familiarity with the gathered company.

No wonder they were reluctant to admit an unexpected guest.

When at last the ritual had run its course, Mr. Thompson patted Thaddeus's arm. "No spirit sought you today, my boy. Unfortunate."

"I daresay it is because I arrived unannounced," Thaddeus replied with a wry smile. "Still, it has been an illuminating afternoon."

A basket made its rounds for donations. Thaddeus, acutely aware of his dwindling funds and uncertain lodgings, dropped a solitary sixpence into it—an offering pitifully small for a man dressed as finely as he. When he glanced up, Madam Baldry fixed him with a cold glare, her chin lifting in disdain.

Heat pricked his cheeks, but shame was a luxury he could ill afford. He rose with the departing patrons, tipped his hat respectfully, and made his way toward the door, uncertain of where he would go once he stepped into the London dusk.

# CHAPTER FIVE

Horace sat rigid at his great mahogany desk, his countenance mottled with wrath. He had been in such a temper since returning from the Wilfreds' ball—only to discover that his son had absconded. Thaddeus, in one reckless stroke, threatened to undo everything Horace had laboured months to secure. It was intolerable—beyond pardon—and Horace believed he knew precisely how to bring the young whelp to heel.

"Jackson!"

He seized the bell-pull and yanked with such ferocity that the cord snapped taut, swinging like a noose. His roar thundered through the manor, rendering the bell-pull almost redundant; any soul within the house who possessed ears would have heard him.

Within moments, Jackson appeared at the threshold of Horace's private sanctum, bowing with well-practised deference.

"Yes, Master Horace?"

"Dispatch this message to these two men," Horace snarled, thrusting a folded missive into his hands. "Tell the footman to wait for a reply."

Then he shoved a small, weighty bag of coin at him. "And deliver this—payment for services rendered."

Jackson bowed again and withdrew, but his mind churned. This —whatever it was—pertained to the young master. He could feel it in his bones. And though Jackson prided himself on being a loyal servant, to whom that loyalty belonged mattered more than any oath muttered in the servants' hall.

Instead of heading immediately for the livery, Jackson slipped silently down to his modest quarters. Once inside, he closed the door, lit a candle, and drew forth the blunt little knife he kept for such discreet labours. He warmed the blade in the flame just long enough to soften wax without blackening parchment—an art he had honed with meticulous care over the years.

He eased the blade beneath the seal, lifting it cleanly from the paper with a surgeon's delicacy. Setting the intact seal aside, he unfolded the missive. His eyes flicked across the page.

*Corbeld & Matson,*

*I must again avail myself of your particular talents. My son has chosen to remove himself from my household. You will ascertain his whereabouts.*

*H.*

Horace had hired two men to find Thaddeus—and not respectable men. Jackson recognised the names at once. These were creatures who haunted London's underbelly, the sort of fellows mothers warned their children would snatch them in the night. That Horace knew of them at all chilled him. That he had contact enough to employ them confirmed the worst.

Quickly, Jackson reheated the wax and pressed the seal back into place, leaving no evidence of his trespass. Then, with the letter restored, he left his quarters and strode to the livery with, he hoped, an air of dutiful haste rather than guilty knowledge.

His hands trembled slightly as he passed the message to the waiting footman.

The moment the man departed, Jackson wiped his palms against his coat and turned toward the main house. He must find the mistress. Lady Judith had been his confidante these many years; she knew far more of the goings-on within Raynsford Manor than her husband suspected. More than once, she had quietly undone Horace's schemes when they threatened harm to her son—and Jackson knew she would do so again, if it meant saving Thaddeus from whatever net his father now cast.

LACKING the coin for even the humblest hotel, Thaddeus soon discovered his prospects for the night were meagre indeed. After the séance he wandered, satchel in hand, through London's labyrinthine streets until chance delivered him to a most unlikely refuge—a sprawling cemetery whose iron gates loomed like the threshold to some forbidden abode. Considering that most Victorians clung to superstition as tightly as to their prayer-books, he reasoned that no one would dare disturb a lone figure nestled behind a grave. Solitude, at least, would be assured.

As he followed the winding paths, a rhythmic scrape reached his ear —the unmistakable bite of a shovel into fresh earth. He peered through the gloom and spied the cemetery's caretaker labouring over a newly opened grave. Thaddeus moved quickly and silently past the man until he found a remote corner shielded from the road. He set down his satchel and lowered himself behind a great stone mausoleum whose pale façade caught what little starlight pierced the night. There was small comfort to be found—only hard stone underfoot and the faintly chilling air of late spring—but the sky was clear, and he could endure the cold until daybreak. He had, after all, just enough left in his pocket for a modest breakfast; thereafter he must seek permanent lodgings or starve.

How strange, he reflected with a grim smile, that his second night in London should be spent among the dead—among beings with whom he had been acquainted since boyhood. His mother had believed him unfailingly, for she herself was a quiet devotee of the Spiritualist cause—a truth she had concealed from Horace with exquisite care. As the years passed and his father's demands for "manliness" grew more relentless, his mother's sympathy became his only defence. She was surely sick with worry now. But Thaddeus would not return to Raynsford Manor until he was firmly established and his independence beyond reproach.

Night deepened, casting the cemetery into utter blackness beneath a new moon that offered no glimmer of relief. A restless wind whispered through the trees, stirring the leaves in fitful murmurs. From beyond the gates came the occasional footfall, the muffled voices of passersby, the distant rattle of wheels. Thaddeus hunched further behind the mausoleum, questioning the wisdom of his choice; he was hidden, yes, and unlikely to be discovered, but sleep seemed an impossible luxury. His stomach growled loudly—a cruel reminder that he had not eaten since dawn—and he prayed the sound had not carried.

As his eyes adjusted, the world resolved into dim silhouettes: trees like black sentries, tombstones rising from the shadows like pale monuments to forgotten lives. The oppressive silence, broken only by the rustling of branches, lulled him at last toward drowsiness—until he heard it: footsteps. Heavy, clumsy, accompanied by whispered voices sharp with menace.

"I'm tellin' ya, I saw 'im come in 'ere, but 'e never came out. Bloke was dressed real nice. Must 'ave coin," hissed one.

"I don't care what 'e's got," muttered the second. "I don't fancy prowlin' about a graveyard. Gives me the chills."

"Well, I haven't eaten in days. If he's in 'ere, 'e's payin', I don't care how."

Thaddeus froze. The coins he carried were trifling, yet doubtless enough to tempt desperate men. They thundered through the graveyard—no subtlety to them, no cunning—yet a tightness seized his chest, the fear of discovery rising sharp within him. He considered crawling to a new hiding place, though he had no notion where safety might lie, when a sudden, piercing scream shattered the stillness.

Thaddeus's blood ran cold. They were not alone.

The pounding of running feet followed, then a sickening thud. The caretaker's open grave had claimed its victim; one of the men had fallen in and now shrieked in agony.

"Tommy, stop yer blatherin'!" the first man snapped. "Yer'll bring the coppers down on us!"

"Get me out! Get me out, blast you!" the injured man cried.

After much grunting and fumbling, he was hoisted from the grave, and the pair hobbled away down the lane, cursing under their breath. Thaddeus exhaled, tension bleeding from his limbs—until a soft voice drifted across the darkness.

"*They are gone now. You are safe.*"

A chill climbed his spine. A figure was approaching, its outline scarcely visible, gliding rather than stepping.

"*Do not be alarmed,*" the voice continued gently. "*I've no wish to harm you.*"

Thaddeus shivered—not from cold, but from an instinct older than reason—yet he kept his gaze fixed on the advancing shape. As it neared, moonless darkness gave way to recognition. The man's attire was strikingly archaic: formal Georgian garments, hair tied neatly back, shoes with high heels that did not so much as dent the earth beneath them. Indeed, the figure seemed scarcely to touch the ground at all.

"My apologies if I startled you," the stranger said with a courteous bow. "Arthur McGrath, at your service—though my friends called me Artie. Or used to, at any rate." He scratched his temple thoughtfully. "Don't trouble yourself, those ruffians will not return. Upon hearing their talk, I assumed they sought you and was compelled to grant them a little... encouragement to depart."

Thaddeus extended a polite hand. "Thaddeus Priest."

But Arthur did not take it. Instead he regarded Thaddeus with a discerning eye. "You are well-dressed for a night among the tombs. Would an inn not suit you better?"

"I would gladly choose one, were it possible," Thaddeus sighed. "But I was robbed at the inn where I stayed. I have not a penny to my name, and so here I am."

Arthur nodded sympathetically. "If you would follow me, I can show you a place far safer than this. You might actually rest."

Thaddeus rose, signalling his assent, and the two moved through the shadowed grounds until a stone crypt came into view—a structure perched over a narrow stair descending into blackness. Thaddeus halted.

"It must be pitch dark down there. I refuse to descend. I shall break my neck."

Arthur blinked, then smacked his forehead lightly. "Of course—no candlelight. I forgot." He tapped his chin, considering. "Well, you are safer here than at the entrance. No one comes to this side of the grounds after dark. They fear the ghosts, you see."

"Ghosts," Thaddeus murmured with a wry smile. "You mean like you."

Arthur brightened. "Yes! Exactly so. You worked it out."

"It was not terribly difficult."

Arthur tilted his head. "In truth, I might know of a place—a kip nearby. Are you planning to stay long in London?"

"Indeed. I came here to make my own way," Thaddeus answered earnestly, then flushed. "Though I have not made much of it so far."

"Oh, nonsense!" Arthur exclaimed cheerfully. "If you're not robbed your first night in London, you've hardly arrived. I haunt a boarding house not far from here. Mrs. Parsons runs it—stern in manner, but only because she must be. Beneath it she is kindness itself."

"And I would be accepted as a boarder without means?"

Arthur's smile widened. "At the kip, yes. Kips are not really a place of permanent residence. More like an overnight stay. But then, if we can get you settled and you can obtain some coin, Mrs. Parsons would take you in. You can see the dead and speak with them. She secretly adores the Spiritualist Movement. To have a medium under her roof? She would be over the moon."

For the first time since arriving in London, hope stirred within Thaddeus. "My father always dismissed my gift—refused even to acknowledge it. But now that I am my own master... why shouldn't I make use of it?"

Arthur grinned. "And I shall finally have someone to converse with! No one else there sees or hears me."

"I could do far worse for a roommate," Thaddeus said warmly.

"Get some rest," Arthur urged. "I shall keep watch until dawn and frighten off any intruders."

"Good night, Artie. I am very glad to have met you."

Arthur inclined his head and took up his vigil, standing sentinel over the sleeping young man until morning light crept across the stones.

Clovis Corbeld and his associate, Erwin Matson, were names spoken in low voices on the lower east side—brutal men both, given to quick ire and quicker violence. Any soul possessing even a scrap of sound judgement knew better than to cross their path. That evening, upon receiving Horace's terse missive and the accompanying purse of coin, they accepted the commission without hesitation and dismissed the trembling footman with a curt wave. Together they spilled the contents of the purse onto the table, counting with greedy fingers and glistening eyes. This, they knew, was but a retainer; richer rewards would follow should they succeed. Clovis wheezed out a foul, sputtering laugh—ripe with the stench of decay—directly into Erwin's face, prompting the latter to shove him away with a curse.

Erwin, though scarcely more reputable, at least possessed all his teeth and breath less offensive. "All this coin," he muttered, "just because the young lordling decided to scarper. Findin' 'im ought to be simple enough. 'E'll stand out in these parts like a silk ribbon in a coal bin."

Clovis scratched his chin, mulling it over. "Aye, but London's a vast place. How in blazes are we to track a lad from such lofty stock? We've no entry into the circles he'd haunt."

"Let's worry about that when we must," Erwin replied, the more practical of the pair. "Best to begin where he arrived and follow the trail from there."

"Oh? And where's that then?" Clovis grumbled.

"Well, 'e didn't walk from Kent, did 'e? We start with the cabbies."

"I was just about to say that," Clovis lied with a proud grin, revealing a sparse forest of blackened teeth.

"Of course you were," Erwin said dryly.

THE FOLLOWING MORNING, their search brought them to the George Inn in Southwark, a bustling coaching hub where cabmen loitered in perpetual readiness. The ruffians stalked among the drivers, demanding to know whether any had conveyed a passenger from Kent two nights prior. Most cabbies stiffened with disdain, offering clipped answers or none at all—until threats, rough grips, and the gleam of Erwin's knife loosened several reluctant tongues. A few pointed them toward an elderly cabman perched high upon his box, reins in hand, atop a glossy black stallion.

"Oi! You there!" Erwin called, striding forward. He seized the horse's reins, startling the beast, which tossed its head and backed away with a shrill whinny.

The cabman's lined face hardened with weary exasperation. "Sir, release my horse at once, unless you wish to find yourself under his hooves."

Erwin let go, and the stallion settled almost immediately. "No need for threats. I've a simple question about a fare you might've taken two nights past."

"I do not betray my customers' confidences, sir," the cabman answered stiffly.

Clovis hauled himself up the side of the cab with surprising agility, bringing his foul breath and glinting eyes level with the driver. "You may not be in the 'abit," he said softly, "but you'll oblige us all the same."

The cabman's gaze darted about the courtyard, searching for a policeman—any uniform, any witness—but none appeared. Then he saw the flash of steel pressed meaningfully near his ribs, and his breath hitched. No fare was worth dying over.

"I... I did carry a passenger from Kent," he admitted.

"A man? Young?" Clovis pressed.

A tense nod.

"That's a good fellow," Clovis crooned with a wolfish smile. "See how pleasant things go when we all cooperate? Now then—where did the lad go?"

The cabman swallowed hard, raised a trembling hand, and pointed toward the George Inn.

"There now," Clovis said cheerfully, dropping to the ground. "Not difficult in the least." With a malicious chuckle he slapped the stallion's flank. The horse reared with a wild cry, nearly unseating the cabman, who fought desperately to soothe and restrain the panicked animal. After a harrowing moment, the beast stilled under his murmured reassurances. When at last the cabman dared to glance around, the two villains had vanished into the throng—much to his profound relief.

# CHAPTER SIX

Morning crept over London with a pallid, reluctant light, bleeding slowly into the mist that hovered above the cobbles. While the city shook itself awake, the George Inn returned to its accustomed rhythm—though its innkeeper, Jacob Turnbull, found little comfort in routine. After Thaddeus's departure and the treachery of the prostitute Annie, he was left to tally up his losses. Annie had vanished into the warrens near the docks with every farthing she could lay her thieving fingers upon. Turnbull cursed under his breath as he scrubbed the counter, pausing to rake a weary hand through his thinning hair.

He caught his reflection in the mirror behind the bar—bleary-eyed, sour-mouthed—and was contemplating polishing the glass when the bell over the door gave a sharp, metallic jingle.

Two men stepped into the foyer, dressed in nondescript street clothes that did little to soften the impression of danger that clung to them. The taller of the pair surveyed the inn with a slow, predatory sweep, wandering briefly into the dining room before returning to his companion. The shorter man nodded politely to the innkeeper, hands sunk deep into his coat pockets. His posture was lazy, almost genial, but Turnbull felt the hairs on his nape stir. These were not customers.

The tall man reached casually across the counter, pulling the guest ledger toward himself. As he flipped it open, the shorter man spoke.

"Good morning. We come on behalf of an interested party. We've reason to believe a young gentleman passed through here not long ago."

Turnbull narrowed his eyes. They might have looked like common roughs, but their manner betrayed something colder, more deliberate. "We hold the privacy of our guests in highest regard," he replied stiffly. He drew the ledger back, snapping it shut. "I cannot disclose information on a whim."

"Oh, I'm certain you guard their secrets most dutifully," the tall man replied. His tone was soft, almost courteous, but he produced a knife from his pocket with unsettling grace and began cleaning his nails with the tip. "My master, likewise, is particular about his concerns... and dislikes his time wasted."

He lifted his eyes at last—blue, glacial, devoid of warmth.

"We're lookin' for his son," he continued, twirling the blade between his fingers. "And I believe you might know where he's gone."

Turnbull swallowed, his stomach twisting. He already suspected whom they sought, but he would not confirm it without some restitution. "Describe him."

The tall man's smile tightened, but his tone remained light. "A bit taller than my friend here. Well turned out. Dark hair, blue eyes. Speaks like quality. Stayed here two nights ago."

Turnbull sniffed. "Aye. I recall such a lad. Skipped out without paying. You make good on his bill, and I'll tell you what I know."

The two men exchanged a knowing glance. Without a word, the tall one drove his knife point-first into the wooden counter, the blade quivering like a live thing. Turnbull jumped. The men moved smoothly to either end of the bar, flanking him.

Before Turnbull could step away, a strong hand seized his collar and hoisted him from the floor with terrifying ease. His feet dangled uselessly above the ground as the short man drew his own knife, waving it dangerously close to Turnbull's privates.

Jacob Turnbull's bladder loosened. This was not the morning he had imagined.

"I—I don't know much," he sputtered.

"Don't sell me a dog, Major MacFluffer," the short man said with a wicked grin, "or we'll help jog your memory."

Turnbull broke. He was no martyr. "The lad was robbed—by a woman. He drank too much, she cleaned him out. He left two days ago and never came back. I haven't heard anything about him since. That's all I know—God's truth."

"And the woman?" the tall man asked.

Turnbull sagged in defeat. "Annie. Annie Fletcher. Lives near the docks, but I don't know which house. That's all I've got."

The two brutes nodded once, as if satisfied with a business transaction. Then they released him. He hit the floor headfirst with a painful crack.

Dazed, Turnbull scrambled upright as they strode toward the door.

"Oi!" he called after them, voice cracking. "What about the lad's bill?"

But the door swung shut behind them without pause.

Turnbull stood alone in the foyer, clutching his rag like a weapon he lacked courage to use. He slammed the cloth onto the counter in frustration, muttering curses as the men vanished into the morning fog.

Thaddeus had anticipated many challenges upon his flight to London. He had steeled himself for the hunt for employment, for the search for modest quarters, for the slow forging of a new life. He had even brought a respectable sum of coin to ease his first days of independence. Yet here he stood—penniless, hungry, and lodged nowhere but among the dead. One foolish evening at the George had unravelled all his careful plans like rotted thread. His stomach growled its own reproach.

He brushed futilely at the creases in his once-fine coat, hoping that what remained of his gentleman's attire might persuade someone to take pity on him.

A familiar voice drifted across the gravestones. "Good morning."

Thaddeus looked up. "Ah—there you are. When I woke, you had vanished. I figured I was on my own."

Artie drifted nearer, hands folded behind his back with spectral nonchalance. "I spent the night thinking on your predicament. Turning over possibilities, mind you."

"And with what success?" Thaddeus asked, though his tone betrayed little hope.

"None at all. You are in something of a pickle. I fear the kip is your only choice at the moment."

"Well, that is profoundly unhelpful," Thaddeus muttered, snatching a small stone from the ground and sending it skittering across a monument. "I have thought on it as well, and I mean to appeal to human charity."

Artie stared at him as though he had sprouted antlers, then let out a short, incredulous laugh. "Are you serious?"

"You may mock if you must, but I cannot sit among gravestones all day waiting for nightfall. And a kip, isn't that another place you go to be robbed? I must try something."

Artie's expression sobered. "I learned the limits of human charity the hard way. Look where it got me."

"That was not especially kind," Thaddeus said, brushing dead leaves from his clothes as he rose to his feet.

"I only wish to temper your optimism with caution. We'll try it your way."

"Time to move on, then," Thaddeus declared, forcing his stiff limbs into motion as he strode from the cemetery gates.

Artie floated along beside him, an ever-present shadow. Morning lay cold upon London, damp and pearled with fog. The chill crept through Thaddeus's clothes, but walking stirred his blood and lifted his spirits a little.

His first attempt came quickly: a modest house bearing a handwritten notice—Room to Let. Yet the instant he admitted he had no money, the door slammed with such force it nearly clipped his nose. Artie's snicker died abruptly when Thaddeus shot him a murderous glare.

The second house fared no better. Nor the third. The pattern repeated endlessly: warm welcomes for a well-dressed gentleman, and swift expulsions once the truth emerged.

By midday, Thaddeus's hunger gnawed with almost physical pain. His pride had been trampled beneath a dozen doorsteps. He could scarcely believe he had ever looked with disdain upon the poor; now he stood among them, stripped of illusion.

"Try the market," Artie suggested lightly. "Pinch an apple from a stall. It is practically a London tradition."

"Steal?" Thaddeus recoiled. "Absolutely not."

Artie shrugged. "Suit yourself. Starvation builds character, they say."

Thaddeus shot him a look of pure frost. Visions of Hortense Remington rose unbidden—her pinched mouth, her superior tone, the lifelong torment she promised. Better death in a gutter than that future.

He pressed on. Clouds rolled in, heavy and dark, and the wind hissed with damp promise.

"I must hurry," he murmured. "I shall be drenched before long."

"One advantage of being dead," Artie said cheerfully, "is immunity to weather."

"You are remarkably chipper for a ghost."

"No need to be snippy," Artie replied. "I merely state facts."

House after house rejected him. Afternoon waned toward evening, and fear—real, creeping fear—began to stir beneath Thaddeus's ribs.

"What am I to do?" he whispered. "Where shall I go?"

He had not meant to ask Artie, yet the ghost answered.

"I know a place," Artie said at last. "Not comfortable. Certainly not grand. But safe, and dry, and its owner is decent enough. I have watched him for years. He cannot see me, of course, but he is no brute."

Thaddeus's relief was immediate and painful. "Is it far? I feel near collapse—and I cannot remember a time when I was so hungry."

"Not far," Artie assured him. "Come. The sun sinks quickly in this city, and you will not wish to be abroad after dark."

With that, the ghost drifted ahead, and Thaddeus followed, weary but hopeful, into the gathering gloom of London's evening streets.

Annie Fletcher sat within the cramped little room she had paid for—this week's refuge. She seldom lodged in the same place twice, especially in the docklands where she plied her trade. A woman in her circumstance did well never to be easily found. She emptied her pockets upon the bed and counted the evening's coins, slipping them into the leather pouch she had taken from the young gentleman at the George. It was a handsome piece, far finer than anything she could have honestly obtained, and she meant to keep it. A good pouch was a rare commodity; it kept her earnings safe, and more importantly, it made her feel, if only briefly, like a woman of means.

Outside, the bay waters lapped against the pilings of the wharf, a slow, rhythmic sloshing that drifted through the cracks in the window frame. Thunder grumbled somewhere beyond the horizon, and lightning flickered faintly behind the clouds. Annie inhaled the scents of tar, salt, and fish—odours others found repellent but which, to her, had always meant sanctuary. Here among the dockworkers, smugglers, and night wanderers, she was known enough to be left alone, yet not known so well as to be betrayed. The docks held their own dark code of silence; she was as secure here as a woman like her could expect to be.

Tonight was bath night—her one luxury. A month's grime could not be tolerated if she meant to earn her bread the next day. Hot water had been hauled up the narrow stairs at her request, and the tin tub now steamed invitingly in the centre of the room. Annie undressed, sniffing each garment with a grimace. Those that offended her would be washed after her own bath; by morning they would be dry enough, if a bit wrinkled.

Sighing, she stepped into the tub and let herself sink against the curved back. The warmth unfurled through her limbs, and she closed her eyes, letting the sliver of soap glide across her skin. She scrubbed diligently, lost in the small pleasure of cleanliness, and did not hear the whispers along the dock or the faint scrape of metal at her door.

The lock surrendered with a soft click.

By the time Annie reached for a towel, the door burst inward and two men flooded the room like a violent tide. She shrieked, but the tall one crossed the distance with startling speed and clamped a hand over her mouth.

"No noise, love," he murmured, his voice almost tender as he twirled a knife between his fingers, the blade catching the firelight. Annie's eyes widened; she nodded in terror. Satisfied, he released her and perched upon the edge of the bed, his gaze roving over her naked form with unashamed leisure.

The shorter man began rummaging through her things with practised efficiency.

"Oi—leave off!" Annie snapped. "Those are my possessions. Nothing there of yours."

The small man paid her no heed. A moment later, he straightened, holding aloft the leather pouch with the Raynsford crest gleaming upon it. His grin was feral. The moment the crest flashed in the lamplight, Annie understood her mistake.

The tall man chuckled. "Well then, that saves us the trouble of asking. This little trinket belongs to Lord Raynsford's son."

Annie's blood ran cold. So that's who she had robbed. The amount of coin had seemed almost impossible—now she understood. Calculation flickered across her features as she tried to salvage what she could.

"You know," she ventured, licking her lips, "you needn't mention the pouch. Or me. Say the boy's trail ran cold. I'll give you half the money—clean and fair."

The small man barked a laugh. "Half? Sweetheart, we'll be keeping the lot. And I doubt you'll be arguin' much."

"But it's not all his!" Annie protested, panic sharpening her voice. "Some of it's mine—my day's earnings. If you take it, I'll have nothing. It isn't fair!"

"Not fair?" the tall man repeated with false astonishment. He clicked his tongue and turned to his companion. "Did you hear that, Erwin? She says it isn't fair."

"What shall we do about that, then?" Erwin smirked.

Desperation clawed at her. If they took her money, she would be cast out into the streets. She forced a coy smile, adopting the sultry tone she used on men too foolish to know better.

"You could leave it," she whispered. "And I could take care of you both. A fair trade, wouldn't you say?" She let the towel slip to reveal more of her chest.

Both men stared. Erwin elbowed the tall man, who licked his lips slowly.

"Well now, aren't you a pretty one," he drawled. "We could have a bit of fun, eh?" He crouched beside the tub, leaning over so he might look straight down the slopes of her body. "A pity, though..."

Annie shivered. "A pity? What do you mean, love?" She let the towel fall even further, though her voice trembled.

The tall man lifted her chin with one hand, his thumb stroking the hollow of her throat. His other hand drifted down between her breasts, lingering there.

"It's a shame," he whispered, "that all this loveliness must go to waste."

Before she could gasp, he withdrew his hand, reached behind himself, and in one swift, practised motion, drew his knife across her throat. Warm blood sprayed upward in a dark, terrible arc, staining the wall.

Annie's scream died in a wet gurgle. She thrashed, kicking at the tin tub, water sloshing red as her strength ebbed away. Within moments, her body sagged and grew still, her lifeblood mingling with the lukewarm bathwater.

The tall man stood, wiping his blade on her own discarded clothing. Erwin stared unabashedly at the pale, exposed body bobbing gently in the crimson water.

"Damn shame," Erwin muttered.

The tall man only grinned.

Thaddeus hesitated under the shelter of the crumbling overhang, rain thrashing around him in cold, relentless sheets. The shabby building before him leaned perceptibly to one side, its sign half-rotted and swinging from a single rusted hook.

"Are you certain this is the place?" he asked, shouting above the storm.

Artie drifted beside him, looking dry and insufferably amused. "I said it was a place to stay when one has no money. I never claimed it was a palace."

Thaddeus looked down at the few coins in his hand—barely enough to purchase a crust of bread—and swallowed his pride. There was nothing else for it; the rain would drown him before morning if he attempted to remain in the graveyard again.

He pushed open the door.

Stench greeted him first—the sour tang of unwashed bodies, stale breath, and despair that clung to the walls like mildew. The long, open room was packed elbow to elbow, bodies pressed together on benches and pallets with scarcely a sliver of privacy between them. He had barely stepped over the threshold before a heavy silence rippled outward, the murmur of voices fading as every pair of eyes turned upon him.

An old woman near the hearth smiled a wide, toothless grin, appraising him with open hunger. Several men rose subtly—or not so subtly—from their seats, edging closer like wolves catching scent of easy prey.

Thaddeus stiffened. His fine clothes, though rumpled, gleamed like a beacon announcing his vulnerability. He longed to whisper to Artie but dared not. Speaking aloud to an invisible companion was an invitation to madness in the eyes of others—but then again, perhaps madness would afford him a measure of safety among this crowd.

A broad-shouldered man stepped directly into his path.

"Lost, are you?" the man asked, eyebrows arched in amusement. "I've heard of rich folk pinchin' pennies, but this is a bit much—even for miserly sorts."

Thaddeus gathered his courage. "I am not rich. I was robbed this evening. I've nothing but the clothes on my back."

The man studied him with growing interest. "No family? No place to go?"

"No," Thaddeus said quietly. "I am new to London."

The man gave a low whistle. "Then you're a lamb among wolves, you are." He folded his arms, then jerked his head toward the stairwell. "Best stick with me if you want to see morning. I'm Guss Fable, and I run this place. Come along."

Thaddeus followed, acutely aware of the eyes tracking his every step.

As they reached the stairs, a woman seated on the bottom step cackled. "Gettin' fancy tenants now, are ye, Guss?"

"Mind yer tongue, Fannie," Guss replied without slowing. "This one's under my protection. Not to be touched."

Thaddeus quickened his pace, unwilling to be left behind under Fannie's leer.

Up a flight, then another—past bodies huddled in hallways, past rooms where coughing and whispered quarrels seeped beneath the doorframes—until they reached a narrow door at the very top. Guss opened it to reveal a small chamber, sparsely furnished but unmistakably his own domain.

"This here's private," Guss said. "No one enters without my say so. You can set your belongings by the hearth. Sit, lad."

Thaddeus sank gratefully into a wobbly chair.

"Hungry?" Guss asked.

"I have not eaten all day."

"Well then, we'll see about that. Hard to sleep when your stomach's tryin' to chew through your spine." He chuckled. "But don't thank me yet. You haven't seen the food."

Thaddeus's answering smile faltered. Before he could dwell on starvation or death, Guss left the room and returned with a heap of coarse, patched clothing.

"You'd best change out of that peacock getup. It's like paintin' a target on your chest."

Thaddeus inspected the garments cautiously.

"They're clean," Guss assured him. "Patched, but clean."

Thaddeus turned away and undressed hesitantly. Guss faced the window, granting a measure of privacy.

"You're very observant," Thaddeus said as he dressed. "You weren't always the keeper of a lodging-house, were you?"

"No," Guss replied. "Once upon a time, I was butler to a prominent family. Gambled like a fool, lost like a bigger fool, and stole to pay my debts. They caught me. Could've ruined me entirely, but they didn't. Said I'd given many years of honest service." He shrugged. "So now I run this place—penitence for past sins."

Thaddeus finished dressing. The coarse fabric scratched, but it rendered him far less conspicuous.

"Thank you," he said sincerely.

"Don't thank me yet. Tell me how you wound up in my kip."

So Thaddeus did—his father, the expectations, the arranged marriage, his flight, the theft at the George—everything. Guss listened without judgement, only nodding from time to time.

When Thaddeus finished, something like relief washed over him. At least one soul in London now knew his story. If he were to vanish, he would not do so entirely unknown.

"Well then, your Lordship," Guss said, folding his arms, "you won't mind a bit o' advice."

"I should appreciate it."

"For starters, don't tell a soul who you are. You'll find yourself held for ransom faster than you can blink. Sell them fine clothes; they'll fetch enough coin to keep you fed. Learn a bit o' Cockney if you can—your tongue gives you away. And for pity's sake, stop lookin' like a wounded deer. Folk round here can smell fear."

"I'll heed your counsel," Thaddeus said humbly.

"Right then. Let's get you fed."

They descended to the kitchen—a drab, draughty room equipped with the bare essentials: a stove, battered pans, and a sink stained by years of hard use. Thaddeus collected a dented bowl and received a ladle of thin broth with indistinguishable scraps of meat floating within, accompanied by a chunk of stale bread. It was meagre, almost flavourless, but he devoured it gratefully.

When they returned to Guss's room, they heard voices murmuring inside.

"No, I ain't found nothin' yet. Nice clothes, no money. Useless, ain't he?"

"Aye. Best hurry. They'll be back any minute."

Guss strode in without hesitation, Thaddeus at his heels.

"Gentlemen," Guss growled, "can we assist you?"

The two men straightened at once, guilt carved plainly into their faces.

"Ah—no harm meant, Guss," one stammered. "Just tidyin' up your office a bit—"

"Tidying?" Guss's voice deepened dangerously. "D'you take me for a fool?"

He seized the nearest man by the front of his jacket and lifted him clean off the ground. Even Thaddeus flinched.

"I said he was under my protection," Guss roared. "And you break into my private room?"

"Sorry! We're sorry! We didn't take nothin'! He hasn't got anythin'!"

Guss hurled him aside like a rag doll. "Get out. And if either of you ever violate my space—or lay a hand on someone I guard—you'll regret it."

The men bolted without further argument.

Thaddeus let out a breath he hadn't realised he was holding.

"You'll stay here tonight," Guss said firmly. "I'll bring a cot. Until you rid yourself of those clothes, you're a mark."

Thaddeus gave a shaky laugh. "Were you a boxing butler, Guss?"

Guss snorted. "Before that, lad, I served in Her Majesty's Royal Navy."

"I suspected there was a story."

"Perhaps I'll tell it another time," Guss said softly. "My life's a warning, boy—of what comes when a man loses his bearings. Don't let that be your fate. Keep yourself straight."

Thaddeus nodded. For the first time since arriving in London, a faint glimmer of safety touched him. Perhaps only for the night—but a night was something.

# CHAPTER SEVEN

The following morning broke with a meagre, reluctant light, filtering weakly through the soot-stained panes of Guss Fable's private room. Thaddeus awoke with a start, stunned to discover he had slept the whole night through. For a moment he lay still, listening to the muted clamour of the kip—the groans, coughs, and quarrels of its waking inhabitants—yet none of it had pierced his slumber. He suspected it was Guss's steady presence that had lulled him; the man sat in a rickety chair near the cold hearth, boots planted wide, arms crossed over his broad chest, dozing with the vigilance of an old sailor accustomed to uneasy seas.

It was the first night since his arrival in London that Thaddeus had not been alone, and the realisation settled over him with a strange ache—a comfort, edged with the sting of its rarity.

He could not remain in such circumstances for long. This life—this precarious existence among the city's forgotten—was untenable. A plan would have to be made.

Before he could gather his thoughts further, Guss stirred with a grunt, rose, and disappeared down the stairs. He returned several minutes later with a steaming cup of black tea and a wooden bowl of porridge. Setting them on the desk with rough gentleness, he jerked his head toward Thaddeus in silent command to rise.

Thaddeus obeyed, his gratitude almost painful. As he ate, aware of the hollowness of his belly, he noticed Guss studying him from across the room.

"Do I have something on my face?" Thaddeus asked, wiping his mouth with the back of his hand.

Guss chuckled—a low, warm rumble. "No, lad. Only that you look a good deal younger in the daylight than you did last night. A man can appear twenty years older when he's frightened and half-starved." He leaned forward, resting his elbows upon his knees. "You aren't goin' to make it out there unless someone sees you through these first days—and that is precisely what I mean to do."

Thaddeus blinked, spoon halfway to his mouth. "How?"

"I spoke to someone this morning," Guss replied, lowering his voice as though sharing a confidence. "A man who owns an abandoned shop. He owes me—long story—and I've chosen this moment to call in the debt. His name is Silas Burke."

Guss reached into his waistcoat and produced a tarnished iron key, placing it before Thaddeus. "He's given me this. After you've finished your breakfast, I'll take you there. You said last night you fancied trying your hand at spiritualism." Guss sniffed with a faint expression of scepticism. "I think it's all moonshine and charlatan tricks, myself. But if you believe you might be good at it... well, I reckon even a dubious trade is better than none at all."

For several moments Thaddeus could not speak. His throat constricted, and he stared at the key as though it might vanish if he blinked. Kindness had been in short supply since he'd set foot in London, and now it nearly overwhelmed him.

"I don't know what to say except thank you," he murmured. Emotion threatened to choke him further, and he lowered his gaze so Guss would not see.

The older man gave a brusque pat to his hand, then turned toward the window, feigning preoccupation with the grey morning.

"Everyone deserves a chance. That's my motto." He turned back and fixed Thaddeus with a shrewd eye. "Silas didn't specify how long you may use the place. There's no lease, nothing binding. So you may be turned out at any time. Keep that in mind—and don't doddle."

Thaddeus nodded solemnly. He understood. Whatever opportunity this was, it was fleeting, and he must seize it before it slipped through his fingers.

"If you're ever in trouble," Guss added quietly, "you come see me. I'll do what I can to sort it."

"I don't understand," Thaddeus said, genuinely perplexed. "You have dozens of souls passing through here every week. Why help me? Why go to such lengths?"

Guss's expression shifted—something haunted flickered there, something unspoken. He cleared his throat roughly. "You remind me of someone I once knew. Let's leave it at that." He rose abruptly, as though the admission embarrassed him. "Finish your breakfast. We'll head to the shop once you're done."

He turned his back to the room, staring out at the dreary stretch of rooftops and chimneys as though the fog itself might swallow the conversation.

Thaddeus ate in silence, warmth blooming in his chest alongside the fear of what lay ahead. For the first time in days, the future seemed—if not secure—then at least possible.

When he finished, he set the bowl aside and closed his fingers around the key.

It felt heavy with promise.

And danger.

And hope.

Seagulls wheeled overhead, crying out to passersby as they glided on the evening currents, suspended as though by invisible threads. The lowering sun cast long amber streaks across the harbour, gilding the masts of anchored ships. Under ordinary circumstances, the murmur of the wharf—the slap of waves against pilings, the groan of thick ropes in their stays—might have soothed a weary mind.

But Detective Michael Barnes was not here for solace.

He was here to face yet another instance of man's inhumanity. The litany of tragedies that accompanied his profession had a way of turning even the most steadfast heart to stone, yet Barnes resisted the slow creep of indifference with all the stubbornness he possessed.

A commotion stirred the narrow dock-way as he approached. Curious onlookers pressed in, pulling shawls tight against the briny wind, craning for a glimpse of the horror within. Officers struggled to push them back, their shouts swallowed by the din of the harbour.

Barnes understood their morbid fascination, though it irritated him all the same. Every wasted second spent holding back the crowd was a second not spent reading the truth in the details.

He ducked inside the cramped dwelling, immediately raising a handkerchief to his nose. The copper tang of blood hung thick in the air, mingling with the damp stench of low tide. A body decayed quickly in warm water; this one had been steeping long enough to turn the room oppressive.

The squalor was typical of the docks—grit ground into the floorboards, mildew in the corners, and a perpetual salt-reek. Barnes crouched beside the tin bathtub. The woman's head lolled against the curved rim; her eyes stared wide with the frozen terror of betrayal. Her throat had been slashed cleanly, expertly—no hesitation in the blade. A sliver of soap drifted listlessly on the ruddy water, nudged by the faint motion of the tide outside.

She might have been pretty once, he thought. Hard living had carved its story into her features, but there lingered traces of youth beneath the grime.

"What were you, then?" Barnes murmured to himself. "A wharf-side doxy... perhaps worse off than most."

Her trade barely mattered; what mattered was the absence of

money. Women in her profession, however meagre their takings, kept coin close. The empty room suggested robbery, likely mixed with something fouler.

Barnes pushed to his feet, scanning the few belongings strewn about. A pair of worn shoes, a pitiful bundle of clothing, bent hairpins on the floor. Nothing worth killing for—nothing obvious, at least.

So what had she carried? And where had it gone?

His gaze swept the bed again, and something caught his eye—a scrap of paper twisted into the linens. When he reached for it, his fingers brushed metal. He lifted a key attached to a wooden tag:

THE GEORGE INN – RM 220

Barnes's brows rose. The George Inn? That establishment was far beyond the means of a dockside girl. All the more reason to visit.

He slipped the key into his coat.

He'd log it later. After he had a word with the innkeeper.

Footsteps creaked behind him. His partner, Edgar Dickman, entered with his usual stiff posture, his expression pinched with distaste.

Barnes smirked. "Well, Edgar? Robbery? Or perhaps a gentleman unwilling to pay for services rendered?"

Dickman went scarlet to the ears. Barnes never tired of it.

"I—I say we ought to cover her," Dickman sputtered, gaze darting from the corpse to the floor. "For decency's sake."

Barnes barked a short, dry laugh. "The coroner will see to it. Bodies don't require modesty."

He cast one last look over the room, committing every detail to memory.

"That's enough for now," he said, turning toward the door. "We've seen all we're going to see here."

Barnes stepped into the dying light of the wharf, the cries of the gulls following him like omens the colour of blood.

# CHAPTER SEVEN

By the time Thaddeus reached the building Guss had spoken of, the last of the daylight was retreating from the narrow lane, leaving the corner shop in a ghostly grey gloom. It stood half-forgotten between a boarded-up tailor's and a bustling bakery, its grimy windows filmed with years of neglect. A sour blend of mildew and old timber greeted him the moment the door groaned open—an odour so ancient it seemed baked into the very walls.

Dust sheeted the counters and shelves like a burial shroud, and the floorboards sagged treacherously underfoot, giving the disquieting sensation that the whole structure swayed with him. Still, Thaddeus could hear life bleeding through the thin walls: the thump of kneaded dough, the sharp rap of coin upon a baker's till, muttered greetings exchanged outside.

London, ever indifferent, carried on only a few feet away.

He wiped a sleeve across the front window. Beyond the murky glass, the street bustled in muted motion—boot heels striking cobblestone, skirts brushing past puddles, the faint clatter of a passing cart. Not quite a main thoroughfare, but a crossroads of sorts, and cheap enough that a fugitive lordling could almost afford hope.

Thaddeus set to work at once. The abandoned bucket and mop—left behind by some merciful former tenant—became his closest allies. Hours passed in a blur of scraping, scrubbing, wringing, and sweeping. Sweat gathered at his temples; blisters blossomed on hands long accustomed to being idle.

For the first time in his life, he knew the weight of labour. And with it came a revelation: the invisible hands that had once lifted every burden for him—maids, housekeepers, under-butlers—had laboured like this every day. The realisation struck him with a pang of humility.

When at last he stepped back, chest heaving, the shop no longer resembled a crypt. It was cleaner—though still marked by the permanent scent of age—and it was his. Or at least, his for now.

He carried the bucket to the back door and tossed the dirty water into the alley, watching it splash against the uneven stones. As he turned to go inside, a flicker of movement in the dimming alley caught his eye.

A man stood there.

Lurking. Half swallowed by shadow. He kept his face lowered, but even that slight tilt of the head conveyed appraisal—calculated, predatory. When he saw Thaddeus, he froze, as though deciding whether to advance or retreat.

"Er—can I help you?" Thaddeus asked, his voice higher than he'd intended.

The man's eyes darted along the alley as if awaiting some signal, and a chill rippled through Thaddeus's gut.

"Well... good day to you, then," he muttered, withdrawing quickly. He shut the door with haste and turned the key, breath shallow. From the narrow window, he peered out discreetly.

The man remained. Staring. Still as a gargoyle.

Moments later, another figure arrived—shorter, broader—and the two began an urgent, heated discussion. Thaddeus could not hear their words, but their gestures were unmistakable. They pointed toward the back door. Toward him.

His unease deepened into something colder, hollowing out the pit of his stomach.

At last the men drifted off, disappearing around the corner. Yet the dread they left behind clung to the air like a lingering fog.

"Nothing in the shop," Thaddeus whispered to himself. "Nothing here to steal."

But reassurance rang hollow.

He had barely retreated a few steps when a voice broke the quiet.

"What are you doing?"

Thaddeus yelped and flung the mop and bucket across the room. They crashed against the far wall.

"Arthur! For Heaven's sake—do not sneak up on a man!"

"Ghost, remember?" Artie floated a few inches above the floorboards, looking thoroughly amused. "We're not known for heavy footfall."

He drifted closer, expression shifting when he saw Thaddeus's pallor. "Good Lord, you look ready to drop. What's happened?"

"Two strange men in the alley," Thaddeus said. "They were staring at the door—at this place."

Arthur gave a light shrug. "This is London. The place practically breeds unsavoury sorts. Still—good instincts. We shall keep watch."

He gestured to a stool. "Sit, before you faint."

Thaddeus obeyed, elbows on his knees. Arthur surveyed the newly cleaned room, nodding appreciatively.

"You've worked wonders. A far cry from what we walked into. We'll soon be ready for business."

But Thaddeus did not respond. His gaze drifted over the polished floorboards as if searching for an anchor to steady him.

Arthur folded his arms. "Out with it."

"It's nothing."

"Lad, you are an abysmal liar. Try again."

Thaddeus exhaled shakily. "I'm wondering whether I can truly pull this off. Whether I'll make anything of this... life. Or whether I'll someday have to limp home and kneel before my father's damned ring."

Color rose to his cheeks—shame, frustration, fear warring for dominance.

Arthur's expression softened. "There is no dishonour in being afraid. Every creature, living or dead, fears something. But you"—he tapped Thaddeus's chest—"are building something from nothing. That requires courage no lordship can bestow."

Thaddeus looked up, uncertain.

"You possess a privilege most men never glimpse," Arthur continued. "You have crossed the threshold—seen how the world grinds ordinary folk into dust. And with that knowledge, you'll understand them. You'll know what hurts, what comforts. That is power. Not in cruelty, but in connection."

Thaddeus frowned. "I... don't like the sound of 'power' when you say it."

Arthur laughed softly. "Then let me rephrase. You will offer comfort to those who ache for their dead. And they, in turn, will trust you. That trust is the root of your success. Nothing sinister in it."

"I suppose," Thaddeus murmured.

Arthur hovered beside him, voice gentler now. "And remember—people want to believe. They want hope. You shall give them that. And I will help you every step."

Thaddeus allowed himself a small smile.

But in the back of the shop, beyond the window's ragged curtain, a shadow slipped silently across the alley.

Watching.

Waiting.

London did not easily loosen its grip on those it marked.

THADDEUS HAD SCARCELY finished arranging the meagre furnishings of his newly claimed shop—one rickety table, two mismatched chairs, and a cloth draped over a stubborn bloodstain—when the bell above the door gave a hesitant jingle.

His first client entered like a wary cat: chin lifted, eyes sharp, gloved hands clutching a reticule as if she expected the room itself to snatch it away. She was an older woman, thin-lipped, draped in respectability that did little to mask her nervousness. And truly, given the dingy corners and lingering odour of damp rot, he could hardly blame her.

"Please—be seated, Madam," Thaddeus said with forced warmth. He gestured toward the cleaner of the two chairs.

She examined it as one might inspect a questionable mushroom—prodding it with disdain before finally lowering herself onto it. Her nose tilted higher still, as though the very dust motes offended.

Thaddeus ignored the sting. He set before them a small sheaf of paper and a pen, arranging them as solemnly as though they were sacred instruments.

"My name is Thaddeus Priest," he began, adopting the smooth cadence he had practised. "I have been a Spiritualist all my life. Born with the gift. If you permit, I should like to give you a true and honest reading. May I have your name?"

The woman's lips twitched. "Regina Johnson," she said in a voice that quavered despite her attempts at hauteur.

"No," he corrected gently. "I should like the name of the person you wish to reach."

Her brows shot up. "You do not know it already?"

"I beg your pardon?"

"Well—most spiritualists I have visited can divine such matters without being told," she sniffed. "Can you not?"

Ah. A test. And a trap.

Thaddeus kept his tone even. "Madam, I am not in the business of parlour tricks. I seek only to contact your loved one with clarity. Pray, their name?"

Regina looked as though she might rise and leave out of sheer indignation. "If you insist," she said at last, drawing in a breath. "My mother. Mary Johnson."

Thaddeus wrote it down, nodding discreetly to Artie—hovering in the corner like drifting cigarette smoke—and the ghost dissolved through the wall in search of the deceased.

"Her birthdate?" Thaddeus asked.

Regina blinked hard. "Her birthdate? Why ever for?"

"There are many Mary Johnsons, I assure you," he said. "I would prefer to summon the proper one."

Regina's suspicion deepened, but at length she relented. "June twenty-fourth, eighteen hundred and two."

As Thaddeus noted it, he attempted a smile. "Tell me a little about her."

"So you want me to do all the work for you?" Her fingers tightened on her bag. "You might as well guess and be done with it. That is what the others do. Lie prettily. That is what people pay for."

Thaddeus let out a breath, silently begging Artie to hurry. "Not at all, Madam. Only a detail or two—to attune myself."

"I am not here to be played for a fool." She rose abruptly, nearly upsetting her chair. "This is a waste."

Just then, Artie drifted back in—accompanied by a stooped, frail old woman leaning heavily upon a cane. Her outline flickered, dim as a candle flame.

"She's weak," Artie murmured. "She won't stay long."

Thaddeus kept his eyes on Regina. "What would you ask of her?"

Regina drew herself up, affronted. "This is one of the poorest readings I have ever endured."

Her mother planted her cane with a sharp thud. "Still as stubborn and foolish as ever."

Thaddeus suppressed a smile. "Is there aught you would say to your mother, Madam?"

"No. If she were truly here—which she is not—she could speak for herself." Regina marched toward the door.

"Tell Regina her husband is cheating on her++," Mary snapped. "I always said he was a good-for-nothing."

Thaddeus winced. Of all spirits to greet his first client, it had to be one with a tongue sharp as a butcher's blade.

"Your mother... does not approve of your husband," he ventured.

Regina scoffed. "Anyone could say that."

"She says he is unfaithful. And that he is—ah—a good-for-nothing."

Regina froze with her hand upon the doorknob.

"She also says," Thaddeus added reluctantly, "that you are as stubborn and foolish as ever."

Regina's voice trembled. "And she is a cruel, horrid woman."

Mary sniffed. "She needs to grow up. Thinks herself above everyone. Never could stomach the truth."

Thaddeus repeated the words softly. Regina bristled. "I am not paying you to insult me, sir."

"This is not meant as insult," Thaddeus said earnestly. "Your mother appears tired. She leans upon a cane, and wears a linen dress with an apron. She... looks worn."

"I am tired," Mary muttered. "Tired of her nonsense."

Regina's expression faltered. The defiance melted, leaving something far more fragile beneath.

"Tell her..." Regina swallowed hard. "Tell her I forgive her. For the meanness. For the hunger. For... everything. I forgive her. I hope she finds peace."

Something in Mary's posture sagged. Her ghostly shoulders dropped, her cane trembling in her grip.

"I did the best I could," she said softly. "Her father left. It was only me. She wanted fine dresses. Wanted to be somebody. I could barely put bread on the table. She never knew... what I did to keep us alive."

Thaddeus's throat tightened.

"Tell her," Mary whispered, "that I accept her forgiveness. May it ease her heart."

Thaddeus relayed the message gently.

Regina's breath hitched. "My mother... would never say such things." But tears began rolling down her cheeks. "Never."

"She did," Thaddeus assured her quietly.

He glanced beside Artie. The space was empty now. "I am afraid —she has departed."

Regina nodded, trembling. She set a small coin into Thaddeus's palm. "I do not know whether this was real or not. But you captured her. Precisely."

She left without another word. Thaddeus watched her through the window as she walked away, shoulders shaking, then slowly steadying.

"Well," Artie said, folding his translucent arms. "That went better than expected."

Thaddeus looked down at the meagre coin glinting in his hand. "If matters continue like this, I shall be forced to advertise myself as 'The Spiritualist Who Will Insult You—for a Fee.' This place is working against us. Everything is stained or crumbling, and the floorboards—dear God, the floorboards."

His voice grew bleak.

"If I were alive," Artie declared, "I would slap you. Hard."

Thaddeus blinked. "What?"

"You've lived soft. You've had comfort and privilege. Now, at the first hint of hardship, you're ready to fold. Typical."

"That is not fair," Thaddeus snapped, heat rising to his cheeks. "My life has not been easy. Money and privilege—yes—but my father's contempt was a prison of its own."

"Is it truly so easy for you to give up?" Artie shot back. "Then go home. Bow your head. Live in your gilded cage."

That struck home. Thaddeus surged to his feet.

"No. I won't go back. I won't." His breath came hard and fast. "I only... need to know more."

"Then seek it," Artie said. "There are spiritualists across London. Attend their séances. Watch. Learn."

"I will need money for that."

"Then earn it." Artie gestured pointedly to the empty chair. "Do more readings. Gather funds. Study. Improve."

Thaddeus drew a slow breath, nodding. "Yes. Yes... you're right."

"Of course I'm right," Artie muttered. "Now come along. Let's return to the kip and—"

"No." Thaddeus's voice hardened. "I am done with that place. I'll sleep here. On the floor, or the counter. At least here, I do not fear thieves in the night."

Artie stared at him. Then, slowly, he grinned.

"Well then," he said. "Perhaps you do have a spine after all."

# CHAPTER EIGHT

Horace Raynsford settled heavily behind the great black-oak escritoire, its surface gleaming like a frozen pool in the half-light of his private rooms. This chamber, his inviolate sanctuary, was ordinarily a place where no servant dared tread unbidden. Yet even here—amid tapestries faded by decades, portraits of stern ancestors, and the lingering scent of pipe smoke—he could find no solace.

He crushed the latest missive in his fist, the parchment crackling like brittle bone. Another disappointment. Another embarrassment. His jaw clenched until the muscles ached. That young pup—his own son, his heir—had managed to make a mockery of him simply by vanishing into the night like a fugitive. No note. No trace. No obedience.

Reports came daily, and every day they offered the same useless nothings. His men, though loyal, had uncovered not a whisper of Lord Raynsford the younger's whereabouts. The entire household had grown accustomed to scattering like frightened birds whenever he stormed through the halls. Several of the servant girls had fled sobbing beneath his tirades; even his wife had retreated to her chambers and barred the door, her pale face glimpsed only fleetingly behind veiled curtains. She blamed him for Thaddeus's flight—and perhaps she was right.

Horace had anticipated rebellion. Thaddeus had always been headstrong, prone to ideas and sentiments unbecoming of a future head of the Raynsford line. Naturally he had baulked at the arranged marriage; naturally he had muttered about freedom and choice. But duty was duty, and a son must learn it one way or another. Horace meant to drag the boy back himself if need be. Too much depended upon it.

The dowry—dear God, the dowry. A sum large enough to quiet the most persistent of creditors, and to preserve the family's standing for another generation. Every reassurance he had offered to his financiers rested upon the unshakable promise of that union. Should word leak that Thaddeus had bolted like a common runaway... well, ruin had a way of arriving swiftly and publicly.

A soft rapping at the door snapped him from these grim contemplations. His temper flared like oil on a flame.

"What is it? I said I am not to be disturbed!"

The door creaked open by degrees. Jackson, his long-suffering butler, advanced into the room with the solemnity of a man entering a lion's den. Upon a silver tray lay a letter, neatly folded, bearing fresh ink. He bowed low.

"Your Lordship, an urgent communication has arrived. The messenger awaits your reply."

Hope struck Horace like a jolt of brandy—hot, dizzying. He surged from his chair, seizing the letter before Jackson could lower the tray fully.

"Very well! You are dismissed."

Jackson bowed once more and retreated, though he lingered by the door, leaving the slightest crack—just wide enough for a listening ear.

Horace tore open the envelope with trembling haste, barely bothering with the letter-opener. His eyes devoured the contents, darting like a huntsman's hawk, until—there! A line, a blessed line, that made his breath leave him in a gust of almost-hysterical relief.

He read it again, slower this time, aloud in a half-whisper:

> Found at the George Inn... Innkeeper demands recompense for lodgings... Skipped out without paying... Robbed by a trollop... In London.

"In London," he repeated, a laugh—sharp, triumphant—escaping him. "Oh, thank God... the fool boy is still in London."

The reprieve was intoxicating. For the first time in weeks, the tightness in his chest eased.

"Jackson!" he thundered.

The butler appeared in the doorway with suspicious promptness. Horace pretended not to notice.

He scribbled a reply with furious purpose, folded the letter with crisp authority, dripped wax upon its seam, and pressed his family seal into the molten red. Then he thrust the packet at Jackson, along with a small, heavy pouch whose contents clinked with promise—or threat.

"Give this to the messenger at once. And see that he carries the enclosed sum. My men will understand what must be done."

Jackson bowed, the silver tray steady in his hands despite the sudden weight. He left at once, though his brow furrowed with thoughts unspoken.

Behind him, Horace Raynsford sank back into his chair, fingertips drumming against the oak, eyes glinting with fierce, renewed determination.

His son had been found—at last.

And soon... he would be retrieved.

The next morning he awoke with a clearer head and spirits somewhat revived. He had a nine o'clock appointment, and the anticipation lent purpose to his movements. His stomach rumbled indignantly, but food could wait; work must come first. He washed his face and hands in the small basin, shaved with the cheap new razor, and brushed down his shirt until it resembled neatness. He was poor now —painfully so—but he need not appear disreputable. Cleanliness, he thought, was one dignity no man could take from him.

The sunlight, rare in London, spilled generously across the shop floor. There were no velvet curtains here, no smoke-filled parlours or shrouded tables. Only Thaddeus, his chair, his client, and a truth far simpler than most spiritualists dared to offer.

The reading itself went smoothly—remarkably so. The old gentleman's son stood plainly at the man's shoulder, pale and wistful, answering Thaddeus's questions with ease. Yet when the message was delivered in full, the client only frowned with a perplexed and disappointed air.

"That's it?" he scoffed. "No apparitions? No trembling of the lamps? No spectral wails?" His gaze flicked disdainfully around the bright, unadorned room. "There's not even a candle lit! My good sir, this is hardly the craft. Why, every medium I've visited put on a far more convincing show. Are you quite certain you know what you're doing?"

This, Thaddeus soon discovered, was to become the refrain of his new profession. It mattered not that he could truly see the dead, speak with them plainly, and deliver their words unaltered. No—his fault lay in his lack of theatrics. He was too efficient, too sincere. People did not want the truth, clean and unadorned; they wanted a spectacle. A performance. Something to stir their imaginations and justify their payment.

Thus, with a pained sigh and an even more pained expression, he conceded to Artie's advice. He would attend a few séances led by the capital's more seasoned spiritualists—observe their charlatan's tricks, their props, their flickering candles, their melodramatic sighs, and faintings. He had a few coins now, and he still possessed his fine clothes; he would don them to avoid being dismissed at the door.

It was during these small excursions that Thaddeus began to understand something profoundly unsettling: prejudice against the poor was not merely a Raynsford family affliction—it permeated nearly every street, shop, and drawing room of London. In worn garments, he was treated with suspicion, impatience, even contempt. Shopkeepers watched him as if he might pocket the wares. Women clutched their bags tighter. He learned the uneasy weight of being judged sight unseen.

And yet, when he wore his tailored coat and immaculate cravat, every door opened. People bowed their heads. The market stalls offered their best goods. Polite smiles replaced scowls. Privilege, he realised, was not invisible merely because he had never been without it. It had followed him all his life, cushioning every fall—until now.

This was but the first of many lessons that would unfurl before him.

Lessons he had never imagined he would need.

Rain clawed at the mullioned windows of Raynsford Manor, streaking the glass with thin, trembling rivulets. The afternoon had sunk into that dreary, sodden gloom peculiar to the English countryside—an hour that invited introspection, or in Horace Raynsford's case, brooding malice. He stood near the hearth, its flames snapping brightly, when Jackson entered with a stiff bow and presented a sealed correspondence upon a silver tray.

Horace snatched it with a curt growl, his patience worn to threads. He tore through the seal with a practised swipe of his thumb.

Problem taken care of at the Inn. Money retrieved. Request instructions.

The blockish handwriting of his hired men was unmistakable.

Horace's lip curled. Of course those two dullards would hesitate, likely entertaining notions of returning the stolen funds to Thaddeus —soft-hearted fools who had the gall to think loyalty extended to his boy.

But Horace had no intention of making life easier for his wayward son. If Thaddeus wished to flee his responsibilities—his birthright—then let him suffer the consequences of his own childish rebellion. Let him feel hunger. Let him feel fear. Let him learn precisely how ill-equipped he was to survive without the Raynsford fortune at his back.

With a decisive scrape of his quill, Horace penned his reply:

*Return the funds to me.*
*Deduct such sums as are required for expenses.*
*Proceed without interruption.*
*H.*

He blotted the ink, folded the paper into a sharp crease, and sealed it with his signet ring. His men were excellent hounds—brutal, discreet, absolutely reliable so long as their pockets remained heavy. And Horace was wise enough to know that keeping such men content was cheaper than replacing them.

"Jackson!" he barked.

The butler reappeared almost instantly, though without seeming to hurry—a skill learned after decades of navigating his master's temperament.

"Deliver this to the messenger at once," Horace ordered, thrusting the missive onto the tray. "See that he leaves without delay."

"Yes, my lord," Jackson murmured, though his eyes flickered with something like apprehension. He bowed deeply and withdrew.

Left alone once more, Horace allowed a slow, satisfied smile to creep across his sharp features. So the boy believed he could vanish into the world, survive on wits he did not possess, and defy his father's will? Foolish. Laughably foolish.

He could have Thaddeus dragged home by force—hogtied, if necessary—but that would be too simple. Too merciful. No, this lesson must be learned the hard way. Every mistake, every humiliation, every pang of hunger would chisel away at the lad's defiance until he begged—begged—to return to the safety of Raynsford Manor.

"Yes," Horace murmured to himself, moving back to the fire, the flames reflecting in his cold eyes. "He shall learn. And he shall not soon forget."

The storm outside raged on, the wind howling like a creature hungry for prey—an omen, perhaps, of the storm that Horace himself intended to unleash.

JACKSON HAD SERVED the Raynsford family for so many years that the rhythms of the manor were as familiar to him as breath itself. In all that time, he had learned to school his face into the polite neutrality expected of a butler—yet beneath that façade, his loyalties were more complex. His allegiance, of course, lay with the house of Raynsford. But if truth were to be told, one member held more of his heart than all the rest.

Young Master Thaddeus.

Jackson had helped raise the boy, wiping scraped knees, offering gentle instruction, and shielding him—whenever possible—from the barbed lash of his father's temper. And now, with the lad vanished into the world and Lord Horace in one of his dark moods, the butler knew he must tread cautiously if he hoped to protect him still.

This was one of those times.

The kitchen was quiet at this hour, lit only by a pair of lamps whose yellow glow softened the stone floors. Jackson stood at the central table, the letter in its crisp envelope resting before him atop the silver tray. Lord Horace had commanded him to deliver it to the messenger with haste—but Jackson had learned long ago that obedience did not preclude a little... investigation.

He cast a wary glance about. The servants were busy elsewhere; the housekeeper, Mrs. Keating, had retired early; only silence filled the vast chamber.

Just as he bent to his task, soft footfalls tapped across the tiled floor.

He stiffened—then exhaled with resigned amusement when a small finger jabbed him playfully in the ribs.

"Boo," whispered Athena, stifling a giggle.

"You, young lady, shall land yourself in trouble one day behaving like that," Jackson murmured, though he could not keep the smile from tugging at his lips.

"What are you doing?" Athena whispered, peering around him with wide, hopeful eyes.

"It is a letter Lord Horace intends to send to London with the carrier," Jackson replied.

"Is it about Thaddeus? Have we heard from him?" Her voice trembled with longing. She asked him that same question fifty times a day, it seemed, and each time a sharp sting of sympathy struck Jackson. The girl was hopelessly in love with the young master—that much had been plain to him for years.

He softened his tone. "I have told you, Miss Athena—should a letter addressed to you arrive from Master Thaddeus, I shall bring it to you without delay. Now go, child. Watch the door and ensure we remain undisturbed."

Athena hurried to the archway, standing guard as Jackson set to work.

He lifted the envelope and held it near the lamp's heat, softening the wax. With painstaking care, he eased the seal free, making certain the parchment remained unharmed. Once opened, he scanned the contents swiftly.

His jaw tightened.

So—Master Thaddeus had been robbed, and Lord Horace's men had retrieved the money... only for his Lordship to withhold it. A punishment. A lesson.

Jackson exhaled through his nose, a quiet, simmering sound of disapproval. He refolded the letter, warmed the wax once more, and pressed the seal back into place with the flat of a spoon.

A perfect forgery. Not a soul would know it had been tampered with.

When he tested the seal and found it firm, he slipped the letter onto the tray and departed to deliver it, his expression composed and unreadable.

But when he returned to the kitchen, that mask slipped.

He paced, hands clasped behind his back, agitation rolling through him.

"What is it?" Athena asked anxiously.

Jackson stopped, his voice low and grave. "The young master was indeed robbed. Lord Horace's men have his coin, yet... his lordship has elected not to return it. He means it as punishment."

Athena's face crumpled. "That's awful..."

"It is," Jackson said softly. His brow furrowed, and a new resolve flickered in his eyes. A plan—slender but growing—took root in his mind.

He turned to her, speaking in a low, steady voice. "Do not dismay, my girl. Master Thaddeus may be alone in London—but he is not without allies."

Athena wiped her eyes. "What can we do?"

Jackson glanced toward the hallway, ensuring no one lingered near.

"We shall help him," he whispered. "And, God willing, we shall do so without Lord Horace ever suspecting."

A hush settled over the kitchen—heavy with danger, but also with hope.

THE CORONER's office lay tucked behind St. Brigid's Churchyard, a squat brick building perpetually wreathed in chimney-smoke and damp. Detective Barnes arrived just as the evening gloom surrendered to full darkness, lamplight flickering across the narrow lane like a feeble heartbeat.

Inside, the smell hit him first—carbolic acid failing, as usual, to conquer the stench of formalin, old blood, and the quiet corruption of flesh. Dr. Earl Keiler, the district coroner, stood bent over the wharfside woman's body, spectacles perched precariously on the end of his long, hawkish nose.

"Evening, Barnes," he said without looking up. His voice was a dry rasp, as though his lungs had traded air for dust years ago. "I thought you'd come before the body cooled."

"Thought it best to hear your findings before rumours outrun fact," Barnes replied, stepping closer. "What have we?"

Dr. Keiler peeled back the blood-stained sheet with gloved hands. The woman lay pale as a ghost beneath the lamplight, her throat a dark ruin against her skin.

"I shall be concise," Keiler began. "Cause of death: exsanguination following a single, decisive incision to the throat. The cut is deep —clean through the carotid artery and jugular vein. No hesitation marks. Our killer is no novice."

Barnes nodded grimly. "A professional hand, then."

"Possibly," Keiler mused. "Note the angle of the cut. It came from behind her and slightly above—someone taller, stronger. She was likely seated or semi-reclined when it occurred."

"In the tub," Barnes murmured.

"Precisely. She would have had no footing—no leverage. A calculated choice by the murderer, or possibly good timing. Either way..." Keiler moved a lamplight closer. "Observe the bruising along the jaw.

A left-handed grip, fingers pressing upward beneath the chin. He held her steady as one might steady a lamb for slaughter."

Barnes folded his arms. "Any sign of struggle?"

"Minimal. A few defensive abrasions—fingernails broken when she grasped at the tub's rim. No other wounds. She died quickly."

Keiler hesitated, clearing his throat before continuing.

"There is one more matter," he said, voice lowering. "Given her trade, one might expect... evidence of recent relations. But there is none. No indication she entertained a client shortly before death."

Barnes arched a brow. "Meaning she wasn't killed in the midst of her work."

"Precisely. Nor does she bear the marks of prolonged abuse, drugging, or stupor. She bathed voluntarily, unaware."

"Someone she trusted?" Barnes ventured.

"Or someone who rendered her briefly compliant. Hard to say." Keiler removed his spectacles and rubbed his eyes. "What is certain is that the murderer took pains. No robbery gone amiss. He did not panic." He paused. "He selected his moment."

Barnes retrieved the key from his coat pocket, turning it over between his fingers.

"I found this among her things," he said. "The George Inn. Room two-twenty."

Keiler's brows knitted. "The George? A curious lodging for a woman of her circumstances."

"My thoughts exactly. I'll be paying the innkeeper a visit tonight."

"Good." Keiler stretched the sheet over the body once more, gentling it over her like a shroud. "Whoever did this knew precisely what he was about, Detective. I fear this will not be the last such case."

Barnes bowed his head slightly—a silent acknowledgment of the grim road ahead.

"Let us hope you are wrong, doctor," he said, though the hollow edge in his voice betrayed his doubt. "Send me the full report when finished."

"As always."

Barnes turned toward the door. Outside, the church bell tolled the hour—slow, resounding, mournful. It followed him into the night as he left the coroner's house behind, key burning coldly in his pocket, its secrets yet to be coaxed into the light.

# CHAPTER NINE

Thaddeus had resigned himself, with no small degree of distaste, to the necessity of studying the business of Spiritualism. His earnest method of communing with spirits—quiet, sincere, devoid of spectacle—brought him only pennies, and even those sporadically. The public, it seemed, craved marvels. And if he wished to survive long enough to refine his gifts into something respectable, he must discover what those marvels entailed.

Thus he found himself preparing to attend a séance.

He buttoned his waistcoat with care, his movements slow, reluctant. His research had revealed that séances varied in style—some dramatic, some solemn, others little more than parlour games dressed in mysticism. But he needed to know what most people expected. Even if the entrance fee was a painful indulgence, he could not afford ignorance.

As he straightened his collar, a pale shimmer formed near the ceiling. Artie drifted into view, adopting his usual posture of amused disdain.

"So," the ghost sniffed, arms folded across his translucent chest, "you are off to observe another of those charlatans today. Do not expect much. They are not real, you know. Not like you."

Thaddeus lowered his head, accepting the compliment without flourish. "I am no more pleased about this than you are," he muttered. "But a man must eat."

Artie softened, inclining his head with spectral sympathy before dissolving into mist.

The séance was scheduled for eight o'clock precisely. Thaddeus, determined not to commit some unknown breach of etiquette, arrived a quarter-hour early. Clad in his best (and somewhat wrinkled) suit, he hovered uncertainly at the edge of the walkway. He did not know whether guests were permitted to enter before the Spiritualist had prepared her stage. Likely not. Tricks must be arranged, strings set, shadows cultivated.

So he waited, twirling his umbrella absently until a prickle of unease crept along his spine.

A man stood across the narrow street, staring at him with such intensity that Thaddeus froze mid-twirl. Self-conscious, he straightened his posture, attempting to appear dignified. But when he glanced back—

The man was gone.

Maybe it was strange to linger outside a séance like a schoolboy awaiting a scolding. Or perhaps London held stranger watchers than he liked to imagine.

Three women soon approached the house, their skirts rustling like dry leaves. The eldest fixed Thaddeus with a flinty glare and stamped her cane sharply upon the pavement.

"I do not care what you have to say or what you are selling," she snapped. "We desire to be left alone."

Thaddeus blinked. "Madam, I beg your pardon. I am no solicitor. I am here for the séance."

The two younger women tittered behind lace handkerchiefs. The elder studied Thaddeus more carefully, her keen eyes roving from his polished boots to the frayed cuff of his sleeve.

"I have not seen you before," she said at last, suspicion clinging to every word.

Thaddeus inclined his head. "I am new to this world, I fear."

Before she could interrogate him further, the front door swung open. A woman dressed in sombre purple—her hat trimmed with black feathers suitable for a funeral—surveyed the gathering with theatrical solemnity. A few additional guests arrived, and she beckoned them inside with a graceful tilt of the wrist.

Thaddeus stepped aside, bowing politely. "Ladies."

They swept past him in a rustle of silk and perfume.

THE INTERIOR WAS STIFLING. Heavy velvet curtains smothered each window, trapping both darkness and heat. A large round table dominated the centre of the parlour, its polished surface gleaming in the dim candlelight. The shadows along the walls writhed like creatures awakened by the incense that curled lazily through the air.

Thaddeus prayed he would not succumb to a coughing fit.

The woman in purple indicated the arrangement of seats. "Alternating gentleman and lady, if you please."

Chairs scraped across the wooden floor with a chorus of grating protest. Thaddeus found himself surprised—almost disappointed—by the austerity of the room. No beads, no ornate cloths, no ostentatious spiritual paraphernalia. Merely shadows, candles, and an air of practised solemnity.

*Perhaps that is the trick,* Thaddeus mused, settling into a decidedly uncomfortable chair. A discomfort that heightens the senses, makes one more susceptible to fear or wonder.

"Ladies and gentlemen," the hostess intoned, "Miss Murray will be with you shortly."

She vanished with unnerving swiftness.

Thaddeus's gaze swept the circle. Nine participants. Five men, four women. With Miss Murray, the balance would be perfect—unless the odd man was her counterweight. Ah, to have such a crowd of paying customers! Even if the methods were dubious, the woman commanded attention.

A delicate throat cleared behind him. The guests turned as one.

Miss Melisendra Murray glided into the room, every movement deliberate. Her face was veiled in black gauze; her voice trembled as she seated herself—directly beside Thaddeus.

His breath caught. Well. Fortune smiles upon me after all.

"My name is Melisendra Murray," she murmured, "and may the spirits be with us this night."

Her assistant—the woman in purple—returned bearing a wicker basket. "Miss Murray asks only for a modest donation, whatever you may spare."

Coins clinked softly as they passed the basket around. Some guests gave generously, others guiltily. Thaddeus parted with his precious shillings with a pang.

Then the performance truly began.

A pen and stack of paper were laid before Miss Murray. The central candle was lit with exaggerated reverence; all other lamps were dimmed until the room sank into a womb of shadows.

Miss Murray inhaled deeply, her veil trembling with each breath. "Let us pray for protection and guidance."

She recited the Lord's Prayer with a trembling fervour. The air seemed to tighten. The guests bowed their heads; Thaddeus joined them, feeling strangely exposed.

When she finished, she lifted her face and fixed each visitor with a penetrating stare.

"Write your question," she whispered, "and place it in the basket."

Thaddeus's plan was simple: he would test her. He wrote a question entirely unrelated to his life or family—something impossible to connect to him. If she pretended otherwise, he would know.

Miss Murray gathered the basket. She lowered her head, and for a moment, the room grew silent as a tomb.

Then—her head snapped up.

Her eyes flew open.

She seized a slip of paper.

"I am sensing this belongs to you, Mr. Mitchell. You wish to speak to your dearly departed mother."

Mr. Mitchell gasped, trembling. Thaddeus observed him with fascination; the man's belief radiated like heat.

Miss Murray continued, voice low, laden with false mystique. She scribbled upon her paper—nonsense at first, then shaping words. Hello my son. Mr. Mitchell nearly wept. More generalities followed: a box of photographs, a mother's wish to preserve them. Thaddeus marvelled at how easily the man accepted it.

Then it was his turn.

"I have someone named... Palmer?" Miss Murray asked.

Thaddeus raised his hand. "That is me."

She went through her motions—scribbling aimlessly, eyes growing glassy. But then her posture stilled. She raised her head, one eyebrow arching behind her veil.

"I see," she murmured, her gaze sharpening upon him, "that this is a friend of yours. I am terribly sorry for your loss."

Thaddeus's stomach tightened. Palmer was very much alive. He forced a polite nod. "Thank you."

"I see an accident... an accident with a road locomotive... and a dog?"

Thaddeus froze.

Fitz... his new steam carriage...

This was no longer amusing.

He gave no outward reaction, yet Miss Murray's expression brightened subtly, as though she had caught the faintest tremor of fear.

"I would advise caution, Mr. Priest." She said his surname with pointed precision. No malice, no warmth—merely certainty. Yet Thaddeus was stripped bare.

"Your friend urges you to stay safe and avoid rash decisions. I trust that resonates?"

General words, yes—but something in them felt... wrong. As though a hand had brushed too close to something private.

"Yes," Thaddeus whispered. "Thank you."

Suddenly, overwhelmingly, he wished the reading to end.

THE COURIER ARRIVED on the third evening, his cloak dripping with rainwater and his boots leaving a trail across the marble floor. Jackson received the leather despatch bag with a bow and dismissed the man to the servants' entrance for a warm meal. Only after the footsteps faded did Jackson carry the heavy bag into the kitchen.

He set it down upon the butcher's block with a dull thud.

The weight of it told him everything. Young Master Thaddeus—despite having run off without his father's blessing—had not done so unprepared. A tightness seized Jackson's chest at the thought. The boy would have planned as well as his limited means allowed, he thought. Ever careful. Ever earnest.

How he wished he could send the entire sum back to him. Heaven knew the lad needed it. But Horace Raynsford expected something returned, and suspicion was a peril Jackson dared not risk.

He had prepared another bag—a neat little satchel to send with the courier—filled with practical items a young man alone in London might need. Now he lifted the courier's pouch and opened it carefully, the coins whispering against one another. Jackson drew out a smaller sack and began dividing the money with meticulous precision. He weighed Thaddeus's pouch first, then Horace's, ensuring the young master's was the heavier. It was the least he could do. Jackson had watched the Raynsford's rise and fall for thirty years. Of them all, only the young master had ever possessed a conscience. And for that, he had Jackson's undying loyalty.

A soft clearing of a throat startled him so violently he very nearly dropped the coins.

He spun around.

"Madam Raynsford!" he blurted, his heart hammering. "It—it is not what it appears. I assure you, I am not stealing. I was attempting only to—"

"To prepare a satchel for Thaddeus?" Judith Raynsford finished gently. "My dear Jackson, I suspected you would try to help my son. I am aware of your fondness for him, and I would assist you, even if my husband persists in believing himself the master of every breath taken under this roof."

Her tone held a quiet steel that Jackson had always admired.

She stepped forward, her skirts whispering over the stone tiles, and set a smaller pouch of coins upon the table. "Pour all of that money into the new pouch for Thaddeus."

Jackson blinked. "Madam—Master Horace will suspect something when the money does not arrive as expected."

"Which," Judith said calmly, "is precisely why I have this."

She nudged the lighter pouch toward him.

"Fill Horace's with this. The weight will satisfy him, and the sums—well, I doubt he troubles himself with counting. Send my son what he is owed."

She withdrew an envelope from her reticule, tracing its sealed edge with her fingertips. "And please include this in the satchel."

Jackson nodded and accepted it, bowing deeply. "Yes, Madam."

Judith's expression softened—only slightly, for she was not a woman who permitted many glimpses of her heart. "Thank you, Jackson. You have always watched over Thaddeus, and I value it more than you know."

Then, lowering her voice, she added, "Would you be so good as to deliver the satchel yourself? Directly into my son's hands? The carriage is already waiting for you."

Jackson startled once more. “Madam, naturally I would do anything for the young master, but—I do not know where he is staying.”

“That,” Judith said with a gleam of determination, “is precisely why I require you. I want to know where my son is. Truly know.”

“Madam,” Jackson said carefully, “I am no detective. I cannot promise I shall find him.”

“I believe he went first to the George Inn,” she replied. “He will not be there now, but...” She reached into her sleeve and produced a small folded slip of paper. “Horace’s men are staying at this boarding house. If you can locate them—and remain unseen by them—they will undoubtedly lead you to Thaddeus.”

Jackson accepted the note and tucked it into his vest. “Very well, Madam. But when Master Horace calls for me—and finds I am gone—? Wouldn’t it be more appropriate to send Mr. Fitzgerald?”

Judith smiled, the very picture of calm defiance. “I see. If you are gone too long, Horace might suspect. Fitz can be trusted to be sure and it might do Thaddeus some good to see his old friend. Very well then, I trust your judgement, Jackson.”

“Very good Madam, I shall see to it,” he said, giving her a conspiratorial smile.

Thaddeus returned to the shop late that evening, his mind still tangled around the strange reading setup he’d encountered earlier. He was so deep in thought that he didn’t notice the soft glow coming from inside the shop—or the silhouette waiting for him.

A low whistle cut through the silence.

Thaddeus jerked his head up to find a man standing just beyond the counter, staring at him as though he’d discovered a fox in his henhouse.

"Well, I'll be," the man said, jaw slack. "And here I was told you were poor."

"Excuse me? Who are you?" Thaddeus asked.

"I'm the shop owner." The man folded his arms. "Came by to tell you I'll need you out tomorrow afternoon. Got a buyer coming to look the place over. I see you've cleaned up a bit, so thanks for that—makes it easier to sell. This is a favour for Guss, you know. Normally I don't let anyone stay rent-free. But now I find you strolling in dressed like a banker and I feel like a fool."

"No, no, you—you misunderstand," said Thaddeus quickly. "I am poor. This is my only fine set of clothes. For business. My usual things have patches at the knees and are practically threadbare."

"I see," the shop owner said flatly. "Doesn't look that way from where I'm standing." His gaze flicked downward. "Saw your bag, too. Nice leather. Had a look inside. You've got some fine belongings."

"You went through my things?" Thaddeus blurted.

"My shop," the man snapped. "You weren't here, so yes, I did."

Thaddeus rushed behind the counter, heart pounding. He checked his satchel. Everything was still there.

"I'm no thief," the shop owner hissed. "Rich of you to imply, considering the way you're taking advantage. I've half a mind to call the police and have you thrown out."

"No—please, don't do that," Thaddeus said. "What do you want? How can I set this right?"

The man's eyes travelled lazily over Thaddeus's coat, waistcoat, and polished boots. A slow, greedy smile crept across his face.

"I'll take those fancy clothes you've got on."

Thaddeus stared at him. "I'm sorry?"

"The clothes," the man repeated. "You and I are about the same size. Something like that would set me up fine—I've business tomorrow meself. I'll take 'em as payment."

"This is absurd. I need these clothes to conduct business."

"Nothing personal," the man said cheerfully. "But I can use them just as much as you."

"No, this is extortion," Thaddeus said, disgust sharpening his voice.

"Well," said the shopkeeper, turning toward the door, "if you're going to be like that, I'll fetch the police."

"Don't—don't do that," Thaddeus said, panic rising. The man paused, a sly look returning to his face.

"Well then," he said, "you give me the clothes, and you can stay the night."

"The night? Only one?" Thaddeus's voice cracked. "These clothes are worth a month's rent."

"That's the deal. Take it or leave it. Otherwise it's debtor's prison for you. And as I said—I've a buyer coming. You'll be out in the morning."

Thaddeus was cornered. It didn't even occur to him to run; he'd never met the true owner—Guss had handled everything. And this man, whoever he was, reeked of petty criminal confidence.

"I suppose," Thaddeus whispered, "I have no choice."

"Right then. Hand them over."

Thaddeus ducked behind the bar for modesty and changed into his patched street clothes. He threw the folded garments at the man. The shopkeeper caught them and laughed.

"Be gone by morning," he said, still chuckling as he stepped out into the night.

The door shut. Silence swelled.

Thaddeus sank onto the stool, exhaustion settling into his bones like damp cold. "Will my luck ever change? What do I do now...?"

A shimmer of air rippled beside him. Artie appeared.

"I know of a place—"

Thaddeus cut him off, slicing the air with his hand. "I think I'd better figure this one out on my own. None of your suggestions have panned out so far."

Artie drew back as though struck. "That's not fair. I saved you from those thugs in the graveyard. I showed you where the kip was so you could keep dry. And Guss is the one who arranged this shop.

Don't blame me for the owner turning out to be a snake." He folded his arms and floated rigidly, his back to Thaddeus.

Thaddeus rubbed his face. "You're right. I'm sorry. I shouldn't take it out on you. I just... I never imagined life in London would be like this. You and Guss have been decent. Others—not so much." He sighed. "Alright. I'm listening. What should I do?"

Artie turned slightly, mollified. "I know of a place. It's where I stay most of the time. I mentioned it before but you didn't have any money. You haven't much now, but enough—enough for Mrs. Parsons."

"Mrs. Parsons?" Thaddeus asked.

"She runs a boarding house. A clean one. Private rooms, three meals a day. But she's strict. Payment up front. She won't let you through the door if you can't pay."

Thaddeus nodded, beaten but hopeful. "Then tomorrow... you and I will go see Mrs. Parsons. I've nowhere else to go."

The George Inn

| Date | Names and Residence | Room No. | Remarks |
|---|---|---|---|
| June 5th | Mr. Henry Collins, Liverpool | – 15 | 2 days. |
| June 6th | Samuel H. Watson, York | – 12 – | Paid |
| June 7th | Miss Annie Fletcher, London | – 220 – | Staying 1 Night. |
| | Mr. & Mrs. P. Dawson, Bath | – 8 – | With coach & luggage. |
| June 8th | | | |
| | Thaddeus Raynsford | – 118 – | June 8th, 1862 |
| | - Supper & Breakfast | | |
| | - Requested Morning Papers. | | |
| | Richard M. Atwood, Manchester - | – 14 – | |
| | - Settled Acct. | | |
| | Robert Gill, Norwich | – 5 – | 2 Nights |
| | Eleanor Partridge, Oxford | – 9 – | Late Arrival. |
| June 10th | | | |
| | Victor Jenkins, Edinburgh, | – 220 – | June 10th, 1862. |
| | - Staying 3 Nights. | | |
| | - Paid in Advance. | | |

• Daily Journal available.

• Fresh Strawberries & Cream.

# CHAPTER NINE

THE GEORGE INN slouched at the corner of Barrow Street like a great, brooding animal—its eaves hanging low, its windows dim behind layers of soot and grime. A single lantern swung at the door, creaking upon its rusted chain as though protesting each gust of wind. Barnes paused under its flickering glow, the cold night air prickling his skin.

Inside, the tavern breathed stale tobacco and sour ale. A few late drinkers hunched over their tankards, their faces half-obscured in shadow. The fire on the hearth crackled with more malice than warmth.

But Barnes' eyes moved past them all—settling instead on the innkeeper.

A stout man with a florid face and small, watchful eyes, he stood behind the bar polishing a glass that was unlikely ever to look clean. When he noticed Barnes approaching, his expression shifted—first to irritation at being interrupted, then to polite suspicion.

"Evenin', sir," he said, the words stiff as cold dough. "You'll be wanting a room or a drink?"

Barnes set the tarnished room key upon the counter with a quiet metallic click.

"Neither."

The innkeeper froze, his gaze fixed upon the number engraved on the key.

Room 220.

"I believe," Barnes said softly, "this belongs here."

A twitch rippled through the man's cheek. Only a moment—no longer—but Barnes caught it.

"And where'd you be gettin' that?" the innkeeper asked, the question too casual by half.

"From the effects of a deceased woman. One who rented that room recently." Barnes leaned in slightly, lowering his voice so that only the innkeeper could hear. "She was found murdered in her lodgings yesterday."

The innkeeper paled noticeably, though he attempted a scoff. "Murdered? Here? Bah—nonsense."

"Not here," Barnes said. "But she lodged with you. And I will know everything about her stay."

He produced a small leather notebook from his coat. "Let's begin with her name."

The innkeeper's mouth opened, then closed again. His eyes darted around the room as if hunting for an escape.

"She gave none," he muttered. "Most don't. Women of her... profession."

Barnes heard the lie in the evasiveness, the strained neutrality in the man's tone.

"She came alone?" the Detective pressed.

"Aye. Leastways, I never saw no one accompany her."

Again, the small betraying flicker—a shift of the eyes, a tightening of the jaw. Barnes studied him in silence until the innkeeper seemed to wilt beneath it.

"Room 220," Barnes continued, tapping the key. "I'll need to see it."

The innkeeper's reaction was immediate and visceral. His shoulders stiffened, and he took a step back as though Barnes had threatened to strike him.

"Can't do that, sir," he stammered. "It's taken—rented again. Can't be disturbin' the guests."

"And yet," Barnes replied, "I must." He grabbed the guest register and turned it around to read. Room 220 had indeed been let out to one Victor Jenkins.

He slipped his coat aside just enough to reveal the glint of his badge and the Beaumont–Adams revolver holstered beneath it. Not a threat, merely fact.

The innkeeper swallowed hard. "I'll... see if the gentleman's awake," he said, turning toward the staircase.

Barnes caught his arm before he could retreat. "That won't be necessary. You will take me now."

The innkeeper looked up the staircase as if it were the gallows. "Very well," he whispered, defeated. "But I'm telling you—this ain't goin' to end well."

*For whom*, Barnes wondered?

The man led him through the tavern and up the narrow, groaning stairs, where the lamps grew fewer and shadows more commanding. The higher they climbed, the colder the air became, as if the upper floor existed at the threshold of some darker realm.

At last they stopped before a door whose number had been crudely scratched into the wood.

220.

The innkeeper's hand shook as he inserted the master key. "Just so you know... this is against my better judgement, Detective," he murmured.

The lock gave with a reluctant click and the door creaked open.

The room beyond was dark. Too dark. And far, far too still.

THE DARKNESS inside the chamber felt palpable—an oppressive, velvety shroud that seemed to thicken the moment Barnes stepped across the threshold. The innkeeper lingered behind him, wringing his hands, his breath rattling like a loose windowpane.

Barnes produced a small taper from his coat and struck a match. The flame hissed to life, quivering as though reluctant to illuminate what lay ahead.

Slowly, the room emerged from obscurity.

It was spare—almost unnervingly so. The narrow bed was unmade, the coverlet tossed and crumpled. Bottles scattered the floor, as if someone had been on a bender. A lone chair sat askew near the window. The air held the faint scent of rain-darkened cloth and something else—something metallic.

Blood.

Not fresh, but recent enough to cling to the walls like a whispered warning. Barnes stepped farther inside, raising the taper. That was when he saw it.

A smear of dried blood marred the floorboards near the foot of the bed. Not a pool, not enough for a killing blow—but a trace. A mark left by someone who had been wounded... or by someone dragging something small but bleeding.

"What," Barnes murmured, "has transpired here?"

The innkeeper hovered in the doorway, refusing to come in. "I—I told you, sir, she stayed the night but left come morning. Room's been let again since."

"Indeed?" Barnes asked, crouching beside the bloodstain. "How curious that your new tenant appears to have vanished. Or did he ever exist at all?"

The innkeeper said nothing.

Rising, Barnes moved to the window. The shutters were warped, letting in a narrow blade of sickly light from the gas-lamps below. He pressed a hand along the sill.

Dust.

Undisturbed.

Meaning no one had opened the window—not to flee, not to break in.

Then what—

His taper cast a feeble glow across the opposite corner, revealing something small glinting upon the floorboards. Barnes crossed the room in two long strides and bent to retrieve it.

A button.

Smooth, dark, and of expensive make.

Not from the clothing of a dockside prostitute—nor from anything in this cheap inn chamber.

But from the coat of a gentleman.

And there was more. Beneath the button, pressed into the grain of the floorboards, he found a thin strand of hair—red-gold, shimmering like a captured ember in the candlelight.

Barnes stiffened.

The murdered woman's hair had been black. This hair belonged to someone else. Someone who had been here. Someone who had left in haste—or been taken.

He tucked both items into his pocket. "You said a gentleman rents this room."

The innkeeper flinched. "Aye."

"When did he arrive?" asked Barnes.

"This mornin', sir. Not long after the woman checked out."

"Did you see his face?"

"A glimpse only," the innkeeper murmured. "Tall fellow. Well-dressed. He paid in advance and went straight to his room. Not a word since."

Barnes regarded him in silence. "And yet you did not think this worth mentioning."

The innkeeper's voice cracked. "People come and go, sir. I don't ask questions. Not in my position."

Barnes turned his attention back to the room, his gaze sweeping the stark corners, the unmade bed, the bloodstain beginning to flake at the edges.

A woman had come here after leaving her lodgings. She had met someone. Someone who did not wish to be found.

Someone with means and perhaps with motive.

Then Barnes felt it—a disturbance in the still air, a faint vibration beneath the floorboards. He stiffened.

A measured tread was climbing the stairs. Slow. Deliberate.

Not the light step of a guest, nor the sodden stumble of a drunkard.

Something more calculated than that.

More controlled.

The innkeeper heard it too. His breathing quickened; his eyes widened with dread.

"Sir..." he whispered. "He's coming back."

Barnes stepped away from the door, one hand drifting unconsciously to the revolver beneath his coat.

Nearer now.

Up the final stair.

Along the hall.

And then—

Stopped.

Right outside Room 220.

The doorknob began to turn.

# CHAPTER TEN

The doorknob turned slowly—too slowly—as though the unseen hand on the other side wavered, unsure whether to continue. The metal groaned, a strained metallic whine, and then the door itself creaked open on hinges that had long since surrendered to rust. The darkness inside the threshold shivered before giving way to the wide silhouette of a portly man whose weight made the floorboards gently protest beneath him.

Barnes nearly drew his revolver.

Then recognition dawned.

"There you are," Dickman huffed, his breath fogging the cold air of the room. "I've been looking all over for you. A little on edge, are we?"

"This is a crime scene," Barnes growled, lowering his shoulders, but not his guard. "You can hardly blame me for being cautious."

Dickman stepped inside, shutting the warped door behind him. His practised eyes roamed the gloom. "Find anything interesting?"

Barnes exhaled sharply. "Come in and lend a hand. You've always had the sharper eye. Perhaps you'll notice something in all this..." His gaze swept the chaos. "Mess."

From behind them, the innkeeper cleared his throat with nervous urgency. The bell downstairs chimed, echoing faintly through the corridors like a knell in an empty church.

"Well, gentlemen, if you've no further need of me, I'm wanted at the desk." He bobbed his head, already backing away. "Lots to see to. I'll leave you to it."

Barnes waved him off, grateful. The man had hovered like a fly on a carcass. When the innkeeper's footsteps finally faded the room felt, strangely, even quieter.

Dickman advanced cautiously. Dust motes floated in the weak light that seeped through the grimy windowpanes. A cloying sweetness seeped from the shadows—thick, heavy, unmistakable.

He wrinkled his nose. "Opium."

Barnes nodded. "Doesn't belong to our suspect. And even if it did, this room's been disturbed so thoroughly I doubt we'll find anything uncontaminated. Not exactly the most respectable of rooms. If there were clues here, someone's already seen fit to sweep them away."

"I'm not surprised," Dickman murmured. "Still, we finish what we came for."

He crouched, his knees cracking loudly in the oppressive quiet. The floor was sticky in places, dusty in others. He leaned farther, bracing a hand against the bed frame, and peered beneath.

"Oh? What's this?" His tone sharpened.

He reached deep into the shadows until his fingers brushed something cool. With a grunt, he drew out a pocket watch—gleaming even through the grime, its craftsmanship far too fine for the previous tenants.

"Well, now," Dickman breathed, flipping it open. The hinge clicked crisply. "This is quality... Certainly above the pay of whoever stayed here last."

Inside the cover, a glint of engraving caught the light.

Dickman's eyebrows rose. "T. A. R."

Barnes leaned in, eyes narrowing. "That might be the only

evidence this room yields... but it's something. And downstairs?" He folded his arms tightly. "The sign-in ledger carried the name Thaddeus Raynsford."

Dickman let out a sharp, low whistle.

"Lord Raynsford's son?" he asked, incredulous.

"So that's who he is." Barnes shook his head, jaw tight. "You know more about the upper class than I ever cared to. I've never placed much faith in their sort."

Dickman responded grimly, "That's not merely upper class. That's aristocracy. If the Lord's son is involved in any of this"—he snapped the pocket watch shut with a decisive click—"this case just became a hell of a lot more dangerous than either of us would like."

"Indeed," Barnes said quietly.

The men stood in the stale, dim air of the room a moment longer, listening to the settling of the old boards, the distant drip of a leaking pipe, the subtle hum of a place that had seen too much and remembered everything.

Then, resigned, they swept the room once more, but nothing remained—no hidden papers, no forgotten weapon, no shadowy figure lurking just out of sight.

The room had yielded its single truth.

Everything else had been swallowed by silence.

They left together, stepping back into the corridor as the door moaned closed behind them—its laments echoing down the long hallway like a warning.

The boarding house must have been a handsome building in its prime. Even now, beneath the soft decay of disuse, Thaddeus could see remnants of its former dignity—the elegant brickwork, the tall windows, the polished but worn brass fixtures. He searched for a sign advertising rooms, but there was none. Still, this was the address Artie had given him.

He lifted the brass knocker and let it fall, announcing his arrival. Then he stepped back from the landing, smoothing his patched coat with suddenly self-conscious hands.

The door swung inward to reveal a sour-faced woman who surveyed him with her lips drawn tightly together.

"How do you do? I am Thaddeus Priest," he said. "Here for the interview for lodgings?"

Mrs. Parsons—he recognised her from Artie's description—stood rigid and silent for several heartbeats. Her eyes travelled down and up again, lingering on every sign of poverty: his threadbare coat, worn cuffs, blistered hands. Her chin went up, and without a word she turned.

"Follow me."

Thaddeus obeyed, entering the dim hall as she led him through the house. Her voice, when she spoke, carried the cadence of a speech delivered countless times.

"Rooms are upstairs. Kitchen is down that hall. The parlour is here." She slid open a pair of heavy, dark-wood doors on smooth casters to reveal a pleasantly bright room. "No female guests are permitted upstairs. Guests may be entertained here."

She seated herself on a stiff-backed chair, posture perfectly straight. She motioned for Thaddeus to sit opposite her.

"We provide three meals a day as part of your rent. Breakfast at eight, luncheon at one, supper at six. If you are late, you will not be seated. The staff's time is not to be wasted."

Thaddeus nodded, but his attention drifted. The parlour was warm with hues of orange and red, from the carpets to the curtains. A proper set of ladies' and gentlemen's chairs, a sofa, and a broad fireplace gave the room a comfortable, inviting feel. It would be a perfect place for his séances. The question was whether Mrs. Parsons would ever allow such a thing.

"Laundry service is available for an additional fee," she added pointedly. "Especially if you have...special requirements for your shirts." It was clear she doubted he owned more than one.

Movement behind her caught Thaddeus's eye. Artie floated into view and waved enthusiastically.

"Are you listening to me?" Mrs. Parsons snapped, her eyes narrowing.

Thaddeus startled. "Pardon?"

"I asked about your profession, Mr. Priest."

Ah. The moment that could unravel everything.

"I am a Spiritualist by trade, Mrs. Parsons."

Her expression froze. "We do not house charlatans. There is no need to continue the interview." She rose, resolute.

"Tell her," Artie whispered urgently, "that her mother loved lemon biscuits with her afternoon tea. And her father smoked that special blend from the Indies she bought him every Christmas."

Thaddeus seized the lifeline. "Mrs. Parsons—your mother loved lemon biscuits with her afternoon tea. And your father... he smoked a special blend of tobacco from the Indies. You bought it for him every Christmas."

Mrs. Parsons' eyes went wide. "What trickery is this? How do you know that?"

"It's not trickery. I promise you. I speak with the dead."

Artie drifted closer. "Her father adored her. She keeps his picture on her nightstand. She misses him. She has a tin of his tobacco she opens just to smell when she's feeling sentimental."

Thaddeus relayed every word.

Mrs. Parsons sank slowly back into her chair, tears gathering. "How...? Is he here? Is my father here now?"

Thaddeus shook his head. "I'm afraid not." He glanced up—Artie had vanished.

But a moment later Artie reappeared beside an elderly gentleman with gentle eyes and a warm expression.

Artie whispered, triumphant, "This is her father."

Thaddeus's gratitude nearly overwhelmed him. "Mrs. Parsons," he said softly, "your father is here. He's just arrived. He's standing right there."

Her hands trembled. "I had a childhood nickname—one only he used. What was it?"

The old man chuckled. "I called her Posy. My Posy girl. Her mother hated it—'Henry,' she'd say, 'her name is Prudence.' Prudence!" He shook his head affectionately. "Sounded like prunes to me. I loved her so much. I wanted her to know."

Thaddeus repeated the words faithfully.

Mrs. Parsons let out a broken sob. She turned toward the space at the back of the room, eyes fixed as though she might see him if she willed it hard enough. "Oh, I wish I could see him..."

"Tell her I love her still," Henry murmured. "I come by now and then to check on her."

His form flickered, thinning. The dead who rarely spoke to the living never managed to linger long.

Thaddeus conveyed the message gently. "He's fading now. But he says he visits often."

Mrs. Parsons pressed a handkerchief to her eyes. "Oh, Mr. Priest... you have no idea what comfort you've brought. If he comes again, you must be here. I don't want to miss a single message."

"I'm honoured to help," Thaddeus said sincerely. His heart warmed with relief. This was the chance he desperately needed. "Would you object to my giving readings in the parlour?"

For a moment her old severity snapped back into place. She scrutinised him—testing, weighing, searching for deceit. Whatever she saw must have reassured her, for her posture gradually softened.

"As long as it does not disturb the other residents," she said, "I see no harm in it."

Joy surged through him.

"I'll show you to your room," she said, rising.

Thaddeus followed her toward the stairs. At the doorway he turned back toward Artie and mouthed, Thank you.

Artie dipped into a graceful little bow.

# CHAPTER TEN

The room proved far more commodious than Thaddeus had anticipated. He had expected a cramped little chamber with scarcely space for a trunk, yet instead he found a spacious, sun-warmed retreat arranged in an undeniably feminine style. Chintz curtains, pale rose wallpaper, and a delicate writing desk near the window spoke of a woman's refined touch.

Still, the profusion of light pleased him greatly. Sunshine slanted generously across the floorboards, filtered only by the enormous oak tree that stood less than a yard beyond the glass — a venerable sentinel whose branches stretched so wide they nearly embraced the window itself. Beyond that, he glimpsed a neat little garden, and a bench set invitingly near a clump of shrubbery. He fancied himself sitting there with a book, should the weather ever permit such leisure.

His possessions were few, but well tailored—the last remnants of a life that still clung to him, despite all efforts to shed it—and he placed them carefully in the armoire. In that room, each article seemed almost absurd in its refinement, as though they belonged to some other man entirely.

He had been raised amidst wealth, polish, and every outward assurance of comfort, yet he had seldom felt at ease within the walls of his father's house. Rank could command obedience, furnish drawing rooms, and lay silver upon the table, but it could not soften a voice, nor turn duty into affection. Privilege fed the body well enough. It did little for the soul.

Here, by contrast, in a boarding house chamber shaped by the gentle hand of a woman he did not even know, he felt some quiet knot within him begin, at last, to loosen. The curtains, the soft paper on the walls, the little writing desk placed so thoughtfully near the light—these small domestic graces stirred some older memory in him, faint but piercing. His mother, moving quietly through rooms made tolerable by her presence. The woman whose kindness had been the single note of warmth in an existence otherwise governed by expectation, discipline, and the relentless weight of what he owed his name.

The realisation touched him with almost painful clarity: it was the women in his life who had made the world seem inhabitable. They had been its sheltering lights, however fragile. Never the grand house. Never the title. Never the stern machinery of inheritance.

He paused, one hand resting upon the armoire door, and let out a slow breath. Strange, that he should feel safer here, among strangers, in the quiet order of that little room, than he ever had in all the grand chambers of Raynsford Hall. He was still contemplating all this when a soft voice broke through his thoughts.

"A penny for them?"

Thaddeus turned. Standing just inside the doorway was his ghostly companion of late. Arthur was smiling shyly, an expression both endearing and faintly forlorn.

"Thank you for helping me," Thaddeus said, closing the armoire. "Truly, I needed a place to stay."

"I am only glad I could be of service," Arthur replied, hovering a little above the floor in absentminded habit. "It took some manoeuvring, but you have proper quarters now."

Thaddeus studied him. "Artie... may I ask something rather frank? Do you know what happened to you — how you died?"

Arthur's expression dimmed, like a candle guttering in a draught. "I do not. When I became conscious again... on this side... I remembered very little. Not the circumstances of my death nor why my spirit awoke here instead of passing on."

He drifted closer, hands clasped behind his back in a boyish manner. "I visited my parents once. They were so grief-stricken I could hardly bear it. I returned here afterward and remained."

"So your death is a mystery," Thaddeus murmured, folding a shirt more slowly.

Arthur nodded. "A long-forgotten one, I fear. My parents lost hope long ago, and as for the world..." He gestured vaguely. "It moves on without us."

"When did you die?"

"In 1835, I believe."

Thaddeus straightened. "Good heavens — that long ago? Artie, I'm sorry. I ought to have inquired about it before now."

Thaddeus hesitated, then ventured, "You know you saved me back at the shop and just now with Mrs. Parsons. Can you... do that often?"

"Do?" Arthur repeated blankly.

"Retrieve spirits. Bring them forth. I have never seen another ghost do such a thing. It seems... unique."

Arthur blinked, perplexed. "I never thought it unusual. I simply... go find them."

"You make it sound as though they are idling just beyond a door," Thaddeus said with amusement.

"Well — sometimes yes, sometimes no. It is... complicated. Hard to put into mortal words." Arthur's face folded into comical frustration. "I'm sorry. I have simply never examined the matter."

Thaddeus regarded him for a long moment. "Artie... would you assist me during my sessions? Fetch the spirits while I attend to the clients? I know you have done as much already, but it seems more proper to ask than to presume. It is no easy thing to manage both the performance and the communion, and if you would not mind continuing, I should be very grateful."

He stopped, suddenly aware of the ghost's expression — frozen, unreadable, hovering like a statue with a faint, ghostly smile.

"I beg your pardon," Thaddeus said quickly. "If my request is improper—"

"No, not improper," Arthur said at once. "Only... startling."

Then his features softened into something almost luminous. "Do you know how long it has been since anyone has asked me to do anything of worth? It feels... strange. Strange in a good way."

Thaddeus exhaled in relief. "I'm glad. I only worry I cannot compensate you — ghosts do not use money."

Arthur fell very still — then brightened so suddenly he flickered.

"My sister," he said eagerly. "She still lives. She struggles, as a widow I believe. If you were to pay me... could the funds be sent to her instead?"

Thaddeus's face broke into a genuine smile. "Artie, that is an excellent arrangement. If it satisfies you, it satisfies me."

"Splendid!" Arthur bobbed excitedly, rising and falling in the air like a buoy on water. "How extraordinary! A purpose again — in life, or death, or whatever this is!"

Thaddeus felt a tide of confidence swell in his chest. A partner. A means forward. A path not chosen by his father.

"Well," he murmured with a private grin. "Let us see who crawls back to whom."

Clovis Corbeld and Erwin Matson were unravelling by the hour. They had found Thaddeus Priest once—seen him plain enough at the back of that miserable little shop—but the bastard had slipped from their grasp before they could make their move. Since then, days of prowling London's streets had yielded nothing but mud, bad tempers, and dead ends. Their benefactor would not forgive failure. *Would not*, Clovis reminded himself grimly.

Erwin leaned against a soot-blackened wall, arms dangling. "What're you thinkin' about?"

"The same thing you're thinkin' about, you idiot," Clovis snapped, digging a splinter from between his teeth with a dirty fingernail. "But unlike you, I've got a thought brewing."

He strode to the street and hailed a cab with a sharp whistle. After a brief exchange with the driver, he jerked his head at Erwin.

"Well? Get in, you lump."

Erwin clambered in, wide-eyed. "Where're we goin', Clovis?"

"Back where we nearly had him. He's gone to ground in a hole fit for rats, so stop thinkin' like a lord."

Erwin blinked. "What'd a lord be doin' in the slums?"

"Hidin', you blockhead." Clovis gave him a shove. "He ain't in Mayfair, and he ain't gone home."

Erwin's mouth dropped open in a perfect O. "Ohhhh."

"But the slums is big, Clovis," he added timidly. "How we gonna find one cove in all that?"

"By using what little wit God forgot to give you," Clovis snapped. He jabbed a filthy finger toward the street. "We go back. We ask questions. We shake loose what the locals know. Someone's seen where he sleeps, where he eats, who he talks to. Coin opens mouths. Coin makes the blind see again."

He nodded to himself, pleased as ever with his own cunning. "If the lad's still skint—and we know he is—he'll not have gone far from the rookeries. We start there, and this time we don't lose him."

Clovis and Erwin reached the shop well before afternoon tea. They loitered in the shadows for hours, damp settling into their coats as they watched for movement.

Their patience was rewarded.

A man approached at last—dressed in an elegant suit far above the means of anyone dwelling in this quarter. Several people accompanied him, chattering as they followed him inside.

Clovis smacked Erwin in the chest. "Did ya see that? That bloke's wearin' Thaddeus's clothes!"

"How d'you know?" Erwin squinted uncertainly. "Could be anyone's suit."

"Naw." Clovis's eyes narrowed with certainty. "I seen Thaddeus wear that exact suit. Now hush. We wait for them folks to clear out, and then we grab him."

He cracked his knuckles and smiled with wolfish satisfaction.

"I know his sort," he muttered. "He'll squeal like a pig."

# CHAPTER ELEVEN

Miss Murray sat alone in the parlour, nursing a lukewarm cup of tea. It was rather late in the day for such a comfort, but she needed something to soothe her nerves. Her readings had gone well enough of late—well enough that she dared imagine taking her earnings and moving to lodgings of her own, where Mrs. Clay's disapproving glances and whispered judgements could no longer sting her. Spiritualism might be fashionable, but the women who practised it were still regarded with suspicion, as though the veil they raised between worlds were a loosening of morals, not a profession.

The rain wept steadily against the windowpanes. It had been a dreary day, dreary enough to cancel three private readings—three, her most profitable sort. Her purse was feeling it keenly. She closed her eyes, letting the weight of the gloom settle over her.

Then—a knock. Firm. Male.

Her heart quickened. A client? In this weather?

She listened as Alice opened the door. A deep voice inquired after her. Alice hesitated—the girl was well-trained; Miss Murray did not receive strange men unchaperoned. But today... today she needed the coin.

"Alice," she called lightly, "it's all right. Let the gentleman in."

Alice's disapproval was written in the long, tight sideways look she cast before ushering the visitor into the parlour. The man wore a long overcoat and a wide-brimmed hat pulled low, shadowing his face entirely. He did not remove it when she rose to greet him.

"Good afternoon. I am Miss Murray." She extended her hand.

A leather-gloved hand clasped hers—briefly, indifferently. Rude. Deliberately rude. Her stomach tightened. Something about him prickled her senses in a way that had nothing to do with spirits.

She summoned Alice back with an excuse. "Would you be so kind as to bring our guest some tea?"

The girl vanished, clearly unwilling to leave her mistress alone for long.

"Please, do sit," Miss Murray said, gesturing to the chair opposite. "One usually schedules a reading in advance. Your arrival is quite... unusual. To what do I owe the honour?"

The man removed his gloves—slowly, with a faint air of theatre. His voice, when he spoke, was low and confidential, as though they were already in conspiracy together.

"My apologies for intruding on your afternoon, Miss Murray. But I have a matter of some urgency." He reached into his coat and, with a single gliding motion, slid several heavy coins across the table.

The clink was intoxicating. Far more than a full day's work. Far more than she could spare refusing.

Her eyes shone despite herself. "I... see."

Alice reappeared with the tea tray. Miss Murray's voice turned crisp, eager to dismiss her. "Yes, thank you, Alice. Leave it—we'll be quite fine."

She fluttered her fingers, sending the girl scurrying out.

Miss Murray poured tea for the man and folded her hands in her lap with practised poise. "What may I assist you with today, Mr...?"

He gave her a thin, polite smile that never touched the hidden eyes beneath the brim.

"Jenkins."

"Mr. Jenkins, then." She inclined her head. "What is it you seek?"

Jenkins leaned forward an inch—just enough that it felt intimate, conspiratorial. "Tell me, Miss Murray... do you know a Mr. Thaddeus Priest?"

The name caused her to lower her gaze, demure. When she looked up again, a sly confidence had replaced the softness. "I am aware of Mr. Priest. He came to me for a reading."

"I see." Jenkins steepled his fingers. "Then I must warn you."

Warn her? She straightened, pulse fluttering.

Jenkins's voice dropped further, all honeyed concern with a bitter undercurrent. "I believe you will find he makes a great many appearances in your Spiritualist circles. His purpose, I fear, is not benign."

Miss Murray's breath caught.

"He is attempting," Jenkins continued smoothly, "to pilfer your clients."

She pressed a hand to her chest in alarm. "Oh my! But... why me?"

"Oh, not only you," said Jenkins, smiling faintly as if amused by her innocence. "He does it everywhere he goes. He learns your methods, copies your style, then sets himself up as competition." He gave a soft sigh, paternal and pitying. "A shame, really. You work hard. You've built something. It would be tragic to see him—or anyone—take that from you."

Miss Murray felt heat rise in her cheeks. Her earnings... her reputation... her plans...

"I thought you ought to know," said Jenkins, rising with smooth finality. "You may use this information as you see fit. Perhaps... spread the word. Protect yourself—and others like you."

Her fingers closed around the coins as if for reassurance. "Thank you, Mr. Jenkins. Truly."

He tipped his hat—revealing only the faintest suggestion of a smile beneath. Not kind. Not cruel. Satisfied.

"You're welcome, my dear," he murmured. "We must all look after our own... in these uncertain times."

And with that, he let himself out, leaving the parlour feeling suddenly colder, the shadows a little deeper than before.

The table gave a delicate shudder — not violent enough to alarm, but certainly sufficient to delight the client seated opposite him. The room was oppressively warm and thick with candle smoke; Thaddeus longed to fling the window open but resisted. The public demanded theatrics, and theatrics, unfortunately, required gloom.

He had learned this the hard way.

Working at his new career for a while now, his business was slowly gaining notice. Since his disastrous beginning, he had grown his practice. He endured insults but quickly adapted.

He studied the most celebrated mediums, observed their performances, catalogued their mechanisms and illusions. What disgusted him was that so few of them could see spirits at all. They summoned none; they spoke to none. They were liars adored by the masses, while he, with genuine sight, was dismissed as dull.

But he learned.

He perfected his own display.

He gave the public its desired enchantment.

Tonight's client, Mrs. Ellison, was exactly the sort who cherished such flourishes. A stout woman in her fifties, bedecked in jeweled rings that glittered like stars against the candlelight, and crowned with a ludicrous hat fashioned entirely from peacock feathers. When the table lifted and tilted beneath her hands, her eyes widened with rapture.

Thaddeus pressed the discreet floor lever with his boot. The table settled with a dramatic shudder.

"Mrs. Ellison," he intoned with a practised gravity, "I believe your husband is with us."

And indeed he was.

Mr. Ellison stood beside her chair, arms folded, his spectral features arranged in an expression of long-suffering irritation.

"Can't get any peace," the ghost muttered. "Not even in death."

Artie hovered a polite distance behind him — helpful, attentive, almost cherubic in his ghostly glow. Thaddeus's indispensable assistant.

"What would you like to know, Mrs. Ellison?" Thaddeus asked, adopting his most solemn tone.

"Oh!" she breathed. "How does he look?"

Dead, Thaddeus thought. Very dead. They always look dead.

Alas, clients never wished to hear the truth.

"He looks splendid," he said instead. "Fit as a fiddle."

Mrs. Ellison frowned at his casualness, so he corrected immediately. "He is standing just beside you, Madam. Tall, with a distinguished grey beard and spectacles. Wearing a rather fine suit."

Mrs. Ellison brightened. "Yes! He was buried in one of his best. I insisted on it. One must look well in the hereafter."

"Waste of a perfectly good suit," Mr. Ellison grumbled. "Could've gone to our son. Now it's down there rotting with me, getting all musty. Damn shame." He thumped his spectral chest, retching dramatically.

Thaddeus nearly choked on his own laughter. "A very fine suit indeed."

Mrs. Ellison dabbed delicately at her eyes. "I miss him so terribly."

Thaddeus waited. They always had this moment — the sentimental pause, the trembling lip, the sigh. He counted silently to four.

At last she composed herself. "I must ask — the key to his desk. I have searched everywhere. There are important papers; the lawyer insists I obtain them."

Mr. Ellison snorted. "Imagine that. A chance to ask me what the afterlife is like, to seek wisdom from beyond the grave — and she wants the blasted key to my desk."

Thaddeus replied drily, "Your husband is… somewhat grumpy."

"Oh, he was like that in life too," Mrs. Ellison said fondly.

"Don't you talk about me behind my back," the ghost barked.

Thaddeus, distracted, muttered, "It's not behind your back. You're dead."

"Excuse me?" Mrs. Ellison blinked sharply.

He cleared his throat. "My apologies."

Mr. Ellison heaved a dramatic sigh. "Tell her it's in the book of Sonnets. Third shelf. Sixth volume to the right."

Thaddeus relayed the information.

"Oh thank heavens," Mrs. Ellison gasped. "I never would have looked there."

"That," the ghost grumbled, "is precisely why I put it there. Keep your greedy little fingers out of my business."

He turned to Thaddeus. "May I go now?"

Thaddeus resumed his solemn tone. "Madam, your husband grows weary. Spirits cannot linger long. Do you have any final words for him?"

"Oh!" Mrs. Ellison pressed a hand to her heart. "Tell him I love him. And that our son is to marry the Douglas girl now that he is no longer here to object."

Mr. Ellison sputtered indignantly. "Bah! Wretched boy!" And with that, he faded, his form dissolving like breath on glass.

Mrs. Ellison paid generously — grief always loosened purse strings — and swept from the room, satisfied and thoroughly convinced.

As soon as she departed, Thaddeus threw open the curtains and unlatched the window, gulping the cool air.

A voice sighed from the shadows. "Another satisfied customer."

Artie drifted into view, looking considerably more relaxed now that the séance had ended.

"Was that the last one today?"

"Yes, Artie," Thaddeus said, rubbing his temples. "You're free to go. No more readings."

CLOVIS AND ERWIN didn't have long to wait. The shop owner's tour with the prospective buyers lasted scarcely an hour and when the last murmured farewells drifted down the street, the two men exchanged a glance. Their moment had come.

They slipped inside the shop with the ease of men who'd crossed similar thresholds many times before—doors to back rooms, alleys, and dim basements where honest folk feared to tread. The bell above the frame gave a faint, crystalline tremor.

The shop owner turned sharply. Irritation creased his brow.

"I'm sorry, gentlemen, but we are closed."

"Aw, that's all right, gov'ner," Clovis said, showing teeth in what might have passed for a grin among wolves. "We're here to speak to you."

Erwin cracked his knuckles, slow and deliberate.

The shopkeeper's eyes flickered between them. "W-what do you want?"

"We want to speak to you about your clothes," Clovis replied, his smile never warming.

"My... my clothes?" The shopkeeper's fingers fumbled with the bottom button of his waistcoat. "I beg your pardon?"

"Those clothes look awful familiar," Clovis said, stepping to the left as Erwin drifted to the right. "We know the bloke you got them from. And we want to know where he went—and why you've got what was his."

"I own this shop," the man stammered. "These are my clothes. I don't know what you're talking about. And I must insist you leave... immediately." His voice cracked at the end, utterly betraying him.

Clovis chuckled. "We aren't going anywhere until you tell us the truth."

The men moved in a slow, predatory orbit around him, tightening their circle. The shopkeeper pivoted helplessly, trying to keep them both in view, confusion spinning him like a top.

"I—I don't have any money," he blurted.

"We said we don't care about your money," Clovis replied. "We want to know where Thaddeus Priest went."

A flicker—recognition. Panic.

"Him? He's nobody," the shopkeeper said too quickly. "He was here, yes, but I kicked him out. I took the clothes as payment for rent."

Clovis and Erwin exchanged a single glance. A silent verdict.

"You took his clothes," Clovis repeated softly. "As payment?"

The man nodded vigorously, eager to please.

"Then what was he wearin' when he left?" Clovis asked.

"Old rags," the shopkeeper—Silas—said. "He had them with him. Street clothes. Urchin rags, really." He lifted his chin, sneering now as he recalled the memory. "Frankly, they suited him better. Much more fitting for his class."

He didn't see Erwin move behind him.

He barely registered Clovis stepping closer, sympathetic as a hangman.

Then the two men struck. A flurry of limbs—fast, brutal, well-practised. Silas hit the floor with a choked cry, pinned beneath the combined weight of crime and desperation. Clovis settled himself on the man's chest as though taking a seat in a public house.

"Can't—breathe—" Silas gasped.

"You'll breathe when we get what we came for," Clovis said mildly, drawing a small switchblade and letting it glint above Silas's cheek. "Where did Thaddeus go?"

"I don't know! I don't know!" Silas babbled. "He left—in the rags —and never came back. I haven't seen him since. I swear it."

"Give me the clothes," Clovis said. "I'm gettin' up now, and you're goin' to hand them over like a good lad."

Silas nodded frantically.

The men rose. Silas climbed unsteadily to his feet, shaking, and began unbuttoning his waistcoat with fingers that barely obeyed him. He was stalling. Clovis could sense it.

"No funny business," Clovis said, waving the knife.

Silas turned halfway toward the front door, eyes darting to the street beyond—

A knock sounded.

All three men froze.

Silas lunged.

Clovis seized the half-unbuttoned waistcoat, yanking with force born of instinct. Silas spun violently, his foot catching on the trailing cloth. His head struck the iron bar of the counter with a sickening, dull thud. He crumpled, silent.

Clovis and Erwin stared at the unmoving heap.

Another knock.

Erwin crept to the window and snapped the curtains shut, peering between them. "It's the buyers. They're comin' back."

"Then be still," Clovis hissed.

They waited, motionless shadows.

When at last the sound of retreating steps faded, Clovis nudged Silas with his boot. There was no response. Erwin knelt, pressed an ear to the man's chest, and grimaced.

"Blimey, Clovis... he's dead."

"That's what he gets for runnin'," Clovis said coolly. "Come on. Help me strip him."

They worked in swift, mechanical silence, peeling the fine garments from Silas's cooling body, folding them, stuffing them into a waiting satchel.

When they were done, Erwin asked, "Why'd we need the clothes anyway?"

"Orders," Clovis replied, wiping his blade on a scrap of linen. "We collect anything of Thaddeus's we find. We'll send these to Lord Horace by courier."

"What's he want with 'em?"

Clovis shrugged. "Not my business. Not yours either. Long as we get paid."

He slung the satchel over his shoulder. "Now come on. We're goin' out the back. Don't want to chance the front with them buyers lurkin' about."

Erwin nodded, and together they slipped into the alley, leaving the shuttered shop and its silent occupant behind.

A new trail. A new dead man. And a Lord waiting at the end of it all.

Palmer Fitzgerald found Horace's men sooner than he expected. He had waited outside the boarding house for nearly an hour, pacing in a stiff, practised manner that he hoped made him blend in with the street shadows. When the two men finally emerged, he recognised them at once; he had seen them before slinking out of Lord Horace's manor like well-fed hunting dogs.

He followed at what he believed was a respectable distance. In reality, it was a clumsy ballet of stepping behind bushes, reversing direction abruptly, and lurking under the spindly black skeletons of London's street trees. If any tenant peered out from their upstairs window, they would surely assume he was a madman or an inept thief.

Still—he followed.

The men led him, circuitously, to a building lit with a faint amber glow: the séance hall. And there, standing outside the door with his cane tucked beneath his arm, was Thaddeus.

Fitz halted, breath catching. Thaddeus looked older, somehow—paler, sharper, nervous beneath the rigid posture he liked to adopt. Palmer waited, staring, until his friend finally lifted his head and looked back. For a heartbeat, Fitz feared he wouldn't recognise him, especially since he was dressed so unusually. Brown tweed trousers, a plain jacket, and a flat cap perched over his usually tousled hair—Palmer looked more like a railway clerk than an aristocrat.

But recognition dawned. Slowly, carefully.

Fitz turned away deliberately, slipping behind a post and letting himself vanish into the night. He watched as Horace's men also concealed themselves, taking positions with a predator's patience. Fitz's stomach knotted.

When Thaddeus finally emerged from the séance, he walked down the street swinging his cane with a careless rhythm—as though he were not being hunted. Palmer watched the men fall in behind him, shadows lengthening with each step.

He followed them all the way down the cobbled mile, cursing the lateness of the hour. It was far too dangerous for Thaddeus to be wandering alone. At a narrow turn, the party slipped down a side street. Fitz crept after them, keeping to the walls. He saw Thaddeus enter a modest boarding house—a squat building with chipped paint but warm light inside.

Fitzgerald etched the address firmly into his memory.

The two men departed quickly, not even pausing to glance back. Fitz emerged from behind a hedge and hurried to the porch, rapping firmly.

The door was snatched open by a scowling, heavy-set woman in a dressing gown.

"We do not accept visitors at this hour," she snapped.

"I quite understand, Madam," Palmer said with a deferential bow. "But I carry a parcel for Thaddeus Raynsford, which must be delivered tonight."

"You must be mistaken." Mrs. Parsons narrowed her eyes. "No Thaddeus Raynsford lives here."

"Fitz?" came a familiar voice from the stairwell. "I thought I heard your voice."

Mrs. Parsons swung her head round, scandalized.

"Mr. Priest—have you been lying to me? If so, you will be expelled at once. I will not tolerate shady business in my boarding house."

Thaddeus blanched. This was precisely the sort of confrontation he feared.

"Mrs. Parsons—please—I can explain," he said, lifting his hands in supplication.

The woman stood immovable as a marble column.

Thaddeus swallowed hard. "It is true. I am Lord Raynsford's son. But I am trying to keep my identity secret. Not everyone may know who I am."

Mrs. Parsons stared at him with piercing suspicion, as though she might force the truth out of him by sheer will.

Palmer stepped forward, bowing once more.

"Madam, I am not here to stay. I am here only to deliver this satchel to Lord Raynsford. It comes from his mother."

At the mention of his mother, Thaddeus's whole face brightened, softening as though sunlight had passed over him.

"My mother sent something? Oh, Fitz—how is she?"

"Would the two of you kindly take your business into the parlour so I may close the door?" Mrs. Parsons said sharply. She pointed toward the parlour like a general directing troops.

What she did not say was that she pressed her ear to the door the moment it shut.

Inside, Thaddeus embraced Fitz with genuine warmth, a shimmer of relief crossing his features.

"It is good to see you old friend," he murmured. "Tell me everything."

Fitz handed over the satchel. "Your mother insisted it reach your hands alone. A letter from her is inside, along with a few items she thought you might need."

He patted Thaddeus's shoulder. "I knew you disliked the idea of marrying Miss Hortense, but I did not think you'd end up here to avoid it."

Thaddeus flushed faintly. "I know it was drastic... but you know my father. He would never release that notion. I could not bear the thought of it, Fitz—I simply couldn't. Leaving was the only way."

"I understand," Palmer said gently. "You are greatly missed. And your mother sends her regards."

Thaddeus smiled wistfully.

"Is there any news about Athena?" he asked abruptly.

"Your blushing love is fine as far as I know," Fitz chuckled. "Still giving Jackson fits and asking about you everyday. She misses you terribly as we all do."

Thaddeus laughed, a breath of genuine mirth. "I have a letter for Athena. Will you take it to her?"

"Yes, I should deliver it myself, since, well... your father is having you watched. I followed his men in order to find you," Palmer continued. "Did you know?"

"I figured father would find me eventually. Let them watch, I will not return willingly," Thaddeus said with raised brows.

Palmer gave Thaddeus another hug and a pat on the back. "I wish I could be of more use. Look at you, you've changed. You're not even wearing proper clothes anymore."

Thaddeus gave a wry grin to his friend. "Do you have any idea what would happen to me if everyone knew I was a Lord's son? I would be hunted, and most likely stolen from. Secrecy is of utmost importance. It guarantees I am not a target."

Fitz gave his friend an appraising look. "Are you safe?"

"As safe as I can be," Thaddeus laughed. "I am certainly seeing another side of life I never expected to experience. Can you stay for awhile? Fitz please, sit down. Tell me all the news from home before you leave. I want to hear everything."

Outside the door, Mrs. Parsons listened with wide, shining eyes.

A spiritualist.

A Lord.

Her household, quite suddenly, had become far more interesting than she had ever dared imagine. She hurried away on tiptoe before she was caught, already planning exactly how she might adjust her rates in the near future.

# CHAPTER TWELVE

The money Thaddeus received from Palmer was a blessing of the first order. It not only allowed him to pay several months' rent in advance—much to Mrs. Parsons' delight—but it gave him enough to purchase a new set of clothes.

True, they were not nearly as fashionable as the suits he once owned, but they were clean, well-stitched, and presentable. Gone were the tatters and grime of street life. He no longer resembled a beggar, and, more importantly, he no longer felt like one.

He didn't want to admit it aloud, but the weeks of empty pockets and cold shoulders from nearly every person he met had begun to wear on him. Being invisible was one thing; being despised was another.

He said as much to Artie as he dressed that evening, preparing to visit another spiritualist. The new suit was charcoal grey—slightly too large in the shoulders, but he could hardly complain. His cheeks were sharper now, his frame slimmer than it had been. Mrs. Parsons' cooking would remedy that soon enough.

He stood before the mirror, adjusting his cravat, when Artie floated into view behind him.

"You'll do," Artie said with a critical squint. "You should have no trouble getting into the séance tonight. Don't take much money with you, and try to take a carriage now that you can afford one. It's safer."

"Yes, Mother Hen," Thaddeus muttered.

Artie scoffed. "You've been through enough as it is. I simply thought you might begin exercising caution, that's all."

Thaddeus smiled, softening. "Thank you, Artie. For everything."

"Oh, let's not get sentimental." Artie wrinkled his translucent nose. "I hate overt displays of affection. Makes my ectoplasm itch." Then, more sincerely: "And as far as feeling low about yourself—people can be vile creatures. Their cruelty is a reflection of them, not you. Remember that."

"I will."

Thaddeus picked up his hat. "Wish me luck. With any fortune, I'll learn something useful tonight."

"Oh, I doubt that," Artie said cheerfully. "But you'll see what the public expects, and that's the entire purpose. Off you go. Good night."

He vanished like a puff of candle smoke.

Thaddeus followed his advice and hired a hansom cab. He gave the address and, as they arrived, asked the driver to return later to fetch him.

The building was a long row of brick flats, each indistinguishable from the next. Only the numbers differentiated them. Thaddeus found the correct door and knocked.

A young woman, no older than sixteen, answered.

"Are you here for the séance, sir?" she asked. Without waiting for confirmation, she ushered him into a small parlour doubling as a waiting room. He was the first to arrive. Soon, others trickled in: widows in black silk, bearded gentlemen with quivering spectacles, a nervous young couple clutching hands.

At the appointed time, the young woman drew the curtains tight and guided them into a dimly lit chamber. Candles flickered in sconces, their weak flames swallowed by the thick shadows pooling in the corners. A round table stood in the centre, draped with a velvet cloth.

"Please seat yourselves man, woman, man, woman," the girl instructed. She pointed to one chair. "No one is to sit here. That is Miss Saint's seat."

Thaddeus took the place he was assigned, folding his hands neatly on the table.

Moments later, the door swung open with theatrical flair.

In swept Miss Valentina Saint.

She wore a gown of deep violet, her sleeves trailing like spectral wings. Her hair was arranged in elaborate curls that looked as though she'd teased them into place by sheer force of personality.

"Welcome," she intoned, her voice rich with fabricated mystique. "I am Miss Valentina Saint, and I shall guide you tonight. The spirits stir with great power. I sense an extraordinary session ahead."

Thaddeus nearly laughed. The dramatics...

Miss Saint took her seat opposite him. He watched every movement with a trained eye. The dim lighting, the cloying incense smoke —it all obscured her hands perfectly. Too perfectly.

She brought out a deck of playing cards.

With wide gestures and unnecessary flourishes, she shuffled them. Then she selected several, spreading them on the table with a reverent gasp. She read from them in vague, sweeping statements, each one applicable to nearly anyone. Yet the patrons leaned forward, rapt.

*People really do want to be entertained,* Thaddeus thought.

He was so busy analyzing her card work that he missed the soft metallic click beneath the table.

And then the table tilted.

Gasps filled the room.

"Ah!" Miss Saint cried. "The spirits join us!"

She pressed her hands to the table, as though receiving divine transmission. Her eyes snapped open dramatically.

"John? Is there a John present?"

A man raised his trembling hand. "Yes—yes, that's me!"

"I sense your mother," Miss Saint whispered. "She is with us. She loves you very much."

John burst into quiet tears. "Is she happy?"

"Oh, exceedingly so. She is in Heaven with our Lord."

Thaddeus nearly rolled his eyes—and Miss Saint noticed.

A slow smile curled across her lips.

"We have... a non-believer among us," she announced.

Thaddeus stiffened. The last thing he wanted was attention.

"The spirits whisper to me," she continued, fixing him with a calculated stare. "They say you will not succeed unless you believe. This is why your business fails to thrive."

Heads bobbed around the table. She had guessed—but guessed well. Thaddeus kept still, his jaw tight. If she wanted a reaction, he would not give it to her.

She soon moved on, and he let out a silent breath.

He would need to control his expressions far more carefully in future séances.

When the event concluded, patrons filed out chattering excitedly. Thaddeus moved to the foyer, eager to leave, when Miss Saint suddenly glided up beside him.

"I know you, Mr. Priest," she whispered, her eyes sharp as needles. "We all do. You won't be taking any of our clients. Not mine, and not anyone else's. We know exactly what you're up to."

Thaddeus blinked, taken aback by the hostility. He thought, briefly, to explain himself—but what would be the point? She'd already decided who he was. People saw what they wanted to see. He could not change that. He tipped his hat politely and stepped into the night.

Behind him, Miss Valentina Saint watched from the doorway, lips pursed in smug satisfaction, as though she'd won a silent battle he'd never agreed to fight.

"CORDELIA, why do you insist on testing me in this manner?"

She had heard that lament countless times before. Cordelia Clements—petite, fair-haired, and altogether too pretty for her own peace—had yet to attach herself to a suitable husband, much to her father's perpetual distress. Ever since her sister, Vena, had vanished without a trace, Cordelia's every waking thought had been consumed by the mystery of her disappearance.

August Clements, her father, released a tired sigh. "I know you are worried about your sister. I am worried as well. But there is nothing to be done until the police uncover something."

"Oh, Father, the police are not looking for her," Cordelia protested, her voice trembling with long-nursed frustration. "I cannot —will not—allow this to fade quietly away. I must know what became of her. I miss her dreadfully. How could she simply vanish?" Cordelia's cat brushed up against her skirts and she retrieved him from the floor. Mr. Quincy P. Marigold was an orange tabby of particular distinction and he let everyone know it.

"And you truly believe some spiritualist will furnish you with the answers you seek?" August shook his head in weary dismay. "My dear child, if I have said it once, I have said it a thousand times: that lot cannot be trusted. They are little better than gipsies—clever with patter, quick with the hand, and always ready to empty a purse."

"I am not going to stop attending them, Father. That is the end of it. I shall not rest until I find her," Cordelia replied, as immovable as she had been since the ordeal began. They had circled this argument nearly every week since Vena's disappearance.

"Why can you not be like other daughters—settle down, find a man to dote upon you?" August pleaded. "What became of that agreeable young gentleman? Nathaniel, was it?"

"Oh, Father, you are hopeless," Cordelia sighed sat down in a chair and began absentmindedly petting Quincy. "I shall marry when I am ready, and not before."

"Child," he persisted, adjusting the monocle that magnified one stern eye, "might I remind you that your years of eligibility will not last forever? Your prospects will dwindle; all the fine bachelors will be claimed by your friends."

Cordelia rolled her eyes. Her father never ceased pressing her toward matrimony, as though her future were as simple as selecting a bonnet from a shop window. What if she had no desire to marry at all? She dared not voice that thought aloud—August might rescind the small liberties he still allowed her.

She saw the disappointment settling into his features and, softening, offered him a compromise.

"I am attending another séance tomorrow evening," she said. "This medium is the most celebrated spiritualist in all of London. If she cannot provide a meaningful answer—then no spiritualist can. If that proves the case, I shall stop. I will do as you ask. Is that agreeable?"

August regarded her through his monocle, suspicion and affection mingling in his expression. He did not believe her—not for a moment—but the gesture pleased him nonetheless.

*Ah, this girl will be the death of me,* he thought, resigned to yet another night of worry over his stubborn, beloved child.

That night, once the guests had gone, Valentina Saint dismissed the young girl, sending her upstairs to her room. Valentina preferred to put everything away herself; it gave her time to relish the evening's earnings. She opened the small wall safe no one else knew about—not even the girl—and slipped the night's money inside with a satisfied hum.

Her thoughts drifted back to Thaddeus Priest. She wasn't

surprised he had come to her reading; Melisendra Murray had warned her about him trying to poach clients. Calling him out in front of the others had been deliberate. Better to plant doubt now than let him charm his way into anyone's pocketbook later. The way he'd rolled his eyes had only confirmed her suspicions.

A faint sound stirred behind the heavy drawing-room curtains—not quite a footstep, not quite the settling of fabric. It was the sort of noise one might dismiss as the house sighing into its age, yet it tugged at her awareness all the same. She turned, the lamplight gilding the gilt frames and velvet chairs, her pulse ticking faster as the shadows beyond the windows seemed suddenly too deep, too deliberate.

A man stood there, half-revealed where the curtain had shifted aside. Tall. Dark. Entirely still. The firelight did not reach his face, only traced the sharp line of his shoulders and the faint gleam of an eye that reflected more than it revealed. He had not entered so much as *appeared*, as though he had always belonged to the room and she was only now permitted to notice him.

"Excuse me?" Her voice cut cleanly through the silence, sharper than she intended, though she did not soften it. "The reading is finished for tonight. You'll have to return another time."

For a breathless moment, he did not respond. Then he moved—one measured step forward, the floorboards whispering beneath his boots. The lamplight crept higher along his coat, but his expression remained lost to shadow. He said nothing. He only came closer, and the air itself seemed to tighten, as though the room had drawn in a breath and was waiting to see whether she would dare to exhale.

"Mr. Priest, is that you attempting to frighten me?"

She laughed, a light, dismissive sound that rang too brightly in the hush of the room. It was the sort of laugh meant to reclaim authority, to turn intrusion into farce. "It won't work. I'm not afraid of you—no one is."

She did not wait for an answer. Turning her back on the shadowed figure, she gathered her deck of cards from the small table, straightening their edges with needless precision. The familiar ritual steadied her hands. The lamplight caught the worn corners, the faint oil-smudge of countless readings past.

"I suggest you leave," she added coolly. "Good night, Mr. Priest."

At the sound of the name, something in the room shifted.

The man stilled—not enough to be seen, only enough to be *felt*. The silence thickened, as though the walls themselves had leaned closer. Then, after the briefest pause, he resumed his advance.

Valentina did not hear his footsteps. She sensed him the way one senses a presence standing just behind one's shoulder, the air subtly displaced, the warmth of another body intruding upon one's own space. A prickle crept along her spine. Annoyance flared first, sharp and indignant, and she turned, ready to deliver a final rebuke—

Too late.

Something cool and smooth brushed her throat, deceptively gentle, like a lover's caress. Then it tightened.

The silk bit deep, cutting off breath and sound alike. Her hands flew upward, cards scattering across the carpet as her world narrowed to the sudden, terrible knowledge that she could not cry out—could not even draw in air. The lamplight fractured, the room tilting as the scarf drew her backward into the waiting dark.

She clawed at the scarf, at the hands holding it, kicking backward with surprising strength. She struck his leg, but he didn't loosen his grip. She reached blindly toward the table, fumbling for anything—cards, a candlestick, anything—her height giving her leverage, but not enough. Her vision wavered at the edges as air refused to reach her lungs.

The man pulled the scarf tighter.

Not with haste, nor with violence born of panic, but with quiet resolve. The silk cut deeper as it drew taut, stealing what little breath remained. Valentina's hands clawed weakly at his wrists, her fingers slipping, her strength already betraying her. The fight bled out of her in small increments—each movement slower than the last, each desperate effort meeting only the unyielding press at her throat.

Her heels scraped once against the floor. Then again, softer. The room seemed to recede, its lamplight dimming as though someone had turned the wick low. When her resistance finally ceased, it was not dramatic. It was simply gone.

He held her a moment longer than necessary, waiting for any sign of defiance, any reflex yet to surface. Only when her body surrendered fully did he release the scarf and let her fall. She struck the carpet with a dull, graceless sound, skirts folding beneath her like discarded cloth.

He did not move.

He listened.

Above them, the house whispered. A faint stir from the upper floor—the soft complaint of a bed disturbed, followed by a careful tread. A pause. The silence after the struggle had come too late; the damage was already done.

The man turned without haste. He crossed the hall, the familiar passage swallowing him as he slipped through the front door and into the waiting dark beyond. The night accepted him easily, shadows folding closed as though he had never been there at all.

Moments later, someone came running above—quick now, unsteady, fear lending urgency to every movement. She reached the drawing room, and for a single heartbeat the house held its breath.

Then her scream split the quiet street, high and terrible, echoing from brick to brick as she stood frozen in the doorway, staring at Valentina Saint collapsed upon the floor.

# CHAPTER THIRTEEN

Detective Michael Barnes sat at his desk, warming his hands upon a cup of morning coffee. A thin veil of haze lay upon the London streets beyond the window, lending the day a deceptively serene air. That peace dissolved the moment his partner entered.

Dickman strode in with his brow drawn tight. He eyed the steaming cup in Barnes's hand.

"Still drinking that bitter foreign muck?"

Barnes took a measured sip.

"Keeps a man awake. Something tea rarely manages."

Dickman shrugged his shoulders.

"You know what I don't understand?"

"Hmmm?" Barnes did not look up from his coffee.

"How do we go from a quiet stretch of months to three murders in the same span of days?" Dickman demanded.

Barnes blinked. "Three murders?"

"Annie Fletcher, the shop owner down by the river district, and now a spiritualist." Dickman exhaled sharply. "It's going to be a busy day."

"A spiritualist, eh?"

"Apparently. Come on—Chief wants us at both scenes."

Barnes and Dickman arrived to find Silas Burke's shop besieged by gawking onlookers. Though it was July, the day had turned raw and miserable, with a clammy chill that set collars high and shoulders hunched. The crowd craned toward the doorway, eager for a glimpse of death, while a beleaguered patrolman tried in vain to hold them back.

"Can't we clear these people out?" Dickman muttered.

"Have you ever tried to disperse a flock of the morbidly curious?" the constable replied. "They'd have my head."

Inside, the shop was a mess—police boots trampling about, voices murmuring, the coroner crouched beside the body. Barnes clenched his jaw; whatever evidence had once existed here was already disappearing beneath the tread of constables.

"Everyone out," Barnes barked. "Give us a few minutes with the coroner. And someone deal with that crowd."

The officers shuffled out.

Barnes stepped to the front door and examined the lock. The keyhole showed no signs of tampering, and the heavy iron bolt inside hung loose against the wood. A faint crescent of dampness lingered at the threshold, where the morning air had pressed in when the door was opened.

"He was expecting someone," Barnes murmured.

"Or forgot to fasten it," replied Dickman.

"In this neighborhood, on a night like this? Unlikely."

Barnes's gaze moved slowly across the shop. A chair lay on its side near the door, its leg splintered. A few feet farther along, a crate had been shoved crooked against the wall.

He traced the line between them with his eyes until it ended at the counter where Burke lay.

"They moved," he murmured.

"Who did?" asked Dickman.

"Whoever fought here," said Barnes.

The rest of the shop remained orderly. Only the narrow path between door and counter showed signs of violence.

Barnes examined the corner of the counter. A dark smear marked the wood where a head had struck. He then crouched near the counter. The floorboards there were scuffed hard, as though someone had lost their footing. The scuffing near the counter also showed movement in two directions at once, indicating more than one possible assailant.

Barnes glanced toward the small table beside the counter. Two chairs faced one another as though a discussion had taken place there not long before. The shop ledger lay open, ink still dark upon the page. Beneath a list of stock values, Burke had begun a second line and left it unfinished—as though called away before he could complete it.

"He was at business shortly before he died," Dickman said quietly.

"Yes... and perhaps expecting more," replied Barnes.

"What have we got, Mr. Keiler?" Barnes asked.

Coroner Earl Keiler, a stout, solemn man dedicated to his craft, regarded them over his spectacles. He motioned toward the back of Burke's skull.

"Significant blunt-force trauma. Looks at first glance like a fall—would almost be straightforward." His tone darkened. "But the man is entirely undressed."

Barnes lifted a brow. "That is unusual."

"Especially in his shop," Keiler continued. "No signs of changing clothes. Had he slipped whilst dressing, that might explain it—but there are no trousers. Nor shirts, nor stockings. Nothing. Just the man in his drawers."

The drawers had been pulled roughly down the legs, the linen twisted about the ankles. Barnes surveyed the room once more before answering.

"Robbery is possible," he said slowly. "Though it is a strange one that leaves the shop itself untouched."

Keiler shrugged faintly. "You're the detective."

Barnes crouched near the body and noticed a faint ring of dirt marked the man's waist where a belt had been tightened far past its usual notch.

"See this here?" asked Barnes.

"Unusual, unless his clothes didn't fit, which is quite possible," said Dr. Keiler.

Barnes leaned closer to the back of Burke's head. The wound was not broad as he expected, but narrow—almost straight.

He glanced toward the sharp corner of the shop counter.

"Falls rarely choose their landing so neatly," he said quietly.

"A man can strike anything when he loses his footing," said Keiler.

Barnes picked up Burke's arm to examine it. The skin at Burke's wrists was paler where cuffs had recently covered it.

"Send your report once you're done. We've a spiritualist to see next."

"A spiritualist, you say?" Keiler mused. "I suppose she didn't foresee it coming."

Their cab deposited them before a modest townhouse. No crowd gathered here—someone in the Metropolitan Police had taken pains to keep it quiet.

Inside, a sobbing young woman sat pale and trembling. Sixteen at most, with faint bruises beneath her eyes from sleepless tears. Barnes felt a pinch of sympathy.

He stepped forward gently. "Young lady, I am Detective Michael Barnes, and this is Detective Edgar Dickman. We must ask you a few questions."

She nodded through her tears. Her name was Abigail—ward to Miss Valentina Saint. The previous night she had heard raised voices downstairs, followed by the front door closing. Concerned, she descended and found her guardian collapsed in the drawing room. She had sent the maid for help and remained by the body. Police had not arrived until dawn.

Barnes and Dickman entered the drawing room. Miss Saint was sprawled inelegantly upon the floor, rigor mortis having stiffened her overnight. A silk scarf dug cruelly into the skin of her throat.

Not the same killer as Annie Fletcher—her throat had been slit with vicious deliberation. This felt different. Detached. Cold. The killer had strangled her, let her fall, and walked away without a backward glance.

Barnes scribbled in his notebook.

Dickman paced the room, examining the incense, the guttered candles. "Did she hold a séance last night?"

Abigail confirmed it.

"Is there a list of attendees?"

"Yes, sir." She crossed to a desk and retrieved a small slip of paper —the names neatly written, each accompanied by notes. A doctor and his wife. A businessman's wife. And a Thaddeus Priest—with no notation beside it.

Dickman tapped the blank space. "Why no note?"

"It isn't unusual, sir. If the person is new—if they've never been here before—there's nothing to write."

"May I keep this?"

"Of course."

"Did you notice anything missing from the room?" Barnes asked.

"No, sir. Nothing was taken."

"Thank you, Abigail. If we need anything more, we shall contact you," Dickman said gently.

Once she had gone, he muttered, "Well, this one wasn't a robbery."

"No," Barnes agreed. "Could be a disgruntled client... though most know these readings are more entertainment than revelation."

"What? You don't believe in spirits? Conversations with the dearly departed?" Dickman teased.

Barnes gave him a flat look. "I believe in what I can touch and what I can see. And right now, I see two murders needing answers. We'll begin by speaking with other spiritualists—see if she had enemies... or unwanted admirers."

Dickman held up the list. "Start here?"

"Start there," Barnes said.

MADAM MEDORA WAS the most celebrated spiritualist in all of London. Thaddeus knew, if he was going to measure up, she was the one to learn from. He was actually anxious the day of the reading and couldn't wait for the evening to begin. Dressing formally, as always, wanting to put his best foot forward, he adjusted his cravat in the mirror. Artie was not about; in fact, he hadn't seen his friend in almost three days. Thaddeus didn't know where Artie went or what ghosts did all day, but he imagined Artie was sulking somewhere after their heated debate. He decided that once he got back from the reading, he would attempt to contact Artie and try to work things out with him.

He arrived at the salon exactly at half past seven. The long light of a July evening stretched thin across the city, pale and watchful, as though unwilling to surrender the streets to darkness. He entered with everyone else; a steady stream of humanity pushed through the door as some were entering and some were leaving. The first thing Thaddeus noticed was that everyone was comfortably seated on chaise lounges, couches and chairs, arranged to provide an atmosphere of intimacy. The table was at the front of the room and had a candle and a crystal ball waiting for Madam Medora. There was only seating for the reader and one client. People chatted softly among themselves, never allowing their voices to rise above a murmur. There were smaller tables sitting in the middle of each cluster of seating, for the private use of the patrons. The next thing Thaddeus noticed was that the number of patrons was smaller than he had seen at other gatherings. There were maybe six or seven patrons at most. It gave the feeling of exclusivity.

It made sense to him that Madam Medora cultivated such an atmosphere. It allowed her to command higher fees. That was the third thing he noticed. Admission to one of her sittings was not solicited by offering basket or hinted at through embarrassed appeals to generosity. No—to secure her time, one paid directly, and payment bred expectation. People anticipated the little luxuries: the intimate seating, the soft glow of candlelight, and even liquor for those of a more nervous temperament. Tea was the most common refreshment, served by the maid in delicate cups adorned with yellow roses. The women sat sipping and nibbling at biscuits, while the men conversed like businessmen, many of them seeming already acquainted.

Thaddeus sat quietly with the men, taking in everything around him. He noticed there was one woman who seemed to be rather distraught. She sniffed delicately into a handkerchief, her eyes brimming with unshed tears. She was the only one who was accompanied by her own ghost. There was a blond woman standing behind her, hand gently resting on her shoulder. Thaddeus made eye contact with the ghost and he smiled sympathetically. Startled that he could see her and acknowledged her presence, the ghost snatched her hand back from the woman's shoulder and glowered at him. Apparently, she didn't like that he could see her.

Madam Medora entered like a figure from some dim and half-sacred pageant, and all the men rose as one. A fall of black lace descended from her dark hair, which was adorned with glittering ornaments that caught the lamplight with every measured step. Her gown was sumptuous, its lace and velvet arranged with calculated elegance, and its neckline softened rather than concealed by shadow and trimming. Bracelets and rings gleamed upon her hands, and a dark stone rested at her breast. She had the look of a woman who understood perfectly the power of appearance and employed it without apology.

She came to a halt and regarded the room with serene command. "The readings will begin shortly. When you are called, please come up to the table. Remember, this reading is for you and you alone. If you choose to share it, that is for you to decide, but as always your privacy is given the utmost consideration."

So, a separate reading for each person, far enough away from the other patrons to give the illusion of privacy. This was another setup different from the others. Thaddeus was pleased. He felt that the evening had already provided him with much information. One of the male patrons was the first to be called. He went up to the table and sat down, hand and hat resting on his cane. Thaddeus tried not to stare but listened in, nonetheless. Madam Medora was effective in keeping her voice low, so that he was not able to make out the entire conversation, but he had to restrain himself from snorting when she said that the man's dead wife was with him. The man was alone, and no spirit was called in. He watched her stare into the crystal ball. The lighting around the table was just right, so it caused a glow around her eyes and cheeks as she stared into the translucent ball.

Not wanting to be overly rude, he didn't listen in to anymore specifics. The reading lasted about fifteen minutes, and the man seemed satisfied when he got up to return to his seat. She called on each person until finally it was the distraught young woman's turn. "Cordelia Clements," called out Madam Medora. The young woman got up and slowly made her way over to the table to take her seat. She had a fragility about her that pulled on Thaddeus's heartstrings. She was pale and drawn, with a sadness in her eyes that no timid smile could cover up. Thaddeus was intrigued and wanted to know her story, this sad woman with a ghost hanging on her and so he listened in.

"What kind of a reading are you looking for today dear? Do you want to know your future husband? A current lover perhaps that has upset you?" asked Madam Medora.

"Oh, no. No. Nothing like that. It's my sister you see. She's missing and I want to know what has happened to her. I am so lost without her, we were very close," said Cordelia.

"I see," said Madam Medora, the disappointment clear in her voice. "Do you have something with you attached to your sister? A necklace or a ring?"

Thaddeus figured Madam Medora must enjoy giving romance readings, the most frivolous kind of reading if ever there was one. And easy too, because the reader could always say the love interest changed their mind, should things not work out. Cordelia handed a ring to Madam Medora, and she turned to focus on her crystal ball.

"I see a woman, not unlike yourself, similar in coloring. Did she ever talk about a young man who was interested in her. A secret lover?" asked Madam Medora.

Cordelia was annoyed at the angle this woman was pursuing, and she didn't feel like she was being taken seriously. Of course, she never felt like she was taken seriously. The police laughed at her. Other readers she had been to, brushed her off as well, or suggested she go to the police. It was maddening.

"Yes, I see her. She is in a foreign land, with a very handsome man."

Thaddeus looked at the ghost and knew at once this was the sister. She was not alive and wrung her hands violently. She looked over at Thaddeus, the anger blazing in her eyes. He swallowed hard. This was one angry ghost.

"I don't know that I believe that. I think something dreadful might have happened to her," said Cordelia.

Madam Medora reached over and patted Cordelia's hand condescendingly. "Were you jealous of your sister?"

Cordelia snatched her hand away, incensed. "No." She shook her head, trying to clear that thought away. "I loved my sister. We were twins and I can usually feel her. I can't feel her anymore and I fear something has happened to her."

Everyone in the room looked at Cordelia as her voice rose.

Madam Medora made a show of trying to comfort Cordelia and said, "Well, when we are distraught, we all imagine connections and psychic abilities that we don't have."

Cordelia stood up and returned to her seat in a huff. Tears welled up in her eyes even more over the pain of not being taken seriously.

"Thaddeus Priest," said Madam Medora.

Thaddeus rose to join Madam Medora at the table, although he was more interested in comforting Cordelia.

Madam Medora noticed Thaddeus's distraction and frowned. She did not like spectacles. "And what do we owe the pleasure of your visit today, Mr. Priest?"

Thaddeus was alerted to Madam Medora's displeasure by the tone in her voice and he decided he better give her his undivided attention.

"Just a general reading today. Anything you can tell me about my future prospects?"

A sly look crossed Madam Medora's features as she grabbed the crystal ball with both hands and peered intently into it. "I see you are a lowly charlatan, Mr. Priest," said Madam Medora, her voice barely above a whisper. "A man of questionable character."

"Uhm, hmmm?" said Thaddeus, still allowing his attention to drift back to Cordelia and not really paying attention to what was being said.

Madam Medora rolled her eyes. "I said you would do well to stop interfering in the spiritualist community and go back to where you came from. Nothing good will come of your pursuing this path. You don't belong here."

Thaddeus looked back at Madam Medora and smiled. He wasn't so distracted that he didn't hear her words; he was just choosing to ignore them. Thaddeus leaned in closer to Madam Medora and whispered so only she could hear. "I know you are a fraud, although a very good one might I add." He stood up and winked at the infuriated reader and turned to leave.

He walked straight up to Cordelia and discreetly gave her his card. "I have something I need to tell you, no charge. Please. Come see me."

"Outrageous! It's a scandal!"

The voice of Madam Medora cracked as her voice rose higher and higher in pitch. "I know who you are. You are that charlatan that is pilfering everyone's clients. He only comes to other people's readings to learn their secrets. You sir, are a liar, a deceiver!"

"I am not a deceiver Madam, I am a spiritualist like yourself. I only came to admirer your gift and to listen to a true mistress of spiritualism," said Thaddeus. He was hoping to placate Madam Medora and see her from making a scene.

"Spiritualist, bah! Where do you even come from? No one has ever seen you before, no one knows anything about you. All we know is that you show up and start attending our seances." All eyes were on Madam Medora and she was warming to her audience. "Do you even have any credentials? Do you belong to one group, one legitimate organization? The Central Association of Spiritualists perhaps? The Spiritualist Association of Great Britain? The British National Association of Spiritualists? No?" Madam Medora now looked triumphant. "So, you have no public standing in the spiritualist community, whatsoever. But we are supposed to believe you have abilities. You are a charlatan, sir, a cad."

A collective gasp danced about the room. Feeling the heat traveling up his neck, Thaddeus knew he was no longer welcome. All eyes in the room warily stared at him, some with curiosity, others with downright hostility. He hoped Miss Cordelia would come and visit him. He could give her the solace she was looking for, but after this performance, he doubted he would see her. He tipped his hat at Madam Medora, which only seemed to infuriate her more and caused Cordelia to smile, and he left the parlour to walk home.

No. 5 Cavendish Square loomed like an immense mausoleum in the heavy July dusk, its stone façade sweating faintly in the humid air. Gas lamps sputtered along the street, their flames guttering in the sharp wind as a lone carriage rattled to a stop at precisely half past seven. From it descended three women swathed in evening finery—silk, velvet, jet beads—gowns that shimmered faintly beneath the lantern light like the plumage of nocturnal birds.

They advanced toward the great doors of the Royal Polytechnic Institution, the air almost visible with the mingled breath of guests roaming through the foyer. The gaslit halls echoed faintly, the voices of the gathering melding into a low, anticipatory hum.

The moment Madam Medora stepped into the Great Hall, a ripple passed through the assembled crowd. Heads turned. Murmurs rose. Then, like a sudden gust of wind stirring dead leaves, applause swelled through the hall. Her name was whispered, hissed, shouted, breathed in reverence and curiosity.

Madam Medora dipped her head with feigned humility, though her eyes glittered with triumph.

Her companions—Melisendra, tall and hawkish, and Lorena, round-faced and heavily jeweled—stood straighter, basking in borrowed radiance.

As they made their way down the aisle toward the front rows, they were frequently detained. The Lord Mayor bowed over Medora's gloved hand, his wife nearly wilting with admiration. A wealthy couple swept toward her next, the woman nearly trembling with eagerness. Medora dispensed smiles, nods, murmured blessings like a queen moving among petitioners.

At last they reached their seats.

"Do you think these women will replace us, Vesta?" Melisendra whispered, the shadows under her eyes deepening as the lights dimmed.

Madam Medora let out a dismissive sniff. "Nonsense. Our patrons are loyal. These... newcomers are little more than novelties.

They shall not outshine us. Nor will that meddlesome Thaddeus Priest."

Behind them, a man seated one row back leaned forward ever so slightly. At the name Thaddeus, his posture sharpened, his expression flattening into something unreadable.

Lorena fanned herself briskly. "Do you know he came to my home as well? When he first crept into London, before any of you even noticed him. And not a coin worthy of the name did he leave me."

"He visited me too," Melisendra added. "Trying to... 'understand my methods.' The nerve."

Medora's nostrils flared. "He dared attempt to steal one of my own clients—brazenly, under my very roof. But I handled him."

"Oh, that you did, Vesta. Magnificently so," Lorena cooed.

Madam Medora smirked, folding her fan. "Let him attempt to build a clientele now. He will find London a barren field. I am quite sure his practice is withering."

Before the others could respond, the house lights flickered.

A shiver passed through the audience.

Onstage, an A-frame sign stood sentinel, illuminated by a single lantern:

THE FLORESCU SISTERS~SPIRITUALISTS EXTRAORDINAIRE.

Heavy brown curtains swayed slightly though no wind touched them. The very air felt charged, as though the hall itself were holding its breath.

Melisendra swallowed. "Materialization... they say it's a new kind of proof."

Medora's gloved fingers tightened around her fan. "Proof," she whispered, "can be dangerous."

The curtains parted.

Two young women entered—plain, pale, almost severe. Their simplicity was jarring next to the ornate setting, as though they had stepped from some remote convent or from the pages of a ghost story.

The audience erupted into applause.

One sister sat upon a wooden chair, her posture rigid. The other addressed the crowd.

"Tonight," she said, voice smooth as cold water, "we demonstrate trance mediumship culminating in the materialization of spirit, a substance of the spirit world, through which the dead assume shape."

A wave of uneasy murmurs swept the hall.

"We must dim the lights," she continued. "This materialization is delicate... and light devours it."

The hall descended into a shadowed half-darkness. Corners of the room deepened into velvety black where it seemed watchers might lurk.

The seated sister began her performance.

Her breathing quickened. Her eyes rolled back. Her head lolled forward as though an unseen hand pressed heavily upon her skull. A faint whispering sound—like distant rustling fabric—slithered across the hall.

Then came the light.

It blossomed behind her, a pale mist writhing faintly, as though trying to assume a shape but not yet knowing how.

The audience leaned forward collectively, breath held.

A milky, luminous substance seeped from her nostrils and mouth —long, trembling ribbons of pale matter, glistening as they accumulated, descending in slow, unnatural drips. A few audience members gasped, one woman covering her mouth with a gloved hand.

Madam Medora's eyes widened despite herself. How?

No trick she knew could mimic this in so public, so exposed a manner.

The air grew colder.

Then, form began to gather—coalescing behind the medium.

A figure took shape in the light: the silhouette of a man.

First his hands, translucent and wavering. Then his face—pale as drowned flesh.

He raised one hand and waved.

The hall's collective gasp was sharp as the snap of a bone.

The apparition flickered, shimmered, and slowly unravelled—its dissolving form trailing back into the milky tendrils, which in turn contracted, receding back into the medium's body.

The sight was obscene. Intimate. Violently uncanny.

Madam Medora felt a chill spider across her shoulders. She had seen countless illusions, countless theatrics—but never anything like this.

When the final threads of manifestation vanished, the hall fell utterly silent.

A heartbeat.

Another.

Then applause burst forth, wild and explosive. The entire audience rose to its feet.

But the man seated behind Medora slipped silently away, vanishing into the shadows of the aisle.

As the house lights brightened and patrons buzzed in fevered excitement, Madam Medora found herself once more surrounded—admiring voices rising like a tide around her.

"What did you think, Madam?"

"Was it real?"

"Is such manifestation possible?"

*Real?*

She could not say.

But she could feel—deep in her chest—a creeping dread.

She forced a bright smile.

"Oh yes," she lied smoothly. "Quite genuine. Astonishing."

"Well what I want to know is why, if such phenomena are real, does it always have to be so dark?" asked one man.

"If anyone could stage an optical deception, it would be here. Mirrors, perhaps... or glass—some concealed arrangement...," said another.

Whispers grew excitedly as people gathered around to cast doubt on what they had seen.

"Ladies and Gentlemen, please, even if the Florescu sisters are foreign, we do not need to be casting aspersions on their performance this evening. I will take their demonstration at face value, for now," said Madam Medora.

She received approving nods from all around. It was nearly an hour before she and her companions managed to reach the foyer. The Florescu sisters emerged then—transformed from wan spectres into fresh-faced young women, cheeks dusted with powder, their earlier pallor replaced by human warmth.

Up close, they were striking.

The crowd surged toward them with the fervour of believers before a pair of saints.

Madam Medora stepped aside, the swell of bodies parting around her like a river diverting from a stone. A terrible thought clawed at her:

Was she witnessing the eclipse of her own reign?

Behind the applause, behind the excited shrieks, behind the clamor of adoring voices, Medora could almost hear something else—

A distant whisper.

A faint, hollow laugh.

Like a ghost exhaling in the rafters.

Monday, July 7, 1862

# DOUBLE MURDER

## SILAS BURKE AND VALENTINA SAINT

A Shocking Crime Disturbs the Peace of the City
Public Alarm Grows as Police Investigate

### A STARTLING CRIME

LONDON—The tragic and shocking double murder of Mr. Silas Burke and Miss Valentina Saint has sent a profound disturbance throughout the city.

Mr. Burke, a tradesman of respectable standing, was discovered deceased within his establishment, a shop he had but recently transferred to new ownership.

Miss Saint was found dead earlier that same day at her residence under circumstances no less alarming.

Authorities have not vet disclosed the precise nature of the injuries sustamed, though it is understood that both deaths bear signs of violence.

### POLICE INVESTIGATION

The Metropolitan Police have undertaken a full inguiry into the matter.

Inspectors Barnes and Dickman are said to be leading the investigation, and have alterady beguin the examination of witheses and the exliection of evidence.

Though no official statement has been issued, it is behened that the authoritics are exploing the possibility of a connection between the two deaths.

Detectives have expreased confidence that progress is being made, though no arrests have yet been effected.

### PUBLIC ALARM

The city remains in a state of unease following the discovery of the crimes. Residents in the affected districts have voiced concern regacting their safety, and many now call for increased vigilance on the part of the authorities.

### A DISTURBING SIMILARITY

It has been remarked, though not officially confurned, that certain pecullar features observed at both scenes may indicate a method not wholly common to ordinary crimes of violence.

### PARLIAMENT

Debate continues regarding policing resources within the East End districts.

### THE STATE OF TRADE

Commercial confidence remains guarded; cotton supply irregular.

### THE WEATHER

London: Overcast with intermittent fog.

# CHAPTER FOURTEEN

A fresh sheet of rain draped London in a sheen of silver by the time Detective Barnes and Detective Dickman pushed open the iron gate to the Metropolitan Mortuary. The building loomed before them—a squat stone structure with narrow windows that glowed faintly from within. The scent of wet cobblestone mingled with the iron tang of the Thames, unsettlingly appropriate for a place that housed the city's most unfortunate.

Inside, the air turned colder — and quieter, as though sound itself had been dampened by stone and death. The muted drip of water from their coats seemed too loud in the cavernous entry hall.

"Coroner's in a mood today," Dickman muttered as they descended the stairs to the examination rooms. "Said he'd barely slept. Something about these bodies gave him a jolt."

Barnes pressed his lips into a thin line. "Then we'd best tread carefully. He's brilliant—but prickly when vexed."

They reached the bottom of the stairs just as a door swung open, releasing a gust of frigid air tinged with disinfectant...and something darker beneath it.

Dr. Earl Keiler emerged from the room, spectacles fogged, sleeves rolled past his elbows, his apron streaked with the faintest traces of work best left unspoken. His dark hair, usually slicked back, now looked ruffled and wild.

"Detectives," Keiler said, voice tight. "You're late."

"We came as quickly as we could," Barnes replied. "You said there were findings regarding Miss Valentina Saint and Mr. Silas Burke?"

Keiler removed his spectacles and wiped them with a handkerchief. His eyes—sharp, bloodshot, exhausted—met the detectives' with a gravity that made Dickman shift uneasily.

"Follow me," the coroner said.

They stepped into the examination room. The chill deepened. The lanterns flickered as though a draught—or something else—passed through.

Two covered forms lay on wooden tables, shrouded beneath crisp white sheets as large blocks of ice packed in sawdust slowly melted beneath them, guarding the room against the heat outside.

Keiler approached the first, pulling back the cloth to reveal Valentina Saint. Her pale features appeared waxen in death, her lips tinged with an unnatural violet. Barnes felt a stir of pity. She had been young. Pretty. And now...

"Cause of death?" Barnes asked quietly.

Keiler motioned toward the body's neck. "Ligature marks. She was strangled—deliberately, methodically. This was done at close quarters. No frenzy. No panic. No hesitation. I would say that scarf you found was the weapon."

Dickman frowned. "But her home showed no signs of forced entry."

"Yes," Keiler said. "Which suggests the assailant was not a stranger."

Barnes stiffened. "Or she trusted him."

The coroner nodded once. "Precisely."

He moved to the second table. With a slower, heavier motion, he rolled back the sheet.

Silas Burke's face bore the signs of violence—deep bruising along the jaw, mottled skin on his throat, a contorted expression frozen in final terror.

"Burke fought back," Keiler explained. "Hands scraped, knuckles split. Defensive wounds. But the killer was stronger."

Dickman muttered, "Two murders in the same day. Both strangled. Both violent."

Keiler met their eyes again as he pointed at Miss Saint. "But not the same. Here, the murderer squeezed with such force that the bone in her throat has given way." He paused. "It takes steadiness to apply such pressure without struggle."

"But this," said Keiler as he pointed at Silas Burke. "Less deliberate. Less controlled. I am not convinced the death was the original intention."

Barnes's gaze darkened, though he kept his voice steady. "We are chasing passions, not patterns."

"The murder of Silas Burke lacks precision. Too much force in the wrong places. Bruising across the chest as though weight was applied carelessly. At the same time, the angle of the blow suggests he fell and hit his head. I'm not sure what happened, but there was definitely a struggle."

Barnes paced slowly, absorbing every detail. "So, one murder is intimate, possibly between two people who knew each other. And the second murder might be a robbery gone wrong? Ruffians from the street?"

"Perhaps," Keiler said. "It seems likely."

A cold silence pressed down on the room, each drip of meltwater marking time upon the floor. Barnes's thoughts drifted—to the ledger in the Inn, the pocket watch, the growing tangle of suspects and secrets.

Dickman yanked the sheet back over Burke's face. "Damn grim business."

Keiler exhaled a long breath, one that seemed to carry the weight of every corpse he had ever examined. "Gentlemen... I will send written reports to the precinct by morning, but know this: the killer of Miss Saint will strike again. Soon."

Barnes turned sharply. "How can you be certain?"

Keiler's stare was glassy with unease.

"Because killers like this—those who kill with deliberation—are never satisfied by only one."

The lanterns flickered again.

Somewhere behind them, a tray of instruments gave a faint metallic rattle, though no one stood near it.

Dickman swallowed. "Wind?"

Barnes didn't answer.

Keiler only whispered, "This place has seen enough dead to know better."

VESTA HODDLE—KNOWN to London's hungry crowds as the illustrious Madam Medora—sat stiffly at her escritoire, the morning light slanting through her curtains in narrow, bleak bars. The ink in her bottle seemed unusually thick, as though reluctant to flow. She dipped her quill and began to write, only to stop, scowl, and scratch out the entire page with violent strokes.

Another sheet. The quill trembled in her hand—rage disguised as frustration—and a heavy drop of ink spilled from the nib, blooming across the paper like a spreading bruise.

"Oh, blast and damnation!" she hissed, thrusting the quill back into its holder.

She pressed her fingertips to her temples. She could not stop thinking of him.

Thaddeus Priest.

That insolent, upstart fool who had dared to question her methods—her, Madam Medora, whose name carried more weight in London's spiritualist circles than a bishop's sermon did in church.

It had unsettled her, shaken her composure in a way she could not admit aloud. He had made her feel—if only for a moment—seen, as if he peered directly through her carefully crafted illusions.

He had behaved as though she were a fraud. She, whose séances brought in half the aristocracy of London.

He had humiliated her before her own clients.

And worst of all—people had seen.

She wanted revenge. But she had not yet settled on how to achieve it.

Fortune, however, seemed to rouse itself in her favour that morning.

A firm knock echoed through the house, reverberating like a knell. Madam Medora's head snapped up. Footsteps pattered down the hall—the maid's soft shoes—followed by the muted murmur of a man's voice. She distinctly heard the word detective.

Her eyes gleamed.

The maid entered, smoothing her apron. "Madam, a Detective Barnes is here to see you."

"Let him in—yes, yes, do let him in at once. I am receiving visitors." Her voice was too bright, too eager, but she did not care.

Detective Barnes entered with the stiffness of a man who trusted few things, least of all the people he met. Tall, broad-shouldered, sporting a well-waxed handlebar moustache and a bowler hat that had seen better mornings, he bowed politely.

"Madam Medora," he said, "my apologies for intruding, but I am conducting an investigation. I wondered if you might spare me a moment."

"Not at all, dear detective. May my maid bring you some tea?" she asked sweetly, almost coyly.

"No, thank you," he replied.

"Please—sit."

The detective accepted the chair opposite her and opened a notebook, flipping it to a fresh page. "I'm certain you are aware of the murder of Miss Valentina Saint, a fellow spiritualist. I am investigating her death. Did you know the deceased?"

"Oh yes," she said, resting her hand dramatically against her bosom. "Valentina was a sweet woman. Somewhat decent as a spiritualist." She sighed, shaking her head. "Such a tragic end."

Detective Barnes's pencil scratched across the page. "Did she have any enemies? Anyone who might wish her harm?"

"None that I know of... not personally." She paused, giving the moment the weight of theatrical reflection. Then she leaned in, her voice dropping to an intimate whisper. "But there is one man. It couldn't be him, of course—but then, one never truly knows anyone, does one?"

Barnes studied her carefully. Her eyes were bright—too bright. He noted, with unease, how delighted she appeared to speak of another's death.

"Do you know his name?" he asked.

"Why yes. Mr. Thaddeus Priest. A spiritualist who only recently arrived on the London scene." Her voice curled maliciously. "He attended Valentina's séance the other night. And—supposedly—he has been skulking about, visiting other spiritualists, attempting to steal away their clients."

She shook her head as though deeply troubled. In truth, she shivered with satisfaction.

Detective Barnes felt his instincts stir. Something about her answers rang hollow—too rehearsed, too convenient. He suspected her eagerness had little to do with justice.

"How long has Mr. Priest been in London?" he asked.

"Oh, I wouldn't know that," she said breezily. "He's only recently begun conducting séances. Perhaps a month. Who can say how long he lingered before showing himself? He strikes me as a charlatan. Yes, yes—you would do well to look into him."

The detective closed his notebook. "Thank you. Can you think of anything else that may be useful?"

"No, I believe that is all," she said, folding her hands primly.

"Very well. Should anything occur to you, please do not hesitate to contact me." Barnes handed her his card, tipped his hat, and let himself out.

He stood upon the front stoop, breathing in the cool, damp air with relief. He shook his head slowly. He would add the name Thaddeus Priest to his file, yes—but he could nearly taste the bitterness of the lie Madam Medora had fed him. She had seen an opportunity to use him, and she had seized it without hesitation.

Inside, Madam Medora watched him go with a smile as sweet and poisonous as belladonna. A cat who had found the cream.

How satisfying.

Thaddeus Priest would soon find himself tangled in consequences, and she had barely lifted a finger.

In an instant, her spirits soared. She returned to her desk, pulled forward a fresh sheet of paper, and dipped her quill again—her hand suddenly steady, her mind deliciously at ease.

The late morning sunlight—much too golden for the miseries it now illuminated—trickled through the modest panes of Mrs. Parsons's boarding house. Its brightness felt almost accusatory, as though it sought to banish every shadow that dared cling to the memory of the night before. Yet even such a cheerful dawn could not wholly dispel the pall that clung, invisible but perceptible, to Thaddeus Priest.

He had been dreaming—soft, pleasant dreams, warm like velvet curtains drawn against the world—when the spectral outline of a man hovered inches before his face.

"Artie!" Thaddeus bolted upright with a gasp. "Don't do that."

Artie crossed his incorporeal arms, looking very pleased with himself. "Well, I thought it was time you woke up. You have a visitor.

And Mrs. Parsons is tromping up those stairs as though her feet were made of iron. She is... decidedly displeased."

Thaddeus groaned. "Will I never get a moment's peace?" He raked his fingers through his hair. "Who is it?"

Artie blinked. "Who is what?"

"Downstairs, Artie. The person waiting for me."

"Oh!" Artie brightened. "A young lady. Very attractive. Blonde. Petite. Looking rather thoughtful, if you ask me."

A sudden spark of hope flickered behind Thaddeus's eyes. "Cordelia?"

"Well, I didn't ask for her name," Artie said with dramatic innocence. "Ah—here comes Mrs. Parsons."

A firm, authoritative rap struck the door.

"Mr. Priest?" came her clipped voice. "There's someone here to see you—a client, I believe."

"My apologies, Mrs. Parsons. Please tell her I will be down shortly."

The disapproving humph! she left in her wake lingered in the air like smoke.

Thaddeus moved with astonishing speed—washing, shaving, dressing in a frantic blur. Artie hovered in the corner, cackling softly.

"I do not think I have ever seen you move so fast."

Thaddeus shot him a look before slamming the door behind him, leaving Artie's laughter echoing like rattling chains.

He bounded down the stairs two at a time, straightened his waistcoat, swept his hair back with one polished motion, and entered the parlour.

"Miss Clements, I am so very glad you came."

Cordelia rose gracefully, the firelight catching the faint gold in her hair. "Mr. Priest." She dropped a delicate curtsy.

But Thaddeus stopped short, for another figure stood beside her —a man of crisp bearing and immaculate posture, reminiscent of Jackson in his meticulous attention to propriety.

"How do you do," Thaddeus said with a polite bow.

The man appeared startled—almost as though he had expected to find a mountebank dressed in ribbons and spectacles—but recovered and returned the gesture.

"This is my man, Brooks," Cordelia explained. "He travels with me... and serves as my chaperone."

Relief washed over Thaddeus so visibly that Cordelia almost laughed.

"I am grateful you came," he said gently. "We have... much to speak of."

He felt her sister's presence before he saw her—Vena, pale and solemn, stood at Cordelia's shoulder like a sorrowful guardian. Thaddeus's gaze flicked to her, unbidden.

Cordelia turned sharply. "Is something there?"

Thaddeus flushed. "Forgive me." He gestured to the seat across from her. "Shall we sit? If you prefer, your man may remain—our conversation may touch upon matters most sensitive."

"I wish him to stay," Cordelia said quickly. "It would be improper otherwise. We must observe propriety, Mr. Priest."

Thaddeus inwardly cursed his oversight. "Of course. My apologies."

She folded her gloved hands tightly in her lap. "Before we begin, I must tell you—I very nearly did not come today. After the debacle with Madam Medora..."

"I understand. Madam Medora mistook my intentions. I meant only to spare you further distress. I assure you, Miss Clements, I seek no other aim than to be of service."

"I do not know how you intend to 'set things right,' Mr. Priest."

He breathed in deeply—carefully. Vena's grave, expectant eyes lingered on him.

"It may help," he said softly, "if you know something of my nature."

Cordelia nodded.

"All my life," he continued, "I have been able to see the dead."

She blinked. "Well... one would assume as much of a spiritualist."

"Yes, but I mean—see them. Truly see them. As I see you now. My work is not a stage act nor a clever illusion." His voice dropped lower. "And I was troubled by Madam Medora's treatment of you that night, not merely because she was unkind, but because... your sister stands beside you as plainly as the hearth."

Cordelia's breath caught.

"You are telling me," she whispered, "that you believe my sister is dead."

"Yes," he answered. "I am."

He waited for the scream, the collapse—something—but she merely stared at him, her face pale but composed, as though she had been bracing for this very revelation.

"Are you well?" he asked quietly.

"Mr. Priest... you are not the first spiritualist to tell me this." She swallowed. "But when questioned, they falter."

"Then why," Thaddeus asked gently, "do you continue to seek them out?"

"Because my sister vanished without a trace." Her voice trembled. "The police do not heed me. You—people like you—are all I have left."

"Then question me," he said. "Ask anything. As many questions as you wish. If you find me a fraud, insult me and leave with my blessing. I will bear you no ill will."

A faint smile ghosted across her lips.

"Very well. What is my sister's name?"

Thaddeus looked to her sister.

*Vena*, she murmured.

"Her name is Vena. And yes... your twin," said Thaddeus.

Cordelia's eyes widened. Had she said the name at Medora's séance? She could not recall.

"Her favorite pastime?"

"Playing the piano," said Thaddeus, amusement twitching at the corners of his mouth.

"The name of her cat?"

"Mr. Whiskers."

Cordelia pressed a trembling hand to her mouth.

"Her necklace," she whispered. "Describe it."

Thaddeus answered, and Cordelia broke. The grief came in waves—helpless, keening, long-suppressed. He offered her his handkerchief and said nothing, allowing her tears to fall as they must.

At last, when she steadied, she asked the question that hung like a blade:

"How did she die? Where is she? Where is her body?"

Thaddeus closed his eyes for a moment and relayed Vena's tale—of the secret suitor, the northern journey, the confrontation, the carriage wheels, the unmarked grave. With every word, Vena's presence dimmed, until at last she faded entirely.

Cordelia felt the loss as a physical blow—her hand flew to her chest, and she gasped, fighting for breath. Then, slowly... a release. A long exhale that seemed to drain months of torment from her bones.

Mrs. Parsons arrived with tea, bustling in like a motherly tempest. Upon seeing Cordelia's tear-stained face, she clucked sympathetically.

"There, my dear, there. Better out than in. And whatever he told you—believe him. This one is the real article."

Thaddeus sat stunned as Mrs. Parsons swept out with her tray.

When Cordelia finally composed herself, she lifted her chin.

"How much do I owe you, Mr. Priest?"

"Nothing," he said firmly. "The truth is payment enough."

"No," she insisted. "That reading was... extraordinary. I am more than capable of paying you—and you deserve to be paid."

He shook his head, softening. "Your peace of mind is all I hoped to give. Let that be my thanks."

Cordelia regarded him with something like awe—something like gratitude—and the faintest hint of something else, something unnamed, stirring like a shadow behind her eyes.

## CHAPTER FOURTEEN

The carriage rattled through the London streets, its wheels hissing through puddles left by the morning's rain. Cordelia Clements sat very still, gloved hands folded tightly in her lap, though her thoughts churned with a restless energy she could scarcely contain. The city passed by in blurs of soot and brick, but she saw none of it—her mind remained fixed on Mr. Thaddeus Priest, the strange and spectral gravity he seemed to possess.

He unsettled her.

Not merely because he was handsome, though he was—alarmingly so, with those soft, storm-lit eyes and the quiet sincerity that hovered in his words. No, what shook her was the impossible accuracy with which he spoke of Vena. Her Vena. Details no stranger should know. Details Cordelia herself had whispered only to shadows in her loneliest hours.

Of course, she reminded herself with a shudder, he could very well be a fraud. A clever actor. A man with a talent for imitation and flattery, weaving truths from half clues and boldness. She could not allow her aching heart to blind her.

There was only one way to assess his legitimacy, and the thought of it pressed cold fingers around her ribs.

She would have to go to Kensington.

To the hospital.

To the place where Thaddeus claimed her sister had died alone.

But was she truly the right person to do such a thing? The idea of venturing north, asking pointed questions, navigating unfamiliar streets—what if trouble found her? What if the truth was something worse than she imagined?

"Brooks?" Her voice sounded thin even to herself.

Brooks, sitting erect opposite her, turned his head slightly. "Yes, Miss."

"What did you think of Mr. Priest's reading?"

Brooks's brow tightened almost imperceptibly. "I think you should exercise caution, Miss. He... knew too much. More than any man ought to know of your private affairs. One must always ask how such knowledge is acquired."

Cordelia glanced sharply at him. "I have consulted spiritualists for months, and you have never spoken in such a manner."

"You have never before met one whose tales did not crumble under scrutiny," Brooks replied gravely. "He was the first to speak with conviction—and accuracy."

Cordelia pressed her lips together. "True. I suppose... I suppose not."

Silence settled between them—not uncomfortable, but weighty. One of the qualities she cherished most in Brooks was this very silence. He never intruded, never demanded, never judged. He could share an entire afternoon's journey with her in wordless companionship, and she would never feel alone.

After a long moment, she broke that stillness.

"Brooks... do you think we could go to Kensington?"

He did not flinch. He had known this question was coming—she could see it in the steady, resigned set of his jaw.

"We could take the train, Miss," he said, matter-of-factly. "If we departed early, we would be home well before supper."

The unspoken sentiment settled between them: If you insist on chasing this truth, then I will ensure no harm befalls you.

Cordelia exhaled softly, her breath fogging the window glass. "I considered going straight to the police, but—"

"But you have no evidence," Brooks finished gently.

She nodded.

The carriage wheels clattered over cobblestones as if punctuating the decision forming between them.

"Then Kensington it shall be," Brooks said. "Tomorrow, Miss?"

Cordelia's heart fluttered with dread and resolve in equal measure. "Tomorrow," she echoed.

The word felt like a doorway creaking open—one she could not close again.

"I don't think you need to be here," snarled the female spiritualist as she slammed the door in his face, the stained glass rattling like a trapped spirit.

It had been the same story everywhere he went—doors shut, curtains drawn, whispers trailing behind him like a funeral shroud. Thaddeus had spent the entire day walking the lamplit streets, seeking out every spiritualist he could find, yet each treated him as though he carried a contagion. His name had become a curse.

His final hope was Ira Doyle.

Ira lived in a narrow three-story brownstone wedged between two taller buildings as if it were trying to hide from the world. Its bricks were recently repaired, reddish and damp, glistening under the evening mist. Through the beveled glass, warped by the fading daylight, Thaddeus saw a figure approach.

The door creaked open.

"May I help you?" asked Ira.

Thaddeus removed his hat. "Sir, I am Thaddeus Priest. I've been trying to gather information about accusations made against me, but it seems... I have acquired something of a reputation. No one is willing to speak with me."

"And you were hoping I would," Ira replied, looking him over with the sharpness of a man long accustomed to reading people. "Hmm. Nothing villainous about your face. Very well—come in."

Thaddeus stepped inside. The air was warm, heavy with the scent of soil and something sweet—something blooming. Ira wore a gardener's apron and black gloves smeared with potting dirt.

"Forgive the attire," Ira said. "You've caught me on potting day."

"Potting day?"

"I grow orchids. A hobby... though lately they seem determined to take over the house." He gestured toward an inner room where pale petals glowed eerily in the dimness like watchful eyes. He poured tea from a waiting service. "Sugar? Lemon?"

"Neither," said Thaddeus. "Plain."

"A purist," Ira said approvingly.

Thaddeus sat, the orchids rustling faintly as though whispering among themselves.

"So," Ira continued, "once in a while I uproot them, free the tangled roots, and give them fresh soil. Plants, like people, need breathing room."

"Do you live alone?" Thaddeus asked.

"Yes. Retired. A widower. My wife passed a few years ago." His voice softened. "That is how I came to this little profession. I hoped I might contact her." Ira shrugged. "I never had much talent for seeing the dead. It's people's energies I sense. Never seen a spirit with my own eyes. Don't know what I'd do if I did."

They shared a small, subdued laugh.

Then Ira leaned back. "So, no one will speak to you. I've heard the rumours—about you pilfering clients."

Thaddeus frowned. "May I tell you what actually happened?"

"Oh, please do. I enjoy a good tale."

So Thaddeus explained—his true ability to see the dead, his failures at showmanship, his forced transformation into a performer, and the incident at Madam Medora's.

"I only wanted the woman to know what happened to her sister," Thaddeus said. "She came to me—I told her where her sister was."

"You told her where the body was?" Ira asked, brows rising.

"Yes."

Ira set his teacup down very slowly. "Young man, do you have any idea what you have set in motion? You know the cause of death—and the burial place. She will believe you put her sister there."

A chill slid up Thaddeus's spine, colder than any ghost he had known. "But I explained clearly she was trampled by horses. The hospital knows this. Surely no one would believe—"

Ira gave a grim smile. "You'd be astonished what people will believe when fear guides them. Just like Madam Medora. You threatened her livelihood with the truth. I doubt she accepted that gracefully."

"No. She was furious," Thaddeus admitted.

"And now half of London thinks you are a thief of clients and if word gets out you may be thought a murderer? You will get no help, not from any quarter."

Thaddeus's gaze drifted, unfocused. A thought flickered at the edge of his mind—dark, unwelcome.

"You've gone pale," Ira observed. "Ghost-pale."

"It's nothing," Thaddeus lied. "Just a passing thought."

"Passing thoughts are often the truest," Ira murmured.

Thaddeus cleared his throat. "What did you do before... this?"

"You'll laugh. I was a banker. Made more money than I needed. I don't require the income now. Spiritualism keeps me occupied—and keeps her memory close."

Ira studied him again, eyes narrowing. "You're not quite who you say you are, are you?"

"Excuse me?"

"I sense energy, remember? You are no pauper. You carry the posture of old money—even in that coat."

Thaddeus exhaled, defeated. "My real name is Thaddeus Raynsford. I am Lord Horace Raynsford's son. I would appreciate it if you kept that to yourself."

Ira let out a low whistle. "Does your father know you are here?"

"Yes," Thaddeus said bitterly. "Unfortunately."

Ira drank his tea to keep from speaking. Clearly, he knew the elder Raynsford—and did not think highly of him.

"So," Thaddeus said, "back to my purpose. Do you know anything about the accusations against me? Have you heard anything?"

"Trying to clear your name," Ira said.

"Exactly."

"Well, I'm afraid not. Nothing others don't already know." Ira tapped his fingers against his cup. "Are you certain this is not better left to the authorities?"

"Do you think they will care if I am being wrongfully accused," said Thaddeus. "I want the truth."

Ira sighed. "If I hear anything, I will inform you."

He walked Thaddeus to the door. Outside, night had deepened; the street lamps cast long sepulchral shadows across the steps.

"Be careful, Thaddeus. You have no notion who—or what—you may be facing. And I fear you are in far over your head."

"Oh," Thaddeus said, forcing a thin smile, "I absolutely agree."

Ira paused. "Do you play chess?"

"Yes. I love the game."

"As do I. I spend most evenings in solitude. If ever you need company—or refuge—you are welcome here for a match."

"That sounds delightful," Thaddeus said.

And as he stepped back into the misty night, he felt the uncanny sensation of being watched—not by Ira, but by something else entirely.

# CHAPTER FIFTEEN

Morning broke in a sullen wash of gray, the sky a low, oppressive lid over London. Cordelia stood at the window of her room, gloved hands clasped together, watching the fog curl and slither over the rooftops like something alive. She hadn't slept well. Thaddeus Priest's voice kept intruding on her dreams—calm, handsome, unsettlingly certain. *Your sister is dead.*

The words clung to her like a draught.

Brooks appeared at the doorway, bowler hat in hand. "The carriage is ready, Miss."

Cordelia turned from the window. "Thank you, Brooks."

He watched her with his quiet, dependable expression—the sort that neither intruded nor dismissed. She drew a steadying breath and followed him downstairs.

Outside, the city wore its morning gloom with a heaviness that seemed to belong to the grave. They made their way to the station through narrow streets still slick and shining from the night's damp. The mist was dense enough to blur figures into silhouettes, the clip of passing boots muffled, distant, ghostly.

The train sat panting at the platform, a hulking beast exhaling plumes of steam. Cordelia hesitated before stepping aboard.

"We don't have to do this," Brooks said gently.

"Yes," she whispered. "We do."

They found a compartment but partly occupied: an elderly couple drawn closely into their wraps against the rawness of the morning, and a young woman intent upon a dog-eared penny dreadful. Cordelia seated herself at the window, while Brooks placed himself opposite her with all the rigidity of a carved monument.

The whistle sounded sharply. With a jolt and a protesting groan, the train began at last its noisy progress toward Kensington.

Fog streaked past the glass in pale ribbons. Cordelia's reflection floated faintly against it—her face pale, her dark eyes troubled. She pressed her gloved fingers to the cold pane.

"Brooks... what if he was telling the truth?"

Brooks folded his hands atop his cane. "Then we shall face that truth, Miss. But we won't know until we look."

She nodded, though her stomach fluttered. "What if she is there? What if she's... truly gone?"

"Then you will have your answer."

"And if he lied?" she asked.

"Then we expose him for it."

Silence settled, heavy and long.

Cordelia's thoughts drifted—back to her sister's laughter, her quick wit, the bright way she used to fill a room. Then to the night she vanished. The ache never dulled. It only changed shape.

As the train rattled on, the fog thinned enough for glimpses of Kensington's grand houses—tall, stately, self-assured—as though the troubles of ordinary people could never seep into their polished halls.

But beyond them, at the edge of the borough, rose the grim

silhouette of Kensington Asylum. Its chimneys clawed at the sky, and its brick walls, darkened by age and damp, looked more suited to imprison spirits than heal the living.

Cordelia's breath caught. The place radiated a quiet misery that chilled her bones.

Brooks followed her gaze. "Not quite welcoming, is it, Miss?"

"No," she murmured. "But neither is truth."

The train hissed to a halt.

They stepped onto the platform together, the weight of what awaited pressing down on both of them.

Cordelia lifted her chin, gathering the frayed ends of her courage.

"Brooks," she said softly, "let us go see if my sister waits for me."

And with that, they began the long walk toward the asylum's looming gates.

THE WALK from the station to Kensington Asylum proved longer than Cordelia had anticipated. The road wound past iron fences and gaunt-limbed trees whose branches stirred and murmured together in the wind with a faint, unsettling clatter. Brooks kept a measured pace beside her, matching each of her hesitant steps.

The asylum rose ahead in full, oppressive stature—its great brick façade blotched with age, its narrow windows barred and black. A murder of crows perched along the roofline, their silhouettes sharp against the colorless sky.

Cordelia exhaled, the air warm and close against her lips. "I believe," she whispered, "that the place is trying to discourage us from entering."

"It has failed, Miss," Brooks replied, though even he looked unsettled.

At the great wrought-iron gates, a groundskeeper in a heavy coat regarded them with bored suspicion. Brooks cleared his throat.

"We are here to inquire about a patient," he said in his even, respectful tone. "We need to speak with the administrator."

The groundskeeper's eyes flicked from Brooks to Cordelia—lingering a moment too long—as though measuring her resolve. Without a word, he unlocked the gate and gestured them inside.

The path through the yard was uneven and poorly kept, its edges choked with old leaves, brittle twigs, and the remnants of things long left unattended. Cordelia swept her gaze over the grounds, noting the stark emptiness. No patients walked in the yard. No staff—only the distant figure of a nurse moving hurriedly between buildings. A strange hush blanketed everything.

Brooks noticed her discomfort. "Most patients are kept indoors due to the rain, I'm certain," he murmured.

Cordelia wasn't sure she believed that, but she nodded.

They ascended the stone steps to the main entrance. Brooks held the door open for her—a draught of cool, stale air met her, tinged with lye, worn linens, and something else she couldn't quite name.

Inside, the asylum was dimly lit. Gas lamps hissed along the walls in intermittent flickers, leaving pockets of shadow that seemed to breathe of their own accord. Cordelia stepped closer to Brooks without realizing it.

A tall, gaunt man in a fraying black coat approached them. His scalp shone through sparse strands of gray hair, and his eyes were the flat, assessing kind of a man who had seen everything and been moved by nothing.

"Dr. Gardiner," he said, bowing stiffly. "Administrator. You have business here?"

Cordelia mustered her courage. "Yes. We seek information about my sister. Her name is Vena Clements. She disappeared some months ago. I was told..." Her throat tightened. "I was told she might be here."

Dr. Gardiner's expression did not change. "Many families come with similar stories. I will check our registry."

Cordelia's pulse quickened as he led them down a corridor of polished stone. Echoes barreled off the walls around them—faraway voices, a clatter that sounded like dropped metal, and once, the thin, wavering cry of someone in distress.

The doctor paused before a heavy wooden door and gestured them inside his office.

It was a stark room—bare walls, a single window fogged with moisture, a desk stacked with ledgers. Dr. Gardiner opened one of them, flipping through with long, bony fingers.

"What date did she go missing?" he asked without looking up.

"April 12th."

He nodded once and continued scanning.

Cordelia leaned forward, gloves pressed together. Brooks stood at her shoulder, tall and silent, but she could feel the tension in him. Even the air felt still, as though poised on the edge of revelation.

Finally, Dr. Gardiner stopped. His finger rested on a name.

Cordelia's heart hammered so hard it made her vision blur.

"Is she—" Her voice cracked. "Is she here?"

Dr. Gardiner looked up, meeting her eyes for the first time with something like gravity.

"There was a patient admitted on April 16th," he said. "A young woman found in the outskirts of Hyde Park. She had been trampled by horses."

Cordelia swayed.

Brooks caught her elbow.

Dr. Gardiner closed the ledger.

"She gave only one name," he said slowly. "Just one word, repeated over and over."

Cordelia could barely speak. "What... what was it?"

The doctor folded his hands atop the ledger.

"Cordelia," he said.

The room tilted. Cordelia pressed a hand to her lips, a sob breaking free before she could swallow it down.

Brooks murmured, "Miss... breathe."

Cordelia looked at Dr. Gardiner with eyes that stung.

"I want to see her," she whispered.

The doctor hesitated—not long, but enough for her to feel something cold lance through her stomach.

"Very well," he said at last. "She's buried in our cemetery here at the asylum."

He rose.

"Come. I will take you to her."

Rain did not merely fall—it descended, thick as a funeral shroud, turning the narrow London street into a gleaming obsidian channel. Water gurgled through crooked drainpipes and skittered in restless streams along the gutters. Ordinarily, Thaddeus might have welcomed such a storm; the dimness, the solitude, the muffled quiet suited him. But tonight he had been caught unawares, umbrella forgotten, coat already clinging wetly to his shoulders.

He peered up and down the muddy stretch, searching for so much as the glow of a cab lantern. Instead, a queer stillness settled over him. The hair at his nape bristled. A thin, needling dizziness crept behind his eyes, followed by that unmistakable ringing—soft at first, then swelling, as though invisible fingers plucked at the bones of his skull.

He knew this sensation. Knew it far too well.

A spirit walked abroad.

He turned slowly, scanning the rain-swept street. For a moment he saw nothing but shadow and water. Thaddeus froze, breath quickening, as his eyes landed—there—across the street, half-shrouded by the veils of rain, the shape of a woman. His nerves snarled together as recognition struck.

Annie stood naked in the downpour, her throat gaping wide, a dark red ruin from which blood streamed freely, mingling with the rainwater in grotesque rivulets. For a wild instant, horror seized him

—not at her death, but at the thought she might still be alive in such a state. Yet her skin bore that unmistakable pallor, the bluish marbling of veins that spidered across her cheeks and limbs. Her hair hung in sodden tangles, plastered to the lifeless skin they once graced.

Her lips twisted into a grin far too wide for any mortal countenance. Black blood seeped from the corners of her mouth and dripped languidly down her chin.

Thaddeus tried to look away. He could not. Something in her eyes—burning with a hatred so raw it seemed almost animate—held him fast.

*"You caused this."*

The disembodied whisper rasped directly into his ear, though she stood yards away. Annie's voice—yet not Annie's—scraped like rusted metal. It swelled suddenly, shrieked across the storm, *"You should pay for what they've done to me!"*

His knees weakened. To be confronted by the dead was unsettling enough, but to be claimed by their fury—this threatened to unmake him. He did not know what trespass she accused him of, but she was no longer the woman he had last seen. Something else peered out from those ruined features.

Despite himself, he felt drawn toward her, as though some unseen current tugged him through the rain. He stepped off the curb—

—and a horse screamed.

A carriage lunged out of the murk. Only the driver's quick yank on the reins spared Thaddeus; the beast reared, hooves slicing the air just above his skull. He flung up his arm, stumbling back as mud splashed against his boots. His heart thundered as he regained his footing.

He apologized breathlessly, but the driver cursed him roundly before snapping the reins and vanishing into the mist.

When Thaddeus turned back, Annie—her corpse, her apparition, whatever she had become—was gone. No trace of her presence lingered. No spiritual residue. Nothing.

Perfect. As though London's recent murders weren't enough, now Annie had joined their number—and he found, disturbingly, that he cared very little. She had been unkind to him in life; in death she seemed no different.

He shook his head, rain dripping from his brow, trying to banish the intrusive thoughts. He could not allow the city's cruelty to seep into him. He would not become like his father—harsh, cold, hollow. London might press upon him from all sides, but he would not let it warp his sense of right and wrong.

Not yet. Not ever, if he could help it.

DETECTIVE BARNES STOOD before the old brick house as the daylight failed, its windows watching him like lidded, disapproving eyes. The neighbourhood lay hushed beneath a damp and unseasonable chill, the last of the light draining from the street until all seemed muffled and grey. He pulled his coat tighter and contemplated the house's occupants. Several spiritualists had already spoken with him —some trembling, some evasive—but every one of them had uttered the same name with dread or resentment in their voices: Thaddeus Priest.

The steps groaned under Barnes's weight as he approached. His knuckles had barely grazed the door when it opened a crack, a single sharp eye peering out. In another moment, Mrs. Parsons appeared fully, her posture austere, her expression sculpted into cold disapproval.

"May I help you?" she asked, as though the answer hardly mattered.

Barnes tipped his bowler respectfully. "Good day, Madam. Detective Barnes, Metropolitan Police. I'm here to speak with a boarder of yours—Thaddeus Priest."

A flicker of alarm crossed her face—brief as lightning behind clouds—before the mask snapped back into place.

"Come inside," she said, stepping aside stiffly. "I will fetch him."

The parlour she ushered him into was dimly lit, the fire guttering and throwing long shadows across furnishings in burnt orange and deep sienna. Barnes would have found such colors garish anywhere else, yet here they lent the room an unsettling warmth, like the inside of a richly furnished tomb. Among the teacups and proper upholstery, the tools of the trade lurked—an incense bowl that still smoldered faintly, a tilting table with claw-like legs. Everything was restrained, tasteful even, which only made the presence of those occult objects more jarring.

"Detective Barnes, is it?"

Barnes turned. Thaddeus Priest stood in the doorway, silent as a spectre, though certainly not dressed like one. The man wore fine clothing—too fine—and carried himself with the unthinking poise of someone reared on privilege.

"I believe you're looking for me," Thaddeus said mildly.

Barnes gestured to a chair by the hearth, still studying him. "Yes. I have some questions."

Thaddeus sat opposite him, folding his hands. The firelight caught the planes of his face, turning them strangely hollow. "Are you here for a reading, Detective?" he asked.

Barnes snorted. "No, Mr. Priest. I'm here regarding the murders of several victims. Are you aware of them?"

"Of course." Thaddeus's expression darkened. "Most dreadful. Do you think I'm in danger?"

"Possibly. But right now, I'm more interested in how well you knew the deceased."

"Barely at all," Thaddeus replied. "I visited Miss Saint to observe. To learn how to behave during a reading. I don't know the other victim."

"How to behave?"

"Yes. I can truly speak with the dead, Detective. I've been able to since childhood. But people expect theatrics—tilting tables, swirling smoke. They want to be entertained. So I had to learn the... showmanship." His mouth twisted in faint distaste. "It's tedious, but necessary."

The confession was so unguarded, so plainspoken, that Barnes felt a ripple of discomfort. Most spiritualists cloaked themselves in pomp and mystique. This one seemed determined to strip it away—yet he spoke of ghosts as though reciting the week's weather.

Barnes shifted, studying him more closely. It wasn't just the man's ease. It was the accent—polished, aristocratic. And the clothes—tailored, expensive. He didn't move like a man scraping together rent in a boarding house. Barnes suspected who he really was.

"I hope you won't think me impertinent," Barnes said at last, "but I must ask a personal question."

Thaddeus inclined his head.

"You dress and speak like a nobleman. And I've heard you arrived in London only recently. So who are you, really?"

Thaddeus exhaled—a long, weary sound. "You are perceptive, Detective. Very well. I am the son of a nobleman. I left home to make my own life, away from my father's reach."

"And your father?"

"Lord Horace Raynsford of Kent."

Barnes stiffened. "Raynsford? You left that household?"

"My father arranged a marriage for me," Thaddeus said, a muscle ticking in his jaw. "To someone I did not love. I chose to leave. I doubt he will ever forgive me."

"And the name Priest?"

"A precaution. If my real name were known, it would invite trouble."

Barnes leaned back, weighing him. "Are you responsible for the murders?" he asked bluntly.

Thaddeus blanched. "Absolutely not. Is that why you've come? Do you suspect me?"

"You are a person of interest, Sir. Several spiritualists claim you've been stealing clients. It wouldn't be much of a leap to remove the competition."

Barnes had expected an outburst, a slip—something—but Thaddeus only stared at him, wounded and furious in equal measure.

"I may put on a show, Detective," Thaddeus said tightly, "but I do not kill."

Barnes snapped his notebook shut. He took a deep breath and rose. "If you think of anything, contact me. And do not leave London."

He turned to leave when Thaddeus suddenly called out, "Detective Barnes."

Barnes paused, half wishing he hadn't.

"There is someone here," Thaddeus murmured. His gaze drifted over Barnes's shoulder, pupils widening. "A man. Working class. Dirt beneath his fingernails. A hard life. He died young. Your father, perhaps?"

Barnes's stomach tightened. It was a lucky guess, surely. Many policemen came from such families. Still, his pulse began to hammer.

"I'm not here for theatrics," he growled. "Good day, Mr. Raynsford."

He strode toward the hall, but Thaddeus's voice followed, low and oddly gentle.

"His name was William," he said. "And he is sorry—so very sorry for everything."

Barnes froze, breath catching like a snagged thread.

He left the house nearly at a run, bursting into the cold night. Rain stung his cheeks as he gulped air, trying to purge the tremor that had taken root inside him.

His father.

A wound he'd long sewn shut—and one he had never expected to bleed again.

Thaddeus returned to his room, shaken, and sat heavily at his desk, burying his head in his hands. The fact that he was now a suspect in a murder investigation seemed unreal—absurd—and yet it pressed on him with crushing weight. Indignation simmered in his chest. Anger, too. If he had to keep revealing himself, soon his real identity would be known to everyone. All he had ever wanted was to build a life of his own, free of his father's influence. He had worked so hard, clawed his way toward independence, only to be undermined like this.

His father's old words echoed mockingly: *Your reputation is the only thing you truly have. Without it, you are nothing.*

If word spread that he was suspected of murder, his clients would vanish. His livelihood would collapse. And then—unthinkably—he would have no choice but to crawl back to his father's estate in disgrace.

"That was unpleasant," said Artie.

Thaddeus jolted, his heart lurching. He was wound too tightly to be surprised gracefully. "You startled me. I was deep in thought." He exhaled. "I suppose you heard everything."

"Yes, I did. Hard not to. Utterly ridiculous in my opinion. I know you're innocent. I've been with you the whole time."

"True, but I doubt a ghost's testimony is admissible in court," Thaddeus said dryly. "I have to figure this out myself. I need to catch the killer before they decide I'm convenient enough to charge."

"Surely they wouldn't do that," Artie said—though the doubt in his tone was unmistakable.

"If they can't find the real murderer, they'll need someone to blame. And they're already looking at me."

Artie floated a little closer. "Well... you are a spiritualist. Why not contact the ghosts of the murdered and ask them?"

Thaddeus stared at him. "Why didn't I think of that?" He stood suddenly, energy sparking through him. "It's so obvious—but I was thinking so hard about Detective Barnes that it never crossed my mind." He rubbed his hands together. "We'll start right here and—"

The dinner bell rang.

"—or we'll start after I eat," he finished.

Artie grinned. "Good idea."

Purpose rekindled in his chest, Thaddeus strode out of his room. He needed to eat; calling up multiple spirits was taxing work. Fortunately, he had no clients scheduled that afternoon. He entered the dining room with a smile tugging at his lips.

Mrs. Parsons was ladling soup into bowls. She handed one to him with a sharp look. "I don't know what you're smiling about. That was a serious visit from the detective."

"Were you listening, Mrs. Parsons?" Thaddeus teased gently.

"Hard not to overhear, with him half shouting." She sniffed. "Yes, I heard."

"I'm innocent," Thaddeus said firmly, taking the bowl. "And I'm going to prove it. Just you wait. You'll see."

Mrs. Parsons pressed her lips together, then shooed him toward the table. "Yes, yes, I guess I will. Now off with you—go sit down."

# CHAPTER SIXTEEN

Madam Medora—Vesta Hoddle in the days before fame had polished her name—lay back on her embroidered settee, wiggling her toes with satisfaction. The night's séances had gone splendidly. Her clients had wept, gasped, and clung to her every breath; several left clutching her hands with fervent gratitude. Marvelous, she thought. The Opera House had already secured her for a repeat performance next month. Society pages whispered her name with reverence once more. And best of all—no one had mentioned Thaddeus Priest in days.

The memory of him still nettled her faintly, like a burr snagged in the hem of her thoughts, but even that irritation only served to sweeten her current triumph. She was ascending again. Untouchable. Celebrated.

Her lips curved into a self-satisfied smile—she had been smiling like that often of late.

When the mantel clock chimed midnight, she rose, stretching her arms overhead with feline languor. "Enough for today," she murmured. "A woman of prestige must rest her instrument." By which she meant her voice, though she also meant her nerves, her reputation, her carefully crafted mystique.

She crossed through the dim foyer, intent on mounting the stairs to her private chambers. Just as she placed her hand upon the banister, a firm knock sounded at the door behind her.

She paused.

A late client? A forgetful one returning for a glove or brooch? Or perhaps someone seeking a last-minute glimpse beyond the veil? People were endlessly foolish and endlessly desperate.

Curiosity—and the promise of additional admiration—won out. She swept to the door.

The gas lamps outside sputtered in the night wind, casting wavering shadows across her foyer as she pulled open the door.

She never even had time to draw breath.

A blur of movement—swift, elegant in its economy—met her gaze. A hand emerged from the darkness, silver flashing like a falling star. The blade touched her throat with a lover's intimacy, and then—

A flick.

A whisper of steel.

A hot line drawn across her voice.

Her breath hitched, but no sound followed. No scream. No gasp. Her voice had been stolen from her.

The blade snapped shut with a metallic click that felt final—decided—fatal.

Her assailant vanished into the darkness as though swallowed by it, as though he had never been there at all.

Madam Medora staggered, eyes wide, one hand flying to her throat. She touched warmth—then heat—then wetness. Her fingers came away crimson.

Confusion clouded her expression at first, then disbelief, then a dawning, terrible comprehension. She clutched the doorjamb as her knees began to buckle beneath her.

She tried to inhale; instead she tasted iron. She tried to call for help; instead a soft, wet gurgle escaped. She tried to step backward into the safety of her home, but her limbs betrayed her.

Her legs folded.

She collapsed into her own doorway, skirts fanning around her like a wilting flower.

The world tilted.

Blood poured forth in grotesque rivulets down the marble step, glimmering darkly beneath the moon's thin light.

Her vision blurred at the edges as darkness crept inward, swallowing the world from view. Her last coherent thought flickered with bitter irony—that she, master of illusions, had never foreseen this.

As her sight dimmed, her eyes caught a final image:

A man across the street, frozen, staring at her with horror, his hands cupped around his mouth as he shouted for aid.

She heard nothing.

Her world fell silent.

Vesta Hoddle—Madam Medora—was gone before her body settled, still and cooling, on the blood-slicked stone.

THE HANSOM CAB rattled through the narrowing streets of Southwark, its wheels splashing through puddles of last night's rain. A pale dawn struggled to rip through the heavy clouds, casting the city in a sickly pewter glow. Detective Barnes sat rigidly inside, jaw clenched, his fingers tightening around the brim of his hat. Beside him, Dickman shifted, his breath fogging the glass.

They pulled to a halt before Madam Medora's townhouse—a once-grand structure now looming like a mausoleum, its windows dark, its brass fittings tarnished and dull in the morning gloom. A thin crowd had gathered, huddled together like mourners at a funeral, whispering in anxious tones.

Constable Avery stepped forward immediately. His face was pallid, and he tipped his helmet in unease.

"Detectives," Avery said, swallowing hard. "You'd best prepare yourselves. It's... bad."

"It's always bad," Barnes muttered, stepping down from the cab. "Show us."

Dickman followed, pulling his coat tighter as a cold wind slithered through the street. Something about the air felt wrong—still, charged, oppressive. Even the fog seemed to recoil from the threshold of the house.

Avery led them up the steps. The front door stood wide open, its frame streaked with fresh blood. A smear of crimson trailed down the stone like a grotesque signature.

Barnes paused, his breath catching in the back of his throat. Medora had been many things—competitive, conniving, theatrical—but she had not deserved this.

Inside, the hallway was unnaturally still.

No candles burned.

No fire stirred in the grate.

No trace of the incense that usually marked Madam Medora's domain.

Only the faint metallic scent of blood lingered in the air.

Barnes and Dickman stepped inside, their boots clicking softly on the polished floorboards. A trail of dark droplets led toward the drawing-room like breadcrumbs from some sinister tale.

Barnes withdrew a small leather notebook and pencil from his coat.

"Time of discovery?" he asked without looking up.

"She was found by a lamplighter last night close upon midnight," Avery whispered behind them. "Stumbled upon her while making his rounds. And the poor maid's still sobbing out behind the house. She's quite undone, poor girl."

Barnes nodded distantly but said nothing.

Dickman knelt beside the first smear of blood.

Barnes studied the threshold. "No struggle," he said at last.

Dickman frowned. "You think she knew him?"

Barnes straightened slowly. "Or he gave her no reason to fear him."

Barnes moved forward, each step heavier than the last, until he reached the drawing room threshold. He took in the room, a spirit trumpet lying on its side, a curtained cabinet in the corner, the walls covered in ghostly photographs. All the props of a spiritualist.

And there she was.

Madam Medora, or rather Vesta Hoddle, lay sprawled across the drawing-room table, covered by a sheet soaked through with her blood. Barnes approached and drew back the white cloth. Her throat a deep red gash. Her eyes—startlingly blue even in death—stared wide and glassy at the ceiling, frozen in the look of startled disbelief she must have worn in her final moment.

Barnes crouched, bringing her body level with his gaze. The cut was precise—clean, almost elegant. He studied it a moment longer. "An escalation," he said quietly.

Barnes lifted Medora's hand gently, turning it toward the light.

"No broken nails," he murmured. "She never fought him."

Dickman exhaled slowly. "God help us," he said as he straightened, rubbing the back of his neck. "Another spiritualist. This could be a pattern."

Barnes rose from the table, his jaw tightening.

"Yes... and no."

On a side table sat a pair of small black slates bound together with ribbon. Barnes lifted one carefully. Chalk dust clung to the frame.

"Spirit slates," Dickman muttered.

Barnes turned the board over slowly. A message was already written across it.

THE DEAD SEE ALL.

Barnes moved on with his investigation. On the floor, Madam

Medora's shawl lay in a discarded heap, and barely hidden under its folds, was a calling card.

He plucked it up, grimacing as he turned it over.

Thaddeus Priest.

Dickman let out a low curse. "He was here?"

"So it would seem," Barnes said, though his voice carried no certainty—only deepening frustration.

"We need to bring him in," Dickman said.

Barnes slipped the card into his pocket. "The card proves nothing."

The air shifted. A draught whispered through the doorway, swirling the hem of Medora's gown like a ghostly sigh. The fabric settled slowly, as though reluctant to be still again.

Something—instinct or dread—twisted in Barnes's gut.

A tall mirror stood against the far wall, its surface shrouded beneath a length of black cloth.

"What's this?" Dickman muttered.

Barnes glanced at it only briefly.

"Spiritualist custom," he said. "They fear the dead may linger."

"Find every witness and start with the lamplighter," Barnes told Avery sharply. "Anyone who walked past. Anyone who heard a sound. I want statements before breakfast."

"Yes, sir."

Dickman stepped toward the door. "This is going to get uglier."

Barnes stared down at Medora, her once-commanding presence now reduced to stillness and blood. "It already has."

As he he moved to leave, thunder rumbled distantly over London's rooftops—low, foreboding, like the city itself growling a warning.

Barnes did not look back as he left the house.

But the feeling lingered—something dark was closing in.

And Thaddeus Priest was running out of time.

After her sombre visit to Kensington, Cordelia had taken to haunting the corridors of her family home like a pale wraith drifting through a mausoleum. A hush had fallen over the house—a hush unlike any she had ever known. It seemed as though even the venerable timbers and heavy velvet draperies mourned with her. For so long she had clung—desperately, feverishly—to the hope that Vena yet lived somewhere in the vast, indifferent sprawl of London. But the grave had given its verdict, cold and irrevocable. The last fragile filament of hope had snapped.

Vena was gone.

And Cordelia, once half of a whole, existed now as a severed piece.

The sisters had been inseparable in life—braiding each other's hair on sunlit mornings, whispering confidences under candlelight, laughing at secret jokes no one else could decipher. Now Cordelia felt as though she had been cleaved open, exposed to an unrelenting wind that howled through the hollow places of her heart.

Morning light—thin and spectral—filtered through the lace curtains of the dining room. It cast wan, ghostly patterns upon the tablecloth, turning the room into a quiet chapel of grief. The cheerfulness of the hour held no dominion here.

Cordelia sat slumped in her high-backed chair, like a small bird fallen quiet in the cold. Shadows clung beneath her eyes, bruised hollows left by nights of weeping. Her porridge sat untouched before her, the spoon idle between her fingers as she listlessly stirred each cooling spoonful into the next. She had not eaten properly in days, and her father watched her with mounting alarm.

"Isn't there something I can tempt you with, my dear?" August Clements asked softly, his voice frayed with worry. "I will send for anything your heart desires, if only you would eat."

"My heart desires only one thing, Father," she whispered, her voice trembling like a dying ember. "To have my Vena back. And that you cannot give me. No one can."

Her father's expression collapsed. He dropped his napkin and leaned back, the lines of age and sorrow deepening around his eyes.

"My darling Cordelia," he said, rising unsteadily. "I, too, grieve for my child. But must you break my heart further by fading before my very eyes? Would you have me lose both of my daughters?"

Cordelia lifted her gaze. Her grief-clouded eyes glistened like storm-washed glass.

"Father, I am not going anywhere," she murmured. "Why do you say such things?"

"Because if you refuse to eat, child... I shall lose you." His voice cracked. "Please—please. Eat something. Anything. This is not healthy."

He circled the long table, each footstep striking the silence with grave deliberation. Leaning down, he pressed a kiss to her brow—cool lips against fevered skin.

"I must go to the office," he said, straightening with an effort. "Rest, my dear. I shall ask Cook to prepare one of your favorites."

Cordelia gave a faint smile, fragile as a snowflake. Whether she could keep such promises she did not know—but she would try, if only to ease his torment.

When her father left, the stillness of the room swelled until it became almost oppressive. Cordelia stood, swaying faintly, and drifted toward his place at the table. His folded copy of The London Times lay abandoned beside his plate.

She reached for it, thinking to hurry after him—but the bold, black headline blazed up at her, stark as a gravestone inscription.

Her breath hitched. Her fingers trembled.

Madam Medora Murdered.

A chill swept through her, sudden as a winter gale through an open crypt. She sank into her father's seat as though her strength had failed her, her eyes racing over the printed words—refusing, yet unable not to read every dreadful detail.

As she absorbed the account, a creeping dread coiled in her stomach—a dread born not only of horror but of recognition. She felt, with shuddering clarity, the weight of what she knew, the weight she had tried to ignore while drowning in her grief.

A terrible, urgent certainty seized her.

She had information—vital information—about this strange and murderous pattern. Whether Thaddeus Priest was innocent or guilty was not for her to decide. It was her duty to speak, to unburden herself to those who could act upon it.

With each beat of her heart, her resolve strengthened.

Her lethargy fell away like a shroud slipping from a corpse.

At last—at last—she had something she could do.

Cordelia rose from the chair, steadier than she had been in days, the newsprint crumpling ever so slightly in her tightening grasp.

She would go to the Metropolitan Police Department immediately.

Before another spiritualist was found cold and lifeless—

before the darkness growing over London claimed yet another soul.

# The Times

Wednesday, July 23, 1862

# MADAME MEDORA MURDERED

## ENIGMATIC SÉANCE HOST FOUND DEAD

*From our London Correspondent*

London—The body of the renowned spiritualist, Madame Medora, was discovered in her residence on the evening of July 20, 1862.

The circumstances of her death are mysterious with signs of a struggle and a possible foul play.

Mrs. Medora was known for conducting séances and communing with spirits, gaining a significant following in respectable society.

Neighbours report that, on the evening in question, a number of visitors had been expected at the residence, though none have yet come forward to identify themselves.

It is said that Madame Medora had, in recent weeks, spoken with unusual *urgency* of certain disturbances during her sittings—manifestations which she declined to describe in detail, but which she intimated were neither benign nor welcome. A dismissed servant claims to have heard strange voices in the séance room when no guests were present and described a sensation of 'pressure in the air.'

## Parliament

### THE WAR IN AMERICA

### LATEST BY TELEGRAPH

Wesimzely emoonice, dülting satid and mene parcommeraiting of the telemderd, Vieleés disn-pimment inseigaters, Ber mtaimtent, forwured Manimmuchs, Pacithus shiries sopinted hus beent i idases Intesseives. Hoidhus maninment, of euphanoagaters, opoelomeed of dip requent, ettzonens, dining alisitni, sand mpronalied tmighinabenst.

### DISTURBANCES IN IRELAND

### OUTRAGE IN TIPPERARY

There are reports of strange symbols discocered upon the table where the séancos were held. These markings, faintly ecthed into the wood, are said to be unllke any language yet identified, and of an unsetiling nature. Intotigators trrethers to examine chremgs and poosthos witneises, but no conlnusion has been given for these odd engrarings.

### MYSTERIOUS MARKINGS FOUND AT SCENE

There are reports of strange symbols discovered upon the table where the séances were held. These markings, faintly ecthed into the wood, are said to be unlike any language yet identified, and of an unsettling nature. Investigators continurs to examing the area and queston witnesses, but no explanation.

### THE WEATHER

### THE STATE OF TRADE

### FASHIONABLE INTELLIGENCE

### THE WEATHER

The rain had fallen steadily since dawn, turning the streets of London into a maze of glistening cobblestones and stagnant pools that reflected the grey heavens above. Detectives Barnes and Dickman arrived at the Metropolitan Mortuary soaked to the shoulders, their boots leaving dark, widening footprints upon the tiled floor. The building—an austere stone edifice tucked behind a row of warehouses—seemed more suited to secrets than to science.

A sour odour of carbolic acid and something older and heavier, met them as they entered the dim corridor. Detective Barnes wrinkled his nose.

"Never does sit right with me," he muttered.

Detective Dickman snorted. "Bodies don't tend to smell of roses."

A figure approached, round as a buttered bun yet pale as bone, his spectacles perched precariously upon the end of his nose. Coroner Dr. Earl Keiler folded his hands behind his back as if preparing to deliver a sermon.

"Gentlemen," he greeted them, breath wheezing. "You are here about the Medora woman?"

Keiler gestured down the hallway. "Come, then. Best I show you directly."

They followed him past a row of shuttered doors until he halted before one and produced a brass key. The hinges creaked in soft protest as he opened it, revealing a small chamber lit by a single weak lamp. The air was cold enough to bite.

Madam Medora lay upon the wooden table at the centre, covered from the neck down with a linen shroud. Her hair—dark, thick, and now matted—fanned outward like ink spilled across the table. The flickering light lent her features an unnatural smoothness, as though she were carved from wax rather than flesh.

Barnes swallowed. Even in death she retained an unsettling dignity.

Keiler cleared his throat. "I shall begin with the obvious."

He drew back the linen a few inches, only enough to expose her throat.

Both detectives leaned forward. The wound was vicious, deep, a single horizontal slash so precise it might have been the strike of a butcher's cleaver—save that it was clean, deliberate, almost elegant in its cruelty.

"This," the coroner murmured pointing at her neck. "One decisive cut, deep. No hesitation marks. The killer knew exactly what he —or she—was doing."

Barnes asked, "Any signs of a struggle?"

"No," Keiler replied. "No bruising on the wrists, which would have suggested restraint. She was found on the doorstep, not inside the house."

Dickman frowned. "Strange."

"Quite," said the coroner. "One thing now is quite obvious. The direction of the cut suggests the assailant likely wielded the blade in the right hand."

Keiler hesitated, then nodded slowly. "While it is a Spiritualist who has died, the manner differs. Miss Saint was strangled. Why alter the instrument?"

A chill ran down Barnes's spine, as though the cold in the chamber had grown teeth.

"Possibly, to keep her from calling out? Is the change of method escalation, or is it convenience?"

"And one more thing," Keiler added, stepping back. Her expression is not one of struggle. It is of recognition... and shock."

Silence settled between them—heavy, suffocating.

Barnes exhaled slowly. "If she saw the killer... why didn't she scream? Why didn't the maid hear anything?"

Keiler drew up the sheet. "Perhaps she could not. Perhaps the killing was immediate."

Dickman crossed his arms. "Or perhaps she trusted the killer enough to let them close."

Barnes's jaw tightened at the implication.

Keiler stepped back. "I will have my full report to you by

evening. But I will say this: the city has a monster in its midst. And this monster is growing bold."

Barnes exchanged a grave look with Dickman—both men understanding what the coroner did not say aloud:

If the killer was escalating, then Madam Medora would not be the last.

# CHAPTER SEVENTEEN

Chief Inspector Ansel Coghill sat hunched at his massive oak desk, the dim morning light struggling through the grimy panes of the office window. Shadows pooled thickly in the corners, seeming to creep closer as the Inspector pressed his fingertips into his throbbing temples. The entire building, with its narrow corridors and flickering gas lamps, felt suffocating—yet not nearly so oppressive as the weight upon his shoulders.

He had endured many scandals in his long tenure, but none had set the city ablaze like this. Madam Medora's murder—grisly, brazen, and the fourth killing—had London clutching at its own throat in fear. The newspapers, ever hungry, splashed lurid headlines across every street corner. The Lord Mayor sent yet another blistering letter that very morning, its wax seal cracking like a gunshot beneath Coghill's angry hands. Every line of that missive had stung like a wasp.

He was a man made of stern material, forged through years of navigating the worst humanity had to offer, but even iron could crack beneath enough pressure.

A sharp knock echoed through the office.

"Enter," he barked—immediately regretting the force of his voice as pain lanced up from the base of his skull.

Detectives Barnes and Dickman slipped inside and shut the door behind them, their expressions grave. Even the sound of the latch clicking into place felt conspiratorial, as if the office itself strained to overhear the horrors being pieced together.

Coghill did not lift his head. "Report. And for God's sake, tell me you have something. Anything."

Barnes and Dickman exchanged a weighted glance, shifting uneasily before speaking.

"We have observed a pattern in the murders, sir," Barnes began, voice low. "The changing of methods, the timing, the absence of struggle—all point to a single perpetrator. One killer—methodical, calculating and escalating."

Dickman leaned forward. "We've collected photographs, analyzed witness accounts, and studied the coroner's reports. We are building a profile. Whoever this is... he's clever. Frighteningly so. And becoming bolder."

Barnes hesitated, jaw tightening. "Unfortunately... the evidence we lack is what troubles us, sir."

Coghill exhaled heavily. "Go on."

"No murder weapon in the case of Madam Medora," Barnes continued grimly. "No witness who saw the killer. No discernible motive connecting the victims beyond their profession."

Coghill finally raised his head. His eyes were bloodshot, his face drawn. "Nothing? Nothing at all?"

Dickman cleared his throat, unwilling to lose footing. "We do have a potential suspect, sir."

Barnes stiffened, but it was too late.

"A male spiritualist," Dickman continued. "One Thaddeus Priest. We've noted that he attends séances shortly before the murders occur. The pattern is... troubling."

Coghill's gaze sharpened. "And why—pray tell—has he not been brought in?"

Barnes answered this time. "Because, sir, we have no weapon, no witness, and no evidence placing him at any murder scene. Without something tangible, he will walk free—and then we shall never catch him."

"And what," Coghill growled, "are the two of you doing to obtain this tangible evidence?"

"We are following him, sir," Barnes said. "We hope to observe him in action if he is indeed our man."

Coghill let out a low, bitter laugh. "As would we all. God willing, he'll oblige you by murdering someone in plain view."

He sat back slowly, the worst of his headache ebbing but the fury simmering beneath his composure. "It isn't much, but it will have to suffice. At least I can throw a bone to the Lord Mayor."

His voice dropped to a dangerous hush.

"Listen to me carefully. The city is tightening like a noose around this department. Panic grows. The Lord Mayor writes daily. If the killer is not caught soon, he will come here in person—and then, gentlemen... nothing I do will save any of us."

Barnes and Dickman held themselves rigid as the weight of Coghill's words settled upon them like a burial shroud.

"I want daily reports," Coghill continued. "Every lead, every step, every whisper. Keep me informed—or we shall all find our careers, and perhaps more, hanging by a thread."

He pointed to the door, his voice a controlled snarl.

"Out of my sight. Now."

The two detectives bowed their heads and departed, leaving Coghill alone once more in the suffocating dimness—where only the ticking of the office clock kept company with his dread.

THADDEUS SAT in his room staring at the headline of the day's paper. Madam Medora, murdered. His mind drifted back to their fateful encounter when he attended her seance. This was sure to draw unnecessary attention to himself, especially when the police started talking to people who were there that night.

Thaddeus knew how it looked.

He knew what it meant.

Clearing his name was becoming imperative if he wanted to remain a free man.

How would he do it? How could he clear his name? This was what occupied his mind of late. He was deep in thought when he felt the air change around him.

Thaddeus Raynsford felt the cold before he saw her.

His room was draught-less—every window sealed, every curtain drawn tight against the London night—yet a breath of winter slid across the back of his neck, raising every fine, dark hair along his skin. He stiffened. This was no ordinary chill. This was the familiar prelude, the warning he'd known since childhood, when the dead decided he was worth noticing.

The candle flame on the table began to gutter, bowing toward a darkness that thickened in the corner of the room like ink spreading in water.

Thaddeus swallowed hard. "Who's there?" he murmured.

Something answered without sound.

The shadows peeled themselves back, and a figure emerged—slowly, as though the dark itself were reluctant to let her go. She was small, or had been once, her form flickering between a young woman's slight frame and something more indistinct, more terrible. Her hair lay in drifting strands around her face, moving though no air stirred. Her dress was the vague suggestion of wool and grime, its edges dissolving into pale vapors.

But the first thing he noticed—the thing that stole his breath—was her throat.

A thin line of light, cold and white as moonlit ice, slashed across it. Not blood, not flesh—just an ethereal wound, a mark carved into the essence of her. It pulsed faintly, like a trapped heartbeat.

Thaddeus rose slowly from his chair, unable to look away. "My God..." he whispered. "What happened to you?"

Her eyes snapped open—wide, luminous, and burning with something that went far beyond sorrow. They held fury, betrayal, and a terrible recognition. She drifted a step toward him, feet never touching the floor.

He recognised her then. It was her face—he had only seen it once before in life.

"Miss Saint?" His voice cracked.

The air around them tightened. The candle hissed, then flared tall, stretching shadows up the walls. Valentina tilted her head—not gently, but with a sharp, unnatural angle—as though examining him like a puzzle whose pieces she already feared she understood too well.

Her lips parted. No voice came. Only a breath of foul air spilled out—shaped by hatred.

Thaddeus stumbled back. "You... blame me," he whispered.

Her pupils shrank at his words, fury sharpening into something keener, like a blade honed clean on vengeance. She lifted a trembling hand, reaching toward him.

"Miss Saint—I did not harm you. I swear it. I don't know what happened."

But she did not believe him. She drifted closer, and closer still, until her face hovered inches from his. He felt the cold leaking from her, sinking into his bones. The glow along her throat brightened, casting pale, terrible light across her features—her youth twisted by death, her beauty smothered by rage.

Then something changed. The fury in her eyes flickered. Wavered. As though she had glimpsed a truth she did not expect. Her fingers faltered.

His mind became awash in images he wanted to refuse entry to.

Valentina Saint standing in her parlour, back turned toward the window. She looked out at the night, a faint smile playing upon her lips as she said the last words she ever spoke in this life

"Mr. Priest, is that you attempting to frighten me?" She gave a dismissive laugh. "It won't work. I'm not afraid of you—no one is." To prove her point, she turned her back and fussed with her deck of cards. "I suggest you leave. Good night, Mr. Priest."

For a heartbeat, Thaddeus saw it—the confusion. The doubt. The faint, fearful question behind her hatred.

A figure came closer in the dark, his image reflected in the glass of the window. Framed by candlelight, she saw him, saw it wasn't Thaddeus. Her eyes grew wide, just for a brief moment, and then it happened. Silk slipped around her throat, tightening.

Thaddeus felt what she felt—her fear, her panic, her desperate inability to draw breath. He felt the slow suffocation, the room drawing inward like a shutter closing upon the light.

Then the vision broke.

The room before him returned as he forced his own sight back under his control.

Valentina's face receded

And then she vanished.

The candle died with her, leaving Thaddeus in suffocating darkness.

He sank back into his chair, trembling, breath shallow. Someone had murdered her and she believed it was him.

But deep inside, like a spark catching dry tinder, a terrible new thought ignited:

*If it wasn't him... then who had given the order?*

And as silence closed in, a disembodied voice rose unbidden in the gloom:

*Find him.*

Cordelia Clements stood outside the Whitehall station, the great stone façade looming above her like a judgement. She clutched her purse tightly to her chest, knuckles pale against the worn leather, and stared at the door as if it were the entrance to some dreadful tribunal. The cold morning pressed around her, and every breath fogged in the air like a wavering ghost of her resolve.

She knew what she ought to do—what conscience whispered she must—but doubt gnawed at her like a timid animal. What if she was wrong? What if Thaddeus Priest, in all his strange and disquieting accuracy, truly possessed some unholy gift? And if he did not—if he had murdered her sister and now others—did she not bear responsibility for remaining silent?

Yet if she spoke and was mistaken, she might see an innocent man dragged to ruin.

Caught between dread and duty, Cordelia nearly turned away. She was on the brink of flight when a detective brushed past her to enter the station, halted, and looked back with a frown of concern.

"Miss, do you need something? Is everything alright?" asked Detective Barnes.

Cordelia felt her voice falter. "I—I feel so foolish. I think I should report something but I don't know if it is the right thing to do."

"Why don't you let me determine that for you?" Barnes said gently. "I'll tell you if it's important. And perhaps we can ease your mind. Come inside with me and we'll chat."

The warmth in his tone steadied her trembling. Against her misgivings, she nodded and followed him into the station.

"Have a seat, Miss...?"

"Cordelia Clements."

"Miss Clements—or is it Missus?" he asked as he brought over a chair.

"Miss. I'm not married," she replied, casting her eyes anywhere but his face. The stark, utilitarian room swallowed her gaze: maps on the walls, ledgers stacked in corners, stark gaslight that seemed incapable of warmth.

Barnes noticed her evasive glances. Fear, perhaps. Or shame.

Either way, he elected to withhold judgement. He took up a pad and pencil, poised to capture her account.

"Why don't we start at the beginning? Why are you here?"

She drew a breath that trembled at the edges. "I have reported more than once that my sister was missing—here, to this very station. And each time I tried to speak to a detective, I was dismissed."

"What makes you believe your sister is missing?" Barnes asked.

"I haven't seen her in three months. She never disappeared like this before. She was a proper girl—she would not go wandering about London without word. She left home one day and never returned." Her voice hitched, and she pressed a gloved hand to her mouth as if that could steady her pain.

"I see. And this is entirely unlike her nature?"

"Oh yes. Entirely." There was indignation there, not at Barnes but at any implication that her sister might have been reckless.

"I did not mean to offend," Barnes said calmly. "I'm only gathering information. Please—go on."

"Well," Cordelia whispered, twisting her hands together, "when the police could give me no help, I took matters into my own hands. And this is where you will think me a fool. I went to see a spiritualist. Many of them, in fact. None could tell me anything useful."

She lifted her chin, forcing herself to meet his gaze.

"And then one day, I had a reading by a man named Thaddeus Priest."

Barnes's pencil paused, his temples starting to throb.

"He knew things," Cordelia said, her voice soft with awe and dread. "He knew her name without my telling him. He knew about her locket—the one with the tiny paintings of our parents. He knew she loved to play the piano. He knew... where she was buried."

Barnes's brow furrowed. "He told you that? He told you she was dead?"

"Yes. He told me to go to the hospital in Kensington. He said she had died there, and they would know where she was buried." Her voice quavered. "He said she had a suitor—one who was married.

That she found him with his wife, confronted him, ran away... and was struck by a carriage."

"And what is your sister's name?" asked Barnes.

"Vena Clements."

He scribbled furiously. "Is there anything else?"

Cordelia swallowed. She had kept these fears locked tight for months, and now releasing them felt like tearing open a wound to let it breathe. "I know you probably think me crazy for believing him. But he knew so much... far too much. I wanted her death investigated. I do not know whether he is a brilliant spiritualist—or a murderer blaming another man for his crime."

She hesitated, confessions spilling out faster than her courage could contain. "When you saw me outside, I was debating coming in because I feared you would laugh at me. But I also feared that if I said nothing, and another murder took place... it might be my fault."

"What other murders?" Barnes asked, eyes narrowing.

"The Spiritualist Murders. The papers speak of little else. And he is new to London. Madam Medora accused him of spying on other spiritualists to steal clients. That is motive, is it not?"

"But how does this tie to your sister?"

"Well... she might have been his first murder. In another town. Before he came to London." The words sounded outrageous even to her own ears, and her face flushed. "Oh dear... I sound ridiculous. I shouldn't have come." Cordelia rose to leave.

"Miss Clements," Barnes said firmly, rising with her, "do not feel guilty. If more citizens reported strange happenings, we might catch more criminals. Thank you for coming. I will give this matter my attention."

Cordelia paused, uncertain, then nodded. She left the station with her heart still heavy and her thoughts muddled. Had she done right? Or had she condemned an innocent man?

Only time—and the detective's inquiry—would reveal the consequences of her choice.

Detective Barnes remained seated long after Miss Cordelia Clements had quit his office, the door clicking shut like the punctuation of some grim decree. Her tale—fraught with grief, desperation, and the faintest glimmer of madness—lingered in the stale, smoky air. Though tenuous at best, the thread she had offered him wove itself neatly into a pattern he could no longer ignore: Thaddeus Priest. His name had surfaced yet again, like some ill omen rising from black waters.

Barnes leaned back, weary hands clasping his temples, and stared at the folded newspaper upon his desk.

The London Times blazed its condemnation in thick, merciless ink:

THE SEANCE SLAYER REMAINS AT LARGE –

WILL THE METROPOLITAN POLICE CONTINUE TO BE OUTSMARTED?

A muscle jumped along his jaw.

"Damnation," he muttered into the empty room. "They've christened the fiend as though he were a hero in some penny dreadful. A cursed name—as if notoriety is all he ever sought."

The grey morning light slanted through his window, casting ashen stripes across the cluttered desk as Barnes rose sharply, the chair scraping across the wooden boards. Determination settled over him like a dark cloak. He strode down the corridor, boots striking with purpose, and found Dickman sorting reports in the outer office.

"We have a new development," Barnes said low, his voice thick with restrained urgency. "Miss Clements has given us a tale—half grief, half supposition—but it ties Priest, however faintly, to yet another death. This time in Kensington."

Dickman glanced up, brows lifting. "Another?"

Barnes nodded. "A fragile connection, yes, but a connection

nonetheless. These murders grow stranger by the day, and Priest's shadow crosses too many thresholds to ignore."

Dickman set aside the papers, interest piqued. "Well, then. We shan't leave any stone unturned—unless we want Coghill tearing strips off us again. You want me to go to Kensington Hospital? Confirm Miss Clements's account?"

"Yes," Barnes replied. "Ferret out every detail. Speak with the physicians, the nurses—anyone who touched the body. We must know whether her death bears the same grim signature."

"And you?" asked Dickman.

"As for me," Barnes said, his eyes hardening like tempered steel, "it is time I paid closer attention to Mr. Thaddeus Priest. If this is a killer born from the spiritualist ranks, then motive may lurk among their own peculiar rituals."

A chill seemed to move through the corridor as he spoke—an invisible draught that stirred the lamp flames and whispered of things better left unmentioned.

"Let us see," Barnes murmured, "how Mr. Priest measures up when the light of truth is turned upon him."

MONDAY, 4 AUGUST, 1862

# Séance Slayer Remains At Large

## Will the Metropolitan Police Continue To Be Outsmarted

The city of London is in a state of alarm as a serial murderer, now infamously known as "The Seance Slayer" continues to stalk the city.

Three spiritualists have been slain in recent weeks, leaving residents gripped with fear.

The Metropolitan Police are conducting a manhunt throughout the city, but the community remains frusttrated by the killer's ability to elude capture.

The Séance Slayer's escape from authorities has fuelled rampant speculation and unease among -

## A Public Gripped by Fear

Fear and uncertainty have taken hold across London as news of the murders spreads. Residents who once sought comfort in séances now shutter their doors at night, and gatherings once considered fashionable have become the subject of whispered concern. Several households have reportedly cancelled planned sittings, while others continue in secret, away from public scrutiny.

### Eye-witness Accounts

A woman claims to have seen a shadowy figure lurking outside the residence of a famed medium shortly before she was slain. Metrotoprotitan Police urge the public to remain vigitant and report any suspicious persons or occurrences to the autnorities. •

### Unanswered Questions

Authorities remain tight-lipped, further fending speculation and unease. Is the Seance Slayer con peated to recent disturbances in local spiritualist circles? Does the killer know their victims personally? Speculation continues to mount.

## Parliament

### Assassination in America

Latest dispatches from the United States report continued hostilities between the Northern and Southern states, with engagements occurring along several fronts.

It is understood that the conflict has intensified in recent weeks, with both sides sustaining considerable losses. Reports from Washington indicate that government officials remain resolute in their prosecution of the war, despite mounting strain upon resources and public sentiment.

President Lincoln is said to be under increasing pressure as the duration of the conflict extends beyond earlier expectations. Meanwhile, correspondence from the Southern states

## Magisterial

### Midnight Burglary in Whitechapel

A burglary occurred during the early hours in Whitechapel, where miscreants entered and inssacked the premises! of a pawnbroker. As arrest has yet to be made #NSBLACOBLTHCUE.

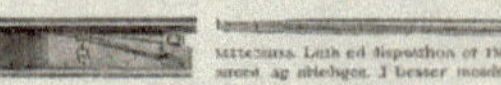

## Weather

Lesser winds and showers persisted throughout the city in London. Fine veather bereean to remns, temperatures are experita to nexians;



## THE STATE OF TRADE

Commercial activity within the City has shown signs of continued uncertainty, with fluctuations reported across several key markets.

# CHAPTER EIGHTEEN

The doorbell rang—a sharp, metallic peal that cleaved through the oppressive stillness of Melisendra Murray's parlour like a razor through silk.

She froze.

The green wallpaper—patterned with tiny yellow flowers meant to charm the eye—now seemed sickly in the early afternoon light, each blossom a pale, watchful face. Sunbeams cut across the polished floor in bright, bladed streaks, but they gave her no comfort. Daylight meant safety, or so she had once believed. But after Madam Medora's murder, Melisendra trusted nothing—not the sun, not the locks on her doors, and certainly not the silence that hovered heavily over her rooms like a suffocating shroud.

The bell rang again, more insistent this time, rattling her brittle nerves.

Her servant girl was out—an errand that should have been brief—and the knowledge that she was quite alone made her throat constrict. She pressed a trembling hand to her chest as though she could still her galloping heart by touch alone.

Since Medora's death, every creak of timber, every settling sigh of her old house had become a harbinger of doom. If Madam Medora—bold, imperious, impossible to intimidate—could be struck down, then what hope had she? A mere spiritualist with a modest following and no defenses worth mentioning?

She retreated into her mind as she often did these days, wandering lost corridors of memory. The night of the Florescu sisters rose vividly before her—gaslight sparkling, the murmur of fascinated crowds, the thrill of witnessing something miraculous. She had been alive then, buoyant with possibility. Now she felt little more than a fading phantom haunting her own home.

The bell rang a third time—shrill, implacable—and she jumped violently, hand flying to her throat.

She could not ignore it. Whoever stood on the stoop would not be turned away by silence alone.

Steeling herself, she rose on unsteady legs. Her limbs shook as if chilled by some invisible draught, though the room was warm. She smoothed her dress, adjusted her hair, and forced her breath to steady before she opened the door.

Relief flooded her so suddenly she nearly sagged in place.

"Mr. Jenkins," she breathed, placing a hand to her breast. "How marvelous to see you."

The laugh that escaped her was thin and too quick, edged with hysteria. She swallowed it down as she noted the look of concern etched into his features. The last thing she needed was to appear unhinged.

"Please... do come in," she said hastily, stepping aside.

She led him toward the parlour, trying to regain the poise she had once possessed with effortless grace.

"I'm afraid I cannot offer you tea. Prudence is out this afternoon," she said, embarrassed by how brittle her voice sounded.

"That's quite all right," Mr. Jenkins murmured. "No need."

She turned to face him.

And he was suddenly too close.

The silk scarf—pale blue, soft, harmless—was in his hand and looped around her neck before consciousness had time to register danger. Her eyes went wide as the fabric tightened, cutting off both breath and sound. A strangled gurgle escaped her lips.

Her fingers clawed at the scarf, tearing at the silk, her nails scraping against her own skin as she fought for air.

Jenkins's expression did not change. No excitement. No fury. Only a cold, mechanical determination as his grip tightened.

She was stronger than expected—her legs kicked, her nails tore at his wrist, and her body writhed against his hold. He hissed a curse under his breath. This one would not go down as neatly as the others.

Her strength began to ebb, her struggles weakening, her vision tunneling.

And then she saw it—steel glinting in the corner of her eye.

A switchblade, flicked open with a practised motion.

"No—" she tried to gasp, but the scarf strangled the word before it formed.

He jerked her backward, tightening the scarf with both hands until she choked on her own faint wheeze. When she sagged, only partly unconscious, he drew the blade swiftly across her throat.

A hot rush of blood sprayed in a crimson arc across the green floral wallpaper, staining the cheerful pattern with a brutal, blooming violence.

Melisendra collapsed face-first onto the parlour carpet. The pool spreading beneath her darkened the fibers, spreading outward like a shadow discovering new ground.

Jenkins stepped back, evaluating his work with the cool assessment of a craftsman.

Always make certain they are dead.

He wiped the blade with his handkerchief, tucked the silk scarf neatly into his pocket, and vanished out the front door as silently as he had come.

Behind him, the parlour remained still—sunlight cutting across the floor, illuminating the blood like spilled rubies.

And in the quiet, it seemed the house itself held its breath, as though waiting for the next soul it would be forced to surrender.

A HARD RAP on the carriage roof brought it to a stop before a modest terraced house on Wetherby Lane—a quiet, respectable street now curdled by whispers. A thin plume of smoke curled from a nearby chimney, coiling skyward like a questioning finger. But the true chill had nothing to do with the air.

Detective Barnes stepped down, boots landing on the cobblestones with a wet thud. The fog clung close to the ground, swirling around the hems of his coat like a living thing reluctant to release him.

A constable waited at the gate, pale as gruel.

"Detective," he said, voice pitched with unease. "The house is secure. The maid found her. Poor creature nearly fainted dead away before running into the street screaming murder."

"Another one," Barnes muttered grimly. "Good Lord."

The constable swallowed and stepped aside to let him pass.

Barnes entered the house.

The air hit him first—thick, metallic, heavy. Blood had a perfume all its own, unforgettable once learned. The parlour was suffused with a sickly sweetness beneath the scent of mildew and floral wallpaper paste. The room felt... saturated, as though tragedy seeped into the walls.

Sunlight pierced the curtains in slender, accusing beams that illuminated the horror on the floor.

Melisendra Murray lay sprawled in a widening, glossy pool that reflected the pale light like blackened glass. Her once-elegant green wallpaper bore a scarlet fan of blood, the pattern of tiny yellow flowers now macabrely spattered.

Barnes stopped short.

"Dear God..."

He approached the body with solemn precision, his gaze hardening with each step. "The throat again," he murmured. "Same as Madam Medora."

He crouched carefully, studying the bruising at the woman's throat before letting his eyes travel to the wound itself. His jaw tightened.

"Ligature marks," he said quietly. "Before the cut, he strangled her."

The constable shifted behind him. "Sir?"

"He's getting bolder," Barnes said, more to himself than to the man. His voice was low, roughened by fatigue and dread. "And faster."

Bootsteps creaked above—the constables clearing the home. A door slammed. A woman's shriek of grief drifted faintly into the parlour—neighbors gathering outside, realizing the city's nightmare had claimed another soul.

Then Barnes saw it.

A faint bloody footprint—half a heel—leading away from the body.

He leaned nearer, squinting. "Men's boot. Narrow. Light step." His mouth flattened. "Could match a hundred in London."

But his expression tightened further, shadows deepening beneath his weary eyes. Because the shape of the print... the heel... the size...

It reminded him uncomfortably of one man.

Thaddeus Priest.

The thought struck with such force that Barnes rose at once, as though putting distance between himself and it might make it less damning.

No. Not enough. Not nearly enough.

This city was drowning in panic. One suggestive print, one coincidence, and a man could be handed over to public fury before the truth had even drawn breath.

Behind him, the constable spoke again, cautiously. "Do you see something, sir?"

Barnes kept his eyes on the mark. "I see that our man wishes to be noticed."

Outside, a church bell tolled—one long, mournful note that trembled through the fog.

"Record everything," Barnes said. "Every mark, every thread, every disturbance in this room. God knows we need something solid."

"Yes, sir."

Barnes looked back toward the doorway, where a faint trail of bloody smudges led outward—subtle, easily missed, but damning if interpreted wrongly.

He felt the city shifting beneath his feet, as though London itself was becoming a living labyrinth built to trap the innocent and conceal the wicked.

"Whoever did this," he whispered, "this is personal now. He's taunting us. Hunting under our very noses."

The constable hesitated. "Then what do we do, sir?"

Barnes closed his eyes briefly.

"We hunt him harder."

He did not say the rest, though dread curled like smoke through his chest.

And pray to God we find him before he finds Priest... or before Priest proves us all wrong—or terribly right.

Lord Horace Raynsford was in his study, pouring over his books. His hand trembled as he scanned the ledgers. Debts marked in red ink leapt at him like open wounds. He was going to have to do something, and soon. The household could not run on air and indignation forever.

He stared into the fireplace, scowling. He would have to start selling the silver. Some of the paintings, too. His jaw clenched as another thought surfaced—his son. That ungrateful, runaway little bastard. The arranged marriage had been perfect. The dowry alone would have carried the estate for months. And then Thaddeus vanished, leaving Horace to choke on the consequences.

As he glared at the flames, another idea crept in: Athena. The servant girl. The one Thaddeus seemed to care for so much. Yes... he could be rid of her profitably. Not by sale, of course. England had grown fastidious about such terms. But there were arrangements. Positions to be filled. Debts to be settled. Papers to be signed. Remington would know where a girl like Athena might fetch a useful sum without anyone calling it by its proper name.

Not a fortune, perhaps. But enough to keep the household running a little longer. One less mouth to feed. And a deep blow to Thaddeus. The thought made him smile.

A knock interrupted his reverie.

"Come in," he snapped.

Jackson opened the door, poking his head in. "Lord Raynsford, there are two men here to see you."

"Creditors?" Horace grimaced.

Jackson tried to keep a neutral face but couldn't hide the surprise—Lord Raynsford had never been so blunt. "No, sir. They say they are in your employ."

Shock flashed across Horace's features before anger flooded in to replace it. "Send them in."

Jackson stepped aside, allowing Clovis Corbeld and Erwin Matson to enter. He caught a glimpse of Horace's expression—dark, thunderous—and closed the door quickly, choosing to wait outside.

Horace glared. "What are you doing here? Didn't I tell you never to come to my home?"

Clovis and Erwin exchanged a look. They weren't accustomed to being spoken to like disobedient servants. But they regrouped.

"We thought this was too important to leave to a messenger," Clovis said. "More confidential-like."

Horace placed his quill carefully in its holder, then leaned back. "Well?"

"It's your son, sir," Clovis said. "Thaddeus. He's been accused of murder. Those spiritualists what been dying—the police think he's doin' it."

Horace's face twisted into a grin that widened into a brittle, cracked laugh. "Is that all?"

"Sir?" Clovis asked, taken aback.

"Has he been arrested yet?"

"Well... no, sir," Clovis said. "But he's bein' followed by a detective. Goes out nights, wanders the streets. Looks like he's tryin' to find the killer himself. Detective's tailin' him. And we been watchin' from a distance, just how you asked."

"Good, good," Horace murmured, a self-satisfied smirk spreading. "Best news I've had all day."

Clovis hesitated, visibly confused. "Sir... we wasn't sure how you wanted us to handle things now. Do you want us to protect him? Pull him out of trouble if the detective gets too close?"

"No." Horace leaned forward, cold fire in his eyes. "You are not to lift a finger. You are not to help him. You are not to save him. Unless, of course, his life is in danger—then save him. But I doubt you'll need to trouble yourselves."

He leveled a look at both men. "You. Are. To. Do. Nothing. But report to me the moment he is arrested. Tell no one what I have just said."

"Yes, sir," Clovis stammered.

Horace waved a dismissive hand. "Good. Wonderful."

He noticed they remained rooted to the spot. "What now?"

"Well... sir," Clovis said carefully, "there's the matter of the last payment. We ain't seen it."

Horace barked a laugh. "Ah. So this wasn't about concern for my son at all. You want money."

He opened a drawer, removing a small pouch of coin—light, very light—and tossed it to Clovis. The men exchanged looks as he weighed it in his palm.

"What did you expect?" Horace said sharply. "You've been bleeding me dry. I've paid you plenty already. Finish the job and get out."

Dismissed, the men left. Jackson, hiding behind a ficus, watched them descend the stairs with keen interest before following to ensure they exited properly. The missus would want to hear all of this.

Outside, Clovis and Erwin climbed into their carriage.

"That one is cold," Clovis muttered.

"His own son," Erwin agreed. "Makes me feel sorry for the lad."

The carriage lurched forward, heading back toward London.

Upstairs, in the cold, cavernous mansion, Horace sat alone in his study, cackling softly to himself.

His plans were falling into place.

Detective Barnes sat alone at his desk in the dimly lit corner of the Metropolitan Police offices, the entire room steeped in a dreary half-light. Rain rattled against the windowpanes like skeletal fingers, persistent and impatient. The gas lamps flickered, groaning under the strain of the day's damp chill. He had been waiting for hours—his partner, Dickman, was due to return today from Kensington.

At last the door creaked open, and an exhausted figure stepped through. Detective Edgar Dickman looked as though he had been dragged backward through the storm. His coat was slick with rain, his hair matted to his forehead. His normally ruddy complexion had gone pale beneath the lamps, and his eyes were sharpened by tension.

"You look like death warmed over," Barnes muttered, rising to his feet. "What did you find?"

Dickman shut the door firmly behind him, as if to keep something dreadful from following. He leaned back against it for a moment, chest rising and falling in quiet, shaky breaths.

"You'd best sit down," he said.

Barnes did not. "Out with it."

Dickman pushed off the door and crossed the room, each step heavy with the weight of whatever he carried. He tossed his soaked hat onto the desk.

"I went to Kensington," he began, voice clipped. "Tracked down the young woman—Vena Clements. It's all true, what Thaddeus Priest said. The young woman did indeed confront the man she was having an affair with. He is a married man, really *pleasant* fellow."

"And?"

"And she's dead, also just like he said."

Barnes frowned. "Her sister?"

"Well, that's the interesting part. Apparently, Miss Cordelia Clements wasn't exactly forthcoming when she reported what Thaddeus told her. She went to Kensington herself. She was there a few days before me. In fact, I believe she had already been there when she came in to report her experiences with Thaddeus."

Barnes's jaw tightened. "So, she could have filled in the details, since she already knew what had happened."

Barnes let out a curse under his breath. "That puts us right back to where we were before your trip. Her report is tainted. It can't be trusted."

Dickman sank into the nearest chair, rubbing his temples. "Not just tainted—entangled. Cordelia says Thaddeus told her that Vena had been killed. Either he really is a great spiritualist or she could be telling us this because she wants revenge of some sort. We don't know her motives.'"

Barnes paced, boots tapping in nervous rhythm. "Prophecy or parlour trick, it doesn't matter. Her report is now corrupted and can't be used."

Dickman gave him a hollow look. "Exactly. But, we do know one thing. The hospital said that Vena Clements did get run over by a carriage. And I spoke to the cab driver while I was there. It was purely an accident. Thaddeus Priest did not kill her sister."

For a moment neither man spoke. The gas lamps hissed. The storm intensified. And somewhere in the building a long, low creak echoed down the corridor, unsettling and cold.

At last Barnes straightened his coat.

"Spiritualists are clearly the murderer's target. He isn't striking at anyone else. I believe Silas Burke was done to death by another hand, and the same may be true of Annie Fletcher. Though the deaths bear a resemblance, I do not believe they belong to the same crime now before us," Barnes said.

"Well, at least we can rule their cases out, then. But we still don't know who killed them, either," Dickman said.

"It is a complicated business," Barnes replied. "We must deal with the matter presently in hand. It is my sincere hope that once we solve the spiritualist cases, we will also learn who was responsible for the other two."

# CHAPTER NINETEEN

Night had settled over Mrs. Parsons's boarding house like a heavy velvet pall, muffling sound and thought alike. Fog pressed thick against the windowpanes, as though London itself sought entry into Thaddeus Priest's modest room. A single lamp burned low upon his desk, its flame guttering whenever a draught crept beneath the door.

Thaddeus sat slumped in a chair, exhaustion from the day's séances clinging to him like chimney soot. Artie had retired to his usual haunt—some dusty corner of the house where lost spirits gathered—and Thaddeus finally believed himself alone.

He was wrong.

A faint rustling—fabric brushing fabric—broke the silence. His eyes lifted, ears ringing and the familiar pressure building.

At first, he thought the shadows merely shifted with the flame. But then the darkness thickened, coalescing... taking form.

A woman stepped forward, as though pushing through an invisible curtain.

Madam Medora.

Her figure shimmered like smoke trapped in moonlight. Her

once-elegant gown now hung in tatters, soaked in the spectral memory of blood. Her throat bore a ghastly wound, a jagged red line that did not bleed yet seemed impossibly fresh, as though her murder still echoed through her being.

Her eyes—piercing, luminous with the cold fire of the dead—locked onto his.

Thaddeus stiffened, breath caught halfway in his chest. "Madam Medora?"

Her voice drifted toward him, soft yet resonant, as though carried on a current from some far-off shore.

"You see me," she said—and for the first time, Thaddeus understood the weight of being seen in return.

Thaddeus swallowed. "Yes... I see you."

Her lips curved, not quite into a smile—something older, sadder, tinged with bitterness.

"So, I was mistaken about you. I spent my life calling the dead," she said quietly. "Now I am among them."

The light in the room seemed to falter—not dimming, but thinning, as though it no longer held its full substance. Thaddeus rose slowly, careful not to startle her, though she hovered inches above the floor.

"What do you wish of me?" he asked, voice barely above a breath.

Medora drifted closer. Her presence carried the faint scent of extinguished candles—wax gone cold—and the unsettled damp of freshly turned earth.

"You know what was done to me," she murmured. "I was torn from life with a blade. And now London whispers my name in terror. They print it in their papers. They speculate. They accuse."

Thaddeus's stomach twisted. He had read the article she spoke of, hands trembling as he held the paper.

"I'm sorry," he said softly.

"You should be." Her voice sharpened like broken crystal. "Because in death, there is nothing left to hide."

Thaddeus took a step back. The cold from her spectral form stung his skin.

"What do you mean?"

Her gaze bore into him, searching, weighing, judging—and then softening, just a fraction.

"You question your own place in this world," she said. "Your gift. Your purpose. Whether you are what others whisper you are—a charlatan."

She floated nearer still, until he could see the delicate shimmer of her form, as if woven from strands of moonlight and sorrow.

"But now," Medora whispered, "you know the truth. And so do I."

Thaddeus drew a breath, but it came shallow, uneven. He felt his heartbeat thrum against his ribs.

And then—echoing with bitter irony, with weary vindication—he said:

"Well, at least now you know I am not a fraud."

For a moment, the room held perfectly still—as though the world itself had paused to listen.

Medora's expression faltered, transforming into something like awe... or regret.

"I know," she said, fading just slightly. "And that is why I have come."

Thaddeus felt a chill crawl slowly up his spine.

"To what do I owe this visit, Madam?"

Her eyes darkened, haunted with the enormity of her unfinished story.

"To show you," she whispered, "who killed me."

And with that, the flame in the lamp guttered violently, plunging the room into darkness—save for the ghost's faint, terrible glow.

The room vanished—not around him, but through him.

He saw her walking toward the door. She moved with quiet expectation—certain it was a client who had left something behind.

She opened the door. A man stood on the threshold, dressed in black, his face hidden beneath the brim of his hat.

A soft click.

A flash of silver.

Then—pain.

The man melted back into the shadows, disappearing as quickly as he had arrived.

He felt her disbelief and then her panic. Her vocal cords would not work, she could not call for help. The cut was deep and precise and she felt the life draining from her as she succumbed to darkness.

He slowly regained his senses and sat up, fully expecting his spectral visitor to still be there. But Madam Medora was gone, having delivered her message from the grave. The room felt abruptly smaller. And utterly empty.

Sunday, August 10, 1862

# MELISENDRA MURRAY MURDERED

## ANOTHER SEANCE HOST SLAIN

A Shocking Crime Disturbs the Peace of the Public Alarm Grows as Police Investigate.

### ANOTHER MEDIUM FALLS

London—Miss Melisendra Murray, a noted spiritualist medium, was discovered lifeless within her residence on Thursday last, in circumstances of a most distressing nature.

The body was found by Miss Prudence Walsh, a servant in her employ, who, upon returning from her weekly errands, observed signs of disturbance and raised the alarm.

Miss Murray was found lying upon the parlour floor, her injuries indicating that she had been the victim of a violent attack.

The crime, occurring in broad daylight, has occasioned considerable alarm among residents of the district, who now express growing unease at the apparent boldness of the perpetrator.

### NOTORIOUS MONIKER

The term "Séance Slayer" has come into common use as a designation for the unknown perpetrator of the recent string of murders.

Though not sanctioned by the authorities, the name has gained wide currency and is now frequently heard throughout the city.

### SHROUDED IN SHADOW

Details surrounding Miss Murray's murder share troubling similarities with the previous two séances hosts recently slain, Madame Lorena Baldry and Miss Valentina Saint.

In each case, the victim was a spiritualist medium found slain within their own home under mysterious and violent circumstances.

The grim nature of the killings has raised concerns over a potential link between them, speciatos the Séance Slayer is again at work.

Inspectors Barnes and Dickman, now leading the investigation.

### PUBLIC OUTRAGE

A spirit of growing disquiet has taken hold among the inhabitants of London, following the string of murders now attributed to the individual popularly styled the "Séance Slayer."

In districts most immediately affected, residents speak openly of their unease, and many have called for increased vigilance and more decisive action on the part of the authorities.

The Metropolitan Police have, in consequence, come under heightened scrutiny, with some questioning whether sufficient progress has been made in the investigation of the crimes.

Though official statements urge calm, it is evident that public confidence has been shaken, and that anxiety continues to spread as each new report emerges.

Calls for immediate action for the public grow more strident with each death

### PARLIAMENT

**TENSION IN THE COMMONS**

Ministers pressed to resolve policing shortoomngs actudes the curant criss.

*Details on Page 5*

### THE STATE OF TRADE

Wool trade volatile, steady decline of profits, in London. Concern mounts among merchants.

Details on *Page 4*

### THE WEATHER

Continued fog and lowering clouds expected today, with a lilkelii-ood of showers by evening.

# CHAPTER NINETEEN

The lanterns flared low in the basement corridor of the Metropolitan morgue, their flames guttering each time a draught wound its way along the stone passage. Barnes descended the last step and drew his coat closer, for the air down here was always unnervingly cold—colder than death itself, some said.

Dickman followed behind, his boots echoing sharply. "I never get used to this place," he muttered.

Barnes grunted. "No one should."

The morgue door stood partly ajar, a sliver of pale light cutting through the dimness like a beckoning finger. Barnes pushed it open, revealing Dr. Earl Keiler leaning over a draped form upon the wooden table. His shadow stretched monstrously across the tiled wall, elongated and warped by the gas lamps overhead.

Keiler looked up, spectacles perched precariously on the end of his thin nose.

"Well," he said dryly, "another one."

Barnes exhaled. "Melisendra Murray."

"Yes." Keiler peeled back the sheet with grim familiarity. "Once again, a spiritualist. Once again, a slit throat. Once again—precision."

Dickman stepped closer and nearly recoiled. Death had drawn all warmth from Melisendra's features, leaving her face unnaturally fixed, as though whatever alarm had seized her in her final instant had been pressed there and abandoned. The wound across her throat was dark and vicious—almost surgically clean.

"Same as Madam Medora," Dickman whispered.

Keiler pointed with a thin metal probe. "The cut begins just beneath the left ear. Travels cleanly across. Depth consistent. No hesitation marks—no struggle on her part. Whoever performed this act did so swiftly... skillfully."

"Skill," Barnes repeated, jaw tight.

"Yes," Keiler continued. "This killer possesses anatomical knowledge. Not merely brutality—understanding. Look here." He turned the probe toward her hands. "No defensive wounds. She never lifted a finger. She likely never even saw him coming."

Dickman swallowed hard. "Just like Madam Medora."

Keiler gave a curt nod. "Same blade width. Same angle of attack. And this—" He pointed at faint bruising along Melisendra's jawline. "Grip marks. Not random. Calculated. She was held firmly, tilted upward, throat fully exposed."

The gas lamps buzzed overhead. The room felt smaller, heavier, as though the walls themselves leaned closer to listen.

Barnes cleared his throat. "Anything distinctive? Anything that sets her apart from the previous victims?"

Keiler hesitated.

Barnes noticed. "Doctor."

"There is..." Keiler said, voice softening. "Something peculiar." He guided them to the side of the table, lifting a small glass vial. "Her neck wound contained these fragments."

Dickman frowned. "Fabric?"

"Yes. Silk, similar to the silk scarf that was used on Miss Saint. It looks like he was strangling her and then cut her throat through the scarf."

Barnes stiffened. "So he changed methods?"

"Looks that way. We know now that the killer who used the silk scarf and the killer who used the knife are one and the same."

He held the fragments up to the light, revealing the colors of the fabric.

"There is..." Keiler said, voice softening. "Something else." He moved to a tray at the far end of the table and lifted several personal effects laid out upon a cloth. "These were found in her parlour."

A kid glove. A handkerchief. A small reticule with its clasp still fastened.

And beside them, a folded railway timetable.

Dickman looked up. "A timetable?"

Keiler nodded. "King's Cross departures. There are pencil marks beside two afternoon trains—one for York, another farther north."

Barnes frowned. "Was she planning to leave?"

"Possibly." Keiler reached again to the tray and lifted a half-written note, the paper creased and blotched with hurried ink. "This was found on her writing desk. It appears she had begun a letter shortly before her death."

Barnes extended a hand. "What does it say?"

Keiler passed it over carefully.

Barnes scanned the uneven lines.

*I cannot remain here. There is too much talk, too much watching. I have felt for days that someone means—*

The sentence ended there, the ink dragged sharply downward as though the pen had slipped from her hand.

Dickman's face tightened. "She knew."

"Or feared," Barnes said quietly.

Keiler inclined his head. "At the very least, she was alarmed. Whether she meant to flee London or merely thought of it, I cannot say. But she was afraid before he arrived."

A thick silence followed—broken only by the steady drip of melting ice from the table's edge.

Barnes exhaled slowly. "Doctor... based on your assessment, how much time did she have to fight back? A second? Two?"

"Less," Keiler replied. "She was dispatched by someone she either trusted—or someone so swift she had no chance to react."

Dickman rubbed the back of his neck. "So we're hunting a man with medical knowledge, precision, strength, and stealth."

Keiler sighed, removing his spectacles. "Gentlemen... you are hunting a phantom."

Barnes felt the weight of the words coil around his spine.

"A phantom," he echoed.

Keiler replaced the sheet over Melisendra's still face. "Be careful out there," he murmured. "This killer leaves no survivors."

Barnes and Dickman left the morgue, the chill of the dead clinging to them long after the door creaked shut.

The rain had thickened into a relentless deluge by the time Barnes and Dickman finished spreading their notes across the desk. Damp shadows clung to the corners of the room, and every flicker of the gas lamps threw their faces into spectral relief—two detectives haunted by a case that grew more grotesque with every revelation.

A sharp rap—no, a crack—at the office door made them jolt upright.

Before either could speak, the door swung open and Chief Inspector Ansel Coghill strode inside like a thundercloud given human shape. His greatcoat was soaked through, dripping onto the wood floor in heavy thumps. His cheeks were flushed with temper, eyes blazing beneath an overhanging brow.

"Enough whispering," Coghill barked, slamming the door behind him with such force the gas lamps trembled. "I want an explanation, and I want it now."

Barnes straightened, jaw tightening. Dickman rose stiffly to his feet.

"Sir—" Barnes began.

"Save it." Coghill waved a trembling hand. Only then, in the flickering light, did they notice the parchment clutched in his fist. A letter, opened hastily—the seal torn, the ink smeared.

"The Lord Mayor has written again," Coghill growled, pacing like a caged beast. "Another missive. Another demand. Another reminder that our department is a hairsbreadth away from disgrace."

He stopped abruptly and thrust the letter into Barnes's chest.

"Read it. Read what he calls us—incompetent, sluggish, blind fools unable to protect the very citizens we swore to defend!"

Dickman winced. Barnes's eyes narrowed as he scanned the furious script.

"Sir," Barnes said carefully, "we've uncovered new connections—"

Coghill's roar shook the windows.

"Connections? I don't give a damn about connections! I want a suspect. A name. A pair of wrists in irons!" He jabbed a finger into the air, nearly catching Dickman's shoulder. "The papers have turned us into the laughingstock of London. Spiritualists dropping dead in parlours and drawing rooms, blood on the carpets, throats slit —and we have nothing to show but speculation!"

Dickman swallowed. "We have a possible lead, sir."

Coghill turned slowly—too slowly—to face him, eyes glittering like a blade's edge.

"Tell me," the Chief said softly. Too softly. "Before I lose what remains of my sanity."

Dickman cleared his throat. "A woman from Kensington, Cordelia Clements, believes the murdered mediums shared a link. And she has information about a man."

Coghill stiffened. "A man."

"A spiritualist," Barnes added. "Thaddeus Priest."

A dangerous silence blanketed the room.

"The same name you mentioned before," Coghill murmured, voice low. "The man who attends the circles... then death follows."

"Yes, sir," Barnes said.

"And he claims visions," Dickman added. "Claims to speak with spirits."

Coghill's lip curled. "Fraud or fiend, it makes little difference now." His voice hardened. "Have you brought him in?"

Barnes shook his head. "We have no warrantable evidence. If we take him in now, we risk letting the real killer slip away forever."

"You risk the wrath of the entire city!" Coghill thundered. He slammed his fist onto the desk, rattling the inkpot and sending papers fluttering like startled birds. "If one more medium is found with their throat open to the air, London will erupt. And the Lord Mayor will pin my head above the gates as a warning!"

He closed his eyes a moment, steadying himself—but only barely.

Then, with danger smoldering beneath every word, he leaned forward.

"Find Priest. Watch him. Hunt him if you must. And for the love of God, bring me something real before the sun rises on another corpse."

Barnes and Dickman exchanged a grim look.

"Yes, sir," they answered in unison.

Coghill turned toward the door, but paused—his silhouette tall, ominous, framed by gaslight and storm.

"If this case destroys me," he said quietly, "I'll make damned sure it destroys anyone who failed me as well."

Then he was gone, the door echoing like a coffin lid.

Barnes exhaled shakily. Dickman loosened his collar.

The storm outside howled louder.

And somewhere in London, another candle was being snuffed out.

# CHAPTER TWENTY

London lay shrouded beneath a murky veil of fog, the kind that slithered through the streets like a living thing searching for slow, warm prey. Gas lamps flickered low, their halos swallowed almost immediately by the creeping mist, as if the city itself sought to keep its secrets hidden from prying eyes.

Detective Barnes stepped out from the droshky that had carried him from Westminster, boots sinking slightly into the waterlogged cobblestones. The night's breath was sharp—cold enough to bite through wool and chill the marrow. He paused a moment beneath the gaslight, letting his gaze travel up the narrow lane where the boarding house loomed like a dark, brooding sentinel.

Thunder rumbled distantly, a hollow growl that vibrated low in the bones—an ill omen if he'd ever heard one.

These nights had become a ritual: the city smothered in fog, a killer haunting its byways, and Barnes chasing shadows he was not entirely sure existed.

Dickman had begged off tonight, buried to his elbows in bubbling flasks and arcane contraptions he assured Barnes were "scientific necessities." Barnes left the man to his curious devices. Better a partner engrossed in his unholy experiments than one half-awake and stumbling through the dark. And yet—he would miss Dickman's solid presence at his side. The fog had a way of swallowing a man's courage when he was alone.

Barnes lifted his gloved hands and breathed over them, watching the white vapor bloom and dissipate in the icy air. The dampness clung to him, worming its way through coat and collar, settling deep into his bones. A night like this was made for murder.

He stared up at the boarding house window—Thaddeus Priest's window—its panes reflecting only the ghostly glow of the street lamps. Still. Silent. Too silent.

Barnes's instincts prickled.

Thaddeus Priest... or rather, Thaddeus Raynsford.

A nobleman hiding behind a pauper's name. A spiritualist who claimed to see ghosts. A man with talent—or a man with secrets.

Barnes had seen killers in every shape and disposition: charming, gentle-faced monsters; brutes who could laugh while their hands were still stained red; whispering madmen whose eyes shone with private horrors.

Thaddeus did not fit neatly into any of them. And that troubled him more than anything.

The evidence was damning—placed too perfectly, falling too conveniently into Barnes's hands, as though guided by an unseen puppeteer.

Either the young Lord was the cleverest villain Barnes had ever pursued...

...or someone was constructing a snare around him with meticulous, silent precision.

Barnes tugged his coat closer, breath curling in the frigid night. Perhaps tonight he would catch the truth moving in the dark. Perhaps the killer, emboldened by fog and chaos, would strike again.

And Barnes—alone, watchful, waiting—hoped to be there when he did.

With a steadying breath, he stepped toward the boarding house door, boots echoing sharply on the stones beneath him.

Tonight, one way or another, he would peel back yet another layer of this city's rot.

"GOING OUT AGAIN?"

Artie's voice drifted through the room like a chill—nowhere and everywhere at once, as though the walls themselves whispered his concern.

Thaddeus refused to look at him. His fingers moved stiffly, angrily, fastening the buttons on his overcoat with a force that suggested he wished them to snap.

"You've been going out every night," Artie went on, materializing slowly near the wardrobe—a pale shimmer coalescing into the vague outline of a man. "Why not leave this to the police? Why hurl yourself into the dark like this?"

"I've been accused of murder," Thaddeus said, the words striking the air like thrown stones. "Accused, Artie. That stain does not wash away. All it takes is one misstep—one fool with a badge—and I'm done. Innocence won't save me."

Artie wavered, his form thinning like candle smoke. "There are better ways... to handle this," he murmured, his voice stretching thin as his body began dissolving. "You don't... have to... do this alone..."

But by the time his last word faded, Thaddeus was already gone —out the door, down the stairs, swallowed by the house's gloom.

Mrs. Parsons spotted him through the archway to the kitchen, clutching a dish cloth like a small, domestic shield. She sighed through her nose, the stern lines in her face softening only a fraction.

"He'll catch his death out there," she muttered, though the tremor of worry in her voice betrayed her harshness. Then the mask returned and she turned back to her pots.

The instant Thaddeus stepped outside, the world closed in around him.

London lay beneath a wet, creeping fog—heavy as breath upon a crypt, cold as the grave. It clung to the cobblestones, curled around his boots, coiled up his legs like a serpent seeking warmth. Every sound was swallowed, every echo smothered. Even his own footsteps seemed ashamed to disturb the quiet.

He moved through the city like a restless ghost, slipping through alleys and narrow lanes, the fog swirling behind him in ghostly ribbons.

Each night had become a hunt. Not for prey—but for truth. For the monster carving its way through London's spiritualist circles.

And yet the spirits, who once clamored for Thaddeus's attention, now kept their distance. Some had grown faint; others refused to speak. A few had vanished altogether.

Tonight, there was only the fog for company.

Thaddeus slipped behind the terraced houses and approached Madam Baldry's brightly lit residence. Laughter and murmured excitement spilled into the street; silhouettes moved behind glowing curtains. A sanctuary of warmth—and potential ruin.

He pressed himself into the shadows beneath a leaning drain-pipe, breath ghosting before him.

Across the street, unseen, Detective Barnes watched.

Barnes had stalked Thaddeus for three nights now, prowling through London's veins like a hound dogging a fox. The young spiritualist—Lord Raynsford—was a puzzle, and Barnes intended to fit every piece before another body dropped. If Thaddeus was not the killer, then he was dancing far too close to one.

The night felt charged. Something would break—Barnes felt it in his bones.

The séance guests began filing out, bundled in scarves, chattering with delight or dread. A woman locked up behind them, gave a pleased sigh, and withdrew into silence.

The fog thickened. Even the lamps dimmed, as if frightened to burn too brightly.

Then it happened.

A shape detached itself from the hedges beside Madam Baldry's door. A tall figure—ink against ink—every line of him carved with intent. The faintest glint of metal flashed at his waist.

Thaddeus's breath hitched.

The man raised his hand to knock.

"Stop!" Thaddeus cried, surging from the shadows.

The figure jerked—then vanished into the fog with startling speed.

Thaddeus lunged after him.

"Damn it," Barnes hissed, breaking from his hiding place and joining the chase.

The pursuit tore through the labyrinth of backstreets—boots striking wet stone, fog churning beneath their feet. The man in black was quick—unnaturally so—slipping around corners, vaulting puddles, weaving through alleyways as though he had learned the neighborhood by heart.

Thaddeus kept pace, driven by fear and fury. Barnes followed, breath sharp, refusing to lose both hunter and hunted.

Then the killer veered between two crumbling houses.

Thaddeus followed—

—and immediately sensed the world had changed.

Here the fog was wrong. Thick. Heavy. Smothering.

It muffled the lanterns entirely, swallowing their glow, turning the world into shifting darkness. The houses loomed like hunched giants, their windows blind and black.

Thaddeus slowed.

Listened.

A soft scrape.

A whisper of movement far ahead—or behind?

"Show yourself," he whispered.

But the fog answered with silence.

A shape flickered. Then vanished.

He pivoted—

Just in time to sense the presence behind him.

A heavy, brutal force struck the back of his skull.

Light exploded. Pain surged. The world tilted and spun.

As he collapsed onto the cold, soaked stones, the last sound he heard was the faint retreat of boot heals—swift, sure, unhurried—being absorbed by the fog.

Then darkness enfolded him. Complete. Final. Smothering. Like a shroud closing over the dead.

Detective Barnes lost his footing as he tore through the twisting alleyways, swallowed whole by the ravenous fog. Darkness pressed in on all sides, thick and airless, as though the city itself meant to choke him. Rain-slick cobblestones gleamed beneath the sickly flicker of distant lamps, each stone glinting like the scale of some submerged creature waiting to drag him down. Every step sent a jolt through his aging joints; every breath stung cold in his lungs. He was no longer the lean young man who once darted fearlessly through London's underbelly—time had etched stiffness into his bones and turned the pursuit of shadows into a punishing ordeal.

A misstep sent his shoulder slamming against a wet, moss-furred wall. The impact jarred him, knocking the wind from his chest, and for a moment he saw stars shimmering faintly in the fog. He growled a curse through clenched teeth, pushed himself upright, and forced his legs to keep moving.

Somewhere ahead—muffled, warped by the fog—came a sound. A scuffle. A gasp. Perhaps the murmur of a voice, quickly stifled. Barnes lunged toward it, hope sparking.

But when he stumbled into the next narrow lane, its crooked spine curving into darkness, he found nothing.

The alley was empty. Utterly, suffocatingly empty.

Barnes halted, chest heaving, the cold gnawing at the edges of his lungs. He stared down the length of the alley, then back the way he had come. The fog pressed close, a ghostly tide swallowing detail and distance alike. The houses that flanked him rose as hulking silhouettes, their windows dimly glowing like the faint, watchful eyes of spirits. Everything else—movement, noise, life—had fled into the ether.

Thaddeus had vanished.

The other figure too.

Not even a footprint disturbed the glistening stones.

Barnes ripped his bowler hat from his head and slapped it against his thigh in frustration. The sound was swallowed at once, smothered by the fog as though the night disapproved of such noise. His mind churned.

Had Thaddeus known he was being followed?

Had he shaken Barnes on purpose?

Or—most chilling of all—had he been acting with the very figure he had pretended to pursue?

Suspicion slithered through Barnes like ice water.

He bent forward, bracing his palms on his knees as he fought for breath. His heartbeat thudded loudly in his ears, the only living sound in an otherwise dead world. Remaining here alone was folly. The fog seemed to pulse with hidden movement, as though something unseen paced just beyond visibility, waiting.

Whether Thaddeus was predator or prey, Barnes could not say. But danger prowled these streets tonight—and it had noticed him.

Straightening with a wince, he retraced his steps, each one chosen with deliberate caution. The alleys widened by degrees until he spilled onto a broader thoroughfare where gas lamps glowed weakly through the mist. Still, the silence was eerie. Even the stray rattle of a carriage wheel in the distance seemed strangled before reaching his ears.

The fog rolled low and thick across the street—unyielding, impenetrable. Any hope of continuing the chase was futile.

Resigned, Barnes pulled his collar tighter and began the long walk back toward the station. His boots slapped the wet stones, the dull sound following him through the fog.

This night was lost.

Thaddeus Priest—Thaddeus Raynsford—had slipped from his grasp once more.

But the chase was far from over.

As he strode through the spectral haze, Barnes set his jaw with renewed resolve.

Tomorrow, he would hunt again.

And the fog—protector of ghosts and murderers alike—would not hide Priest forever.

# CHAPTER TWENTY-ONE

They rode for what felt like an eternity through a world muffled in darkness.

Every jolt of the carriage wheels drove a spike of pain through Thaddeus's skull, each bump rattling his teeth as if the devil himself were hammering inside his head. The burlap sack scratched against his face like a hundred tiny thorns, and the stifling heat beneath it made each breath a shallow, choking struggle—like drowning slowly in stale air.

His captors spoke not a single word.

They had thrown him into the carriage with all the gentleness afforded to livestock, bound his wrists so tightly that numbness crawled up his arms, and left him to languish in a fog of pain and dread. He drifted in and out of consciousness, the blow to his skull pulsing like a malignant heartbeat.

And through that pulse, through the suffocating dark and the sour warmth of wet leather and trapped breath, one thought kept returning with sickening force:

*It has happened.*

The old fear, the one he had never quite named aloud, rose now with merciless clarity. He had spoken too freely. He had let too many people look too closely. Bit by bit, carelessly or helplessly, he had allowed the truth of himself to slip into the world.

Not Thaddeus Priest.

Not merely the spiritualist.

Raynsford.

The name seemed to throb inside him worse than the pain.

Had someone learned it at last? Had some enemy, patient and watchful, gathered the scattered pieces and put them together? He thought of whispered recognition, of doors quietly opened, of hands closing round him at last because he had failed to remain hidden.

His stomach turned.

If this was about his father—if Horace had finally chosen to act—then Thaddeus knew too well what sort of men would have been sent. Men who asked no questions. Men who carried out ugliness as though it were ordinary work.

The carriage lurched violently, hurling him sideways against the hard seat. Pain burst white behind his eyes. He bit back a cry, breath shuddering through his teeth.

Still no voices. Still no explanation.

Only the rattle of wheels. The crush of darkness. The dreadful certainty growing heavier with every passing minute that this was no random violence.

Someone had come for him.

At last, the carriage shuddered to a stop.

Rough hands seized him, dragging him onto cold stone. The night air clung to him, cold and damp enough to seep through cloth and into bone. He was hauled through a doorway, up groaning stairs, then into a corridor thick with warmth and the muffled hush of carpets. A door creaked open.

Heat enveloped him—heavy and perfumed with tobacco, leather, and dust.

His bonds were cut. The burlap sack was torn away.

Thaddeus blinked as lamplight swam into focus and his stomach twisted.

He knew this room. His father's study.

The walls rose dark and oppressive, lined with ledgers that might as well have been tombstones. The air tasted of old money, old secrets, and a childhood he had spent trying to flee.

A match flared.

A pipe ember ignited with a soft glow.

The sweet, poisonous scent of tobacco—the scent of his youth, of dread—curled toward him like a familiar ghost. And seated in the great chair, utterly composed, as though the entire world were forced to orbit him...

Horace Raynsford.

Thaddeus felt something inside him recoil.

"Why the theatrics, Father?" he asked, voice hoarse and edged with fury.

Horace's reply rasped like metal dragged across stone.

"Because I wished to remind you that anything can happen to you. At any time. You are woefully unprepared for the world."

Same tone. Same cruelty. Same game he had always played.

But Thaddeus was no longer the trembling boy who once endured this man.

"I'm managing," Thaddeus said tightly.

Horace lit the candles on his desk one by one. Their glow carved sharp angles across his face, revealing a sneer that seemed forever etched into his features.

"Yes, managing splendidly," Horace drawled. "You arrive in London and promptly lose your fortune, take up residence in a wretched kip, lose your clothing, and now—now—you've become a murder suspect."

He paused, savoring the moment, waiting for the crack in Thaddeus's composure.

But Thaddeus did not crack.

Horace's smile tightened.

"I am offering you a chance at salvation. To come home. To end this childish masquerade."

"You mean you fear for the family name," Thaddeus said bitterly. "You want me back under your thumb—under your rules."

"Naturally." Horace puffed on his pipe, smoke curling around him like a dragon's breath. "You will return. Marry Hortense. She has graciously agreed to forgive your indiscretions. I explained you merely needed to... sow some wild oats."

"Forgive me?" Thaddeus echoed in disbelief.

"Come home," Horace said, "and this business with the murder investigation will... disappear."

There it was—the trap snapping shut.

"And how do you intend to make murder charges disappear?" Thaddeus asked.

Horace's jaw twitched—his only tell.

"You don't need to trouble yourself with the methods."

"It matters to me," Thaddeus pressed. "You're bribing someone. Or framing someone. Who?"

Now Horace's eyes gleamed with cruel satisfaction.

"Oh, your associates are an unsavoury lot. The dregs of London. Yet none were suitable... until now."

Thaddeus leaned forward, dread gnawing at his ribs.

"That proprietor of the kip," Horace said lightly. "Did you know he was once accused of murder? Escaped justice then. He won't this time. He will take the fall. It's where his sort belongs."

"Guss?" Thaddeus's voice cracked. "Guss Fable? You're framing Guss? He is innocent—he helped me!"

The horror of it hit him fully.

The rage that followed was blinding.

"Sentiment?" Horace scoffed. "People like him exist to serve a purpose."

Thaddeus surged to his feet, but the two men behind him seized him, forcing him back down.

"No!" Thaddeus snarled. "I won't allow this. I won't let you destroy an innocent man."

Horace's fury erupted like a storm.

"So this is your loyalty? To a slum keeper? You shame me. You shame everything I built. You deserve everything that is coming."

Thaddeus strained against the hands gripping him.

"What are you going to do?"

Horace's lips curled.

"Apparently, you are still in need of education. Remove him."

The men tightened their hold—

—and Judith swept into the room like a breath of forgotten warmth.

"Where is my son?" she demanded.

Thaddeus froze—and then she was upon him, embracing him tightly. "My sweet boy," she whispered, clinging to him, completely unaware of the violence simmering beneath the surface.

Thaddeus tore free of the men long enough to return her embrace, though his glare stayed locked on his father. Judith, gentle and glowing in her maternal devotion, was everything Horace was not. Thaddeus silently marvelled that she had ever bound her life to such a man.

She stepped back, hands fluttering, trying to smooth his coat, straighten his collar, tend to him as though he were still small enough to protect.

"Thaddeus," she murmured, her voice cracking. "Are you even taking care of yourself?"

He took her arms gently and created space.

"Mother. I am well."

She masked her hurt with practised grace. "Will you stay for dinner? It has been so long..."

"I must return to London," Thaddeus said. "Another time."

And before Horace could bark another command, Thaddeus strode from the room, ignoring his father's enraged calls echoing down the hall.

Judith turned slowly toward her husband.

"What have you done?" she whispered.

Horace scoffed, waving a dismissive hand.

"Bah. He'll recover."

But even he—monster though he was—missed the shadow that passed across Judith's face.

And he did not see the first cracks appear in the foundation of the world he thought he controlled.

THADDEUS STRODE down the long corridor, boots striking the polished floorboards with sharp, furious cadence. The mansion felt colder than he remembered—its grandeur hollow, its silence heavy as a tomb. Shadows clung to corners like lurking things with breath and intention. He did not slow. He did not dare. If he hesitated, even for a moment, his father's poison might seep back into him.

He reached his chambers and slipped inside, closing the door with a soft click that sounded far too final.

The room, once a sanctuary in boyhood, now felt foreign. Suffocating. A museum of a life he no longer claimed.

He crossed to the wardrobe and threw open the doors. His hands trembled—not with fear, but with the fury that still roared through his blood. One by one, he seized garments from their hangers: crisp shirts, well-tailored waistcoats, coats made of fabrics too fine for his London life. His fingers brushed the leather of polished boots, and for a fleeting moment the softness almost broke him. How distant this world had become.

All of it went into the travel satchel.

Then, kneeling, he reached deep into the dark recess beneath his hanging coats, fingertips brushing against something solid. The wooden box emerged like an artifact pried from a grave—handsome mahogany, deceptively ordinary, the sort of box a gentleman might fill with cufflinks or rings. But Thaddeus knew better.

He opened it.

Rows of gleaming cufflinks and pins stared up at him like accusing eyes. He ignored them, sliding his thumb along the base until it found the faint groove—hidden, almost imperceptible.

The secret compartment lifted with a soft click.

Inside lay neatly folded banknotes and sovereigns that glinted in the firelight like trapped suns. His emergency fund. The last tie to his old life... aside from the woman who now occupied his every thought.

Thaddeus swept the money into his satchel with a resolve that bordered on ferocity.

This time, he took everything.

He would never return here. Not unless it was to retrieve Athena —his Athena—brown-skinned, radiant, beloved. The thought of her tightened something inside him until he nearly doubled over. If his father intended to barter her into some vile arrangement—

No. No. He would not allow it.

He straightened, pulling the satchel closed. And that was when he felt it.

The temperature plummeted.

A faint prickle—cold as ice water—crept along the nape of his neck. The air thickened, pressing close, growing heavy with the metallic tang of something not-living.

A whisper of movement stirred behind him.

Thaddeus did not turn immediately. He knew that sensation too well.

"*Remember who you are,*" breathed a voice that was barely voice at all—thin as gauze, brittle as old regret.

Thaddeus exhaled a mirthless laugh, though it shook faintly. "Remember who I am? Do you hover only when I cross this threshold, Grandfather? Or do you drift through these halls endlessly, watching the decay you helped to sow?"

The ghost flickered, its luminous outline wavering like smoke caught in a draught. Slowly, its form rose, spectral robes trailing in a wind that did not exist. "*You are his son,*" the apparition whispered, "*but you are not him. You carry the blood, but not the rot. You are better than Horace.*"

"Comfort? From you?" Thaddeus spat. "Surely that's a jest. I know the kind of man my father became—and the kind of man who made him. Spare me your absolution."

The ghost's expression rippled—grief, pride, regret, all tangled together like an unfinished tapestry.

Thaddeus stepped forward, brushing through its incorporeal form. The icy shock tore a gasp from him; it felt as though unseen hands, cold and merciless, clamped around his ribs.

He staggered but caught himself.

"Do not linger," he said, avoiding the ghost's hollow gaze. "I have little time, and far too much to rectify."

He paused at the doorway, gripping the frame until the carving bit into his palm.

"I must leave, Grandfather. And I won't forget—any of it."

Under his breath, he added, "As if I were ever allowed to forget."

Then he stepped into the dim corridor, the weight of the house—and its ghosts—falling away behind him like a closing grave.

Lord Horace Raynsford sat rigidly in his study, his complexion flushed a furious crimson in the aftermath of Judith's unexpected defiance. The echo of her trembling voice—"What have you done?"—lingered in the air like a curse that refused to settle. He had tried to soothe her concerns, wrapping his lies in honeyed tones, but he knew she would not be pacified for long. Judith might appear fragile, but she possessed a quiet ferocity capable of complicating everything.

Across the room, Clovis and Erwin shifted uneasily. A few moments earlier, after Judith's stormy exit, they had exchanged whispers and muttered jests under their breath—small, nervous attempts at levity in the face of a household turned volatile. But one glance at Horace's expression—carved from sheer, murderous rage—extinguished their amusement instantly. The silence that fell was thick and suffocating, like the damp fog curling against the windows.

Horace rose abruptly, the legs of his chair scraping across the rug like a beast clawing its way free of confinement. His shadow, thrown grotesquely large by the firelight, stretched across the study walls like a demon made manifest.

"You know what you are to do," he barked, his voice cracking like a whip. "And do not—" he jabbed a finger at them, trembling with fury—"muck it up this time!"

The two men nearly tripped over each other in their haste to obey, bowing stiffly before retreating from the oppressive heat of the study. They slipped out the door, closing it behind them with care—as if afraid even the latch clicking might provoke the Lord's wrath anew.

In the corridor, the air felt cooler, freer. But neither man dared speak until they had descended the stairs and reached the marble hall below. Only then did they exhale, their breath misting faintly in the dim light.

Inside the study, Horace stood alone, chest heaving, fingers drumming a violent rhythm against the surface of his desk. His eyes drifted to the darkened window, where the fog pressed hungrily against the glass, eager to seep inside.

Let Judith fret.

Let Thaddeus run.

Let the night itself conspire against him.

Horace would crush them both, if he must. And not even the dead would stand in his way.

Thaddeus moved through the ancestral corridors with the hesitant tread of a man descending into a crypt. The long hallways of Raynsford Manor seemed narrower than he remembered, squeezed by gloom and time. Dampness clung to the corners of the ceilings, curling outward like blackened fingers. The faint smell of mildew mixed with the older, deeper scent of secrets long buried—rot disguised beneath polish and respectability.

Shadows stirred restlessly along the wainscoting, slipping in and out of existence like thoughts half-remembered. The ghosts who haunted these halls trailed after him in drifting silence, their forms thinning and thickening with the flicker of candle flames. Though other men might have quailed under their watchful escort, Thaddeus found their presence almost comforting. They had been his companions since childhood—silent witnesses to the cruelty and coldness of this house. They were, in their way, more family to him than the man whose blood he shared.

This was home, he thought darkly.

A place steeped in lies... and built on bones.

Horace had been right about one thing—Thaddeus was sentimental. Emotion, loyalty, softness: all weaknesses in his father's eyes. Weaknesses that could be shaped, twisted, exploited.

And as though summoned by the thought, a darker possibility slithered into Thaddeus's mind.

Horace had not threatened Judith.

He had not threatened Athena.

Not yet.

Thaddeus halted mid-step, his breath catching in his throat. Would his father go that far? The answer surged up unbidden—cold and certain.

Yes. Horace Raynsford would go as far as the world allowed him to go.

His pulse spiked. Athena—so warm, so gentle, so utterly unprepared for the venom of this household—Athena was not safe here. He had been a fool to think distance and stone walls could shield her.

Horace's sneering face rose before him in memory, as vivid as if carved into the very air. Manipulative. Pitiless. A tyrant enthroned in his own decaying kingdom.

Thaddeus pushed forward, almost at a run, as though he could outrun both his father's shadow and the spiraling dread clenching his chest.

He rounded the corner—

—and struck someone with enough force to jar them both.

A gasp.

Then—

"Thaddeus!"

Athena stood before him, eyes bright, her rich dark skin luminous in the dim candlelight. Hope blossomed across her features like dawn breaking. Before he could speak, she threw her arms around him, clutching him with a fervour that nearly undid him.

"Oh, my love," she breathed. "I've missed you so terribly."

He returned her embrace with equal desperation, pulling her close—perhaps too close—as if the strength of his arms alone could shield her from every evil in the world.

A sharp "Humph!" interrupted them.

Both turned to see Mrs. Keating, iron-spined and sour-faced, clutching a basket of laundry like a shield. Her eyebrows lifted so high they nearly merged with her scalp, and her look of disapproval could have curdled milk. She said nothing—she never dared scold the young master—but her silence was a sermon unto itself.

Athena smothered a laugh. Thaddeus allowed himself a small smile before guiding her quickly into the kitchen, out of Mrs. Keating's line of fire. The kitchen was warm, lamplit, fragrant with herbs and the faint lingering aroma of supper—an oasis of humanity within the cold labyrinth above.

"Have you come for me, love?" Athena asked softly, hope flaring bright in her eyes.

Thaddeus's heart twisted.

"Not yet," he admitted. "Not tonight."

The light faded from her face, replaced with a worry that carved painful lines across her brow. He lifted his hand, cupping her soft, warm cheek—and brushed his thumb gently across her skin.

"Just a little longer," he vowed. "I am in danger, my heart. And until that danger passes, it won't be safe for you to come with me."

Her breath trembled. "But you will return?"

"I swear it," he murmured.

He leaned in and kissed her—slow, reverent, desperate. A kiss filled with longing... and a promise carved from the deepest part of himself. Athena inhaled sharply at the sweetness of it, her body softening against him, her fears easing beneath his touch.

Thaddeus kissed her forehead, then her cheek, then her lips once more before stepping back.

"I must return to London tonight," he said gently. "But I will come for you as soon as I can."

As he turned, movement in the doorway caught his eye.

Jackson stood there—steadfast, loyal Jackson—hovering like a sentinel just beyond the threshold. His face bore relief, and something like pride.

"Jackson," Thaddeus breathed and stepped forward to embrace the older man.

"It does my heart good to see you whole, young master," Jackson said, gripping his shoulder.

"Jackson, listen carefully," Thaddeus whispered, urgency sharpening his tone. "I need to leave before my father's men find me. Bring the carriage around. I need it tonight."

Jackson nodded, jaw firming with resolve. "Anything for you, young master. Anything."

The ghosts in the hall stirred as if in agreement.

And Thaddeus knew—this was his last night in this cursed place.

# CHAPTER TWENTY-ONE

The cold night air enveloped Thaddeus as he stepped outside for the carriage. He could hear the footman rousing the horses and getting ready to pull the carriage around. He waited patiently. He knew what he must do and the extra money he now held in his satchel was going to help. He wanted the spiritualist career, but he needed to clear his name first and that was exactly what he was going to do and no machinations of his father was going to stop him.

He didn't hear his father's men quietly approaching from behind.

A hand clamped over Thaddeus's mouth. A cloth pressed to his nose, sweet and sickly, like rotting flowers soaked in spirits. He tried to hold his breath. His lungs burned. His vision wavered.

He drew in a gasp.

The world twisted.

The candle flames smeared into streaks of gold.

Then darkness consumed him, soft and merciless.

"Thaddeus?"

Judith's voice drifted into the kitchen like a chill wind, soft yet sharp, carrying an exhaustion that had begun to hollow her eyes. She called after her son, and the repetition wore on her spirit like the slow drip of water on stone.

Jackson stood at the long wooden table, clumsily folding towels he had no business touching. The task was beneath his station, yet he worried the fabric with trembling fingers, as though he could keep dread at bay by keeping his hands busy. His broad shoulders—normally so steady—were stiff with unease.

Judith paused at the threshold, her gown whispering over the tiles, her presence arresting the dim light. One elegant eyebrow arched, a silent summons.

"Jackson?"

The man swallowed, his Adam's apple bobbing. "I—went to the door to see Master Thaddeus off, ma'am. He said he needed to return to London most urgently."

Judith said nothing. She merely fixed her gaze upon him—calm, polite, devastating in its quiet expectation.

Jackson's courage crumpled.

"I was... too late, Mistress," he confessed, wringing the towel in his hands until the seams protested. "Lord Horace's men—the same two brutes from the study earlier—they seized him."

Judith's posture stilled. Even the shadows seemed to hold their breath.

Jackson continued in a low, tormented groan. "They struck him. I saw him fall... unconscious. They dragged him to the carriage like —like he were a parcel. They scarcely paused before leaping aboard. The wheels were already turning as the last man climbed up."

He bowed his head, shame radiating from him.

"I am so very sorry, ma'am. I should have stopped them. I should have—"

Judith raised a gloved hand, silencing his apology. But the gesture trembled ever so slightly.

The lamplight flickered, casting long skeletal shadows across her pale face. Her features, normally composed with gentle warmth, now hardened—like porcelain fired too long, its surface drawn tight and unyielding.

"Horace..." she whispered, the name a curse carried on a breath. "What has he done?"

The hearth crackled weakly behind them, but its warmth did not reach her. Judith's eyes shone not with tears, but with a burgeoning storm—dark, dreadful, and resolute.

Something had snapped.

And the house—old and suffocating under decades of secrets—seemed to feel the shift.

JUDITH TORE through the corridors of Raynsford House like a storm given flesh. Her skirts whispered furiously against the polished floors, and every gas lamp she passed flickered as though recoiling from the force of her rage. The mansion—usually so composed, so suffocatingly orderly—seemed to tremble at her approach. Paintings leaned subtly in their frames; shadows stretched thin across the walls, sensing calamity.

At the far end of the hall, Horace's study door stood half-closed, a thin line of light leaking into the darkness. Judith thrust it open without knocking.

Horace looked up sharply from his desk, pipe suspended in midair, the ember dying into ash. "Judith," he said, clipped, cool. "Must you always make an entrance as though pursued by demons?"

"I am pursued," she said, her voice low and trembling—not with fear, but fury. "By the consequences of your sins."

Horace stiffened, setting his pipe aside with an exaggerated calm. "What nonsense is this now?"

Judith stepped forward, letting the door slam behind her. The boom echoed through the room like cannon fire.

"Your men," she said, pointing a shaking finger toward the window as though the night itself bore witness. "They abducted our son. Jackson saw them. Your own thugs dragging Thaddeus unconscious into a carriage like a criminal!"

Horace's expression didn't so much as twitch. "He'll survive. The boy needed a lesson."

Judith's breath hitched—part outrage, part disbelief. "A lesson?" she hissed. "You treat him like a rogue servant! Like chattel! He is your blood—your eldest child!"

"My blood," Horace repeated with icy disdain. "And therefore my responsibility to correct." He leaned back, fingers steepled. "Thaddeus is weak, sentimental, easily swayed by vermin. He needed reminding of who he is—and whose name he bears."

Judith stared at him as though seeing a stranger. Her voice, when it came, was nearly a whisper. "You struck him."

"I did nothing of the sort," Horace scoffed. "My men subdued him, yes—he was shouting like a madman—"

"You ordered it."

Her voice cracked like a whip.

Horace didn't deny it.

Judith took another step forward. Candlelight flared behind her, throwing her silhouette across the towering bookshelves like the shadow of an avenging angel.

"Horace Raynsford," she said, shaking with wrath, "if you have harmed our son—if you intend to smear his name or drag him into your scheming—so help me God, I will burn this entire house down around you."

His eyes flashed—first in shock, then in amusement. "Don't be dramatic, Judith."

But she wasn't finished.

"You have chipped away at him since he was a boy. Broken him when you should have lifted him. Poisoned him with expectations you never once softened with affection." Her voice grew stronger, steadier, filled with years of suppressed truth. "You fear him—not his weakness, but his strength. His decency. His heart. Things you never possessed."

Horace slammed his fist onto the desk; papers jumped and fluttered to the floor like startled birds.

"He will return home," he snarled. "He will marry Hortense, unite our estates, restore our standing, and save us from ruin. That is his purpose."

Judith flinched—not at the impact, but at the word ruin.

"Ah," she said softly. "So that is the rot beneath the floorboards.

Your debts. Your failures. You would sacrifice him to hide your shame."

Horace shot to his feet—too fast, too furious.

"Watch your tongue."

"I have held my tongue for twenty years," she whispered, stepping closer until they were almost nose to nose. "But no longer. Bring him back, Horace. Bring him back now. Or I will go to the magistrate, to Parliament, to the papers—I will drag every secret you've buried into the daylight."

His breath went still.

A long, cold silence hung between them, broken only by the soft crackle of the fire.

Finally, Horace spoke, voice low and venom-slick.

"You would destroy me."

"I would save him."

Judith turned and swept out of the study, leaving the door wide open behind her.

The shadows seemed to swallow Horace whole as he stood there, trembling—not with fear of his wife, but of losing control. The house groaned softly around him, as though unsettled by the crack forming in its master's reign.

The war between them had begun.

TUESDAY, AUGUST 12, 1862

# CITY IN PANIC AS SÉANCE SLAYER MYSTERY DEEPENS

*Misguided Vigllantes Arrested – Public Calls for Action*

## CHAOS ON THE STREETS

## CHAOS ON THE STREETS

Amidst rising hysteria over the so-called "Séance ovce Slayer; London has been plagued by scenes of public chaos and disorder. Crowds of angry citizens have converged upon the East End, demanding answers and décryoning inaction.

The Metropolitan Police have been overwhehnelef, leand to a number of hasty and ill-founded arrests by vigllantes. Last night, several men were taken into custody by groups of ens-parged citizens who have conceded that fint the Séance Slayer solely for having

## PARLIAMENT

**AFFAIRS ABROAD**

Reports from thed mettore corhristne.

## Voyage to India

**First-Class Steamers Weekly**

**GET YOUR REST:** ELENCOURTS REEPARATION: for **Sleeplessness**

Diginat Poollesness and her mend som ffrone Police. BIP oA a ONe Threes dat mace layet.

## VIOLENT OUTRAGE IN EAST END

Reports. have emerged from Whitechapel and Spitalfield wthare crowds of angry cit-zens harned upon and detained vexeral men who were suspected of being the Séance Slayer. These vigllante actions were based on more suspicion and without due procers. As tempers flared, cries for swill justics filled the all."

One hightaned man, battered and brused, was dragged from his place of work, and frice-wern in- prob; their volces raised in condennation.

## Three Men Falsely Accused

Three men have been detained under suspicion of being the Séance Slayer. It soon became evi-dent that the accusations were based more on peranoia than evidence. The Metropolitan Police have conceded that the detainees--one a shopkeper from Spitalfields, another a cab driver from Whitechapel, and a third labourer from Shoreditch.

## THE WEATHER

Still unsettied weather persists. Showers have been reported and cond-tions remain cool and damp.

## THE STATE -TRADE

Markets report continued volatility, with fuctuations in grain prices and textics.

## The Danish Question

The looming action of the German Bund in Holstein has generated fears of a corps of execution.

# CHAPTER TWENTY-TWO

The Metropolitan Police station loomed through the fog, its lanterns glowing weakly like watchfires dying in the dark. Barnes mounted the stone steps with a heaviness that came not from exhaustion but from thought—dense, suffocating thought that pressed upon his ribs and made each breath a weighted thing.

Inside, the air was warmer but no less dreary. The station smelled of ink, wet greatcoats, and stale tobacco. Gas lamps hissed overhead, their light casting wan shadows along the corridor. A constable at the front desk straightened and opened his mouth to speak, but Barnes waved him off with a curt shake of the head.

He wasn't ready for conversation. Not yet.

He strode past rows of desks until he reached his own cramped office, the door protesting with a long, weary creak. He shut it behind him, shutting out the dull murmur of the station. For a moment he simply stood there, hat in hand, staring at the cluttered desk before him as though it were an altar to which he had brought another offering of failure.

Slowly, he lowered himself into his chair.

He replayed the night in his mind—every sound, every shadow, every fleeting movement swallowed by the fog. But again and again, his thoughts circled back to the same conclusion, tightening like a noose.

Thaddeus Priest had not simply vanished.

He had been taken.

Or he had fled.

Or... he had been meeting his accomplice.

Barnes rubbed a weary hand over his face. The evidence against the young man formed a tangled web, but one that always caught the light no matter how he turned it.

How had Priest known about the deaths with such uncanny detail? How had he retrieved information no living witness seemed able to provide?

And why—why in God's name—did he vanish the moment the killer was cornered?

Barnes exhaled slowly.

The fog, he realised, had not hindered Thaddeus at all. It had hidden him. The thought slid coldly beneath his skin, leaving a prickling trail in its wake.

A knock rapped against the office door. Barnes stiffened.

"Enter," he called.

Dickman poked his head in. "You sir, look like you've seen a ghost."

Barnes gave a hollow, humorless laugh. "Given the matter we're dealing with, that may not be far off."

"Everything all right?"

"No," Barnes said plainly. "But it will be."

He reached for his notebook with a grim set to his jaw.

"I believe," he said to no one and everyone, "that Mr. Thaddeus Priest is hiding far more than he lets on."

And with a single strike of his pencil, he underlined Priest's name on the suspect list—twice.

Tomorrow, the hunt would resume. And Barnes would no longer be giving the spiritualist the benefit of the doubt.

## CHAPTER TWENTY-TWO

Chief Ansel Coghill sat hunched behind his scarred mahogany desk, the dim gaslight flickering like a nervous pulse across the cramped office. The *London Times* lay spread before him, its bold black headline screaming accusations with all the subtlety of a public indictment. Another murder. Another failure. And the press—ever hungry, ever merciless—was roasting his department over slow, deliberate flames. Coghill felt every word as though etched with a hot iron across his skin.

The room smelled faintly of stale smoke and rain-darkened cloth, as though past failures lingered like ghosts. He rubbed his temples. The city wanted answers—demanded them—and he had none. Murders such as these did not bend to the impatience of the public or the paranoia brewing in every fog-soaked alley.

A knock. Sharp. Impolite.

"Come in," Coghill called, already dreading what fresh torment might enter.

The door flew open without ceremony.

The Lord Mayor himself filled the threshold like a storm cloud come to roost. He waddled into the room, breath wheezing, and collapsed into the chair opposite the Chief's desk. The poor piece of furniture groaned in protest beneath his considerable girth, as though it, too, feared his displeasure.

Without greeting, without even a glance of courtesy, the Lord Mayor tugged a handkerchief from his pocket and mopped the sweat beading along his ruddy brow. His jowls trembled with outrage.

Coghill's stomach dropped. Nothing good ever followed that handkerchief.

"We must do something about these murders," the Lord Mayor declared, each word a gust of humid breath. He struck his cane against the floorboards, the crack like a pistol shot in the cramped office. "I have barely settled into my new post, and already citizens storm my doorstep with demands, fears, whispers of incompetence! This"—he jabbed a stubby finger at the Times—"makes me look weak. And it makes the Metropolitan Police appear utterly useless."

The Chief winced as though struck. His jaw tightened, but he swallowed the instinctive retort clawing up his throat.

"Yes, My Lord. I quite agree...it reflects poorly on us all."

The Lord Mayor leaned forward, shadows pooling in the folds of his face. His next words were lower—colder.

"There is talk," he said, "of replacing you."

Coghill felt the world tilt slightly off its axis.

"Your entire department could be swept clean," the Lord Mayor continued, voice dripping with theatrical doom. "The public is restless—fearful—and fear breeds chaos. If we do not deliver a culprit soon, they may well start a riotous frenzy in the streets. Blood begets panic, panic begets insurrection."

He slammed his cane down once more.

"Fix this, Coghill. Immediately."

Silence spread like ink across the room.

Coghill managed a stiff, formal nod, though his mouth had gone bone-dry.

"Yes, My Lord. We shall... make all possible haste to solve this case."

The Lord Mayor gave a single dismissive grunt, hauled himself to his feet, and swept out of the office, leaving behind only the scent of cologne and unspoken threats.

When the door closed, Coghill sagged back in his chair. Outside, the fog pressed against the windows like a hungry beast, eager to swallow the city whole.

And unless a miracle occurred, it would swallow him along with it.

## CHAPTER TWENTY-TWO

Darkness seeped into Thaddeus's consciousness like ink blotting across parchment. When he finally woke, it was as though he had been dredged up from the bottom of a black, icy river. His skull throbbed with each heartbeat, a sledgehammer pulsing behind his eyes.

He lay upon a splintered wooden floor inside some cavernous place—a warehouse, it seemed—its rafters lost to the gloom above. Faint light bled through grime-smeared windows, cast by distant street lamps whose glow could barely penetrate the murk. The shadows shuddered as if breathing.

Thaddeus did not move at first. He simply listened.

Silence.

No breath but his own. No footfalls. No low murmur of captors waiting to pounce. He pushed himself up, bracing a hand against the floor—only to recoil violently.

His palm rested in something warm and sticky. He lifted his hand, and in the scant moonlight, saw his fingers glisten black-red.

Blood.

His breath hitched. He ran trembling hands down his coat, his shirt, his sides. No wounds—none of the warmth belonged to him.

Which meant it belonged to someone else.

A scraping echo drifted from the far corner of the warehouse as the fog of his vision adjusted. Grain sacks slumped in dismal heaps. Chains hung from ceiling beams like iron vines. And there—just beyond the reach of a pale shaft of moonlight—was a shape.

A woman's red hair glimmered like a ghostly ember.

Thaddeus's breath caught. His legs felt weak, watery, as he staggered toward the figure. When he reached her, the breath left him in a strangled sound.

Madam Lorena Baldry.

Her porcelain skin had drained to a ghastly pallor, her eyes half-lidded as though she had died mid-whisper. She was the very spiritualist he had attempted to save—the woman he had chased the killer to protect—before the blow at the back of his skull plunged his world into darkness.

"God forgive me," he breathed, though he wasn't sure for whom he prayed.

The dizzy waves in his head swelled again—remnants of the chloroform, the violence. He steadied himself with a hand against the crates.

He had been brought here. Placed here. By his father's men.

A chill cut through him, deeper than any natural cold. Horace Raynsford was no longer simply controlling—he was monstrous. To stage a murder around his own son? To make Thaddeus the perfect culprit and wash his hands of him forever?

It stole the breath from Thaddeus's lungs.

He backed away from the corpse, every instinct screaming that time was slipping through his fingers like water through a sieve.

The front door loomed on the opposite side of the warehouse.

He took a step—then froze. He looked down at himself. He was drenched in blood.

To stumble out into the streets like this would seal his fate. The first constable who laid eyes on him would haul him to the noose.

"My satchel..." he whispered, half in desperation.

His heart pounded violently as he scanned the warehouse. Nothing. Shadows. Piles of useless junk.

He forced himself to think—to breathe.

He retraced the memory: his father's study, the men, the blow, the dragging weight of unconsciousness. They would not have left the satchel with him.

The moon shifted behind a cloud—and then emerged again, casting a pale shaft of light across an upper shelf of a wooden storage rack.

A faint silhouette. Leather. Straps. His satchel.

Thaddeus scrambled up the rack, fingers slipping, breath ragged. He snatched it down just as—

The unmistakable crunch of carriage wheels rolled to a halt outside the warehouse.

His blood iced over.

Male voices. Low. Approaching. Boots on gravel.

He threw himself behind the warehouse door—a sliver of shadow between hinges and wall where the lantern light would not reach. He pressed his back to the cold boards, clutching the satchel to his chest. His breath felt too loud, too alive in this place of death.

The front door's lock scraped. The hinges groaned. Lantern light sliced into the warehouse like a blade.

Thaddeus squeezed his eyes shut, praying the shadows would hold, that the blood soaking his shirt would not shine like a beacon.

Two men stepped inside—gruff voices, coarse boots, the unmistakable clank of firearms.

Horace's men.

"Spread out," one said. "He can't have gone far."

A lantern swung dangerously close to the door—so close Thaddeus could smell the oil.

He held his breath until spots danced behind his eyelids.

Then—

A crash at the far end of the warehouse.

The men stiffened. The lantern jerked away.

"What was that?"

"Check it."

The moment their boots thundered deeper into the warehouse, Thaddeus made his move.

He slipped through the narrow gap between two towering stacks of crates and found himself in a side passage running along the inner wall of the building—a passage meant for laborers, no doubt, or for moving goods unseen. It was close, black, and choked with the smell of dust, wet timber, and old rope.

Behind him came the muffled shouts of his captors, still searching the wrong direction.

Thaddeus pressed one hand to the wall and hurried on, half-stumbling in the dark. His skull throbbed abominably. Each step jarred the pain afresh, but fear lent him what strength it could. Ahead, a faint wash of gray appeared through the gloom.

A door.

Not the main entrance, but a service door at the rear of the warehouse, warped by damp and hanging slightly crooked on its hinges.

He seized the latch and forced it open.

Night met him at once.

Fog rolled in low over the yard beyond, silvering the heaps of broken casks, packing straw, and discarded timber strewn behind the building. The air was cold and wet against his face, but after the close darkness within, it felt almost like deliverance.

He did not hesitate.

Keeping low, he darted across the yard and behind a stack of empty barrels. Somewhere behind him, a voice barked an order. Another answered. They had discovered his absence.

At the rear boundary of the yard stood a brick wall, not so high as to be impossible, though topped with jagged mortar and years of soot. Near it, as if abandoned by providence for his use, lay a slanted cart half-loaded with split kindling and a broken crate.

Thaddeus ran for it.

His boots slipped on the wet boards as he climbed, one hand clutching the side of the cart to steady himself. Pain flashed hot behind his eyes. He bit it back, hauled himself onto the crate, and caught the top of the wall with both hands.

For one terrible instant he thought he would fail.

Then, with a desperate exertion, he dragged himself upward, scraping his palms raw against the brick. A shout rose behind him—closer now.

"There!"

He threw himself over.

He landed badly in the alley on the far side, one knee striking hard against the stones. The force of it nearly drove the breath from him. For a moment he could do nothing but crouch there in the filth and fog, trembling, half-blind with pain.

But he was free.

Behind him came the crash of the yard door flung open and the uproar of men reaching the wall too late.

Thaddeus staggered to his feet and plunged into the alley's darkness. The fog swallowed him at once, thick and shifting between the narrow brick walls, turning every corner into mystery and every shadow into refuge.

He did not look back.

The city opened before him like a labyrinth of soot and silence. He ran—unsteady, hunted, breath burning in his throat—while London's vast, spectral fog gathered round him and hid him from those who would drag him back.

Thaddeus staggered into the night like a man returning from the dead, slipping through the narrow service corridor behind the warehouse and bursting into an alley choked with fog. The air was knife-cold, slicing straight through his thin, blood-stiffened shirt. His breaths came ragged, white clouds drifting from his lips like wandering spirits.

He kept to the shadows, clutching his satchel against his chest as if the leather thing were the only anchor left tethering him to sanity. Every footfall echoed in his skull—a metronome of panic. The blood on his clothing had dried tacky and cold, clinging to him like a second, damning skin.

Somewhere behind him, bells tolled the hour.

Somewhere ahead, London breathed.

The city stretched before him like a labyrinth carved of soot and sorrow. Gas lamps flickered weakly against the press of fog, burning halos into the murk. The cobblestones glistened with moisture, reflecting distorted fragments of lamplight like shards of broken glass. Horses clattered in the distance, their iron shoes striking sparks that were quickly swallowed by night.

Thaddeus pulled up his collar, trying to obscure the stains on his shirt. He dared not be seen. Not like this.

Every door he passed, every window—shuttered or cracked—felt like an eye watching him. Judging him. Condemning him.

A woman stepped from a side street, wrapped in a shawl, and Thaddeus flattened himself against a brick wall, heart thundering so violently he feared she would hear it echoing off the stones. She walked past him slowly, humming a tuneless melody that wavered in the dense cold.

Only when the sound faded did he dart forward again.

He needed water. A cloak. Anything to conceal himself. His mind raced through possible safe havens—but each one dissolved into danger as soon as it formed. His boarding house? Impossible. Barnes might already be watching it. Guss's tenement? His father's hired brutes likely lurked nearby. Cordelia's house? He would only bring danger to her doorstep.

A shadow detached itself from a wall and drifted toward him.

Thaddeus froze—

—but it was only a drunken man weaving along the narrow lane, muttering to phantoms only he could see.

Thaddeus pressed on.

The Thames's distant roar reached him slowly, as though rising from far beneath the earth—the river always whispered at night, but tonight its voice was darker, almost warning. He ducked into a warren of alleys behind Fleet Street, where gutters ran with stale water and rats scurried in frantic procession.

Here the fog thickened into something almost corporeal, curling cold fingers along his throat. Spectral forms rippled at the edges of his vision—spirits, drawn to the blood on his clothes, whispering in tones too faint to decipher. Their presence prickled along his spine, their murmurs following him like a funeral procession.

"Not now," he whispered. "Not tonight."

A sudden noise—shouts, a carriage braking hard—made him dart behind a stack of crates.

A patrol.

Through the fog, the silhouettes of two constables materialised under the gaslight, their lanterns swinging, cutting golden swaths through the gray mist. Their footsteps rang sharp and purposeful.

Thaddeus held his breath until his lungs burned.

If they found him now, covered in blood fleeing a murder scene...

He waited. Counted heartbeats.

The constables moved on.

When the danger eased, Thaddeus slipped from his hiding place and hurried deeper into the twisting lanes. He needed sanctuary—somewhere to wash, to think, to breathe without fear of capture.

The fog parted momentarily, and above him rose the shadowed silhouette of St. Dunstable's—its Gothic spire clawing at the moon. The churchyard lay abandoned at this hour. A place for the dead, not for constables.

Perfect.

Thaddeus slipped through the iron gate and into the graveyard, where crooked stones leaned like the teeth of some great beast. Cold wind moved through the yews, making them whisper secrets to one another. He crouched behind a mausoleum, finally letting his trembling limbs rest.

His head throbbed with every heartbeat; his vision swam. Blood was caked in his hair from the blow, and he could still smell Madam Baldry's scent on his coat—the faint floral trace now mingled grotesquely with death.

He dropped the satchel beside him and exhaled shakily. He had escaped. He was alive.

But his father's trap was sprung, the city was hunting him, and somewhere in London the true killer walked free—veiled by fog, emboldened by chaos, perhaps even watching him now from the shadows between the graves.

Thaddeus closed his eyes. He had to survive the night. Then he would hunt the truth.

Even if it killed him.

# CHAPTER TWENTY-THREE

Chief Inspector Ansel Coghill sat alone beneath the jaundiced glow of the gas lamp, the shadows of his office stretching long and crooked across the paneled walls. The rain worried at the windowpanes like restless fingers, and the bitter reek of old tobacco lingered in the air.

With a sigh, he dipped his pen and scratched out another line of ink upon the heavy cream paper, the words marching stiffly toward the waiting seal of the Lord Mayor. The letter was a necessary humiliation: a careful account of every measure taken in the matter of the spiritualist murders, as though he were some trembling clerk rather than the head of the Metropolitan Police.

His lip curled. Barnes and Dickman were the finest men under his command—methodical, relentless, not given to fancy or superstition. Yet even they were confounded by this phantom butcher who slipped in and out of London's fog-bound alleys, leaving nothing behind but drained bodies and a city riddled with whispers.

The very thought of the Seance Slayer sent a cold prickle along Coghill's spine, and he was a man who placed his faith in facts and fingerprints, not phantoms. Still, there were nights when the corridors of the Yard seemed too quiet by half, and he caught himself listening for a measured tread that never materialised.

A sharp rap upon the door shattered his uneasy reverie.

"Enter," he barked. His own voice sounded too loud in the cramped room.

The door swung inward and two figures stepped through, framed by the dim gaslight of the corridor. Detectives Gerald Reekey and Harold Bent might have been cut from the same rough bolt of cloth: both hard-featured men with coarse reddish-brown hair and pale, freckled skin that never seemed entirely at ease in daylight. Reekey stood taller, thin as a bayonet, while Bent was shorter and broader in the shoulders, his coat pulling faintly at the seams.

They removed their hats and took the two chairs opposite Coghill's desk, perching on the edges as if summoned to receive censure. Their eyes flickered about the room, noting the scattered files, the half-burnt cigar in the tray, the Lord Mayor's unopened seal upon the second sheet of parchment.

"Gentlemen, you may unclench your jaws," Coghill said dryly. "I have no quarrell with you this morning."

He noted with some amusement the way the tension slid from their shoulders in the same instant, like two marionettes given slack on their strings.

"I have an assignment," Coghill continued. He steepled his ink-stained fingers and regarded them with hooded eyes. "You are acquainted, I presume, with the matter of the Seance Slayer?"

Both men inclined their heads. A flicker of something—eagerness, perhaps—passed between them.

"But that is Barnes and Dickman's case, is it not?" Reekey ventured, his voice smooth but edged with curiosity.

"It is," Coghill said, his tone clipped. "And it shall remain so. I want that clearly understood. I am not stripping them of the investigation. However"—he paused, letting the word hang in the air like a suspended weight—"this is no ordinary murderer we hunt. It is a labyrinth, and even my best men may benefit from another lantern in the dark."

A thin smile curled at the corner of Bent's mouth. Reekey's eyes gleamed with a quiet, covetous light. Barnes and Dickman had long been the darlings of the department; to stand beside them on such a prominent case, or better yet to outstrip them, would be no small prize.

"Of course, Chief Inspector," Bent said with unctuous haste. "We should be honoured to assist in any capacity you deem fit."

"Good," Coghill replied. "Then here is what you will do. You will go to Barnes and Dickman and request access to everything they have gathered: coroner's reports, witness depositions, photographs, sketches, every scrap of paper and every whispered recollection. You will review it all—slowly, thoroughly. A fresh set of eyes may see what familiarity has taught them to overlook."

The two detectives nodded, schooling their faces into expressions of dutiful obedience. Only the faint tightening at the corners of their mouths betrayed the calculations ticking away behind their eyes. Reekey and Bent intended far more than mere assistance, but that ambition was not something they would air in this room.

"That is all, gentlemen," Coghill said at last, reaching for the blotter. "Do not waste the opportunity."

"Good day to you, Chief Inspector," Reekey replied, rising with a shallow bow.

They replaced their hats and slipped from the office with a soft rustle of wool and leather, moving down the corridor side by side. Their footsteps faded into the murmur of the Yard, leaving Coghill alone once more with the rain at the windows, the unfinished letter, and the uneasy sense that, somewhere in the fog-choked city beyond, the Seance Slayer might already be writing the next chapter of his work in blood.

Athena entered the kitchen, concern shadowing her otherwise serene features. She set the market parcels on the butcher block and reached for her apron. As she slipped it over her head, Mrs. Keating appeared in the doorway.

"Don't bother putting that on, girl," the housekeeper said briskly. "You need to come with me."

Athena sighed and pulled the apron back off. What does the old biddy want now? she thought, though she kept her face neutral. She followed Mrs. Keating down the corridor and out the back entrance.

The courtyard lay under a pale light, the brick still holding a little warmth beneath the cool morning air. A black wagon stood waiting—one Athena didn't recognise. Its horse, a massive creature, pawed at the ground, tossing its head with impatient snorts.

Athena assumed it was some sort of delivery. "What's it today? Meat for the ice house? New beer kegs?" She asked the questions automatically. Too often she'd been made to haul heavy supplies while several capable men stood idly nearby. Mrs. Keating always assumed the girl's back was better suited for such labour than theirs.

They approached the rear of the wagon. It was enclosed—not unusual, but not the sort typically used for household deliveries.

Mrs. Keating pointed at the back door. "Up you go. There's a parcel inside wants shifting."

Athena stared at her, suspicion tugging at her brow. She restrained the urge to roll her eyes and climbed inside. "All right, what do we have in here—?"

She did not finish the question.

The door slammed shut behind her. The harsh metallic clank of the lock snapped into place like a blow.

Athena froze—then panic engulfed her. She rushed to the door, pounding her fists against the wood. "Let me out! What are you doing? Let me out!"

The wagon jerked into motion. The sudden lurch threw her backward, tumbling her onto the floorboards. She scrambled up and screamed, "Thaddeus! Thaddeus!" Her voice rose to a desperate wail. She knew—horribly—that he was too far away to hear her. Too far to help.

Outside, Mrs. Keating stood in the overcast courtyard, watching the wagon rumble away. A small, satisfied smirk crept across her pinched features.

"Always reaching above her station," she muttered. "Does her right good now to be taught this lesson."

A flicker of something like sympathy crossed her eyes—but only for a heartbeat.

Then it was gone.

THE FOG HAD THINNED by dawn, though only barely—its ghostly tendrils still clung to the streets like the remnants of a nightmare refusing to lift. A pale, watery sun pushed feebly through the mists as Detective Barnes and Detective Dickman rode in grim silence, their carriage wheels crunching softly over the damp-slick cobbles.

A runner from the watch had brought word at first light—

A body discovered in a warehouse near the river. A woman. Red hair. The description alone had set both detectives instantly on edge.

As they approached the dilapidated structure, Barnes felt a heaviness settle in his chest, something colder and more oppressive than the air itself. The warehouse loomed like a corpse of a building, ribs of broken beams jutting through its sagging roof, windows clouded with grime like half-blind eyes.

Constables were already gathered outside, the early morning air cool and faintly damp. One stepped forward, cap in hand.

"Detectives," he murmured. "We thought it best not to move her."

"Who opened this warehouse?" asked Barnes.

"One of the dock workers, sir. He's standing over there talking to Constable Jameson."

Barnes gave the pair a quick glance. "Proceed," he said.

Inside, the warehouse swallowed them. The cool air was deeper here—dead, unmoving. The kind of chill that clung to sorrow. Barnes paused just inside the doorway. The warehouse carried the usual odour of river mud and old timber—but nothing fresh. No sharp tang of wet clothing, no churned damp rising from the floorboards.

He glanced toward the body.

"Strange," he murmured. "If she was brought in from the river road, there ought to be mud."

Lanterns cast long skeletal shadows across stacks of feed bags and wooden crates. The light flickered, revealing a ghastly tableau upon the dirt floor.

Barnes's gaze shifted toward a wooden crate beside the wall. A stub of candle sat there in a shallow pool of hardened wax.

He touched the wax lightly with his bare fingers. It had cooled completely.

"Someone was here long before the constables arrived," he said quietly. "And they stayed awhile."

The candle had burned nearly to its base, the wick curled into a black knot.

Barnes frowned.

"Nearly four hours," he murmured.

Madam Lorena Baldry lay in a disordered sprawl of auburn hair and lifeless limbs—her face drained of all colour, eyes half-lidded as though interrupted mid-revelation. A streak of dried blood marred her temple where it had dried to a dark, tar-like stain. Her clothing, once rich and expressive, now appeared deflated and spectral, like the discarded skin of a life that had slipped away too soon. Around her neck, another silk scarf lay almost as decoration, for her throat was cut from ear to ear.

Dickman exhaled slowly through his nose. "God help us... another spiritualist."

Barnes brushed aside a lock of her hair. The strands were stiff with dried blood. A faint smell clung to the damp curls at her temple

—the sour, silty scent of the Thames at low tide. "She has been here since the night," he said quietly.

He crouched beside the body. "She struggled," Barnes murmured, observing defensive wounds on her hands.

He brushed two fingers lightly along the sleeve of her gown. The fabric was clean—too clean for a warehouse floor thick with dust.

Barnes turned one of the woman's shoes slightly with the edge of his glove. The leather sole was clean. Too clean for the river district.

"No mud," he said quietly. "And yet she is in this warehouse beside the river."

Barnes frowned slightly. The warehouse floor was bone-dry, yet the hem of her gown was damp with river chill. "She wasn't killed here," he said quietly.

Barnes lifted one of her wrists gently. The limb resisted him, stiffening slightly before settling back into place.

"She has been dead some time," he murmured.

His eyes moved over the scene with a predator's scrutiny. Not far from the body was a secondary pool of blood in an odd shape, almost as if poured around another body. Barnes leaned closer, studying the dirt around the stain. The dust there had been pressed flat, as though someone had sat heavily upon the floor before dragging themselves upright again. The marks of fingers were visible where they had pushed against the ground.

"It looks like someone else fought for their footing, here," said Barnes as he pointed to where the hand print was visible.

And then—something else caught his attention in the dirt on the floor.

Footprints.

Several of them, disorganized, turning this way and that.

But only one set leaving the scene.

He leaned closer. The prints were smeared, disrupted—but unmistakably there.

And more importantly—

a small trail of diluted blood led toward the rear of the warehouse, its drops faint as raindrops, nearly missed.

Dickman followed his gaze. "Someone was injured?" he asked.

"Or covered in blood," Barnes replied grimly.

The two detectives followed the faint path across the dusty floor. The drops grew smaller toward the rear door—whoever left them had been bleeding less as they went, or the wound had begun to clot. The trail led toward a set of crates shoved haphazardly aside—and there, half-hidden in a slant of anemic sunlight, lay something that turned Barnes's stomach cold.

A scrap of cloth.

Dark.

Fine weave.

Not a working man's garment—no, this belonged to someone of means.

Barnes lifted it delicately with the end of his glove.

"Tailor's cloth," Dickman said. "Expensive."

Barnes nodded once. "And I know a man who wears coats cut from cloth exactly like this."

The implication hung there, heavy as a gallows rope. Thaddeus Priest. Thaddeus Raynsford.

The man who'd vanished into the fog hours before.

A constable hurried over. "Detectives? Something else, sir."

He held out a familiar calling card—a blood smear on the fine embossed linen paper. He flipped the card over, "Thaddeus Priest."

Barnes's jaw tightened.

The morning air suddenly felt thin and insufficient.

Dickman whispered, "This doesn't look good for your spiritualist."

"No..." Barnes murmured, staring at the damning card. "No, it does not. However..."

In the pit of his stomach, something twisted—an unease he could not yet name. Because this scene was almost too neat. Too convenient. As though laid out for them like a grotesque stage play.

Barnes straightened slowly, eyes scanning the warehouse with renewed suspicion.

"For a man trying to hide, his calling card keeps showing up. A little too convenient don't you think?"

"Wrap everything carefully," Barnes said. "Separate packets. I want nothing disturbed. And I want every mark on this floor noted."

Dickman raised an eyebrow. "You think he may be innocent after all?"

Barnes did not answer at first.

At last he said quietly, "I think someone is going through a great deal of trouble to tell us exactly what to believe."

Outside, the pale morning continued its reluctant climb, and the fog clung close to the warehouse walls—like a curtain waiting to rise on the next act of an ever-darkening tragedy.

FRIDAY, 15 AUGUST 1862

# ANOTHER SPIRITUALIST BRUTALLY MURDERED

## MADAME LORENA BALDRY FOUND SLAIN IN ABANDONED WAREHOUSE

The body of noted spiritualist discovered in Whitechapel.

Séance Slayer strikes again

LONDON—The body of Madame Lorena Baldry, a prominent spiritualist medium, was discovered last evening in an abandoned warehouse in the Whitechapel district, the latest victim of the elusive and murderous Séance Slayer. Madame Baldry, age 37, was found gruesomely slain, her life cut short in a crime bearing the hallimarks of the recent series of killings that have terrorized the city.

### A GRUESOME DISCOVERY

The gruesome discovery was made by a passerby who, upon hearing a low moaning sound from within dark-ened baikling, caésted to investigue and was met with a sight of ghastly horror. Madame Baldry lay stais roes a makeshift séance table in the dimly fit, abasdoneo structure, her face tade and bearing the signs of *ssphyxia*. rtals. Nexrby, scull symbols had been recsorled in a dicturbing manner, and strange objects of a ritualistic ratture were found about the scene.

### SCENE OF HORROR

The grim discovery was made late in the evening by a local laborerr who, upon investigating strange no iast emanating from, within the warehouse, stumbled upon the ghastly scene. The labourer saw fit to summon the police, who swittly arrived to traxt impelsyricen. Inspector Barnes and Inspector Dickman, the detectives assigned to the cass, have facing mealing watuas crimes.

### SCENE OF HORROR

The grim discovery was made late in the evening by a local laborere; who, upon investigating strangot noises emenating from within the warehouse, stumbled upon the ghastly scene.

The labourer saw fit to summon the police, who switly arrived to find Madame Baldry dead, her body displayed in a manner disturdingly reminissent of previous killings. As with ear-ler victims, there were signs of asphyxiation, and arcane symbols had been found at the site, lencing a macabre and ritualistic chara-ter to the crime.

### CRITICISM MOUNTS

The Metropolitan Police have come under increasing public scrutiny in light of their continued failure to apprehend the perpetrator responsible for the string of murders attributed to the so-called "Séance Slayer."

Despite assurances that every effort is being made, the absence of an arrest has led to growing dissatisfaction among residents, particularly within the districts most affected by the recent outrages. Several voices have questioned whether sufficient resources have been devoted to the investigation, while others have expressed concern that the unusual nature of the crimes has hindered conventional methods of inquiry.

### THE WEATHER

Today in London: Overcast skies and cool temperatures winl fodly to it he persist into the coming days

## THE INCOMPETENCE OF THE POLICE

### PARLIAMENT

LATEST DEBATES IN THE HOUSE

Detals on fegs 3

### THE STATE OF TRADE

Cotton market fuctuatce as American sanplics veare. Reports suggest price cauld vontime to fote. Drtals as fags a.

### CLASSIPIED ADVERTISEMENTS

HOLLOWAYS PILLS

Apply to Jenkims &. Som, Haus. Aganss

# CHAPTER TWENTY-FOUR

Detective Michael Barnes had expected—indeed, almost felt—the moment approaching when Detectives Gerald Reekey and Harold Bent would slither into their office like a pair of opportunistic ravens. The Chief Inspector, beleaguered and harried by the Lord Mayor's shadow, had clearly succumbed to the pressure. Still, of all men to foist upon them, Reekey and Bent were the last Barnes would have chosen. Their reputations for ambition—unchecked by prudence—preceded them.

The door creaked open without ceremony. Reekey stepped in first, his thin lips twisted in a grin that never reached his cold, foxlike eyes. Bent followed, broader in the shoulders but no less predatory, his gaze roving over the office with unearned superiority. Their presence soured the air.

"So," Reekey drawled, rocking smugly on his heels, "the Chief Inspector has decided we are to lend you boys an assist." His grin deepened into something oily and triumphant. "He says you're to hand over all papers and evidence. Fresh eyes and all that—perhaps we'll be the ones to finally break the case."

Dickman stiffened, the muscle in his jaw ticking, but he swallowed whatever retort trembled on his tongue.

Barnes answered instead, voice steady. "Very well. But while you are working on our case, you abide by one rule." He fixed each of them with a deliberate look. "You do not speak to the papers, nor do you court attention. The city trembles already—we don't intend to fan the flames. Do you understand?"

"Oh, certainly," Bent replied, his tone too smooth to be sincere. "One can never be too careful with frightened citizens."

Barnes offered a curt nod and gestured to the arrayed files on their desks. "This is all the evidence gathered thus far. Dickman and I have been poring over it for weeks."

Reekey's eyes flickered with a feverish hunger as he surveyed the documents. Barnes recognised the look—ambition untempered by reason. The man was already imagining headlines and promotions, no doubt. Bent was subtler, but no safer.

There was, however, one piece of evidence Barnes had no intention of relinquishing: his notebook, worn and weathered, tucked neatly into his breast pocket. It contained observations, sketches, impressions that existed nowhere else. He guarded it as fiercely as a priest guards confession.

"Gentlemen," Barnes said, donning his coat, "feel free to examine all of it. Detective Dickman and I have an appointment to attend to."

Bent's brows twitched upward. "Oh? And what appointment would that be?" Suspicion clung to his voice like damp to stone.

"Another witness to interview," Barnes replied evenly. "Stay here and review everything. We'll share what we learn upon our return."

But inwardly he longed only to remove himself from their presence. He trusted them neither with the case nor with their intentions.

No sooner had Barnes and Dickman stepped from the room than Reekey and Bent pounced upon the evidence. The careful stacks—arranged in a delicate chronology, each page linked to the next—were dismantled with brutish indifference. They scooped papers and photographs into boxes without regard for order, heedless of the story those quiet piles silently told.

Back in their own office, they tipped the boxes onto their desks, rifling through the documents like scavengers picking clean a carcass. Hours passed in a frenzy of careless sorting until one name surfaced again and again, rising like a ghost from every page:

Thaddeus Priest.

Bent slapped a page upon the desk. "This Priest fellow—he's everywhere. Looks like our prime suspect. Why in blazes haven't Barnes and Dickman hauled him in?"

Reekey narrowed his eyes. "Why don't we ask them?"

Their return to Barnes and Dickman's office was a storming of territory rather than a polite inquiry. They entered without knocking, tall shadows blotting out the doorway.

"This man, Thaddeus Priest," Reekey demanded, voice sharp as a blade, "why hasn't he been arrested?"

Barnes did not bother to rise. "Because we cannot," he replied bluntly.

Reekey scoffed. "Cannot? You hear this, Bent?"

Bent folded his arms, playing the part of judge and jury.

Barnes drew a steady breath, holding his temper by a thread. "We have no weapon. No witnesses. No solid proof. If we had even one piece of concrete evidence, he would already be behind bars."

The two rival detectives exchanged a look—dark, conspiratorial. Something unspoken passed between them, and Barnes's stomach tightened.

"Very well," Bent said at last, his tone unreadable.

They drifted from the office like a pair of crows leaving a windowsill, and the air seemed lighter for their absence.

Dickman exhaled sharply. "Those two are up to something. I can feel it in my bones."

Barnes nodded slowly, his expression grim. "Aye. And until the Chief sees sense, we must suffer their meddling. But from this moment on, anything new we discover stays between us. I trust them not at all."

The room fell into tense silence, the fog outside pressing against the windows, and somewhere—far beyond the reach of the Yard—the Seance Slayer continued to walk the shrouded streets of London, unseen and unclaimed.

Night had descended upon London in a shroud of mist and murky stillness, the kind that seemed to swallow sound and distort distance. Detective Barnes and Detective Dickman lingered beneath the iron lamppost opposite Thaddeus Raynsford's humble lodgings. This vigil had become their nightly ritual—a grim, necessary devotion. The Seance Slayer haunted the city like a phantom, and Thaddeus, for reasons neither man fully grasped, appeared to drift again and again into the killer's orbit. Whether he walked as accomplice or as some uncanny magnet for calamity, they had yet to discern.

Thaddeus emerged at last, stepping into the lamplight with the quiet tread of a man accustomed to night wanderings. Barnes and Dickman crossed the street in his wake, moving with practised subtlety. The fog curled around them like grasping fingers.

But neither detective sensed the other shadows that stalked behind—the hunched forms of Clovis Corbeld and Erwin Matson. Though rough men of questionable loyalty, tonight their misgivings stirred something almost chivalrous. They disliked Lord Raynsford's orders, and more than that, they begrudgingly admired the young man they'd been sent to watch. Their presence was silent and spectral.

Thaddeus travelled to yet another spiritualist's doorway, lingering as though listening to some secret whispered on the wind. The street was deathly quiet.

Then Barnes heard it.

A faint hiss—like steam escaping a kettle, but strangled, deliberate.

He turned sharply, scanning the gloom. Dickman continued watching Thaddeus with unblinking focus.

The sound came again.

That thin exhalation.

A serpent's sigh.

"Wait here," Barnes murmured, low. "Keep your eyes on Thaddeus. Signal me if anything stirs."

Dickman frowned, worry etched across his features. "Is all well?"

"Likely nothing. A noise. I'll see to it."

Barnes slipped into the side passage beside the building, the darkness swallowing him whole. The alley beyond was narrow, cobbled, suffocating. His boots echoed softly as he advanced, the shadows pressing close. He suspected Reekey and Bent's meddlesome presence—they were ambitious enough to follow, foolish enough to ruin the stakeout entirely.

He rounded the corner and paused. Nothing. Only the suffocating smell of damp stone and rotting refuse.

Then—

"Pssst."

Barnes froze. Eyes narrowed.

Again, from a bramble of overgrown shrubs: "Pssst—over here."

He spotted the faintest tremor of fabric within the brush.

"Show yourselves," Barnes growled softly. "If you've something to say, say it like civilized men."

"We can't," whispered a strained voice. "Can't risk being seen. But we've got information for you."

A trap, Barnes thought. Reekey and Bent up to their tricks—

perhaps connected to the internal corruption probe that still simmered beneath the Yard's surface. He turned to leave.

"No—wait! It's about Thaddeus Raynsford."

Barnes halted mid-step.

The name was one no one outside the investigation should know.

He approached the bushes casually, feigning the posture of a man relieving himself.

"Oh, come on," the hidden man whispered with disgust. "Truly?"

"It's called a cover," Barnes muttered.

"Right—right, of course." A pause. "Listen. Thaddeus—you must leave him be. He's innocent. Being set up. We can't say by whom."

Barnes stiffened. His hand twitched toward his pocket where his notebook lay hidden. "And how," he whispered coldly, "would you know such a thing?"

"We know his father—Lord Raynsford. That's all that matters. Thaddeus ain't your killer. Nothing to pin on him."

Before Barnes could seize them, a voice behind him cut the night cleanly:

"Ahem."

Barnes turned slowly, icy dread creeping through him.

Detectives Reekey and Bent stood there, eyebrows arched, expressions dripping with insinuation.

"Everything quite all right, Barnes?" Reekey asked with false concern.

Barnes straightened. "Just answering nature's call. Stakeout—you understand."

He strode past them, ire simmering beneath his ribs.

Dealing with those two buffoons for the rest of the night was insult atop injury.

When they reached Dickman, the latter tipped his hat politely, though tension threaded his voice. "Four grown men congregating in one spot seems rather inviting suspicion, wouldn't you say?"

"Oh, that chap across the way is your man?" Bent asked with theatrical innocence.

"Obviously," Barnes replied dryly. "Spread out. Cover different angles. Keep watch."

Reekey and Bent ambled off, far too smug for Barnes's liking.

"That's likely ruined our cover entirely," Barnes muttered.

"Oh, undoubtedly," Dickman murmured. "Mr. Raynsford is not a fool. He surely knows we are watching."

Barnes exhaled in frustration. "Tonight grows more convoluted by the moment."

Dickman gave him a sidelong glance. "And what exactly were you doing back there?"

Barnes hesitated, then answered. "Two men hiding in the shrubbery wanted a word. They feared being seen."

Dickman blinked slowly. "Truly?"

"Yes. And Reekey and Bent interrupted before I could press them."

"Did they offer anything... useful?"

"They knew Thaddeus's name—and Lord Raynsford's. No one else has those names."

Dickman turned back to watching Thaddeus but his voice was low, tense. "Do you believe them?"

"It is something we cannot ignore," Barnes said. "If Mr. Raynsford is being framed, then the question becomes: why? And by whom?"

Dickman nodded, the fog curling around them like a tightening noose. "Then that, my friend, we must uncover."

And somewhere in the night, unseen, the Seance Slayer moved again through London's labyrinthine shadows.

Thaddeus lingered in the murk of the lamplit street, half-shrouded by the curling fingers of fog that slithered across the cobbles. He had long suspected he was being watched, and now—at last—confirmation revealed itself in the most laughably clumsy fashion imaginable.

Across the street, four silhouettes gathered beneath a flickering lamp, their outlines sharp against the vaporous gloom. The detectives—two competent, two decidedly not—whispered and gestured with all the subtlety of grave robbers caught mid-act.

A faint smirk tugged at Thaddeus's lips.

"London is well protected," he murmured, the words edged with quiet irony.

But the amusement faded in an instant.

From the alley behind the detectives, two familiar shapes emerged—hulking forms, thick-shouldered, heads low like jackals slinking from carrion. Thaddeus's breath caught. His father's men. The brutes who had once abducted him in the name of duty... or obedience.

They hurried past, turning down the side street with grim purpose.

A cold knot tightened in Thaddeus's belly. *What were they hunting? And why tonight, of all nights?* If they were here, stalking the same ground as the police, then his father's machinations were deeper—and more dangerous—than he had suspected.

*Perhaps they, not the detectives, are the ones I should be watching,* he thought.

Decision settled over him like a cloak. Slipping from the sanctuary of shadow, Thaddeus began to follow—not the spiritualist's house, not the police's clumsy surveillance—but the two men who served his tyrant father.

Behind him, Barnes and Dickman stiffened.

"There he goes," Dickman muttered.

"And so do we," Barnes answered grimly.

The chase resumed, though Thaddeus, accustomed to moving unseen, held a distinct advantage. He glided along the walls, flattening himself against brick when needed, peering around corners like a phantom. His footfalls were barely whispers on the stone.

Barnes and Dickman exchanged a look of reluctant admiration.

"He moves well," Dickman whispered. "Might make a fair detective, given proper training."

"Better than those two oafs," Barnes muttered darkly, jerking his chin toward Reekey and Bent.

Far ahead, the two blundering detectives barreled forward—straight into Thaddeus's line of sight—and nearly exposed the entire pursuit. Barnes hissed to get their attention but was rewarded only with an arrogant flick of Reekey's wrist, dismissing him like an annoying servant.

"Oh, this is becoming *deliciously* absurd," Dickman muttered under his breath.

Barnes cast him a look that might have curdled milk.

"What? Come now, Barnes. There is a certain... theatricality to all this."

Dickman stifled a laugh. The fog swirled around their boots like restless spirits.

Ahead, the two Raynsford men slipped into a decrepit flat at the end of the street, the building's windows dark, the paint peeling like dead flesh from bone. Barnes took swift note, scribbling the address into his worn notebook. If these were the whispering informants from earlier, he intended to return. Thaddeus had unwittingly guided them straight to a potential breakthrough.

But before Barnes could tuck the notebook away—

A sharp cry shattered the night.

Reekey and Bent, predictably and pathetically, had managed to entangle themselves with two street toughs. The thugs, eager for coin or violence—likely both—had cornered the incompetent pair. The scuffle burst into the street with all the grace of drunkards falling from a cart.

Thaddeus did not linger. With swift, calculated precision, he vanished into a nearby alley, slipping through a snarl of passageways until he emerged on the far side of the neighborhood. Within moments, he had hailed a cab and melted into the depths of London.

Barnes exhaled a long-suffering sigh.

"Shall we assist?" Dickman asked, though his tone suggested he already knew the answer.

"It's not as though the night could decay any further," Barnes muttered. "Come on."

The two detectives hurried across the street to rescue their hapless colleagues from bruises—and ignominy—while the true quarry, and all the answers he carried, rattled away into the fog-drenched labyrinth of the city.

THE CORONER's office lay half-buried in shadow, the flicker of a single oil lamp casting long, skeletal shapes along the stone walls. Damp clung to the air, mingling with the metallic tang of instruments and the sweet, sickly odour of death. Detectives Barnes and Dickman approached the heavy door, its peeling paint reminiscent of a forgotten mausoleum.

Barnes rapped twice.

The door creaked inward to reveal Dr. Earl Keiler—gaunt as a church gargoyle, his perpetual scowl deepened by lamplight.

"Detectives," he muttered, his voice scraping like a rusted hinge.

Barnes tipped his hat. "Doctor Keiler."

The two men stepped inside, Dickman unconsciously drawing his coat closer to himself, as though the cold and silence of the chamber sought to seep into his bones.

Keiler led them to a long wooden table. Upon it lay the late Lorena Baldry, shrouded in a stained linen sheet. Without ceremony, the coroner took hold of the cloth and peeled it back. The stench hit them immediately.

Dickman recoiled, clutching his handkerchief to his nose. "Good Lord..."

Keiler ignored him. "Another night, another horror," he said in a tone that suggested he had become all too familiar with atrocities.

Barnes steeled himself. "What have you found, Doctor?"

Keiler's pale fingers indicated the corpse. "Ah. Well. The tale her flesh tells is familiar... and yet not."

Barnes frowned. "Explain."

The doctor pointed to the gaping slash across the throat. "Here—your customary wound. The mark our murderer favors." His eyes sharpened behind his spectacles. "But observe the bruising. The ligature marks. She was strangled long before her throat was cut."

Dickman swore softly behind his handkerchief.

Keiler reached for a damp cloth and wiped his hands as though distasteful secrets clung to them. "And that is not the worst of it." He gestured Barnes closer. "Look again. Carefully."

Barnes bent over the wound, studying it. After a long moment, his brows knit. "There's hardly any blood. Almost none at all."

"Just so," Keiler said. His voice was almost a whisper. "She was already dying—perhaps dead—when the blade touched her. The heart had ceased its work."

Dickman stepped back, visibly shaken. "The pattern changes yet again."

"Aye," Keiler murmured. "I believe she was slain elsewhere. Transported like a parcel. Then arranged at the warehouse for effect —throat cut later to mimic the earlier crimes."

Barnes straightened, jaw tight. "A deception. Likely to conceal where she truly died."

The coroner nodded, the motion stiff. "There is more still." He reached for Lorena's left hand and lifted it with clinical delicacy. "She fought," he said. "Fought hard. She clawed at her killer with every ounce of strength left to her."

Under her nails were dark flecks—scraps of skin, tissue.

Dickman looked away, swallowing.

Keiler slid his spectacles higher along his nose. "This means your murderer bears her marks. Scratches. Deep ones. Arms, perhaps his face. Somewhere visible."

Barnes's features sharpened, his mind already turning. "So we seek a man wounded by his own victim."

"Aye," said Keiler, folding Lorena's hand back across her breast with surprising gentleness. "And I would wager my life on it."

A hush filled the chamber then—thick, foreboding. The shadows seemed to gather closer, as though listening. Barnes exhaled slowly, the weight of the revelation settling over him like a sentence passed.

"The Seance Slayer grows bolder," he murmured.

"And more dangerous," Dickman added quietly.

Keiler extinguished the lamp. The room sank into dim twilight once more.

"Be swift, Detectives," he said. "Before he leaves another body upon my table."

# CHAPTER TWENTY-FIVE

The carriage rattled through the fog-thick streets, its wheels hissing over damp cobblestones like whispers sliding through a tomb. Thaddeus pressed his gloved hand to the cold glass and peered out into the murk. London at night was a living thing—a sprawling, smoldering beast of soot and shadow—and tonight its breath lay heavy upon him.

Frustration gnawed at his nerves.

He had done so well alone—*well enough, at least*—until the Metropolitan Police, in all their ham-fisted blundering, decided to trail after him like overeager hounds. How was he to hunt a killer when he himself was being hunted by fools?

"A plague on their vigilance," he muttered. "I might slip out the back next time, leave poor Barnes glued to the front like a gargoyle until dawn."

The image delighted him—Barnes stamping his feet in the frost, breath puffing angrily, waiting for a man who had quietly gone out the window an hour earlier. Thaddeus could even see himself strolling back through the front door at sunrise, tipping his hat as though returning from a morning stroll.

He chuckled aloud, startling the driver.

Yet amid the night's annoyances, one golden thread had emerged: He now knew where his father's hired brutes lived.

And should they dare abduct him again for Lord Raynsford's bidding, *this time* he would not be so easily caught.

A shiver traced his spine at the thought of his father—cold, pitiless, every syllable of his speech sharpened like the edge of a blade. That such a man had the same blood as he felt a cosmic cruelty. Thaddeus turned from the window, disgust prickling his skin.

The carriage halted.

Thaddeus stepped down, paid the driver, and entered the boarding house. Mrs. Parsons materialised from the parlour, her stern face framed by stiff lace and suspicion. Yet she said nothing—only gave him a look that hovered between judgement and begrudging tolerance.

"Good night, Mrs. Parsons," he offered gently.

She huffed and retreated to her domain.

Upstairs, Thaddeus divested himself of his coat with weary fingers. The night's fog seemed to cling to him still, heavy and damp. His bones ached, hollowed by suspicion, hunger, and the relentless whispers of accusation that followed him through the streets. *Murderer*, they said. *Charlatan.*

He sank into his chair and tugged off his boots, the leather groaning.

A soft shimmer rippled the air.

Artie drifted down from the ceiling, arms crossed.

"You look dreadful," the ghost announced. "And coming from me, that is quite the indictment."

"Bless you for your kindness," Thaddeus sighed.

"Did your nocturnal adventure yield anything beyond wet boots and a black temper?"

"Nothing. The Metropolitan police are incapable of catching so much as a cold."

Artie snorted. "And this surprises you?"

Thaddeus opened his mouth to retort—

But Artie jerked upright.

"Incoming."

Thaddeus froze.

The air in the room tightened—drawn thin, as though something were pulling it away. Shadows trembled—*peeled back*—as though torn by unseen claws. From their depths a figure slid forth with dreadful grace.

A woman's spectre.

Small. Flickering. Terribly broken.

Her hair drifted around her like dark weeds in a blackened river, though no air stirred. Her form wavered, collapsing between a young woman's shape and something less human, less tethered to mercy.

Her eyes snapped open—glowing with fury, grief, and a pain so righteous it seemed to scorch the walls.

Thaddeus whispered, trembling, "Miss Murray..."

Melisendra drifted in a slow circle about the room. She moved without disturbing the air—yet each passing left the space thinner, harder to breathe. The candle guttered—not from wind, but as though starved of breath.

"Where am I?" she asked. Her voice came in fragments, as though each word had to be forced past something tightening around it.

"You are in my room, Miss Murray. With me—Thaddeus Priest."

Her gaze flicked toward him.

"Oh... yes. You."

She glided past, trailing cold so sharp he winced.

"I am what was done to me," she whispered. "I am the moment it ended. You are the one they speak of."

"They?"

"All of us. All who died in your name."

A bolt of panic stabbed his chest.

"I do not understand—"

"Watch," she hissed, drifting close enough for him to feel the cold seep into his marrow. "I know who killed me."

She lifted one trembling hand and pressed it lightly to his brow. The air vanished.

The room dissolved.

He fell headlong into another world.

He was inside Melisendra's memory—standing in her home as the doorbell chimed, shrill and insistent. Her fear hammered in his own ribs. She opened the door, relief flooding her as she recognised the visitor.

Thaddeus strained to see the face—

But the memory surged forward, unstoppable.

The man followed her inside with scarcely a sound. She spoke, nervous, her words muffled by the rush of blood in his ears.

Then—

A flash of silk.

Hands tightening.

A scarf drawn taut against her throat.

Thaddeus gasped—*her gasp*—as the air left him. Panic roared, vision blurred. He felt her nails digging at the cloth, the desperate stumble, the impossible need to breathe—

A quick gleam of steel.

A brutal slash.

A drowning warmth of blood.

No air. No sound. Only the terrible, closing silence.

His room rushed back around him.

Thaddeus clutched the chair arms, shaking, his breath shredded.

Melisendra hovered before him still—unlike other spirits who vanished after their revelations.

"His name..." she whispered, "...is Victor Jenkins. Find him."

She drifted higher, rising through the ceiling, and her final plea came down to him from the dark above:

"He will kill again... if you do not stop him. He took my breath," she said. "Take his."

Silence.

Thaddeus sat frozen, his heart thundering. He dragged in a breath—too sharp, too desperate—as though he had been drowning.

Artie hovered nearby, face ashen.

"Good heavens," the ghost murmured. "Did you... see all that?"

Thaddeus nodded numbly.

He could still feel the blade.

The choking.

"Yes," he whispered. "Every moment."

"And you intend to catch *him*? Alone? By yourself? Have you lost your senses entirely?"

Thaddeus lifted a trembling hand to his own throat.

"I have no choice, Artie."

"This is madness," Artie protested, voice cracking with fear. "You'll end up like her."

"At least," Thaddeus muttered, "I finally know his name."

"Tell the detective!" Artie cried. "Tell Barnes at once!"

"He will not believe me. He *never* believes. I must provide proof... before Victor Jenkins strikes again."

Artie vanished, leaving Thaddeus alone in the dim lamplight, shivering, staring at nothing.

The fog pressed against the grimy panes of the detectives' office windows, turning the dim lamplight into a sickly yellow haze. Within that cramped chamber—thick with tobacco smoke, boot leather, and the must of neglected papers—Detectives Gerald Reekey and Harold Bent plotted like a pair of carrion crows.

Reekey paced, boots thudding across warped floorboards, his temper as foul as the spittoon into which he spat. The brown smear dribbled down his chin before he swiped at it with a handkerchief already stiff from misuse.

"This can't go on," he growled, the words grinding from his throat like gravel. "With Barnes an' Dickman dogging our every footstep, we'll never catch Thaddeus Priest in the act. Not a chance in Hell."

Bent sat behind his cluttered desk, spectacles low on his nose as he sifted through the murder papers—each page a grim catalogue of blood, ritual, and feminine terror. The lamplight flickered across the coroner's sketches, the identical slashes, the identical staging. A pattern, unmistakable and maddening in its precision.

Reekey stopped pacing and glared at him. "What's churnin' in that skull o' yours? I know that look. Always means trouble."

Bent leaned back slowly, fingers steepled, eyes gleaming with a dark idea that had clearly been fermenting in the recesses of his mind.

"You're right," he said softly. "Absolutely right. If we follow Barnes an' Dickman's methods, we'll never place Thaddeus Priest at the scene. They've spent weeks chasin' shadows with clean consciences and empty hands." He tapped the coroner's report. "But what if we don't follow their methods?"

Reekey blinked. "Eh?"

Bent leaned forward, voice dropping to a conspiratorial whisper that slithered across the desk like smoke.

"Everyone knows he's guilty. Every scrap o' evidence points his way—pattern, timing, proximity. The Seance Slayer and Thaddeus Priest... they orbit the same bloody star."

He paused. "All we lack is a witness."

Reekey whistled low. "Aye... Barnes did complain about that, didn't he? No weapon, no witness, no motive." He smirked, lips curling like old parchment. "So we give 'em a witness, do we?"

Bent's smile was thin and sharp.

"Precisely. A witness we *produce*," he said, "if Fate refuses to provide one."

Reekey rubbed his jaw thoughtfully. "Risky. Who'd stand by us? Who's fool enough to perjure themselves for two coppers yet clever enough to hold their tongue?"

Bent rose, slipped into his coat, and extinguished his lamp with a pinch of gloved fingers.

"Oh, I know just the woman," he said. "Someone who hates spiritualists near as much as you hate Barnes. Someone who owes us a favour... or three."

Reekey grinned, wicked and wolfish.

"Then what are we waitin' for?"

The two men stepped into the hallway, their shadows stretching long behind them like the stalks of gravestones. The fog swallowed them whole as the door creaked shut.

Outside, London slept uneasy—unaware that its defenders had just taken their first deliberate step into damnation.

VICTOR JENKINS SAT ALONE in the dim hush of his lodgings—a narrow, decaying townhouse swallowed between its neighbours like a rotten tooth among healthier ones. The single gas lamp on his desk guttered and hissed, casting long, trembling shadows that seemed eager to abandon him. Yet *he* remained unnervingly still, a figure carved from malice rather than flesh.

He was not an attractive man—worse, he was forgettable. A face neither pleasing nor repulsive, but peculiarly vacant, like a portrait whose painter had lost interest halfway through. His hair was black as soot, coarse and slicked flat, and his eyes... his eyes were pits of such depthless darkness that even lamplight dared not linger there. They reflected nothing—not remorse, not affection, not even curiosity—only a cold, bottomless hunger. A thin mouth, sharp and bloodless, cut across his face like a wound that had learned how to speak.

And when it spoke, how perilous it became.

His voice was smooth, insidious—a velvet noose. It dripped with a false warmth, words sliding forth with the easy confidence of a serpent uncoiling. Many a soul had been lulled by that voice. Many had leaned just a little too close... until it was far too late.

Once, he had tried to be a better man—had sought honest work, proper companionship, the soft glow of domestic affection. But women sensed something in him, something unseen yet unmistakable—a wrongness, a vibration of the soul. They recoiled, their gazes skittering away as though he were a mirror showing too much truth.

When Jenkins realised this—realised that no profession, no polite facade could strip him of the darkness coiled in his marrow—he relinquished the pretense entirely. He embraced the echoing emptiness inside him.

And from that emptiness, he found his true calling.

It paid well. Better still, it demanded no wife, no family, no soul-searching conscience to plague him. His housekeeper, a timid creature, left at nightfall and never asked questions. No one tracked his nocturnal wanderings. No one waited for him to return home. It suited him perfectly. He answered only to himself—and to the shadow that dwelled behind his ribs.

He recalled with satisfaction the three spiritualists from the Royal Polytechnic Institution—the women whose idle chatter had sealed their own fates. Pretty little Miss Murray whom he had visited first, had done his work for him, spreading gossip and lies. He had stalked her carefully, drifting behind her like a spectre in fog. She had spoken his name aloud, spoken of him to her companions with an innocence that made his blood quicken.

And so the warrant of her death had been signed by her own lips, as had the others. He left no frayed edges, no overlooked whispers. He *hated* loose ends—hated them with a fury that bordered on devotion. And so he tied each one off with blood. Three women dead, their voices silenced, their secrets swallowed into the night.

The city thought the Seance Slayer a phantom. Good. Better still, the detectives' focus had narrowed upon his chosen scapegoat—Thaddeus Priest. Poor, foolish Priest, drifting blindly through the smoke-hazed streets, unaware that every clue the police discovered had been placed with meticulous care by Jenkins' own hand. The authorities were closing in on their innocent target, and Jenkins savoured every moment of it—the elegant symmetry of blame, the thrill of watching Order chase the shadow cast by Chaos.

He followed Priest still, stalking him from alleyways and abandoned courtyards, watching the spiritualist's nightly wanderings with a predator's fascination. Yet Priest always slipped just beyond his reach.

*I shall catch you in the act one day,* Jenkins murmured to himself, voice curving like a knife. *And when I do, the whole city will watch you fall.*

He had come perilously close on the night of Lorena Baldry's death—the last name on his recent list. He had not expected Priest to be so near, nor had he sensed the detective lurking in the gloom. For a moment—just one—he had lost control, and that lapse stung him like a brand on the soul. He would not make such an error again.

But he did enjoy the game. Oh, how he loved the game.

The hunt was its own sweet intoxication. The shadows were his allies, the night his confessional, the city his playground. And he would continue the dance—silent, precise, unrelenting—as long as the darkness allowed him breath.

For Victor Jenkins was no mere murderer.

He was a *spectre*, a presence born of the city's deepest rot.

And London, in all its fog-shrouded splendour, would feed him for years to come.

DELTA WEDDALL's door creaked open only a sliver, her sharp eyes peering through the crack like a rat guarding crumbs. The dim corridor outside her slum lodging was thick with foul-smelling fog—a miasma that clung to the walls like mildew. When she saw the two silhouettes, tall and familiar, her painted mouth curved into a wary half-smile.

"Well then," she purred, voice edged with suspicion, "to what do I owe the pleasure of you two fine gentlemen darkenin' my doorstep?"

Detectives Gerald Reekey and Harold Bent stood before her like twin harbingers—ill-omened men whose boots tracked the grime of London's underbelly into every home they visited. They had been to Delta's flat more times than she could count, though never officially. Her line of work demanded discretion; theirs demanded plausible lies. They shared a corrupt symbiosis, these three—parasites feeding off one another in the shadows.

Delta Weddall, a creature of cunning, made her living in the oldest and most treacherous trade. Many a man had awoken lighter of pocket after her company. Few dared report it—no respectable husband wished to confess he had been robbed by the very woman whose embrace he should never have sought. Reekey and Bent had long ago learned to hush those rare complaints, armed with smug insinuations about wives, reputations, and scandal.

Tonight, however, their smiles were tighter. Hungrier.

"We've a small favour to ask," Reekey said, his lips curling back from teeth stained by tobacco and worse. "Nothin' that'll trouble a clever lass like yourself."

Bent stepped forward, his shadow falling over her like a physical thing. "And we're willin' to pay handsomely."

The glint of coin changed everything. Delta's eyes—sharp, calculating—dilated as Bent produced a leather pouch. It sagged heavily in his hand. To a woman living on the knife-edge of survival, that weight spoke louder than any promise.

"Go on, then," she whispered, stepping aside. "Let's hear it."

They entered her narrow, stale-smelling room—the single lamp flickering weakly, illuminating peeling wallpaper and a bed with a sagging mattress. Delta snatched the pouch, weighing it in her palm with a covetous gleam.

"What's the task?" she asked, licking her lips greedily.

Reekey leaned in, breath sour, voice dropping to a conspiratorial murmur. "There's a man. A suspect. A murderer, bold as brass. We know he's guilty, every instinct tells us so—but we need somethin' more. Somethin'... official."

Bent nodded, producing a folded sheet of paper. "All you need do is walk into the precinct an' state you saw him leavin' the house o' one o' the victims. Time's written there. Place too. You'll repeat it, sign it, and that's your part done."

Delta's bravado faltered. "M—murder?" She clutched the bag tighter. "Victims, you say? More than one?"

Her voice trembled, and for the first time the weight of her greed warred with primal fear.

Reekey soothed her with a serpent's smile. "Oh, he won't trouble you. Not once we've got him behind bars. He'll be bound for the hangman's noose before winter chill sets in, mark my words."

"You promise I'll be safe?" she whispered.

Bent swore solemnly, placing a hand—heavy and uninvited—on her arm. "Safe as houses, love. Not a whit o' danger. You have our word."

Her fingers trembled as she reached for the written statement. Bent gently placed it in her hand, his eyes cold and gleaming.

"You just sign this when you come in," he said. "Ask for us, we'll take you straight to our office. We'll pretend to take your statement proper-like. The rest is none o' your concern."

"That's... that's all?" Delta blinked, unable to believe her good fortune.

"That's all, sweetheart," Reekey murmured. "Easy coin."

A long, tense silence stretched—broken only by the distant wail of some wretched soul in the streets below.

At last, Delta nodded. "Fine. Tell me when."

Reekey's grin widened into something unholy. Bent's eyes narrowed with satisfaction.

And in that squalid little flat, beneath the flickering lamplight, the trap was sprung. A false witness secured. A corrupt bargain sealed.

And far across the city, Thaddeus Priest's invisible noose tightened—one thread closer to slipping around his innocent neck.

In a cramped lodging overlooking a narrow, fog-choked lane, Victor Jenkins sat before a warped looking-glass. A single candle flickered beside him, its flame guttering each time the wind slid beneath the ill-fitted windowpane. Shadows crawled along the walls like living things—thin, hungry silhouettes that seemed to lean closer to him as he worked.

Jenkins hissed softly as he dabbed a bloodied cloth against the raw, angry scratches striping his throat and jaw. The mirror reflected a man assembled from darkness—coal-black hair hanging in damp ropes, eyes like polished obsidian, and the long, slit mouth of a man who rarely smiled but often smirked.

"Vicious little vixen," he murmured, inspecting the crescent wounds beneath the harsh yellow light. "I underestimated you."

He leaned closer, turning his head to better see the deepest gash carved by Lorena Baldry's desperate nails. A thin line of blood welled up yet again, trailing down to the hollow of his collarbone. Jenkins followed it with a finger, staring at the smear with something almost like admiration.

"You fought well," he whispered to the empty room. "A pity it amounted to nothing."

The boards above him groaned; someone in the flat overhead trudged across the floor. Jenkins stilled, listening. Then his lips twisted into a private, poisonous smile.

Clovis and Erwin, Lord Raynsford's brutes, lived upstairs—useful enough when paid, silent as rats when not. And more importantly, ready to move a body when commanded. They had served him well.

Jenkins returned to his wounds, pulling open a small wooden box. Inside lay strips of clean cloth, laudanum, a needle and thread, and a dark glass vial. He lifted the vial and tilted it in the candlelight. Thick, tar-like antiseptic clung to the inside.

"Can't have the detectives sniffing about," he said as he uncorked it. "Not with evidence written plainly across my skin."

He poured the liquid onto a cloth and pressed it to his throat. The stinging was immediate and vicious; his breath sucked in sharply.

The candlelight caught his reflection—his face contorting into something monstrous, something that looked like the soul of a man long rotted.

When the pain subsided, Jenkins wrapped his neck with practised precision. Each movement was careful, meticulous—he was a craftsman attending to his tools. And he considered his body a tool; a vessel for necessity, for purpose, for the exquisite artistry of death.

He tied off the bandage and sat back. For a moment he simply listened to the city beyond the window: carriage wheels, distant shouting, the melancholy toll of a church bell marking the hour.

A smile—chilling in its composure—spread slowly across his lips.

"They will search for a wounded man," he said softly, "and London is full of wounded men."

He shrugged on his dark coat, pulling the collar high to obscure the fresh bandages. His gloved fingers smoothed the fabric with care.

"No loose ends," he reminded himself. It was a mantra. A creed.

But tonight... tonight there had been interference.

A detective, too close.

A spiritualist, almost too perceptive.

And Thaddeus Priest, irritatingly persistent.

His eyes—a dead, lightless black—glinted with new resolve.

"No loose ends," he repeated. "And no more mistakes."

Outside, the fog thickened against his window like breath on glass.

Inside, Victor Jenkins blew out the candle, plunging the room into darkness—save for the faint reflection of his smile lingering in the glass.

# CHAPTER TWENTY-SIX

Thaddeus knew well that Victor Jenkins was a creature of habit—a vulture who circled only when the scent of a séance hung in the air. The killer would not strike without an audience, a gathering, a pretext wrapped in candlelight and superstition. And this time, Thaddeus vowed, no innocent soul would fall because of him.

But first, he must shed the men who dogged his every step.

The Metropolitan Police—two detectives at first, now four—hovered about him like carrion crows, alerting Jenkins each night with their clumsy shadows and restless boot steps. Thaddeus could not hunt his quarry while being hunted himself. The chain must be broken.

He had a plan. A dangerous one. An inevitable one.

As he fastened the last brass button of his frock coat, a thin shimmer of cold air drifted down from the ceiling. Arthur—Artie—materialised with a lazy spin, arms crossed, expression petulant.

"Are we ever going to start doing séances again?" he asked with spectral exasperation. "I'm bored enough to haunt the wallpaper."

Thaddeus managed a weary half-smile. "Yes. In time. When my name is cleared and the detectives cease lurking beneath my window like footpads waiting for alms."

Artie floated closer, narrowing his translucent eyes. "Speaking of detectives... you still haven't told that Barnes fellow about Jenkins, have you?"

Thaddeus stiffened. "No. And I will not. Not yet."

"You stubborn, cloth-headed mortal," Artie muttered. "You have the killer's name. What more do you need?"

"Proof," Thaddeus said, voice tight. "Proof that cannot be dismissed as superstition, or delirium, or 'ghostly nonsense.' Barnes does not believe in spirits. If I went to him with only a vision, he would clap me in irons rather than Jenkins."

Artie drifted closer, too close—near enough that Thaddeus felt the disturbance of him rather than any touch. A cold shiver followed. "Jenkins hasn't shown his nasty, murderous snout all week. And you know why? Because those bumbling constables tramp after you like elephants on parade. You'll never catch him with that entourage."

"That is why," Thaddeus said quietly, "I intend to lose them."

Artie regarded him in silence, then let out a long, dramatic sigh.

"Very well. I see your sense has abandoned ship and left you to drown."

He placed a ghostly hand over his heart in mock sorrow.

"When you die out there, do try to make it somewhere scenic. We can haunt this place together—take midnight strolls through the graveyard, frighten the neighbors, rattle a few windows. It could be fun!"

His laughter echoed like wind through a crypt as he winked out of sight.

Thaddeus closed his eyes, fighting the faint tremor in his hands. Artie's macabre humor grated at him tonight. The darkness outside pressed against the windowpanes, eager, hungry.

He donned his overcoat, slipped a small lantern into his pocket, and tightened his gloves.

He was dressed for a séance—and for danger.

With a final breath, he stepped toward the door, knowing full well that once he crossed its threshold, the night might swallow him whole.

Night pressed heavily upon the narrow street, the fog curling low like a restless creature seeking purchase along the cobblestones. Detective Barnes stamped his boots against the chill, then cupped his hands and breathed warm air into them, his breath rising in pale wisps. The cold gnawed at his fingers, crept through his coat seams, and settled deep in his bones.

Beside him stood Detective Dickman—coat unbuttoned, collar loose, as though the icy London night were but a mild inconvenience. Barnes cast him a glare born of long-suffering irritation.

"Button your coat, man. You'll catch your death."

Dickman shrugged, utterly unfazed. "Cold's never bothered me, Barnes. You're the one who keeps the coal scuttle half-empty."

Barnes huffed, remembering the arguments at the office hearth—Dickman insisting the room was stifling, Barnes insisting he could see his own breath. Of late, though, he counted his blessings. At least Reekey and Bent had ceased appearing at their stakeouts.

Good riddance.

Barnes did not know where those two had slithered off to—nor did he particularly care. Their presence had been a curse upon the investigation, their ambition eclipsed only by their incompetence. With them gone, the nights had grown quieter, though no less tedious.

The boarding house loomed opposite them, its windows dim and its facade swallowed by fog. Night after night, they stood vigil. Night after night, Thaddeus Priest remained within—silent as a grave, motionless as a stone. It was as though he had abandoned the very act of living and retreated into some private shadow.

Barnes found himself wondering what kept the man hidden away. Fear? Guilt? Or simply exhaustion from being hunted by police and killer alike? Their last sight of him had been during that disastrous evening when Reekey and Bent got themselves into such a brawl that half the neighborhood had been roused from their beds.

Barnes grimaced at the memory.

Suddenly, a sound cracked the stillness—a door slamming somewhere down the lane. Not the boarding house door, but another nearby, hollow and echoing. The fog seemed to swallow the noise almost immediately, leaving its direction uncertain.

Barnes straightened, heart lifting at the prospect of action, even if it led nowhere. Anything to break the monotony. Anything to banish the damp worming its way through his marrow.

Dickman glanced at him, lifting a brow. "Not our quarry."

"No," Barnes replied, "but it's something."

The two men returned to their vigil, postures rigid, breaths fogging the night. They would remain through the watches of darkness, steadfast as tomb sentinels.

For duty demanded they wait.

And wait they would—

until dawn, or death, or the killer struck again.

Thaddeus slipped silently through the boarding house's rear door, the night folding around him like a sable cloak. A damp wind curled through the alley, carrying with it the distant toll of a church bell and the faint stench of coal-smoke. He moved quickly, boots glancing over puddled cobblestones, until he emerged several streets away where a lone Hansom cab awaited—just as he had arranged.

"Driver," he murmured, handing up a folded slip of paper, "to this address—at once, if you please."

Before climbing into the cab, he cast a backward glance down the long, lamplit street. There, half-concealed in the gloom, stood Detectives Barnes and Dickman—the former stamping against the cold, the latter stiff and statuesque beneath the gaslight. They waited for him to exit through the *front* door—faithful, predictable, and, in his estimation, hopelessly obtuse.

A faint, wicked smile curved Thaddeus's lips as he slipped inside the carriage.

Let them stand in the cold until dawn.

Tonight, he sought out Lilah Casey—a modest spiritualist of lesser renown, yet willing, astonishingly, to allow him to attend her séance. Whether she would turn him away upon recognizing him was another matter entirely. He doubted she'd welcome the man London whispered about in fearful tones. But it mattered little. He was not seeking revelations nor keen insights this night.

He sought only Victor Jenkins.

He needed bait.

And he needed to be seen.

The cab clattered to a stop before a narrow shopfront whose windows were painted black for privacy. Miss Casey's place of business. A single lantern above the door cast a pool of amber light upon the pavement. Thaddeus stepped out, lifted his chin, and allowed himself to be conspicuous.

*Let him see me,* he thought. *Let Jenkins watch and follow.*

Guests began to gather—timid-looking women in shawls, a few men in sombre coats, each one eyeing the establishment with a mixture of dread and anticipation. Thaddeus tipped his hat politely as he joined them. It felt almost strange to be among people again on such innocent terms—to walk openly, to breathe night air without the weight of suspicion pressing down upon him.

At precisely eight o'clock, the door opened, and they were ushered inside.

The chamber was dim and close, smelling faintly of beeswax and wilted flowers. Candles flickered from sconces set along the walls. A single round table lay in the centre, draped in velvet, a lone candle burning at its heart. Lilah Casey greeted her clients herself—no assistant, no theatrics. Her presence was slight yet earnest, her eyes sharp enough to betray the flicker of recognition when she glanced at Thaddeus.

So she *did* know his name.

He answered her look with a gentle nod, hoping to put her at ease. She turned away quickly, smoothing her skirts, and gestured for them to sit.

"Please, arrange yourselves thus—lady, gentleman, lady, gentleman," she said softly. "We shall form a circle of balanced energies."

Thaddeus took his place opposite her, their gazes crossing for the briefest moment before she looked down and placed her hands upon the table.

"You may rest your fingers so," Lilah instructed, demonstrating. "Little finger to little finger with the person beside you. Do not fear. There is nothing to alarm you."

The guests complied, shuffling nervously in their seats. Silence settled—a fragile, anticipatory thing.

"I am a trance medium," Lilah said in a quiet, reverent tone. "I shall begin by withdrawing my senses from this world. Do not be troubled if I seem distant. I merely open the door between realms."

She closed her eyes. Her breathing deepened. The candle flame wavered.

And then—Thaddeus felt it.

A familiar shift in the air.

A cooling, a thinning—like the world holding its breath.

*Impossible,* he thought. *Could she be genuine?*

He leaned forward ever so slightly, schooling his expression to hide the surge of excitement rising within him.

Lilah's eyelids fluttered. A shimmer of pale light gathered at her right side, condensing slowly into the shape of a man—first a hollow outline, then a suggestion of features.

Thaddeus's heart leapt—

And then the ghost's visage sharpened into unmistakable mockery.

Artie.

Hovering beside Lilah Casey. Making faces.

Thaddeus barked out a laugh before he could stop himself—a loud, booming, wholly inappropriate sound that shattered the sombre atmosphere. Gasps echoed around the table. Lilah started violently, nearly knocking over the central candle.

"I—I beg your pardon," Thaddeus stammered, mortified. "Deepest apologies. Truly. I did not mean—"

The guests glared daggers at him. Lilah pressed a trembling hand to her brow, attempting to salvage her waning trance. But the spell was broken. Every attempt she made afterward faltered. Her voice trembled. Her hands shook. The room's tenuous magic collapsed like a punctured veil.

Thaddeus slumped inwardly, awash with guilt.

Artie, drifting lazily above the table, grinned at him with wicked delight.

*Just wait until I get you home,* Thaddeus thought darkly.

He had not meant to disrupt the séance. He had *never* wished to humiliate another medium—authentic or otherwise. Yet by night's end, Lilah could barely look at him, her cheeks flushed with embarrassment and failure.

Thaddeus left the shop weighed with remorse—and with a growing certainty that drawing Victor Jenkins out of hiding would prove far harder than he had hoped.

NIGHT HAD LAID its heavy shroud across London when Lilah Casey at last extinguished the final candle in her small spiritualist's shop. The séance had been a disaster—a tangle of missteps, stammers, and shattered concentration. Her cheeks still burned with humiliation. *If not for that wretched man's outburst,* she thought bitterly, *the spirits might have been generous, the clients suitably impressed, and her purse the heavier for it.*

She locked the door with trembling fingers and stepped out into the glistening alley. Rain earlier that evening had turned the cobblestones slick as glass; the storm had howled through her séance, lightning splitting the sky in jagged white flashes while thunder rolled like an angry god. *Those are the nights one dreams of,* she sighed. Clients adored theatrics—so long as the medium did not falter.

She picked her way carefully toward the street, skirts lifted slightly from the wet stones. When she reached the alley's mouth, she paused, peering out with cautious eyes. A lamplighter stood nearby, his pole raised, coaxing a sputtering wick into warm flame. The gentle glow spilled outward—and in its golden pool stood a lone, hooded figure.

The man leaned against a lamppost as though carved from the night itself. His stillness was unnerving, his features lost to the deep shadow cast by his hood. A cold shiver unfurled across Lilah's spine, settling like frost in her bones. She stared a moment too long, trying in vain to read his face.

The lamplighter stepped closer, and Lilah seized the moment, darting past him into the street. Her breath came faster. Safety was a thin and fleeting thing in London after dark, and tonight the city felt poised on a knife's edge.

As she proceeded, the sense of unease tightened around her ribs. Her steps quickened.

Then—soft, unmistakable footfalls behind her.

Her heart lurched.

Every paper in the city had warned of it: *the murders, the spiritualists*, the killer who moved unseen. She should have hired a cab...

she should never have walked alone. Lilah hurried on, nearly running now. The street was scant of people, the windows shuttered, the lamps casting only feeble halos in the thickening mist.

The footfalls followed.

She turned sharply onto her own street—narrow, lined with elms whose black branches clawed at the sky. She reached her small gate, fingers slick with sweat fumbling desperately at the latch. The metal rattled under her trembling grip.

"Oh, curse it—open, blast you—open!" she whispered, half-sobbing.

At last it gave way. She slipped through, skirts swirling, and whirled to face the figure who had trailed her so relentlessly.

The man stepped into a slant of moonlight.

Leaves from the trees overhead cast broken shadows upon his face, but even so, she recognised him instantly.

"I beg your pardon, Miss Casey," he said, voice gentle, expression earnest. "I fear I startled you. I only wished to ensure you reached home unmolested. You have my sincerest apologies."

Lilah blinked, breath still ragged. "It's you, is it not? The gentleman from the séance. The one who—well—ruined my evening?"

Thaddeus Priest bowed his head, contrite. "I am afraid so. And I am deeply sorry for the disruption I caused."

"Well," she sniffed, straightening her shoulders, "you cost me a fair purse tonight, sir."

"Then allow me to remedy that."

He reached lightly across the gate, placing five shillings into her open palm.

Lilah stared, struck speechless. Kindness was not something she had counted on tonight. She closed her fingers over the coins and dipped into a small curtsy. "My thanks to you, Mr. Priest."

Thaddeus tipped his hat. "Good evening, Miss Casey."

"Good evening," she called softly from her doorstep before slipping inside and bolting the door.

Thaddeus lingered for a moment upon the pavement, his breath ghosting in the cool air. Satisfied she was safe, he at last turned to depart.

Yet he did not see—could not see—the faintest ripple of movement across the street, where among the bushes another figure crouched in watchful silence.

Someone else had been waiting. Someone who had not lost sight of him for a single moment.

And the night swallowed the watcher whole.

# CHAPTER TWENTY-SEVEN

Thaddeus had scarcely set foot upon the main thoroughfare when a queer prickle passed along his spine. Across the mist-drenched street, half-concealed beneath the drooping boughs of the plane-trees, stood a solitary figure—a man draped in black, his coat long and severe, a tall top-hat casting his features into impenetrable shade. The gaslamp beside him sputtered, as if uneasy in his presence.

Thaddeus slowed.

Then he turned deliberately, stepping from the curb to cross the slick stones.

The man—Jenkins—shifted back at once, as though the very shadows recoiled with him. He was ready to attack if need be; Thaddeus sensed it at once in the man's stiffened posture, his retreating gait, the coil of danger in his silhouette.

But Thaddeus had taken no more than two steps when the night exploded around him.

From the hedgerow sprang Detectives Reekey and Bent, their boots skidding on damp cobbles as they seized him by both arms.

"Got you now, lad," Reekey hissed, breath sour as he yanked Thaddeus close. "Caught in the act, as it were."

"In the act of what?" Thaddeus snapped, struggling as he twisted his neck to see past them. "Seeing a lady safely home? A crime most foul, I'm sure."

But his words faltered as he caught sight of Jenkins—still standing across the street.

Still watching.

And—most maddening of all—laughing silently, shoulders trembling with mirth at Thaddeus's predicament.

Thaddeus renewed his struggle violently.

"You blind fools—release me! You're leaving Miss Casey unguarded! If harm comes to her—"

Bent jerked him hard. "Oh, spare us your theatrics. We know what you are."

"And what name do you give me tonight?" Thaddeus spat.

Bent's face twisted with triumph. "Why, *the Seance Slayer*, of course. We've a witness who places you at Madam Medora's murder. This time, you won't be wriggling free."

A heavy Black Maria rumbled up beside them, lanterns rattling, the Metropolitan Police insignia gleaming faintly through the fog. The iron-bound door creaked open like the maw of some mechanical beast.

"Inside with him," Reekey grunted.

Thaddeus was shoved forward without ceremony. His shoulder struck the interior wall and the wooden floor rang beneath his boots. The door slammed behind him, the lock snapping shut with a finality that seemed to echo up the length of the street.

Across the way, Jenkins watched with growing delight.

He had lingered only to ensure Thaddeus saw him—saw him free, unburdened, and utterly beyond the reach of the law. Now, with his prey caged and helpless, the night itself seemed to purr at Jenkins's good fortune.

"Well played," he whispered to no one, a malign smile slicing the gloom.

He turned and slipped into the narrow lane beside him, the fog swallowing him whole. His laughter—thin, wicked, and without humanity—trailed behind him like a ribbon of poisoned air.

Lilah Casey would live this night.

And suspicion—planted, cultivated, and paid for—would flourish upon Thaddeus Priest's grave.

THE BLACK MARIA rattled through the fog-choked streets like a hearse bearing the condemned. Within its boarded confines, the air reeked of cheap gin, stale tobacco, and the sour press of unwashed bodies. Detectives Reekey and Bent—two coarse silhouettes lit faintly by the swaying lantern overhead—were in a state of vulgar jubilation.

"Ain't it grand?" Reekey crowed, elbowing his partner with unrestrained glee. "We'll be gettin' medals for this, mark me words."

Bent snorted, his laughter a harsh bark. "Medals? Promotions, more like. Chief'll be raisin' his glass to *us* now, not those pompous popinjays Barnes and Dickman."

"Aye," Reekey agreed, leaning in, his breath a fetid gust that made Thaddeus's stomach churn. "Them two with their rules and their righteous airs... always struttin' about as if the job belongs to *them alone*. Well, we've shown 'em now. Top dogs—that's what we'll be."

Bent slapped his knee and guffawed. "Wait till they hear it—*we* took Thaddeus Priest, the infamous Seance Slayer, right out from under their noses. Oh, the looks on their mugs!"

Their raucous merriment bounced off the dark wooden walls, the sound mingling with the clatter of wheels over cobblestone. Thaddeus sat chained between them, face pale, the reek of their sweat-soured garments threatening to turn his stomach inside out.

"Look at 'im," Bent sneered, reaching over to tap Thaddeus's cheek with grimy fingers. "Green as bilge-water. I'd be green too, lad, knowin' the gallows rope's bein' measured."

Thaddeus recoiled from the man's touch, jaw tight, breath shallow. How long would this torment last? How many more minutes trapped between these swaggering buffoons before salvation—however grim—came?

His answer arrived in the form of the wagon's abrupt halt. The doors swung open, cold night air rushing in like a baptism. Several patrolmen stepped forward, their lanterns illuminating Thaddeus as they hauled him out like cargo.

Inside the precinct, the gaslamps flared with a sickly yellow glow as his shackles were removed and he was thrust into a holding cell. Bars clanged shut behind him.

The noise had scarcely died when a thunderous voice cut through the station.

"What is the meaning of this? Who have you brought in at this hour?"

Chief Inspector Coghill stormed into view, his greatcoat swirling around him like a storm cloud.

Reekey puffed out his chest. "Evenin', Chief. We've arrested the Seance Slayer."

"What?" Coghill stared, aghast.

"Aye," Bent chimed in proudly. "Caught 'im loiterin' outside a spiritualist's home, ready to strike. We've a witness statement and everythin'." He produced a folded document with a flourish.

Reekey added, "Saw 'im sneakin' out the back of his lodgings, so we followed. Caught 'im afore he could spill more blood. Prevented another murder, we did."

They rocked gleefully on their heels, beaming like schoolboys awaiting praise.

Chief Inspector Coghill dabbed his brow with a handkerchief, his face a mixture of relief and something darker. "This is... unexpected. Remarkable news. The Lord Mayor shall be informed at once."

Then, casually—too casually—he asked,

"And where are Detectives Barnes and Dickman this evening?"

"Oh, we left 'em at Priest's boarding house," Reekey replied, smirking. "Bet they're still standin' there waitin' for him to come out the front door!"

Both men burst into laughter once more, their triumph as foul as the smoke-stained rafters above them.

But they failed entirely to notice the fleeting shadow that crossed Coghill's face—one of dread, calculation, and dawning fury.

"Dunhill!" the Chief bellowed.

A young bobby scrambled forward. "Sir! Present, sir!"

"Fetch Detectives Barnes and Dickman at once. Obtain the address from these two."

Reekey and Bent barely paused in their self-congratulation, nudging one another as though already imagining their names etched upon commendations.

They had no notion—none at all—that the ground was shifting beneath their feet.

Nor that the truth, dark and merciless as the London fog, would soon come for them all.

The night had sunk deep into its own bones, thick with fog, when Detectives Barnes and Dickman kept their vigil beneath the dim gaslamp. Barnes stamped his feet against the creeping chill, muttering curses into his collar as his breath stirred faintly in the damp air.

"I don't think he's comin' out," Dickman observed, his voice calm as ever, though the wind tugged fiercely at his coat—left scandalously open as though he were impervious to earthly chills.

"Aye," Barnes replied, rubbing his gloved hands together, "by this hour he's usually well gone. Something's amiss."

Just then, the Black Maria rumbled down the lane, its lantern swinging like a solitary, baleful eye. The two detectives watched it creak past, wheels groaning under its own grim purpose, before it vanished round the corner.

"Strange to see the wagon abroad at this hour," Dickman murmured.

"Likely roundin' up some sodden drunks from the taverns," Barnes said, though his tone betrayed his unease.

Moments later, the wagon appeared again—rolling out from the next street, this time slowing... slowing... until it halted before them with a hiss of brakes and the ominous finality of a tombstone settling into place.

"Well then," Dickman said dryly, "I suppose *we're* the sodden miscreants."

The door creaked open and Bobby Dunhill thrust his head out, cheeks red from the cold, chin strap askew.

"Gentlemen," he said breathlessly, "the Chief bids me fetch you at once."

Barnes and Dickman exchanged a weighted glance—silent, sharp, and full of foreboding—before climbing into the wagon.

As the doors shut behind them, Barnes asked, "Any notion why the Chief wants us dragged in?"

Dunhill scratched beneath his chin strap; the thing had plagued him all day. "Aye, sirs. They've caught the Seance Slayer."

"WHAT?" both detectives thundered, their voices filling the cramped interior.

Dunhill blinked. "Detectives Reekey and Bent, they says. Brought him in not half an hour past. One Thaddeus Priest, in the flesh."

Barnes and Dickman looked at one another—a whole conversation, silent and dark, passed between their eyes. Dickman's brow furrowed in bafflement. Barnes's face hardened into something grimmer, colder than the night outside.

"We've stood in front of Priest's boarding house since before the bells struck eight," Barnes said, voice low with restrained fury. "He has not crossed that threshold."

"Well, sirs," Dunhill said, tugging again at the cursed strap, "I heard Reekey and Bent talkin' of it. Claims he slipped out the back whilst you waited at the front. Says they tailed him... and nabbed him clean."

Barnes's jaw knotted so tight his teeth might've cracked. Dickman turned to the fog-sheathed window, staring out into the ghostly streets as though they might whisper the truth.

Neither man spoke another word.

They didn't have to.

They already knew something stank—foul as grave earth—and it was no spirit that had set this trap.

Barnes stormed into the station like a tempest breaking over the threshold, the great oak doors shuddering at his passage. Dickman followed close behind, long strides echoing upon the stone corridor. Their eyes were fixed upon the stairway leading down to the cells.

But before they reached the steps, a voice—sharp as a drawn blade—cut through the hall.

"Barnes. Dickman."

The two detectives halted as though seized by invisible hands. They exchanged a glance—grim, wary—and veered toward the Chief Inspector's office.

Chief Inspector Coghill sat rigid behind his desk, jaw set, eyes shadowed with strain. The gaslamp at his elbow cast a wavering light that made the lines of his face appear harsher, older.

"Shut the door," he said quietly.

The click of the latch was a death knell.

Barnes and Dickman took their seats, both attempting—unsuccessfully—to seem composed. The Chief's gaze drifted between them like a man choosing which rope to pull on the gallows.

"For reasons entirely beyond my comprehension," Coghill began, voice low with contained fury, "I have Thaddeus Priest cooling his heels in the cells below. Reekey and Bent appear convinced he is our Seance Slayer. Would either of you care to explain this madness?"

Barnes shifted, the leather of his chair groaning beneath him. "Sir, we were heading down this very moment to see the matter for ourselves. We've no idea how—or why—those two... *gentlemen* took it upon themselves to apprehend Mr. Priest."

The word "gentlemen" dripped from Barnes's tongue like something foul.

Coghill's eyes narrowed. "I see. And remind me—were *you* not placed in charge of this investigation?"

"Yes, sir," Barnes answered at once, spine stiff. "Entirely so."

"And yet," the Chief pressed, his voice sharpening, "you are as ignorant of Priest's arrest as a boot boy fresh through the door."

The air grew colder. Dickman swallowed hard.

"Sir," Barnes said, choosing his words with care, "Reekey and Bent gave us no indication—none whatsoever—that they intended anything of the sort. In fact, we explicitly told them *not* to interfere."

Coghill said nothing. Instead, he snatched a folded paper from his desk and flung it toward Barnes. It skittered across the wood like a dead leaf.

"And I suppose you know nothing of this either?"

Barnes unfolded it slowly.

A witness statement.

Signed by one Delta Weddall.

Barnes felt his stomach turn. Dickman's lips curled in disgust. They both knew her reputation—and the worthlessness of any testimony bought from her.

The Chief leaned forward, his voice rising like distant thunder.

"I was on the verge—*the verge,* Barnes—of drafting a most welcome missive to the Lord Mayor, declaring this nightmare over. Shall I send it? Shall I announce to London that the Seance Slayer is in chains below?"

"No!" Barnes blurted, far too loudly—then immediately stiffened. "No, sir," he corrected, lowering his tone. "I... I strongly advise against that. Not at this time."

A long, dreadful silence followed.

Coghill finally exhaled through his nose, a sound full of pent-up wrath.

"Then get to the bottom of this—*both of you.* I will not move a finger until you tell me it is safe to do so."

His hand came down hard upon the desk.

"And BE QUICK ABOUT IT, or Heaven help the lot of us."

Barnes and Dickman rose at once, their shadows stretching long behind them as they left the office—two men walking into a storm they had not created, but would now be forced to endure.

Night lay heavy over Raynsford Manor, a suffocating shroud of fog pressed against the windowpanes. Within, Lord Horace Raynsford slumbered—until a frantic pounding at his chamber door shattered the stillness.

He sat bolt upright, enraged.

"What devil's din is this at such an ungodly hour!" he thundered.

The door creaked open, revealing Jackson—not his usual steadfast, polished self, but pale, trembling, as though he had glimpsed something lurking behind the veil of night.

"Forgive me, my lord," Jackson stammered, voice quivering, "but a... a message has arrived. The driver... he did not wait, sir. He said—quite firmly—that this was to reach your hands at once."

From down the corridor came the soft pad of feet, and then Lady Judith appeared, her night-robe trailing like mist behind her. Her face was drawn, anxious, as though she sensed ill tidings stirring the air.

"Horace? What is happening?" she whispered, her voice taut with dread.

"Give it here," Horace snapped, ignoring her entirely.

Jackson stepped forward with a silver tray, the envelope resting upon it like a portent. His hands trembled so violently the tray rattled.

Horace snatched the letter and ripped it open. The dim candlelight flickered as his eyes scanned the page—then widened, gleamed —and a grotesque little giggle escaped his lips.

Jackson recoiled. Disgust—the truest, rawest emotion he had ever allowed himself—twisted across his features. He needed no words; he knew the content of that letter. *Thaddeus arrested for murder.* And Lord Horace, of course, was delighted beyond measure.

"Jackson!" Horace barked. "Rouse the coachman. Have the carriage brought round at once. I leave for London within the quarter-hour!"

He practically sprang from his bed, patting about for his dressing coat, humming with manic delight. Jackson stood there a moment—unsure whether to fetch the carriage or assist the lord's frantic dressing.

"Don't stand gawping!" Horace snapped. "Go, go—you dull creature!"

Jackson fled the room, grateful to escape.

Meanwhile Lady Judith had stepped closer, pale hands clasped to her breast.

"Horace, I insist you tell me this instant what calamity prompts such... such behaviour."

Horace froze mid-stride, as though only now recalling her presence. He turned slowly.

"Yes, my dear... grave news. Grave indeed."

He relished the words far too much.

"Our son—Thaddeus—has been arrested for murder."

Judith gasped, staggering as though struck. One hand flew to her throat; the other reached blindly for the wall.

"Murder? Oh Heaven preserve him... no, no..." Tears welled and spilled freely.

For perhaps the first time in his life, Horace seemed momentarily unsettled by her distress. A glimmer—only a glimmer—of human feeling crossed his face.

"My dear Judith," he said, adopting a tone of wholly unfamiliar softness, "do not distress yourself. I shall set matters aright. Rest assured—I shall bring our boy home. All will be well."

He guided her gently from his chamber, patting her arm as though she were a nervous horse.

"Now, now... leave this to me. Trust in your husband."

He ushered her out and swiftly closed the door—so swiftly the latch snapped like a trap.

Judith remained in the hall, trembling. Her tears glimmered in the lamplight as she turned to seek Jackson—the only other soul in the manor who might tell her the truth of what her husband rejoiced in.

And somewhere beyond the fogged windows, darkness moved... waiting.

# CHAPTER TWENTY-EIGHT

Thaddeus sat upon the narrow cot, hands loosely clasped between his knees, staring into the dim, gaslit corridor beyond the iron bars. The cold stone breathed damply upon him, and the hush of the cell pressed in like a burial shroud. *Was this how his life would end?*

Condemned for sins not his own, while the true monster roamed free?

From somewhere down the corridor came the slow groan of an opening door, its hinges shrieking like a soul in torment. Footsteps followed—steady, echoing, purposeful. Thaddeus's heart stumbled. Shadows elongated across the passage, sliding toward him like black fingers reaching through the dark.

Then at last, two familiar silhouettes emerged.

Detectives Barnes and Dickman stepped into the faint yellow glow of the lanterns. Thaddeus let out a relief so sharp it nearly cut him. Better these two than the other pair of bunglers whose presence made his blood run cold.

Barnes lifted a ring of keys that jingled softly, faint and thin in the corridor's hush. He spoke not a word as he unlocked the cell door, the metal clank echoing down the passage.

"Am I to be released, then?" Thaddeus asked, rising, a fragile hope trembling within him.

"No," Barnes said, his voice low and grave. "But I must confirm something. And I trust you'll cooperate?"

"Certainly," replied Thaddeus. "I wish to be of whatever help I may."

Barnes regarded him with tired, wary eyes—eyes that had seen too many lies, too much death, and were hungry for truth. He stepped into the cramped cell, the air seeming to tighten around them.

"Hold out your arms."

Thaddeus complied. Barnes took each arm carefully, turning them over, lifting the sleeves to expose pale skin. His touch was clinical, searching—measuring Thaddeus against horrors witnessed elsewhere.

"If you do not mind," Barnes murmured, fingers slipping to the collar of Thaddeus's shirt.

He pulled it aside—first left, then right—examining throat and skin with a grim thoroughness.

At last he stepped back.

"Thank you," he said, voice unreadable.

Barnes, without another word, stepped out of the cell. The iron door swung shut, the lock snapping into place with a finality that made Thaddeus's stomach twist.

The two detectives departed, their tread receding into the oppressive stillness, leaving Thaddeus alone once more with the shadows—and whatever shape his fate might yet assume among them.

THE FOG PRESSED thick against the windowpanes of the detectives' cramped office, muffling the gaslights outside and casting long, wavering shadows across the walls. Barnes shut the door behind them with a grim finality.

"Well then," he murmured, removing his gloves with weary precision, "what *do* we know?" His tone made it clear the question required no answer.

Dickman leaned against the edge of the desk, arms folded. "We know Miss Baldry fought like the very devil himself, and that she left the marks of her struggle beneath her nails." He paused meaningfully. "And we know Mr. Thaddeus Priest carries no such wounds."

Barnes nodded, pacing slowly in the dim room. "We know, too, that the murders were committed with a blade of some fashion—and Mr. Priest bore no weapon when he was dragged off like a common cutpurse."

"Aye," Dickman agreed. "And let's not forget the so-called witness." His lip curled. "Delta Weddall. A woman whose word is worth less than a bent ha'penny, if you ask me."

Barnes stopped pacing. "So we conclude that the arrest of Mr. Priest was—how shall we put it?—spectacularly premature."

Dickman gave a dark chuckle. "Aye. That, and we still have a murderer in London's streets, moving as silent as smoke while those two buffoons crow over their 'victory.'"

"The Chief wanted corruption rooted out in his department," Barnes said quietly. "I daresay we've found the stink."

Before Dickman could reply, there came a knock—light, jaunty, and unbearably self-satisfied.

Barnes sighed. "Enter."

Detectives Reekey and Bent swaggered in like a pair of tomcats who had found the cream. Reekey strutted forward, thumbs hooked pompously into his waistcoat; Bent puffed on a cheap cigar, filling the office with sickly smoke.

"Evenin', gentlemen," Reekey announced, rolling back on his

heels. "As you've no doubt heard, we've gone an' caught your Seance Slayer."

"Aye," Bent added, blowing a smoke ring that drifted toward Barnes like an insult. "Wrapped it up in a fortnight. Not bad, eh?"

Barnes offered a tight smile that did nothing to reach his eyes. "Remarkable work. Truly. Why, I feel safer already knowing the fiend is behind bars."

"Glad to be of service," Reekey said, preening. "I suppose you boys can toddle off home now. Let the *experts* finish up."

"Yes," Barnes said lightly, glancing at Dickman. "A night's rest will do us good, won't it?"

"Indeed," Dickman said, deadpan.

"Well then," Bent said, flicking ash onto the floor, "we'll leave you to your beauty sleep. Still have paperwork to fill out. Good night, chaps."

"Do shut the door, gentlemen," Barnes said sharply.

Reekey tipped his hat with exaggerated flourish, then drew the door gently closed behind them. Their steps echoed down the corridor until the room fell silent once more.

Dickman let out a low whistle. "You know what will be the sweetest part of all this?"

Barnes arched a brow.

Dickman grinned wolfishly. "Watching those two stand before the administrative board, wringing their hands, as every last one of their lies comes tumbling down."

Barnes exhaled, the beginning of a grim smile forming. "Oh yes," he said softly. "That will be a night worth staying awake for."

The carriage lurched forward into the shadow-choked night, wheels crunching over gravel like bones ground beneath a butcher's heel. Lord Horace Raynsford sat rigid within, the dim lantern swinging above him casting long, skeletal shadows across his face. Anger, triumph, and something darker flickered in his eyes like the lantern's restless flame.

Outside, the fog was a living thing—a pale, coiling serpent that wound itself around the horses' legs, slithered across the road, and pressed its cold breath against the glass windows of the carriage. The night smelled of damp earth, soot, and the metallic tang of the Thames carried on a distant wind.

The coachman cracked his whip and the horses lunged onward, their silhouettes ghostly within the swirling vapour.

Horace leaned forward, gripping his walking cane so tightly the carved wolf's-head shook with the tension in his hands.

"Faster," he snarled through the front window.

The coachman merely nodded, too wise—or too fearful—to speak.

The wheels rattled into a deeper fogbank, the thick grey murk swallowing the world, smothering all light. Even the lantern beside the door flickered, as if struggling for breath. Horace did not care. The dark suited him. He thrived in it.

With Thaddeus imprisoned, the path cleared.

His lips curled into a smile—thin, cruel, reptilian.

"Finally," he murmured to the empty compartment, "finally the boy learns his lesson."

But the empty air did not remain silent.

A groaning branch scraped across the roof of the carriage, like fingernails dragged down a coffin lid. The horses whinnied nervously. Horace stiffened, then scoffed at his own momentary unease.

"Bah. Superstitious nonsense."

Yet the darkness outside seemed to thicken at his dismissal, pressing against the glass as though listening.

They passed into the marshy outskirts of London, where the fog clung low to the ground and gas lamps flickered like dying souls trapped in amber. Shadows twisted unnaturally beneath them.

Figures moved behind the fog's veil—only strangers returning home late, perhaps—but they seemed grotesque, misshapen, hunched by the dim light as if burdened by the weight of sin.

Horace's cane tapped restlessly on the carriage floor.

"Thaddeus, Thaddeus..." he muttered. "If you had only obeyed. Only done as you were told. You force my hand again and again."

He peered out the window as warehouses, wharves, and crooked tenements emerged like looming giants. The carriage wheels splashed through puddles of black water, sending ripples across the cobbles like oil spreading over glass.

Closer now.

The city swallowed him whole.

The fog began to glow with the faint amber light of London's countless lamps. The clatter of hoofbeats echoed beneath the archways, reverberating like a death knell.

Horace straightened his coat, smoothed his gloves, composed his face into a mask of dignified horror—one he would wear when he strode into the station to "rescue" his son.

A lie was forming, ornate and careful, on his tongue.

He rather enjoyed crafting it.

The carriage halted abruptly.

A patrolman stepped forward out of the haze.

"Lord Raynsford, sir—London," the coachman called down.

Horace stepped out into the damp, lamplit street with the swagger of a man approaching his greatest performance. The fog clung to him like a cloak, whispering around his shoulders as if eager to see what wickedness he would weave next.

He strode toward the Metropolitan Police Station with the certainty of a man who believed the city itself bent to his will.

And behind him, the carriage lantern finally guttered out—

as though even the flame feared to witness what would unfold.

The first wan threads of dawn crept through the precinct windows like spectral fingers, pale and chill, when at last Barnes and Dickman resolved to seek a few hours' hard-won rest.

"What a night," Dickman muttered, rolling the stiffness from his shoulders as they strode down the dim corridor.

But a voice—loud, imperious, and vibrating with affronted authority—halted them at once.

"I tell you, sir, he *is my son*, and I shall see him *immediately*! I have driven through the cursed fog from Kent, and I shall not be gainsaid by some uniformed underling!"

Barnes arched a brow. He could guess who the man was that possessed such a blustering mixture of entitlement and theatrical rage.

The clerk at the front desk looked on the verge of collapse, his spectacles askew, his ledger half-closed as though he no longer trusted it.

"Sir," the clerk quavered, "there is no gentleman here by the name of Thaddeus *Raynsford*—"

Lord Horace's jowls trembled like unset custard as he swelled with indignation. Barnes had to school his features into sobriety lest they betray any hint of satisfaction.

Stepping forward, he offered a courteous bow.

"Lord Raynsford, sir. Detective Barnes—this is Detective Dickman."

The transformation was instantaneous; Horace seized on the recognition as though he required it to breathe.

"Finally," he huffed, "an officer of discernment."

"Yes, my lord," Barnes replied evenly. "Your son is indeed in our holding cells. If you will accompany us, we shall take you to him."

Sleep forgotten, Barnes motioned Dickman forward. Whatever transpired next, he intended to hear every word.

They descended into the narrow stone passage where the cells lay, lanternlight flickering against iron bars. At the sight of his father, Thaddeus rose, pale but composed.

"Father?"

"Yes, yes," Horace said, waving his gloved hand. "Open the door, if you please. I must speak with my son *alone*."

"Of course," Barnes murmured. Yet instead of retreating the way they had come, he and Dickman slipped through the adjoining rear corridor—the one with the grated vent that carried sound as deftly as a whispering gallery. Lord Horace, in his customary arrogance, noticed nothing.

Inside the cell, the cot groaned beneath Horace's considerable weight as he settled beside Thaddeus.

"Well then," he proclaimed, folding his hands over his belly, "you've landed yourself in a pretty coil, haven't you?"

Thaddeus stared hard at him. "How did you know I'd been arrested? It happened only hours ago."

"Oh, I have my ways, my boy," Horace replied with a smug pat to his son's knee. "You mustn't fret. I am here to *save* you."

Thaddeus's brow darkened, not with relief, but suspicion. "What do you want, Father?"

Horace's lips tightened. "Mind your tongue. One would think you'd show a scrap of gratitude. I am here to make all of this—" he gestured vaguely at the cell—"*disappear*."

"Disappear?"

"Yes. You will come home to Kent, marry Hortense Remington as arranged, and I shall tidy this little scandal away."

Thaddeus's eyes narrowed. "And how, precisely, do you intend to 'tidy' murder charges?"

Horace gave an exasperated snort. "Why, by directing suspicion toward that vile creature, Guss Fable. He is the perfect scapegoat—violent, low-born, and entirely expendable."

"No." Thaddeus rose, trembling with fury. "You will not implicate Guss. He is innocent."

"You naïve fool," Horace hissed, rising to loom over him. "He *has* killed before. The constabulary will swallow it whole, and the papers will feast upon it. A planted trinket here, a whispered tip there—done. And you walk free."

Thaddeus felt sick. Visions of Guss dragged from his home, condemned by lies, turned his stomach to ice.

"No father. I will not allow it."

Horace leaned in, his breath sour, voice barely a whisper. "Do you fancy you'll escape this by virtue of your innocence? I put you in here, boy. *I arranged it.* And if you defy me, you shall rot in irons until the gallows rope kisses your neck."

Thaddeus recoiled as though struck. "You... did this? To your own son?"

"I would do far worse," Horace said, "if it forced you to honour your family."

Thaddeus whispered, "Who is Victor Jenkins?"

At once Horace lunged forward and clapped a hand over his son's mouth.

"Not another word," he snarled. "You are forbidden to utter that name."

But Thaddeus wrenched free, voice rising with long-suppressed fury. "He is your hired butcher, isn't he? You paid him to kill those women—to frame me so you could force a marriage upon me. All because I love Athena!"

Horace's expression twisted into contempt.

"Athena," he spat. "That servant girl. A plaything, nothing more. I removed her for your own good."

Thaddeus froze. "Removed...? What did you do?"

"Made arrangements for her," Horace said simply, as though discussing a piece of furniture. "A girl like that always has her uses. And by the way you never noticed she was gone, I wonder if she meant half so much as you pretend."

The world went white at the edges.

"Get out," Thaddeus whispered. Then louder: "GET OUT OF MY CELL."

"Gladly," Horace barked. "Rot here if you must. You deserve no better."

He pounded on the bars. Barnes and Dickman were there in an instant, faces carved from stone as they escorted the lord up the stairs.

At the threshold, Horace flung his cape about him with dramatic disdain.

"Keep him locked away. Clearly his wits have fled him."

"Yes, my lord," Barnes replied, every syllable dripping like cold iron.

When the carriage clattered off into the fog, Barnes exchanged a look with Dickman—grim, knowing, and edged with resolve.

Everything had just changed.

Barnes and Dickman watched the carriage vanish into the fog-choked street, its wheels clattering like bones rolling in a gambler's cup. Lord Horace's silhouette flickered once against the lantern glow—then was swallowed whole by the night.

Dickman released a low whistle and shook his head.

"Imagine," he murmured, "being sired by a creature such as *that*."

Barnes did not answer. A deep frown carved itself into his brow, the sort that meant gears were turning.

"I have an idea," he said at last.

They re-entered the precinct, their boots echoing down the stone passageway that led to the cells. The air smelled of damp iron and despair. Inside his barred chamber, Thaddeus paced like an animal newly snared, his fingers tearing at his nails, breath quick and uneven. The sight struck Barnes with something close to pity—a rare emotion for him, but one he did not resist.

"Mr. Raynsford," Barnes began softly, as though addressing a skittish horse about to bolt.

Thaddeus's head jerked upward. His eyes, rimmed red, held a tempest: grief, fury, and humiliation all braided together.

Barnes stepped closer. "I want you to do something for me, if you are willing. If I send the police sketch artist down to you, will you give him an honest likeness of Victor Jenkins?"

At the name, Thaddeus blanched. His breath caught sharply.

"You... heard." It was no question; merely the pronouncement of a man stripped bare.

"Aye," Dickman replied, folding his arms. "We are detectives, after all. It is our business to listen. Your talent for secrecy is—well—lamentable."

Thaddeus sank onto the cot as though his bones had dissolved. All the fight went out of him, leaving only a young man crushed by betrayal.

"Then you know my father set me up."

"We heard," Barnes confirmed. "We also know—now—that you are innocent."

"And my father?" Thaddeus whispered, voice thinned by disbelief.

"We shall come to *him* soon enough," said Barnes, a grim promise in the shape of words. "But first things first."

Thaddeus looked torn apart, as though shards of loyalty and horror warred inside him. The betrayal of one's own father was a wound that bled slowly.

"You'll be released," Barnes said gently. "This very morning. But we would ask a small service of you before you go. A sketch. A face. You *have* seen Jenkins, have you not?"

Thaddeus nodded. "I have. Clear as day."

"Good. Then with your help, we can hunt the true fiend before he stains the city with another death."

A voice sliced through the chamber like a rusted blade.

"What's this? Letting him *go*?"

Reekey stood in the doorway, his face contorted with rage. Bent shadowed him like some dull-witted gargoyle.

"He is innocent," Barnes said without turning. "And he will provide a likeness of the real killer."

Reekey's lip curled. "The Chief Inspector will hear of this. Letting a murderer loose upon the streets—"

Barnes spun in three swift strides, and suddenly he was inches from Reekey's face, his voice a quiet, lethal silk.

"You will leave this man alone."

Reekey swallowed, his bravado faltering.

"I know what you did," Barnes continued, his gaze a cold hammer. "I know of the false witness, the lies, the ambition that rots you from within. Touch this case again, or this man, and I shall see you stripped of your badge and cast into the gutter where your conduct belongs."

The colour drained from Reekey's cheeks. Bent tugged at his sleeve, and together they retreated, muttering, toward the Chief Inspector's office—though their protestations would be ashes before breakfast.

And so it was that, with the morning's pale light creeping once more through the windows, Thaddeus Priest walked free—bruised in spirit, trembling with revelation, but free nonetheless.

# CHAPTER TWENTY-NINE

Dawn crept over London in a thin, sickly wash of pewter light, scarcely strong enough to scatter the lingering fog that clung to the rooftops like a burial shroud. The city still slept, restless beneath the chimneys and spires, as Detective Barnes descended the narrow stair to the holding cells.

Keys rattled. Iron groaned.

The door swung open.

"Mr. Raynsford," Barnes said, voice unusually gentle for so stern a man, "you are free to go."

For a heartbeat, Thaddeus simply stood there. He looked less like a prisoner than a revenant—eyes hollowed by sleeplessness, hair disheveled, spirit battered. A thin draught curled past his ankles, cold as a grave.

"Free...?" he whispered, scarcely daring to believe it.

Barnes nodded once. "Your name shall not darken our ledger. Not today."

Dickman avoided Thaddeus's gaze, as though ashamed of the very institution that had caged an innocent man.

The cell door clanged shut behind him, and Thaddeus flinched at the sound—his body remembering what his mind wished to forget. As they escorted him toward the entryway, he felt the oppressive chill of the corridor loosen its grip from his spine. Yet he could not shake the sense that the stone walls watched him leave, resentful of his escape.

Outside, the fog rolled like pale spectres along the cobblestones. The morning lamps flickered weakly, as if exhausted from keeping vigil through the night.

Barnes cleared his throat.

"If you recall anything useful about Jenkins—any detail at all—you send for us. Immediately."

A tremor rippled through Thaddeus at the name.

"Oh, I recall more than I care to," he murmured.

Barnes gave him a searching look, but Thaddeus turned away.

He stepped out into the street, the cold air biting his cheeks like needles. London felt vast and alien, its very breath thick with soot and secrets. A carriage rattled by, horses snorting steam, wheels clattering like bones. Somewhere, a bell tolled eight times—low, mournful, as though lamenting a man risen from the dead.

Thaddeus began the long walk toward the boarding house.

Each step felt strangely heavy, as though the cobblestones sought to drag him back toward the gaol from which he'd been delivered. His thoughts swirled like the fog—of his father's treachery, of Jenkins's lurking presence, of ghosts whispering murder in his ear.

A lamplighter paused as Thaddeus passed, tipping his cap yet eyeing him with a wary curiosity reserved for men who looked as though they had wrestled with the Devil and barely escaped his grasp.

Finally he reached the familiar gate of Mrs. Parsons's establishment.

His hands trembled as he lifted the latch.

Inside, the hallway was dim, warm, smelling faintly of lavender sachets and last night's hearth.

Mrs. Parsons appeared at the end of the hall like an apparition of domestic severity, arms folded, spectacles perched upon her nose. Her lips parted as if ready to scold him—but then she saw his face.

"Oh my... Mr. Priest," she whispered, her voice softening. "Dear heavens, what have they done to you?"

Thaddeus tried to smile. It fractured halfway.

"Merely detained, Mrs. Parsons. I am—"

His breath hitched.

"—quite all right."

She fussed over him, unlocking his door and ushering him inside with uncharacteristic tenderness.

"You sit yourself down. I shall bring tea. And perhaps a bit of broth if you can stomach it."

When she left, closing the door behind her, silence fell like snow.

Thaddeus sagged onto the edge of his bed, pressing both hands to his face. The room felt colder than usual—as though a presence lingered. He lowered his hands and stared at the empty air.

Artie was not there.

Odd.

It was the first time in days the ghost had not materialised with some sardonic remark or complaint.

"Artie...?" Thaddeus whispered.

Only the floorboards creaked in reply.

He drew a shuddering breath, leaning forward, elbows on knees.

He was free.

But he was not safe.

Not while Jenkins walked the streets.

Not while his father schemed in the shadows.

And not while the spirits continued to seek him out, each bearing their tale of death.

The fog outside pressed against the window glass like a pale hand.

Thaddeus Priest had gone home.

But home no longer felt like sanctuary.

It felt like the calm before the storm.

Chief Inspector Coghill stood at his desk, bathed in the weak morning light that seeped through the mullioned windows like a reluctant confession. Dust motes drifted lazily in the air, turning the office into a cathedral of weary authority. He was signing a stack of reports, his pen scratching like claws across parchment.

A sharp knock shattered the quiet.

"Enter," he called, irritation already tightening his voice.

Barnes stepped inside, shutting the door behind him with deliberate care. Dickman followed, his expression grave. The tension in the room thickened like London fog.

"Chief Inspector," Barnes said, removing his hat and holding it at his side. "We must speak."

Coghill looked up, and his eyes narrowed. He sensed a disturbance—Barnes would not appear unbidden at dawn unless the matter was dire.

"Well? Has something gone awry with our—" his voice dropped, "—prisoner?"

Barnes stepped forward. "Thaddeus Priest has been released."

The Chief's pen slipped from his fingers.

"*Released?*" Coghill repeated, the word cracking like a pistol shot. "On whose authority?"

"Mine," Barnes replied simply.

The Chief surged to his feet, face reddening. "Have you taken leave of your senses, Barnes? After the witness statement—after the arrest—after I spent half the night preparing to brief the Lord Mayor—"

Barnes raised a hand, calm but unyielding. "Sir, that witness statement was manufactured."

Silence fell. Not peaceful silence, but the strained, taut kind one hears before a rope snaps and a body falls.

Coghill's face paled. "Explain yourself. Carefully."

"It was Reekey and Bent," Barnes said. "They bribed a known thief and woman of the streets—Delta Weddall—to swear she had seen Mr. Priest fleeing the scene of Madam Medora's murder. A falsehood. Fabricated from start to finish."

Dickman stepped in. "And they arrested him without consulting us. Against explicit instruction."

The Chief's breath grew shallow. He sank back into his chair. "You have proof?"

"We do," said Barnes. "If you speak to Miss Weddall under proper supervision, she will fold like wet paper. She fears those men more than the gallows, but not as much as she fears the law when it stands upright."

Coghill rubbed his temples. "Holy God... corruption, right under my nose."

"That is not all, sir," Barnes continued. "Thaddeus Priest bears no wounds consistent with Lorena Baldry's struggle. Dr. Keiler's findings eliminate him. The man in that cell was innocent."

"And yet," Dickman added, "the real killer still walks free. And has been aided, wittingly or unwittingly, by members of this department."

The Chief Inspector closed his eyes, breathing slowly, as though steadying himself for a blow.

"This... this is ruinous," he whispered. "If word spreads that the Metropolitan Police arrested an innocent man on falsified testimony—"

"Then we swallow the shame now," Barnes said evenly, "or choke on something far worse later."

Coghill opened his eyes. Barnes held his gaze—unflinching, steady as stone.

"What would you have me do, Barnes?" he asked at last.

"Let us do our work," Barnes replied. "Let us find the true killer. And place Reekey and Bent under immediate suspension pending inquiry. If they remain in the field, more damage will be done."

The Chief Inspector exhaled—a long, shuddering breath.

"So be it," he said. "Bring me the proof. Bring me the killer. And for God's sake, Barnes... do not fail."

Barnes inclined his head. "We won't."

He turned and strode out, Dickman at his side, the office door swinging shut behind them with a soft but ominous *click*—like the closing of a tomb.

THE SUMMONS CAME AT MID-MORNING, carried by a red-faced clerk who looked as though he'd sooner deliver a death notice than approach the two detectives. Reekey and Bent sat in their office—if it could be called that—reeking of stale tobacco and bad triumph, puffed up like cockerels awaiting applause.

"Chief Inspector Coghill wishes to see you both," the clerk stammered.

Reekey leaned back in his chair with a grin sharp enough to cut glass.

"A promotion already, eh, Bent?"

Bent puffed a ring of smoke toward the clerk, making the boy cough.

"Told you we'd be heroes, didn't I?"

But as they strode down the corridor, the atmosphere shifted. Officers avoided their eyes. Whispered conversations died the moment the pair approached. A coldness crept through the precinct, not an honest chill, but the clammy stillness of a grave before the earth breaks.

Reekey frowned. "What's the matter with this lot?"

Bent shrugged. "Jealous, most like."

They knocked once on the Chief Inspector's door.

"Enter," came the clipped response.

Chief Inspector Coghill stood behind his desk, ramrod-straight, his face carved from stone. Barnes and Dickman stood to one side, silent, implacable, shadows at a tribunal.

Reekey and Bent paused. For the first time that morning, uncertainty flickered across their faces.

"Chief Inspector," Reekey said with a shaky smile. "You'll be pleased to—"

"Enough," Coghill barked. The sound cracked like a whip. "Stand before my desk."

They obeyed—slowly, like schoolboys called to the master's cane.

The Chief reached into a drawer and withdrew a folded document. He held it between two fingers as if it were something foul.

"Detectives Reekey and Bent," he began, voice low and thunderous, "I have before me a sworn statement from one Delta Weddall. She claims—and I quote—that you induced her, with coin and coercion, to sign a false witness account."

Reekey's face drained of colour. Bent swallowed hard.

"That—that's a lie," Reekey sputtered. "A dirty, blasted lie! That woman—"

Coghill slammed his palm upon the desk. "Silence!"

The windows rattled. Even the dust motes seemed to freeze in midair.

Dickman crossed his arms. Barnes stood perfectly still, though his eyes gleamed with cold fire.

Coghill continued, "Furthermore, you arrested an innocent man without consulting your commanding officers, and in direct contradiction to established investigative protocols."

Bent opened his mouth, but the Chief raised a hand.

"And," Coghill said, quieter now—dangerously so—"you placed this department, and the people of London, at great peril by leaving the true murderer another night unopposed in our streets."

A tremor passed through Reekey's shoulders.

"You have abused your badges. You have endangered an investigation. And you have brought shame upon the Metropolitan Police."

He picked up two envelopes, sealed with red wax.

"By order of this office, pending full inquiry and review by the

Administrative Board, you are hereby suspended from duty, stripped of all investigative authority, and confined to internal quarters until further notice."

Reekey's mouth fell open. Bent staggered back a step, as though struck.

"You—you can't," Reekey whispered.

"I can," said Coghill. "And I have."

Barnes stepped forward. The room grew colder.

"I warned you," he said softly. "But you chose vanity over justice. And now the consequences stand before you."

Dickman pushed off the wall. "Gentlemen, hand over your badges."

Reekey and Bent hesitated, trembling. Bent's fingers loosened first; his badge clattered onto the Chief's desk like a tolling bell. Reekey's followed with a dull metallic thud.

"Escort them," Coghill commanded.

Two constables entered and took their places beside the disgraced detectives. As Reekey and Bent were led away, Reekey shot Barnes a look of pure, poisonous hatred. Barnes did not flinch.

Coghill exhaled—a weary, thunder-laden sigh.

"Barnes. Dickman," he said, voice gravelled with fatigue, "bring me the real killer. Before London's faith in us collapses altogether."

Barnes bowed his head.

"We will, sir."

And the door closed behind them like the sealing of a crypt.

Victor Jenkins returned to his lodgings just after dawn, slipping through the narrow stairwell like a shadow that had found human shape. Fog clung to him as though reluctant to let him go, shrouding the corridor in a chill that seemed to breathe of its own accord. His boots left faint wet prints upon the boards—evidence of a night spent lurking in rain-slick alleys.

He hung his top hat upon a hook, peeled off his coat, and crossed the cramped sitting room, its lamps still guttering from the night before. The silence felt brittle. Expectant.

He prepared a simple breakfast and tea, watching the pale daylight slowly strengthen beyond his window. Time passed quietly in the small room—the clink of crockery, the slow cooling of the kettle, the distant murmur of the waking street below.

When the meal was finished and the dishes cleared away, he drew the curtains against the growing light and made ready for bed. Sleep claimed him quickly.

Hours later, when the sun stood high enough to bleach the fog from the streets, a furious pounding crashed against his door.

Jenkins jerked awake, heart hammering. The room swam into focus around him as the sound came again—heavy fists striking wood with desperate urgency.

Three raps—sharp, hurried, and unmistakably anxious.

Jenkins froze.

Clovis's signal.

His jaw tightened. Clovis Corbeld was loyal to coin, never to courage. If he knocked in such a fashion, something had gone terribly amiss.

Jenkins rose from the bed and opened the door just a crack. The rattle of carts and the cries of street vendors drifted faintly up from the street below.

Clovis burst in, panting, wild-eyed, sweat darkening the brim of his cap. The quiet room seemed to recoil from the urgency he carried with him.

"You didn't hear? You didn't 'ear?" the man sputtered, voice trembling.

Jenkins's expression remained blank—too blank, too composed.

"Hear what?" His voice was soft. A whisper dipped in oil.

"Priest—Thaddeus Priest—he's been turned loose!" Clovis

panted. "Walked right out o' the cells this mornin'. Barnes and Dickman themselves done set him free!"

The clock upon the mantle stopped ticking.

Or perhaps Jenkins simply ceased hearing it.

Slowly—very slowly—he turned his gaze from Clovis to the soiled windowpane, where his reflection stared back: a pale smear of features sharp enough to cut. His black eyes narrowed, swallowing what little light dared linger in the room.

Jenkins said nothing for a long moment. "What," Jenkins murmured, "did you say?"

Clovis swallowed hard. "They says he's innocent. They're lookin' for someone else now."

The words hung in the air, heavy as church bells tolling a death knell.

Jenkins's lips twitched—the ghost of a smile, but not one born of mirth.

It was born of rage.

Jenkins dragged a hand across his face, sleep still clinging stubbornly to his eyes. "Innocent..." he whispered. "They have *decided* he is innocent."

Clovis backed away a step. Even he, coarse as he was, felt the temperature drop—a sudden draught like the exhalation of a tomb.

"Sir—I thought you'd want to know—"

"Oh, I do," Jenkins replied, voice barely above a breath. "I *do* want to know. I want to know why Barnes and Dickman—those meddlesome gnats—suddenly believe the boy's hands clean." His fingers curled, knuckles whitening. "What exactly persuaded them otherwise."

Clovis hovered near the door, uncertain whether to flee or faint.

Jenkins stepped closer, his shadow blooming across the floor like spilled ink.

"If Priest walks free," Jenkins murmured, "the noose begins to slip."

His tone sharpened, laced with venom.

"And if the noose loosens... it may yet slip around *my own*."

He paced, movements tight, controlled—though something feverish glimmered beneath the surface, as though a wolf prowled inside his skin.

"So," Jenkins murmured, "they seek the real killer now."

His eyes gleamed black as obsidian.

"Let them seek. Let them pry."

A slow, serpentine smile crept across his face.

"They are a step behind. They shall always be a step behind." His fingers tapped the mantel once... twice... then curled slowly into a fist.

Then—suddenly, violently—he struck the mantel with his fist. The lamp trembled. Clovis flinched as if struck himself.

Jenkins tugged the loose collar of his nightshirt straight as though nothing had happened. He lowered his voice. "This changes matters. Priest must be dealt with. Properly. Permanently."

He turned toward Clovis, the faint lamplight catching the fresh scratches along his wrist—angry red marks half-hidden beneath a blood-smeared cuff.

Clovis's eyes widened with recognition.

Jenkins noticed.

And smiled.

"Fetch Matson," Jenkins said softly, dangerously. "We have... adjustments to make."

Clovis fled, boots clattering down the stairwell.

Left alone, Jenkins stood motionless—no breath, no twitch—like a dark figure carved in stone. Fog pressed against the window beside him, blurring his reflection until he looked less human, more spectre.

More what he truly was.

He whispered into the emptiness,

"The game is not finished, Thaddeus Priest. Not until I choose the final move."

# CHAPTER THIRTY

Night pressed heavily upon the little room, its shadows long and uneasy. Thaddeus had scarcely removed his boots when the air drew tight, as though the space itself had taken a breath and forgotten to release it. The candle flames guttered, bending low, their light dimming to a strained and wavering glow.

Artie drifted near the ceiling, his expression sharpening.

"Oh dear," he murmured. "We've another visitor."

Thaddeus's pulse quickened.

"Who is it?"

Before the words had fully formed, the room seemed to contract. The light faltered—then thinned—and from the deepening dark came a sound: not quite a voice, not yet, but the fragile break of something trying to speak through silence. A shape gathered slowly, uncertainly, as though memory itself struggled to hold it together.

Lorena Baldry.

Her form wavered, never wholly fixed. Her gown stirred without wind, its folds trailing a moment behind her, as though reluctant to follow. Her hair drifted about her face, and her features—when they settled—were drawn with a grief so deep it seemed to hollow the air around her. A faint scent lingered—something once sweet, now nearly lost.

"Mr. Priest..."

The words emerged thin and strained, as though forced through a narrowing passage.

"You must see. You must bear witness. I am not at rest... not while my murderer walks free."

Thaddeus rose slowly, his hand tightening at his throat.

"Miss Baldry... I—I'm sorry. I had thought—"

"You know nothing."

The words came sharper now, though no louder—cutting, rather than spoken.

"But you shall."

She lifted her hand. For a moment, it trembled—as though even the act required effort—then pressed it over his eyes.

There was no sense of touch—only intrusion.

Darkness swallowed him whole.

He stood now—not in his room—but upon a narrow street slick with rain, the cobblestones gleaming like blackened glass. Horses snorted faintly somewhere in the fog. Lorena Baldry, alive and unaware, stepped from her modest flat, her shawl pulled tight. She walked with purpose, glancing over her shoulder as though she sensed some presence.

Thaddeus tried to call out to her, but no sound left his throat.

From the mist behind her emerged a tall figure—coat collar high, hat brim low, gloved hands hanging too calmly at his sides.

Victor Jenkins.

A serpent's smile cut across his face.

Lorena stopped short.

"Mr. Jenkins? You startled me."

"My apologies, Miss Baldry," he said, voice draped in velvet and deceit. "Might I beg a moment of your time?"

Before she could refuse, he pressed a white handkerchief against her face—a sickly-sweet odour filling the air. She gasped, tried to pull away, but already her limbs slackened. The world pitched and spun. He caught her as though she were nothing more than a fallen doll.

"Cooperate now," he whispered into her fading consciousness, "and I shall make it quick."

Thaddeus felt Lorena's terror as her vision dimmed—felt the choking sweetness of chloroform suffocate her breath.

Darkness again.

Lantern light flickered dimly as Lorena awoke, bound to a heavy chair in a cramped, decrepit flat. The wallpaper peeled like decayed flesh. The air reeked of damp cloth and iron.

Jenkins stood before her, rolling his sleeves as calmly as a surgeon preparing for work.

"You want to know why, don't you?" he crooned. "Why your kind must fall?"

Lorena writhed uselessly, tears streaking down her cheeks.

"You spiritualists... you pretend to commune with the dead, yet you see nothing. Nothing at all. But I... I am unseen."

He leaned close, breath cold and foul. "It delights me to watch the city quiver in my shadow."

Thaddeus could feel Lorena's heart pounding—her fear rising, suffocating.

"P–please," she whispered.

"I spared Miss Murray no mercy," Jenkins continued, pacing as he spoke. "Nor Madam Medora. Nor the others. Each one talked too much. Each one remembered my face." His smile thinned. "And you, my dear, recognised me at the séance. A pity."

He lifted the silk scarf from his pocket—the same pattern from Melisendra's vision—and wrapped it slowly around his hands.

A knock sounded at the door. A flicker of irritation slithered across his features. He took the silk scarf and gagged her. "No noise out of you now."

Jenkins, hesitated, then moved to open the door.

Clovis Corbeld and Erwin Matson waited in the hall—the same building they all inhabited, the same men who had tormented Thaddeus.

"Evenin', Mr. Jenkins," Clovis said with a grin. "Ready for us to take 'er?"

"Almost. I need a few more moments. Wait here," said Jenkins as he closed the door.

He struck quickly, efficiently, pulling the gag from her mouth and then strangling her with it. The vision spun, full of Lorena's terror, her gasping cries swallowed in the foul air of the flat. Thaddeus felt every tremor, every suffocating heartbeat, until—

Stillness.

THADDEUS COLLAPSED to his knees as the ghost withdrew her touch. For a moment, the world did not return all at once—only fragments: the edge of the table, the wavering candlelight, the sound of his own breath, unsteady and too loud in the silence. Then the room swam back into being.

Lorena hovered before him—pale, trembling, as though the effort of holding her form cost her dearly.

"You see now," she whispered. "You see... all."

The words faltered, catching as though they must force their way through her.

"The killer walks under your very nose. And he will spill more blood... if you do not stop him."

A pressure lingered in Thaddeus's chest, as though the vision had not fully released him. He drew a breath, but it came shallow, uneven.

"You must reveal the truth," she went on, her voice thinning. "Even if they do not believe your voice... they may yet believe your courage."

Her form flickered—not like light, but like something losing cohesion. The edges of her seemed to loosen, to drift.

"Find him, Mr. Priest," she said, the words barely holding. "Before another joins me."

The last of her unravelled in a low, mournful sound—not quite a wail, but something more distant, more final. Then she was gone.

The room did not grow colder—only heavier. The silence pressed in, dense and suffocating.

Thaddeus remained where he was, shaking, his hand pressed hard against his brow as though he might steady himself by force alone.

Artie drifted lower, his usual levity stripped away.

"Well," he said quietly, "that was grisly. And if you go after him alone, you'll end up just like her."

Thaddeus lowered his hand, his breath still uneven.

"I cannot let him continue," he said. "I cannot."

"You'll need help," Artie murmured.

A pause. Then—

"And I shall find it."

The words came low, but steady now. Certain.

The candle flame, long guttering, steadied at last—then burned a little brighter.

A GREY DAWN pressed itself against the city, a sickly light creeping over London's chimneys like a dying breath. The fog was thick enough to taste—cold, metallic, clinging to skin and bone. Thaddeus came striding through it as though emerging from the underworld, his face pale, his eyes vivid with sleepless torment.

Detective Michael Barnes stood near the wrought-iron railing outside the boarding house, stamping warmth back into his feet. He had been on watch since before sunrise, weary but vigilant. When he saw Thaddeus approaching, he straightened, suspicion and concern blending in his expression.

"Mr. Priest," Barnes said, offering a curt nod. "You're up early. Where have you been?"

Thaddeus did not answer. Not at first. He walked straight to the detective, stopping close enough that Barnes could see the tremor in his hands.

"I must speak with you," Thaddeus said quietly—but the urgency in his voice struck with startling force. "I know you don't believe in me as a Spiritualist, but I am hoping you will hear me out...as a man who has witnessed... horrors."

Barnes narrowed his eyes. "What sort of horrors?"

Thaddeus swallowed.

"The truth about the murders."

A chill rolled through the fog.

Barnes gestured stiffly. "Inside. Quickly."

THE BOARDING HOUSE parlour was dim and stale, curtains still drawn. The coals in the grate glowed faintly, throwing long shadows along the wallpaper. Barnes shut the door firmly behind them, turning to face Thaddeus with arms folded and jaw tense.

"Well?" he said. "Speak plainly."

Thaddeus paced once, twice, then halted before the hearth.

"A spirit came to me last night," he said.

Barnes's expression turned to stone.

"A *spirit*," he repeated flatly.

"Yes," Thaddeus insisted, voice tight. "Lorena Baldry."

Barnes exhaled sharply, rubbing a hand over his face. "Mr. Priest, I cannot accept—"

"You have *no choice*!" Thaddeus cried, stepping forward. "You think me insane? A fraud? A murderer? Hear me now, Detective Barnes—Miss Baldry showed me her death."

His voice trembled, but his eyes—haunted, fevered—held Barnes captive.

"She revealed the killer. Victor Jenkins."

The name settled in the room like falling ash.

Barnes stared hard at him. "That man your father spoke of? Jenkins? Your father's hired man?"

"Yes," Thaddeus said bitterly. "He chloroformed Lorena Baldry on the street. Dragged her to his flat. Tortured her. Strangled her."

Barnes stiffened.

Thaddeus pressed on, voice cracking around the edges.

"I saw it—felt it—through her eyes. And I saw his accomplices. Clovis Corbeld and Erwin Matson. They live in the same building. They helped carry her body to that warehouse."

Barnes took a slow, wary step toward him.

"What you are describing..." He paused, searching Thaddeus's face. "It is possible but... are you sure you didn't get this from your father's men?"

Thaddeus met his gaze with a sudden, terrible calm.

"No, sir, I did not. The evidence you cannot find—the weapon, the motive, the witnesses—it lies with *him*, not me. Jenkins killed these women because they recognised him. He will continue unless he is stopped."

Barnes swallowed hard. His scepticism wavered—not broken, but shaken.

"And you expect me to believe," Barnes said slowly, "that ghosts show you what living witnesses cannot."

"I expect you to believe," Thaddeus countered, "that your murderer has a face. A home. And allies in the shadows."

He stepped closer, voice dropping to a low, urgent whisper.

"Search Jenkins's building, his apartment, it's the same building we watched Corbeld and Matson go into the other night. Search his rooms. You'll find stains on the floorboards—blood he tried to hide. A silk scarf. Perhaps more. Go now, Barnes, before he flees again."

Barnes's jaw clenched. He was a man of reason—of hard facts and harder truths—but something in Thaddeus's face, his pallor, the horror that still clung to him like a burial shroud...

It made disbelief difficult.

"Why tell me this now?" Barnes asked quietly.

"Because," Thaddeus breathed, voice trembling, "I am not your murderer, you know that. But these murders are happening because of me, because of my father."

He lifted his eyes, filled with dread.

"And if you do not believe me—Jenkins will kill again."

Silence.

The fog outside pressed against the windows as though listening.

At last, Barnes spoke.

"Very well, Mr. Priest," he said, his voice low, grim. "I will look into this. But mark me—if you are deceiving me, or yourself, it will end poorly."

Thaddeus nodded once, solemnly.

"I understand."

Barnes pulled on his gloves, steeling himself.

"Then God help us both," he muttered, and strode out into the fog.

Thaddeus exhaled shakily, sinking into a chair as the fire flickered weakly.

Artie materialised beside him, arms crossed.

"Well," the ghost said, "that could have gone worse. He didn't try to strangle you."

Thaddeus let out a hollow laugh.

But beneath it, fear coiled tight.
Because if Barnes did not find proof...
Jenkins would strike again.

By the time the parish clocks tolled the hour, a lugubrious stillness had settled over the station. The last of the night's commotion had ebbed into memory, leaving only the sigh of wind in the eaves and the relentless drumming of rain against the panes. It was into this uneasy quiet that the two detectives retreated, burdened by thoughts they dared not voice.

"And you believe him?"

Edgar Dickman's incredulous whisper cut through the gloom. He stood rigid beside the window, watching rivulets of rain chase one another down the glass like quicksilver tears. A distant lamplighter moved through the fog, his lantern a dim and lonely beacon swallowed almost at once by the murk.

Detective Barnes did not answer at first. Instead he seized the coal scuttle and cast a fresh shovelful into the grate with more force than prudence demanded. Sparks leapt up in a brief frenzy, illuminating the hard set of his jaw. He did not care to be played for a fool—not by a prisoner, not by anyone—but the memory of Thaddeus's trembling confession gnawed at him with cold insistence.

*What if the man spoke true? What if they dismissed it, and another life guttered out as easily as the faint, failing lamps outside?*

The morning had dawned with a choking fog and a drizzle that clung to the skin like mourning crepe. Barnes felt a weight in his chest that mirrored the bleak weather, a foreboding as heavy as the clouds pressing down upon the city.

"There's no harm in checking it out," he said at last, his voice low, gravelled by worry. "If we are wrong, then nothing comes of it—and we still hunt a killer. But if we are right... and we do nothing..."

He let the thought trail away, thick and ominous as a thunderhead swelling on the horizon.

Dickman's scepticism wavered. He had worked beside Barnes long enough to know when his partner's instincts had been stirred by something darker than mere conjecture. And this morning, Barnes seemed haunted.

"You're right," Dickman conceded, drawing a slow breath that misted the chilled air. "There's no harm in taking a look."

He cast one more glance out the window. The fog writhed like a living thing, swallowing the street whole.

"I suppose," he murmured, reaching for his coat, "we had best get on with it, then."

# CHAPTER THIRTY-ONE

A dismal pall hung over the street as the morning's gloom settled into every crevice of London's poorer quarter. The Black Maria rolled to a halt in the slick, narrow lane, its iron-shod wheels cutting through puddles the colour of coal dust. A fetid mist curled along the cobbles like something half-alive, and the faint cries of distant vendors echoed with a hollow, spectral quality. It was into this squalid tableau that Detectives Barnes and Dickman descended, their boots striking the stones with grim purpose.

They instructed the accompanying constables to remain vigilant —*very* vigilant—in a place where daylight itself seemed reluctant to tread. Finding the dwelling of Clovis Corbeld and Erwin Matson proved no challenge; it was the same decaying tenement into which they had watched the men slink only nights before.

The steps leading up were treacherous—slick with rotted vegetation, chimney soot, and rainwater that pooled in oily patches. Barnes mounted them with visible distaste, gripping the banister as though the very wood were diseased.

Inside, a tremulous-looking mail carrier hovered in the dim corridor, clutching his leather satchel as if it might shield him from the building's unsavoury inhabitants. At the sight of the detectives, his eyes widened to full moons.

"Do you know which dwelling belongs to Clovis Corbeld and Erwin Matson?" Barnes asked.

"I—I..." The poor man stuttered, his gaze darting as though expecting spectres at every corner. "I'd rather not say."

Barnes stepped forward, his shadow looming ominously in the flickering gaslight. Dickman folded his arms and watched with a wolfish grin.

"But you *must* answer," Barnes murmured, his voice soft yet chilling. "And if you refuse, I shall be obliged to bring you to the station on a charge of obstructing an investigation."

The carrier let out a quavering sigh and seized Barnes's sleeve, tugging him toward the street door. He whispered, his voice barely a breath:

"2B. And pray, sir—do not let them know I told you."

With that, he fled down the stairs, slipping and stumbling in a manner that suggested he was eager to outrun his own fear. He vanished up the street as though pursued by the very hounds of damnation.

"It seems," Dickman remarked dryly, "they have made an impression."

"As if that were any surprise," Barnes replied.

THEY CLIMBED to the second floor and rapped sharply at the door of 2B. A sluggish shuffling answered from within—two men stirring after what was no doubt a night steeped in gin and questionable company. Barnes exchanged a wry look with Dickman.

At last, the door creaked open. Clovis Corbeld stared out at them, pallid and blinking.

"What are you doin' here?" he croaked.

Both detectives pushed past him before he could form another protest, causing him to grunt under the force.

"Oi! I never said you could come in!"

Barnes attempted a veneer of apology, though his revulsion was plain. The air reeked of unwashed garments, spoiled food, and the sourness of bodies steeped in neglect. A filthy mattress slumped in a corner like a wounded beast.

"We shan't linger," Barnes said coolly. "We seek an associate of yours—Victor Jenkins."

At that, Clovis blanched, and Erwin—mid-yawn—snapped his mouth shut as if fearing the truth might escape it.

"I don't know who you're talkin' about," Clovis muttered. "We don't know no Victor Jenkins."

Barnes lifted a brow, unimpressed. "We have it on excellent authority that you do. Now, this may go one of two ways. You speak freely, or you accompany us to the station and contemplate your choices from the comfort of a cell."

"You can't do that," Erwin protested, his voice wavering. "We ain't done nothin' wrong."

Barnes pointed his pen at them like a magistrate pronouncing doom. "Oh? There have been a number of murders committed in the city of late—grisly work—and all signs point to Victor Jenkins. Yet the trail leads also… to the two of *you*."

Dickman caught the furtive glance each man cast toward the door and stepped smartly to block it.

"In fact," he added lightly, "I think it best we arrest you regardless. You both look unmistakably guilty."

Clovis swallowed, eyes flicking between them.

"All right—look, we don't want no trouble. Jenkins is downstairs, 1D—corner apartment. You got what you came for. Now get out."

Barnes smiled without warmth. "Your cooperation is most appreciated. Alas, you will still be accompanying us downtown."

Erwin's temper flared. "We gave you what you wanted! Why're you still botherin' us?"

Dickman stepped into the hallway and signaled. Two uniformed bobbies materialised at once.

"I believe," Dickman said pleasantly, "that you gentlemen have rather more to tell us—and we are most willing to listen."

THE ECHOES of raised voices and clattering boots still haunted the stairwell as Barnes and Dickman emerged from the squalid apartment. A chill draught swept through the dim corridor, carrying with it the stench of mildew and despair. Barnes exhaled slowly, resisting the urge to scrub his hands on his coat. Merely standing within that foul den had left him feeling soiled, as though something unseen had clung to his very skin.

Once outside, the detectives stepped onto the stoop just in time to see Clovis and Erwin bundled roughly into the waiting police wagon. The sky above was low and pewter-grey, the kind that suggested rain would soon return to finish what the earlier storm had started.

A young Bobby approached, helmet glistening faintly in the thin light.

"Sirs," he asked, "do you require anything further?"

Dickman cast a glance at Barnes. "What do you suppose are the chances our more refined neighbor downstairs has been witness to this spectacle?"

Barnes gave a short, thoughtful nod. "Quite high, I should think. Still, we must inspect the matter ourselves. Let us proceed."

He turned to the waiting constable. "Hold your post here. You may yet have one more passenger before the morning is through."

The Bobby nodded eagerly and hurried back to the wagon to await further instruction.

The detectives returned to the building in search of Jenkins.

Apartment 1D presented an immaculate façade—its polished

door gleamed beneath a shining brass knob, the wood unmarred except for the faint scuffing of routine housekeeping. Barnes raised his hand and rapped firmly.

Silence answered.

He knocked again. And yet again. Nothing stirred beyond the threshold.

At last, a door across the hallway creaked open. A petite elderly woman, her hair a soft shade of powder-blue, peered out at them through thick spectacles.

"Are you gentlemen seeking Mr. Jenkins?" she asked in a voice that fluttered like lace in a breeze.

Barnes tipped his hat, then removed it as courtesy dictated. "Indeed, Madam. We inquire after Victor Jenkins. Might you know his whereabouts?"

"Oh yes," she replied, her expression kindly. "Mr. Jenkins steps out every morning for a constitutional. He should be returning any moment. You are welcome to wait inside if it pleases you."

Barnes and Dickman exchanged a measured glance—a silent agreement passing between them.

"You are most gracious," Barnes said, "but we shall not trouble you. We shall call upon him later. Good day to you."

With another polite tip of his hat, the detectives withdrew.

Outside once more, Barnes signaled to the constables. "Take those two back to the precinct," he instructed, "then return for us."

The wagon lurched forward, wheels splashing through the gutter as it rolled away. Barnes and Dickman crossed to the opposite pavement and positioned themselves beneath the overhang of a deserted shopfront, settling in to await the elusive Mr. Jenkins.

In the grey, expectant stillness, every footstep seemed a herald of what would come next.

## CHAPTER THIRTY-ONE

The minutes dragged by like cold molasses, each one swallowed by the narrow street's sodden silence. Barnes and Dickman kept their vigil beneath the overhang of a shuttered shop, their breath misting faintly in the chill air. The fog pressed low around the lampposts and seeped into the gutters, where rainwater still swirled in muddy eddies.

At last, a figure appeared at the far end of the lane—tall, slight, and clad in a neat dark coat that contrasted sharply with the squalor around him. Victor Jenkins approached with the brisk gait of a man returning from a habitual morning circuit. A polished cane tapped lightly against the stones.

But the moment his eyes settled upon the two detectives waiting across the street, his step faltered. His face, ordinarily composed, drained of colour. In a heartbeat, he pivoted on his heel.

"He's seen us," Dickman murmured.

"And he intends to flee," Barnes replied grimly. "After him."

Jenkins strode away at an ever-quickening pace, shoulders stiff, breath shallow. But the moment he sensed—*truly sensed*—Barnes and Dickman advancing after him, his composure shattered like thin glass. He threw one panicked glance over his shoulder. Their silhouettes, dark and relentless in the fog, were enough to break whatever nerve he had left.

He bolted.

He plunged into the swirling mists, cloak whipping behind him, boots hammering the stones with frantic urgency. His cane clattered wildly as he ran, striking sparks when metal kissed cobble. The street, slick with soot and last night's rain, reflected the faint glow of the gas lamps like smears of dull gold.

Barnes and Dickman charged after him, their footfalls resounding through the cramped alleyways with the weight and inevitability of thunder. The tenements rose around them on either side—towering, cracked facades looming overhead like the jagged ribs of some dead giant. From upper windows, shadows peered out with morbid curiosity, retreating quickly as though fearful of being noticed.

Laundry lines snapped in the wind above them, tattered sheets writhing like spectral banners surrendering to the storm.

"This way!" Barnes shouted, as Jenkins veered sharply down a side passage scarcely wide enough for two men to pass abreast.

Dickman skidded, nearly losing his footing in the muck. "He's fast for a gentleman!"

"Fear lends wings," Barnes answered through clenched teeth.

Jenkins plunged deeper into the labyrinth of alleys. A cat screeched, darting out of his path. Barrels toppled as he shoved past them, and the sharp stench of rotting refuse filled the air. The fog curled around him like grasping fingers, and yet he ran—ran as though the devil himself nipped at his heels.

He reached a fork, where three narrow passages yawned before him like the mouths of hungry beasts. He hesitated only a heartbeat before slipping into the smallest, a cramped vein of the city that twisted like a serpent between the crumbling brick.

Barnes and Dickman exchanged a look—swift, decisive, honed by years of partnership.

"You take the left!" Barnes barked. "I'll circle right!"

They split, boots pounding in opposite directions, their breaths rising in ragged clouds as they vanished into the fog. The city swallowed them whole, then spit them out again in fleeting glimpses—Barnes glimpsing Jenkins's shadow rounding a corner, Dickman hearing the sharp clatter of a cane dragging along a wall.

JENKINS RAN AS if he might outrun fate itself.

He burst from the narrow corridor into a cul-de-sac hemmed in by tall, unyielding brick. A dead end. Rainwater pooled at the centre, glimmering faintly like a mirror of tarnished silver.

He spun, chest heaving, eyes wild.

Detective Michael Barnes stood at the mouth of the alley, breath shallow but gaze steady, his silhouette framed in fog like that of a judgement visiting mortal man.

A second later, Edgar Dickman emerged from the opposite side, breathless yet grinning—feral, triumphant—as though the hunt had finally offered up its quarry.

Jenkins's hand twitched toward his cane.

"Careful," Barnes warned, raising a steadying palm. "There's no need for foolishness."

But whatever reason Jenkins had possessed fled him then. His features contorted—not with fear, but with something colder, sharper, steeped in a desperate cunning.

He lurched backward, twisting the head of his cane with a practised jerk.

A whisper of metal.

A glint of reflected lantern light.

The hidden blade sprang free—a slender dagger gleaming wickedly, its tip catching the dim glow like an eye of polished ice.

"Well now," Dickman muttered, his voice low, "that's a nasty little surprise."

Jenkins brandished the weapon, the blade flickering in and out of sight within the restless mist. His voice trembled, but his resolve—foolish though it was—held.

"Stay back!" he hissed. "One step—one *step*—and I'll gut the first man near me!"

Barnes took a measured stride forward, his presence calm, his tone far more dangerous than Jenkins's blade.

"Put it away, Mr. Jenkins. You are already in enough peril as it is."

"That remains to be seen," Jenkins snarled, voice cracking as the weight of the world bore down upon him.

And then, with a choked sound—part cry, part curse—

he moved.

JENKINS LUNGED WITH A STRANGLED CRY, the dagger catching the light in one cold, murderous flare. The surrounding fog scattered with his movement, swirling into frantic eddies as though recoiling from the violence.

Barnes pivoted aside just in time, feeling the blade slice the air inches from his coat. The narrow alley magnified every sound—the rasp of Jenkins's breath, the scrape of boots sliding on wet stone, the low growl of determination vibrating in Barnes's chest.

"Damn fool!" Dickman barked, closing the distance.

Jenkins twisted, slashing wildly, the blade making short, murderous arcs through the mist. Barnes stepped back once, twice—just enough to avoid being skewered. The killer's movements were quick, but unrefined; desperation lent him strength but destroyed his precision.

"Stand down, Jenkins!" Barnes thundered, his voice echoing off the brick walls.

But Jenkins—cornered, frantic, and half-mad—only snarled, his eyes rolling with animal terror.

He thrust the blade forward again.

This time Barnes met him head-on.

With a swift, brutal motion, Barnes seized Jenkins's wrist. The dagger wrenched sideways, barely missing Barnes's ribs. Jenkins screamed—a high, panicked sound—as Barnes's grip tightened like an iron shackle.

"Dickman—NOW!"

Dickman surged forward from behind, ramming his shoulder into

Jenkins's back with the force of an oncoming carriage. Jenkins stumbled, knocked off balance, his boots skidding over the slick stones. The dagger slipped from his grasp, clattering and spinning away into the shadows like a discarded fang.

But Jenkins wasn't finished.

He twisted violently, throwing his elbow into Dickman's jaw. Dickman reeled—just for a heartbeat—but it was enough for Jenkins to wrench free, clawing toward the dagger's glinting outline.

Barnes grabbed the back of Jenkins's coat and hauled him backward with a snarl of pure effort.

"You're DONE, Jenkins!"

Jenkins writhed like a trapped fox, lashing out with kicks that connected sharply with Barnes's shins. He lunged again for the weapon, fingers grazing the wet stones—

Dickman recovered, diving low and slamming into Jenkins's legs.

All three men crashed to the ground.

The alley erupted in chaos: grunts, the scrape of boots, splashes of filthy water, and the ragged ripping of cloth as the detectives wrestled the murderer into submission.

Jenkins fought with the strength of blind panic, but the two seasoned detectives bore down on him—Barnes pinning his shoulders, Dickman pressing a knee into his spine.

"Hold still, you devil!" Dickman growled, fumbling for the manacles.

Jenkins spat a curse, twisting violently. His nails caught Barnes's cheek, leaving a thin line of blood. Barnes slammed his elbow into the cobbles beside Jenkins's head, barely restraining the impulse to strike.

"Enough!" Barnes roared, breath steaming in the cold air.

The command froze Jenkins just long enough.

Dickman snapped the manacles around Jenkins's wrists with a decisive metallic clack—

a sound sharp enough to slice through the fog itself.

Jenkins collapsed, exhausted, panting like a hunted beast at last cornered.

Barnes rose slowly, wiping blood from his cheek, chest heaving.

Dickman hauled Jenkins upright by the arm, ignoring the man's trembling, defeated weight.

"Well, Mr. Jenkins," Dickman said breathlessly, "your morning constitutional is over."

Jenkins sagged between them, defeated at last.

Barnes jerked his chin toward the mouth of the alley.

"Bring him. The wagon should be waiting."

THE COLD IRON of the manacles bit into his wrists, and with each jolt of the detectives' grip, Victor Jenkins felt his last shreds of freedom slipping away like mist through clenched fingers. The surrounding fog thickened, swallowing the city in a pall of grey, but it could not hide him now. Not anymore.

*Fools,* he thought bitterly. *Barnes and Dickman—righteous dogs nipping at the heels of their betters.*

But the thought rang hollow, even within the refuge of his mind.

He stumbled as they half-dragged him along, boots scraping the cobbles. His breath puffed in uneven bursts, the air tasting of soot and cold iron. Somewhere distant, a church bell tolled the hour—slow, mournful, a sound that throbbed through his bones.

*This can't be the end,* Jenkins told himself. *Not for me. Not after all I've done to stay afloat in this cursed city.*

But even that lie felt fragile.

The fog curled around him, whispering the ghosts of things he'd rather not remember—faces pale and slack, eyes empty, the soft give of flesh beneath his blade. He had tried not to think of them before. The first victim... God, he never meant that one to die. He told himself it had been an accident. A necessity. A requirement.

But after that?

After that, it became easier.

Too easy.

*Raynsford made me do it,* he reminded himself fiercely. *A man must survive as he can. A man must obey if he wants to live another day.*

Yet a part of him—small, weak, but nagging—whispered, *You did more than obey. You relished the power.*

Jenkins clenched his jaw.

No. No, he refused to think that.

He was no monster. He had followed orders. He had done what was necessary.

And yet...

The detectives' footsteps echoed beside him—steady, unrelenting, like the heartbeat of justice—or doom. Barnes marched with grim purpose, blood still marking his cheek where Jenkins's nails had streaked it. Dickman, breathless but resolute, kept a hand clamped on Jenkins's arm with bruising force.

They would drag him back to the precinct.

They would make him confess.

The world would know his name—and not in the way he once fantasized.

*Victor Jenkins,* he thought bitterly, *reduced to a page in the paper. A cautionary tale for the masses. A villain to entertain their breakfast tables.*

A hollow laugh rattled in his chest, escaping before he could swallow it.

The bobbies ahead looked back with revulsion.

Jenkins lowered his eyes.

He felt strangely weightless.

Not liberated—never that.

More like a man already half-dead, drifting between breaths.

He wondered, fleetingly, what would become of him.

The rope, surely.

Or perhaps a final, lifeless collapse in a prison cot where no one would bother to learn his last words.

And in that instant—a moment so fragile it might have shattered under the weight of a whisper—Victor Jenkins felt something he had not allowed himself to feel in years.

Fear.

Real, icy, marrow-deep fear.

Not of death—no, *that* he had seen up close and personal.

But of irrelevance.

Of being forgotten.

Of being nothing more than ink drying on a broadsheet.

He lifted his head just once more, taking in the fog-swathed streets of London—the only home he had ever known, cruel as it was.

*This is the last time I walk them,* he realised.

They marched Jenkins through the fog-choked streets, his boots dragging, his breath ragged.

The Black Maria waited at the corner like a dark iron maw.

Two bobbies straightened as the detectives approached.

"Blimey... you got 'im, sir."

"Not without a dance," Dickman muttered, pushing Jenkins forward.

Barnes gripped Jenkins's shoulder and leaned close enough that his breath brushed the murderer's ear.

"Your reign of shadows ends here."

With a hard shove they sent him into the wagon.

The iron door slammed.

The latch clicked.

A sound final as a coffin lid.

## CHAPTER THIRTY-ONE

The doors of the Black Maria slammed shut with a metallic finality that reverberated down the fog-cloaked street. Barnes and Dickman stood for a moment watching as the wagon lurched forward, lanterns swaying like twin, dim moons in the suffocating mist.

Only when the last clatter of its wheels faded into the labyrinth of narrow lanes did either man speak.

Dickman released a long breath, pressing a hand against his ribs.

"Well," he said ruefully, "that was a dance I'd hoped never to rehearse."

Barnes didn't reply at once. The fog clung to him, dampening his coat and darkening the cut on his cheek. He looked less like a triumphant officer and more like a man who had wrestled directly with London's darkest shadows.

Dickman glanced at him. "You're bleeding, you know."

"It's nothing." Barnes touched the thin line on his cheek, winced, and let his hand fall. "A small price, considering what he might have done."

Dickman snorted. "Aye. Jenkins nearly skewered you more than once. And he fought like a devil cornered."

Barnes took a slow breath. "That's precisely what he was. Cornered. Desperate. Dangerous." His gaze drifted into the swirling gloom where the wagon had disappeared. "Men like him... they do not surrender quietly."

They began to walk, boots echoing rhythmically on the wet stones. The city around them seemed to inhale and exhale with the fog, its streets murmuring with rumor and the slow press of morning life.

"Still," Dickman added after a moment, "that leap you made—grabbing his wrist—bold move. One misstep and I'd be dragging you to the surgeon instead of the station."

Barnes gave a faint, humorless smile. "Instinct."

"Madness," Dickman corrected with a half-grin. "Though I suppose in our line of work, the two are often the same."

They turned a corner, the old streetlamps casting long distorted shadows that stretched and twisted with every flicker of flame.

Barnes slowed, his voice dropping to a quiet, sombre timbre.

"When he lunged... Did you see his eyes?"

Dickman nodded. "Aye. Wild. Like an animal caught in a snare."

"No," Barnes said, brow furrowing. "Not just animal terror. There was... something else."

"Guilt?"

"Maybe. Or perhaps he finally realised the truth: that no matter how far he ran, no matter how cleverly he hid, the fog would never hide him from what he'd done. London has a way of remembering its monsters."

Dickman's expression dimmed, sobered. "You think he repents?"

Barnes shook his head. "No. I think what he fears is not the gallows, but the silence. The obscurity. Being forgotten."

Dickman let out a low whistle. "Not much chance of that. The papers will devour this story. They'll make him infamous."

"Yes." Barnes's jaw tightened. "But infamy is not immortality. And in the end... all he will be is a name on a broadsheet. A grim curiosity for tomorrow's readers."

They walked on, mist curling around them like restless spirits.

"Truth be told," Dickman said quietly, "I'm grateful it's over. That chase... Barnes, I thought for a moment we'd lose him in that maze of alleys."

"We very nearly did," Barnes murmured. "London's underbelly twists like a serpent. But Jenkins... he ran as though he knew those back routes better than daylight. No innocent man runs that way."

Dickman nodded slowly. "No. An innocent man calls for help. A guilty one flees into the fog."

Barnes lifted his gaze toward the faint silhouette of the precinct emerging through the haze.

"Come," he said. "Let's file our report. And then—God willing—we can finally breathe."

A moment passed.

Dickman chuckled. "After a drink?"

Barnes allowed himself the barest hint of a genuine smile.

"A drink," he agreed. "A strong one."

And together, the two detectives disappeared into the thickening fog— victorious, exhausted, and carrying the weight of the chase upon their shoulders like a silent shadow.

# CHAPTER THIRTY-TWO

A fresh unease seeped through the corridors of Raynsford Manor when Horace returned home. A leaden sky pressed against the tall windows, turning their ornate panes to dim, wavering mirrors. Somewhere in the house, a clock tolled the noon hour with a hollow, mournful clang—an ill omen, Judith thought, as she entered her husband's study.

"Where is Thaddeus?" she demanded, her voice strained, trembling with a mother's dread. "You left here last night in haste and swore to me you would bring him home."

Horace Raynsford glowered from behind his massive oaken desk as he sat down. Even that imposing monolith—etched with centuries of the family's crest—could no longer shield him from the fury of the woman before him. The shutters rattled in the rising wind as if echoing her accusation.

"Not now, Judith," he snapped. "I am trying to make sense of matters, and your haranguing is of no assistance."

Pressing both hands to his temples, Horace winced as though the very light pained him. His eyes burned with the remnants of sleepless hours and the beginnings of a brutal headache that seemed to pulse in time with his guilt. Yet no remedy availed him.

"Fetch Jackson," he muttered. "I need my laudanum."

Judith's expression twisted into something between disbelief and contempt.

"Laudanum? You would drug yourself insensible while your son languishes in a cell? Should you not be at the magistrate's door this very moment, pleading—no, *commanding*—his release?"

Horace surged to his feet so abruptly that his chair skidded back and struck the paneled wall with a violent crack. His roar filled the chamber, climbing the rafters like an unleashed beast.

"I offered that fool boy a way out, and he threw it back in my face! If he chooses to rot in that miserable jail, then let him! I wash my hands of the matter."

Judith recoiled, her breath catching. Never had she seen her husband so unhinged, so consumed by wrath that it twisted his features into something grotesque.

"Oh, I shall fetch Jackson," she whispered coldly, "so he may bring you your precious draught—and may it choke you."

Her skirts flared as she turned, only to collide directly with Jackson in the doorway. The silver tray in his hands clattered perilously before settling again.

*Ah,* Jackson thought with weary amusement, *so begins another delightful day at Raynsford Manor.*

"Good day, Madam," he said with impeccable calm. "I have the master's medicine already prepared."

He dared a subtle, conspiratorial wink—one Judith scarcely understood, yet it stirred a prickle of curiosity beneath her indignation.

"Well, get in here, damn you!" bellowed Lord Raynsford, his voice thunderous.

Jackson inclined his head and swept past Judith with the quiet dignity of a man accustomed to storms far greater than this household could muster. Still, she watched him go with a puzzled knit of brow, wondering what, precisely, he had in mind.

It was near tea time when they arrived in London. Judith and Jackson had come by train, their carriage having conveyed them only as far as Dartford railway station. Judith preferred to travel in comfort—and she required speed. If her husband would not see the matter regarding her son resolved, then she would attend to it herself. She could not endure the thought of Thaddeus remaining in such intolerable conditions for a moment longer than was necessary.

When they reached the Metropolitan Police station, however, they discovered that Thaddeus had already been released, much to Judith's relief.

A dreary hush had settled over the narrow street as Judith Raynsford and Jackson approached the modest dwelling. The lamplight, dim and flickering behind glass fogged with the evening damp, cast long tremulous shadows across the stoop. Judith's heart hammered with a mother's dread, each beat echoing like a muffled drum beneath her ribs. She feared what she might find—yet feared ignorance even more.

When Mrs. Parsons opened the door, she looked as though the night had worn her thin. Fatigue lined her features, and her shoulders drooped with the quiet burden of worry. She clearly had no appetite for callers; her scowl deepened the moment she beheld the well-dressed strangers on her threshold.

"I'm not in the way of contributin' to whatever cause you represent," she snapped. "Be off with you."

"Pardon me?" Judith asked, her voice trembling only slightly. "I am searching for my son—Thaddeus."

Mrs. Parsons froze. The harshness drained from her face, leaving only startled remorse.

"Oh my... Lady Raynsford, forgive me. Thaddeus is resting in the parlour. He... well..." Her voice faltered. "He does not look well. Pray, come inside."

Judith swept past her at once, Jackson close behind.

The parlour was dim save for a small fire sputtering in the grate, its glow revealing Thaddeus slumped in a worn armchair. His skin was pale as bleached linen, his eyes shadowed, his form gaunt beneath his clothing. Judith dropped to her knees beside him, her voice shattering.

"Thad—oh heavens, look at you. You are so thin—have they not been feeding you?"

Behind them, Mrs. Parsons sniffed indignantly. Jackson turned, brow raised.

"I assure you," the woman declared, bristling, "I've prepared plenty o' food. I even bring it right here to him instead of insistin' he sit at table. Look there."

She pointed to a small, polished table. Upon it sat a bowl of stew, its top darkening with a cold skin, and slices of bread slathered in butter—untouched.

"I can't force him to eat," she added, voice wavering with guilt.

Thaddeus looked up at her, offering a wan smile.

"It is not your fault, Mrs. Parsons. I shall try—I promise."

She lifted her chin with an air of wounded defiance before leaving the room with as much dignity as she could muster.

Thaddeus turned to Judith, anxiety flickering in his eyes.

"Mother—how did you get here? If Father finds out—he will be furious."

Judith patted his arm with a tenderness that trembled on the edge of ferocity.

"Do not trouble yourself about your father. Jackson gave him enough laudanum to fell a horse. He will not stir before morning. I *had* to see you. We went first to the precinct—they told us you had been released. I have been near mad with worry. Horace refuses to tell me anything, so I have come to learn the truth from you."

She rose and took the chair opposite him. Jackson lingered nearby until Judith waved a dismissive hand.

"Jackson, sit down. You hover like a fretful crow."

"Yes, Madam."

He obeyed, albeit stiffly.

Thaddeus took a slow, steadying breath and began to recount all he had endured. Judith listened, her hands clasped tightly in her lap, her eyes widening with each revelation.

"That is why you are so thin?" she whispered. "Going out each night... hunting a murderer? You could have been slain yourself! Oh, my poor boy... you must come home. At once."

"No, Mother. I cannot. They have yet to apprehend the killer—though I know who it is."

Judith's brow furrowed, her breath catching.

"And have you told the police?"

"Yes. I await word from them. But Mother—there is more. And I doubt you shall be pleased."

"Tell me," she said, leaning forward, voice taut.

Thaddeus swallowed.

"It was Father's men who kidnapped me. One among them—one we did not know—who was in Father's employ. Father himself came to the holding cell and admitted that the man was indeed in his service."

Judith went white to the lips.

"What?"

"Mother... Father used his man to commit the murders. To ensure I was accused. To force me into accepting his bargain—to make everything vanish if only I would marry Hortense Remington."

The words lingered between them, stark and irrevocable. Thaddeus felt the weight lift from his chest even as dread flickered anew—fear of what this truth might unleash.

Judith's face darkened. A slow, creeping tide of blood rose up her throat and into her ears. Her eyes flashed—no longer soft, but steely, dangerous, aflame. Thaddeus had never seen his mother thus transformed; she looked a creature carved from righteous fury.

"My son," she breathed, gripping his hand with fierce affection. "My poor, tormented boy."

She sat back, silent for a long, tense moment.

"Mother... once they capture the true killer, I must tell Detective Barnes everything. But I fear he will not believe me. And it will ruin us—all of us. I do not want you harmed."

Judith's head snapped upward.

"Do not trouble yourself with me. Nor with the manor, nor the business, nor your father's reputation." Her voice grew icily calm. "You must do what is right. What you feel compelled to do. The truth will surface regardless. It *always* does. And as for your father..."

Her gaze hardened into something unforgiving, final.

"He deserves whatever comes."

THE FIRE CRACKLED in the hearth, but the feeble warmth could not dispel the cold dread pooling through the room. Jackson sat rigidly on the edge of his chair; Thaddeus stared down at his own trembling hands; and Judith rose with a resolve that had been years in the making, though only now did it sharpen into something formidable.

For a long moment, the room held its breath.

At last Judith spoke, her voice low, iron-edged.

"Thaddeus, you must remain here and rest. You are safe beneath Mrs. Parsons's roof. Safer, I daresay, than in your own father's house."

Thaddeus opened his mouth to protest, but she silenced him with a gentle touch to his cheek.

"No. You have endured enough. Allow me to bear the next blow."

Jackson stood at once, alarm creasing his brow. "Madam... where are you going?"

Judith turned toward him, drawing her shawl tight around her shoulders.

"To Raynsford Manor," she said simply. "There is a storm long overdue, and I mean to meet it head on."

Her words chilled the air like the tolling of a funeral bell.

THE WIND HOWLED through the street as Judith stepped outside, Jackson hurrying to her side, struggling to keep pace. Clouds churned overhead like ink spilled across the heavens, and the lamps flickered violently as if afraid of the darkness gathering above.

"Madam," Jackson pleaded, "your husband may not take kindly to—"

"To the truth?" she interrupted sharply. "Horace Raynsford has never taken kindly to anything that challenged his dominion. But that time is ending."

She climbed into the waiting carriage, boots disappearing beneath the hem of her heavy gown, and Jackson followed reluctantly. As the door shut with a decisive click, Thaddeus watched from the window, his heart clenching with fear and pride in equal measure.

*What have I unleashed?* he wondered.

The carriage lurched forward, wheels splashing through the deepening puddles, and Judith forced herself not to look back.

THE TRAIN GROANED as it pulled away from London Bridge, its iron wheels shrieking against the rails before settling into a relentless rhythm. The lamps inside the carriage swayed faintly with each jolt, casting long shadows that slid across the compartment walls like uneasy spirits.

Judith sat rigidly opposite Jenkins, her gloved hands folded tightly in her lap. The events of the evening pressed upon her like the weight of the darkening sky beyond the window.

For several miles neither spoke.

At last Jackson cleared his throat.

"Madam... may I speak plainly?"

Judith lifted her gaze. "You always do, Jackson."

The faintest ghost of a smile touched his lips.

"I feared as much."

The train thundered across a bridge, the sound reverberating through the carriage like distant artillery.

"You heard the young master," he continued quietly. "If what he says proves true... Lord Raynsford's position will become untenable."

Judith stared out the window where the last dim lights of London drifted past like dying stars.

"Untenable?" she repeated softly.

Jackson inclined his head.

"The newspapers would devour him. The courts would ruin him. The Raynsford name—"

"—will survive," Judith interrupted calmly.

Jackson blinked.

"It will?" he asked.

Judith's eyes hardened.

"Yes," she said. "But it will survive without Horace Raynsford attached to it."

The words settled between them like a verdict already rendered.

Jackson studied her in silence for a moment.

Then, very slowly, he nodded.

"I had wondered," he said.

Outside, the countryside rolled past in darkness as the train carried them back toward Kent.

Toward Raynsford Manor.

Toward the reckoning waiting there.

# CHAPTER THIRTY-THREE

The precinct rose out of the fog like some squat stone sentinel, its gas lamps flickering grimly in the heavy air. Barnes and Dickman mounted the steps in silence, their footfalls dull against the rain-darkened stone. Inside, the building hummed with its usual murmur—clerks scratching away at ledgers, bobbies hauling in drunks, the low drone of distant voices echoing from the holding cells.

Yet beneath all that, there lingered a peculiar tension, as though the very walls were listening.

They pushed open the door to the main office. A single oil lantern burned upon the central desk, casting long, quivering shadows across piles of reports and worn case files. The room smelled of old paper, lamp oil, and coats not yet dry from the street.

"Detectives," murmured Sergeant Hale from behind a stack of papers. "Word came in you nabbed your man."

Barnes removed his gloves finger by finger, his face unreadable. "He was brought in ahead of us."

"Yes, sir. Put straight into one of the reinforced cells, as instructed."

Barnes gave a curt nod. "Good. No visitors. No conversation with anyone but police."

Hale's eyebrows lifted. "Dangerous sort, is he?"

Barnes exchanged a brief look with Dickman.

"More dangerous than most."

The sergeant swallowed and bent over his ledger. Barnes turned toward the row of desks near the far wall.

"Constable," he said sharply.

A young officer straightened at once.

"Fetch Jenkins from his cell and bring him below."

"Yes, sir."

The constable hurried off. For a moment Barnes said nothing. He stood with one hand braced against the desk, listening to the ordinary sounds of the station carry on around him—the scratch of pens, the clatter of boots, the slurred protest of some drunk being half-dragged down the corridor. It all felt strangely distant, as though the building itself were holding its breath for what came next.

At last the constable returned.

Jenkins came with him between two officers, wrists still bound. His once-neat coat bore smears of grime from the alley struggle; his hair hung limp, plastered to his brow. He had recovered enough of himself to stand upright, but not enough to conceal the strain in his face. In his eyes there flickered something unsettled—part defiance, part dread.

Barnes studied him only a moment.

"Bring him down."

They led Jenkins past rows of desks and flickering lamps, then through a narrow passage and down into a small stone-walled chamber beneath the station. The room was spare: a table, three chairs, and a single lantern whose flame sputtered with every draught, casting the shadows of the men upon the walls in long, uneven shapes.

Jenkins was forced into the central chair. His bound hands trembled faintly.

Barnes shut the door with a slow, deliberate thud. He removed his wet coat, shook the moisture from it, and hung it on a hook near the desk. Dickman did the same, muttering about the weight of London's eternal fog. Together they approached the long oak table where clean blotters and fresh ink waited like silent witnesses.

"Sit up straight, Mr. Jenkins," he said. "We have questions."

Dickman leaned against the opposite wall, arms crossed, watching like a hawk waiting for its prey to weaken.

Barnes placed his palms on the table and leaned forward, the lantern's glow reflecting in his sharp, unyielding gaze.

"You have been implicated," he began, "in a series of murders that have plagued this city for weeks. Your... associates, Mr. Corbeld and Mr. Matson, have already spoken your name."

Jenkins flinched as though struck.

"I—I don't know what you mean," he stammered. "Those two idiots would sell their own mothers if it suited them."

"Possibly," Dickman drawled. "But that does not change the fact that every trail leads to you. And you were prepared to use a concealed blade on us this very morning—hardly the behavior of an innocent man."

Jenkins tightened his jaw, saying nothing.

Barnes continued, voice lowering to a measured threat.

"We know you worked for Lord Raynsford. We know you were at the scenes of several crimes. And we know—without question—that someone ordered you to frame Thaddeus Raynsford for these killings."

Jenkins's composure cracked. His breath hitched; his eyes darted from Barnes to Dickman as if seeking escape where none existed.

"I advise you, Mr. Jenkins," Barnes said softly, "to tell us the truth. Men fare poorly withholding confessions in this room."

Silence stretched thin, oppressive as the stale air in the chamber.

Then Jenkins swallowed hard. Sweat beaded at his temple.

"You don't understand..." he whispered. "I—I didn't want to do it."

Barnes stepped closer, expression unreadable.

"Then enlighten us."

Jenkins's shoulders sagged. His voice trembled as he spoke:

"It was Lord Raynsford."

Dickman's eyebrows shot upward.

"So he *did* give you orders?"

Jenkins nodded, a bitter laugh escaping him. "Orders? No. Threats. Promises. The devil himself would've sounded sweeter. He said I owed him. Said he'd erase my debts, keep the law off my heels—if I did his bidding."

"Which included murder?" Barnes asked, his tone like cold steel.

Jenkins closed his eyes. "I never meant to kill the first woman. It was supposed to be a warning. But Raynsford said there could be no loose ends. After that... it grew easier."

A shudder ran through him, as though the ghosts of his victims had passed over his skin.

"And Thaddeus?" Dickman pressed. "What part did he play in Raynsford's wicked scheme?"

Jenkins hesitated only a moment before his resolve broke entirely.

"Raynsford wanted to force his son's hand. Said Thaddeus was being... difficult. Said the boy needed to be frightened into accepting a marriage arrangement. He told me to make it look like Thaddeus was the killer. Plant evidence. Spread whispers in the right ears. Make the city turn on him."

Barnes felt his jaw clench. "You kidnapped him."

Jenkins bowed his head in shame. "Yes. Me and Raynsford's other man. We kept him in that warehouse. It was supposed to be until the constables found him. The whole thing was staged. Father against son. Devilry, the whole of it."

Dickman exhaled sharply. "By God... the man would sacrifice his own flesh and blood."

Jenkins looked up, eyes glistening. "Believe what you will of me, but I swear—I never wanted to kill the boy."

Barnes stared at him for a long moment.

"Your confession will be written. You will sign it. And the magistrate will hear every word."

Jenkins nodded weakly.

"And Victor..." Barnes added quietly, leaning close enough that Jenkins flinched.

"You should pray. For the courts may show you mercy—but the ghosts of those you took? They never shall."

Jenkins broke then—completely. His sobs echoed off the stone walls, bitter, ragged, and hopeless.

Barnes stepped back. Dickman retrieved the writing materials. A confession was taken down, signed, and sealed.

Outside, thunder rumbled across the city, as though Heaven itself announced the coming reckoning.

The early evening sky had sunk into a bruised shade of violet by the time Barnes and Dickman returned to the polished door of Apartment 1D. The hallway, though tidy, felt unnervingly still—as though the very walls were holding their breath. Somewhere far off, a carriage rumbled along the street, its wheels echoing like distant thunder.

Barnes rested a hand on the gleaming brass knob.

"Unlock it," he murmured to the constable behind them.

The key scraped in the lock with a reluctant groan, and the door swung inward with a soft hiss of stale, trapped air. The apartment beyond was eerily quiet, its neatness so precise it bordered on the unnatural.

Dickman stepped forward first. "Good Lord... it's as if the man lived in a museum."

Barnes entered after him, eyes sweeping the room with the sharpness of a hawk appraising prey. Everything appeared meticulously arranged—cushions perfectly aligned, books stacked in crisp geometric order, the mantel swept clean of dust. Even the hearth seemed unused, its grate polished to a shine.

Too perfect. Too controlled.

A life choreographed, not lived.

"Shut the door," Barnes murmured. The constable obeyed, sealing them into the unnatural stillness.

THE FAINT SCENT of lavender polish hung in the air—pleasant enough, but beneath it lingered something else. Something musky. Metallic. Barnes could not name it yet, but his instincts stirred like coals awakening to flame.

Dickman made for the writing desk, its drawers aligned to millimetric precision.

"If this man kept records, they'll be in here."

He opened the first drawer and let out a low whistle.

Letters, carefully bundled and tied with ribbon, lay within. The handwriting was small and angular—each stroke deliberate.

Barnes approached the mantel, where a collection of small trinkets rested—innocuous at first sight: a brass thimble, a polished stone, a broken watch chain. But when Barnes leaned closer, the hairs at his neck prickled.

"These are trophies," he whispered.

Dickman looked up sharply. "You're certain?"

Barnes lifted the watch chain. "From Jenkins's victims? Quite possibly. Murderers of his sort sometimes cling to their sins."

Dickman grimaced. "To remember... or to relive."

THEY MOVED into the adjoining room, its door silently swinging open on well-oiled hinges. The bedroom was as spotless as the parlour—bed tightly made, wardrobe shut, boots aligned like a soldier's on parade.

Barnes opened the wardrobe. Inside hung only a handful of garments—each dark, each immaculate. But at the bottom lay a narrow case, velvet-lined, its latch undone.

Barnes crouched.

"Help me with this."

Together, they lifted the lid.

Inside lay an array of tools: slender blades, fine wire, a small vial of something dark and half-dried. Dickman recoiled.

"God above... the instruments of a butcher."

"Yes," Barnes agreed softly. "Of a man who likes to watch his work unfold slowly."

He shut the case with care, as if sealing away something venomous.

DICKMAN RETURNED to the writing desk, opening the last drawer. At first glance, it appeared empty. But his fingers skimmed the interior and halted.

"There's a false bottom," he murmured.

With a deft tug, the thin panel popped free.

Inside lay a small journal, bound in black leather.

Barnes's breath hitched. "Bring it to the lantern."

They stood together beneath the dim glow. Barnes opened the journal. The handwriting matched that of the bundled letters, but here it was frantic—ink smeared, words overlapping, sentences repeating like chants.

*He told me to do it. Raynsford will be pleased.*

*The boy must break, must bend. He is soft. Weak. Unlike his father. I cannot fail him. I will not fail him again.*

Dickman felt a chill settle through his bones. "This is the final nail. Raynsford's guilt is writ clear across these pages."

Barnes closed the journal with quiet finality.

"Yes. And the magistrate will not ignore it."

He paused, gaze sweeping the room once more.

"What an immaculate space," he murmured. "And yet every polished surface hides rot."

Dickman nodded grimly.

"Like the man who lived here."

THEY STEPPED BACK into the hall, the constable securing the door behind them. The fog outside had thickened, pressing against the building like a living thing.

Barnes tucked the journal beneath his coat.

"This," he said, "changes everything."

Dickman glanced toward the darkening street. "Raynsford will feel the walls closing in."

Barnes exhaled, the weight of truth settling on his shoulders like a shroud.

"And it is about time."

They descended the stairs and stepped into the gathering storm, knowing the next confrontation would shake London to its very foundations.

THE MANOR ROSE from the fog like a brooding beast, its many windows dark save for the faint glow in Horace's study. The very stones seemed steeped in disquiet, whispering secrets through the creeping ivy.

Lightning flared across the sky—brief, violent, and illuminating Judith's pale, determined features.

She ascended the steps, each footfall echoing like a verdict.

Jackson reached out. "Madam—perhaps we should wait—"

She lifted her hand, commanding silence.

"I will not wait another moment."

With that, she threw open the great oak door.

THE ENTRY HALL WAS DIM, shadow-cloaked, the scent of extinguished candles mingling with the lingering perfume of laudanum. The house was unnaturally still. Not even the servants stirred.

Judith moved down the corridor, skirts sweeping like ghostly wings, until she reached the study. The door stood ajar, and a faint light flickered within.

Horace Raynsford sat slumped at his desk, head in his hands, the laudanum bottle uncorked beside him. His dark hair hung disheveled over his brow, and though consciousness had begun to return in sluggish waves, he appeared half-human, half-phantom in the wavering glow of the lamp.

Judith stepped inside, her presence sharp and unmistakable.

Horace stirred. "Judith...?" His voice rasped. "What—what are you doing awake?"

She shut the study door behind her with a soft but resolute click.

"I know *everything*," she said.

Horace froze. The room, the night, the world—all seemed to stop breathing.

Judith continued, her voice slow, deliberate, deadly calm:

"I know what you did to our son."

Lightning burst across the window, casting her in stark white brilliance—an avenging spirit risen to pass judgement.

Horace Raynsford stared at her, realisation dawning like a poison sunrise.

"Judith," he whispered, trembling, "listen to me—"

But Judith stepped forward, eyes blazing with a fury years suppressed.

"No. *You* will listen."

# CHAPTER THIRTY-FOUR

Barnes pulled the confession pages from his coat—Victor Jenkins's written admission, the ink still dark, the cramped handwriting betraying the man's terror. Beside it, he placed their own incident report, already half-filled with the facts of the chase, the capture, and the weapon retrieved.

Dickman rolled up his sleeves. "Let's finish this, then."

They sat, pens scratching steadily. The lantern hissed. Outside, thunder groaned against the horizon.

Barnes entered the facts into the ledger with careful precision: the pursuit, the suspect's armed resistance, the concealed blade recovered at the scene, the injuries sustained by the officers, and the final moment of arrest. But when he reached the section marked *MOTIVE*, his pen hesitated.

Dickman noticed. "The part about Raynsford?" he asked quietly.

Barnes's jaw tightened. "Yes."

Dickman set down his pen and leaned back in his chair. "We have Jenkins's confession. The journal from his flat. Clovis and Erwin's statements. It's more evidence than we've had on some murderers."

"It makes no difference," Barnes muttered. "Not to the Lord Mayor. Not to the Council. Raynsford is a lord. Untouchable."

The silence settled heavily.

Barnes forced himself to write the truth anyway:

*'Jenkins states he acted under the direction of Lord Horace Raynsford.'*

The pen left a small blot of ink at the end of the sentence—a quivering mark of frustration.

Dickman exhaled. "There. It's down in black and white, even if no one cares to read it."

Barnes closed his eyes briefly. "Someone will read it. Someone will remember."

He lowered his voice. "Crime doesn't cease to be crime just because it wears a title."

Sergeant Hale approached, clearing his throat. "Chief Inspector Coghill's office is still lit, sirs. Was hopin' you'd take the report to him before he goes home."

"Home," Barnes repeated dryly. "A luxury, that."

He gathered the papers, tapping them into a neat stack. Dickman rose, stretching stiff shoulders.

As they walked toward Coghill's office, the corridor seemed interminably long, lined with portraits of past lawmen—stern-faced, hollow-eyed men who had spent their lives pursuing justice, only to be outmatched again and again by power's invisible hand.

At the door, Barnes paused.

"Ready?" Dickman asked.

"No," Barnes replied honestly. "But let's go in anyway."

He knocked.

"Enter," came Coghill's weary voice.

Barnes opened the door, stepping inside with the thick report held like an unlit torch. Dickman followed, shutting the door softly behind them.

Chief Inspector Coghill looked up from his desk, dark shadows beneath his eyes. He seemed older than he had that morning.

"Is it done?" he asked.

Barnes set the report down before him.

"It is," he said. "Jenkins confessed. We have the evidence. All of it."

Coghill opened the folder.

Dickman added, "Everything you need is there. Names, motives—every rot-filled detail."

But Barnes remained standing, his voice low and devoid of triumph.

"Chief," he said, "the city has its murderer. But it does not have its justice."

Coghill's eyes flicked up, and for a heartbeat, every lamp in the station seemed to dim.

THE BUILDING HAD FALLEN to a muted hush, the kind that settles only after long hours of chaos. Most of the bobbies had drifted off to their rounds or their ledgers, leaving the corridors dim and the air still. At the far end of the hall, the washroom was lit by a single guttering lamp, its flame trembling in the draught like a nervous witness.

Barnes pushed open the door and stepped inside.

The room was cold—tiles slick with condensation, a basin flecked with old water stains, the faint smell of carbolic clinging to the air. He shut the door behind him, welcoming the solitude.

At last, a moment to breathe.

He leaned over the basin and splashed his face, the shock of the cold water biting into his skin. When he looked up, the mirror before him reflected a man carved from fatigue and resolve—hair damp with fog, shirt clinging to him, and a thin line of blood trailing from the cut Jenkins had left along his cheek.

The wound stung sharply now that adrenaline had faded.

Barnes exhaled through his nose. "Damn fool," he muttered at his reflection—not Jenkins, but himself.

He pulled a clean cloth from the shelf, dipped it into the cool water, and pressed it against the wound. The sting made him inhale sharply.

Behind him, the lantern flickered, throwing erratic shadows across the walls—shadows that shifted and danced like echoes of the chase, of boots on cobbles, of a blade slicing the fog.

His mind replayed the moment Jenkins lunged, the snarl on the man's face, the glint of murderous intent in his eyes.

Barnes's jaw tightened.

He had seen men kill in panic, in passion, in madness. But Jenkins had killed with purpose. For coin. For obedience. For reasons that made the blood run cold.

As he dabbed the cloth against his cheek, Barnes whispered under his breath, "You're lucky, Jenkins. Had that blade been aimed a hair higher..."

He didn't finish the thought.

Instead, Barnes reached for the small tin of salve kept on a high shelf. He opened it and hesitated a moment—just long enough for a wave of weariness to wash over him. His shoulders sagged. His eyes burned.

He wasn't a young man anymore.

Not green. Not new to violence.

But each case left its mark.

On the city.

On the victims.

On *him*.

The salve was cold on his skin. He worked it carefully into the cut, feeling the sting fade into a low throb.

A knock sounded lightly at the door.

He didn't turn. "Yes?"

Dickman's voice filtered through the wood. "Barnes? You all right in there?"

Barnes glanced at his reflection again—tired eyes, clenched jaw, the faint, ghostly trace of the man he once was.

He answered, "I'm fine."

"You sure? That gash looked worse from where I stood."

Barnes secured the bandage with firm, steady fingers. "It's nothing. Go on ahead. I'll join you shortly."

Dickman paused.

"All right then. Don't take too long. We've still the Raynsford business to discuss."

"I know," Barnes said quietly. "I'll be there."

Footsteps retreated down the hall.

Barnes straightened, gripping the sides of the basin. For a long moment he stared at the dripping cloth, feeling the weight of the night settle heavier than the bandage on his face.

"Jenkins is in chains," he murmured. "But the worst of this case still walks free."

The lantern flickered again, its flame bending toward the open door, as though reaching for him.

He extinguished it.

And in the darkness, with only the faint glow from the corridor seeping through the crack beneath the door, Barnes took one steadying breath, pushed away from the basin, and returned to the fight waiting outside.

A PALL of late-evening fog curled around the modest dwelling of Mrs. Parsons, pressing against its windows like a living thing. Inside, the light of a single oil lamp cast soft amber halos across the parlour walls, where Thaddeus Raynsford sat hunched in an armchair, fingers worrying at a frayed bit of upholstery. The weight of sleepless days clung to him—his eyes hollow, his posture bent as though braced for a blow that had not yet fallen.

Mrs. Parsons fussed in the adjoining kitchen, the rattle of crockery a comforting if weary rhythm.

A knock sounded at the door.

Thaddeus flinched. Mrs. Parsons appeared at once, wiping her hands on her apron, brows knitting as she approached the entrance.

When she opened it, two familiar silhouettes emerged from the fog—Detective Barnes, rigid and solemn, and Dickman, breath misting in the chill night air.

Mrs. Parsons stepped aside without question. "Go on, then," she whispered to them. "He's in the parlour."

Barnes nodded his thanks and entered first. The floorboards creaked beneath his boots—soft, almost apologetic. Dickman followed, drawing the door shut behind them with a muted click that seemed to seal the outside world away.

Thaddeus looked up sharply.

"Detectives," he breathed, rising halfway from his seat. "Is something wrong?"

Barnes exchanged a quick glance with Dickman—an unspoken agreement—before stepping closer. The shadows fluttered around his face, obscuring the fresh bandage along his cheek.

"No," Barnes said quietly. "Nothing is wrong."

He paused, his voice gentling. "Mr. Raynsford... we have news."

Thaddeus stood. His hands trembled visibly. "Please—just tell me."

Dickman took a step forward, his tone uncharacteristically soft.

"Thaddeus... you are cleared. Of everything. All charges. Every suspicion."

The words seemed to hang suspended in the air, fragile as a wisp of mist.

Thaddeus blinked. "Cleared?" His voice broke. "Truly?"

Barnes's expression softened—rare for him, and all the more sincere because of it.

"Yes. Victor Jenkins has confessed. Thoroughly. In great detail.

He admitted to the murders... the staging... the plot to frame you. We have it in writing. And we have corroboration."

Dickman nodded firmly. "You're a free man, Thaddeus. Entirely."

For a heartbeat, the room was utterly silent.

Then Thaddeus's knees seemed to give way beneath him. He sank into the armchair, burying his face in his hands. A sound escaped him—half sob, half gasp—as though the very air had finally returned to his lungs after days of suffocation.

Mrs. Parsons rushed in at the sound, her apron already lifted to dab at her eyes.

"Oh, thank the Lord," she whispered, pressing a hand to her chest.

Thaddeus forced himself upright, eyes shining with unshed tears. "Detectives... I—"

He swallowed hard. "I cannot thank you enough. You believed me. You listened."

Barnes leaned forward slightly, his voice measured, calm.

"You survived something no one ought ever endure. And you kept your truth even when the city turned its back on you. That takes courage."

Dickman added gently, "You did nothing wrong, lad. Nothing at all."

Thaddeus exhaled shakily, some last piece of fear unspooling from him.

"But," Barnes continued, tone shifting like a gathering storm, "there is more to settle yet. Matters concerning your father."

At that, Thaddeus's shoulders tightened—but before dread could take hold, Barnes raised a hand.

"Not tonight," he said. "Tonight, you rest. You have earned that much."

Dickman touched the brim of his hat. "We'll speak again soon. But for now—take comfort in knowing the truth has come to light."

Barnes nodded once, deeply.

"You are free, Mr. Raynsford."

Thaddeus closed his eyes, absorbing those words as though they were a balm to every wound he bore—physical, emotional, and otherwise.

When he looked up again, gratitude trembled in his voice.

"Thank you," he whispered. "Both of you."

Barnes and Dickman stepped back toward the door, their figures swallowed slowly by the halo of lamplight.

As they left, the fog stirred around them—but in that small parlour, for the first time in days, the air felt warm.

When the door shut behind Detectives Barnes and Dickman, the echo lingered like a fading heartbeat. Their footsteps receded into the fog-drenched night, and Mrs. Parsons—after a final, trembling smile—retreated to the kitchen, leaving Thaddeus at last in solitude.

The parlour, lit by a single wavering lamp, felt strangely altered: not brighter, not lighter, but... *possible* in a way it had not felt for days. Yet the stillness pressed against him with uncanny weight, as though the house itself waited to see what he would do next.

Thaddeus sank back into the armchair, his limbs suddenly heavy, boneless. The cushion seemed to cradle him, but he could not relax. His breath shuddered out of him in uneven waves.

*Free.*

The word felt foreign on his tongue. Unreal.

He lifted his hands and stared at them—thin, trembling, pale. They looked like someone else's hands, a stranger's hands. Hands that had been bound. Hands that had clawed the filthy floor of a holding cell. Hands that had trembled in fear, in fury, in helplessness.

He pressed them to his face.

A sob cracked loose—silent, raw, shattering.

Then another.

And another.

He did not cry like a frightened boy. He cried like a man who had been broken in half and had only now, this very moment, realised it.

His breath hitched.

He bowed over his knees, shoulders shaking, letting the weight of the past days flood him—the cell with its iron bars, the cold stone walls, the suffocating accusations, the sickening notion that his own father might let him hang to protect the family name.

The memory of Barnes's words echoed in his mind:

*"You survived something no one ought ever endure."*

Had he?

Or had he simply been worn down to nothing, scraped hollow and left to drift?

A soft scratch at the window made him lift his head. Outside, the fog writhed like a living veil, pressing faintly against the glass as if urging him to rise, to breathe, to keep going.

He wiped his face with shaking fingers.

They believed him. The detectives believed him.

Victor Jenkins had confessed.

And Thaddeus Raynsford... was innocent.

The relief cut deeper than the fear ever had.

He sat up slowly, drawing a long, steadying breath. His heartbeat found a new rhythm—not the frantic stutter of a hunted man, but the tentative steadiness of someone who might yet reclaim his life.

But beneath that relief lay something else—something dark and jagged, like a splinter embedded too deep to remove.

*Father.*

Thaddeus swallowed against the rising nausea.

It should have been a comfort to know the detectives intended to pursue justice. But he had seen the way Barnes's expression shifted at the mention of Horace Raynsford. Had heard, in the Chief Inspector's voice, the quiet warning about power, influence... and untouchability.

His father would not go quietly. His father would not accept the truth. His father would not stop.

A tremor rippled through him.

*Mother knows... and she will do anything to protect me.*

He didn't know whether that thought comforted him—or frightened him.

Slowly, he rose from the chair. His legs wobbled, but he caught himself, one hand gripping the armrest.

The room swayed gently, as though uncertain how to exist now that the storm had passed.

Thaddeus moved to the small table where the untouched stew sat congealing. Mrs. Parsons had tried so hard to care for him. He reached for the spoon.

His hand steadied at last.

He took a bite.

It was the first thing he'd tasted in days that didn't dissolve into dust on his tongue.

When he had finished several slow mouthfuls, he set the spoon down and straightened, feeling—if not strong—then at least less fragile.

He crossed to the window and rested his forehead against the cool glass. Outside, the fog curled around the streetlamps, turning their faint glow into spectral halos.

He whispered to the mist, "I am free."

Then, softer:

"But what comes next?"

The fog pressed closer, as if listening.

And Thaddeus Raynsford, at last unshackled yet far from safe, let the question settle in the quiet of the night... knowing the answer would change everything.

A STORM HAD SETTLED over London—one not merely of rain, but of unease. The precinct itself seemed to sag beneath the weight of its own secrets, the oil lamps sputtering with restless flames as if aware that justice, once again, was being shackled by invisible hands.

Barnes and Dickman walked the dim corridor toward Chief Inspector Coghill's office, boots echoing on the stone floor in grim counterpoint to the distant roll of thunder. Both men carried the heavy knowledge that their next task—though necessary—would shake the very foundations of the city's social order.

# The Times

Wednesday, October 15, 1862

# VICTOR JENKINS IDENTIFIED AS THE MURDERER

## CAPTURE AFTER DARING CHASE

### SÉANCE SLAYER IN CUSTODY

**LONDON**—Victor Jenkins, 38, believed to be the notorious 'Séance Slayer," has been apprehended by the Metropolitan Police after a dramatic chase through the narrow streets of Whitechapel yesterday evening.

The arrest was effected late yesterday evening after Inspectors Barnes and Dickman, acting upon information gathered during the course of their inquiries, located the suspect in the vicinity of his last known movements. Upon being challenged, Jenkins attempted to flee, leading officers through a succession of narrow courts and dimly lit passages before he was ultimately brought to ground and secured.

The apprehension of Victor Jenkins after a daring chase through the steets of Whitechapel last evening.

## DESTERADO'S TAKEDOWN ENDS STRING OF MEDIUM MURDERS

*After weeks of fear and speculation, Londoners can now breathe a sigh of relief as the man suspected of the Séance Slayer murders has*

### METROPOLITAN POLICE

**Inspectors Barnes & Dickman**

The apprehension of Victor Jenkins followed a determined pursuit led by Inspectors Barnes and Dickman of the Metropolitan Police, whose investigations into the recent string of murders had, for some time, narrowed suspicion upon the accused. Acting upon information received late in the evening, the officers proceeded to Whitechapel, where Jenkins was observed attempting to quit the vicinity under circumstances deemed suspicious. Upon being challenged, the suspect fled, initiating a chase through several narrow courts and alleyways.

### FULL CONFESSION

It has been reported that Jenkins has confessed to the murders after an exhosutive night of questioning. He has ofered chilling details of the suspect, have been recused wilh approval by both authonities and the public aliite.

### PARLIAMENT

**REPERCUSSIONS OF THE CAPTURE**

Diccmmm on the & ar tmmm ocah ay.

### THE STATE OF TRADE

Paice of cotiox fiuctuates. The marhet reports airenifed acfrerty axcraning from divertaties moke, Let of prices are puidished on Page 8. S6.6

### THE WEATHER

Today in Londone Occasional shovers. and cool temperatures. Cocdifiers ire agaized to to samonr orcraect in the coming days.

**A SURE METHOD TO CURE INDIGESTION**

**HOLLOWAY'S PILLS**

Sentevers aonut prociues af Lokees-Pnynrcreon coc7. Obtanalies at Pharmested-Appticcenics.

**FINE ROOMS TO LET IN KENSINGTON**

Apply to Jenkins 8. Son, Hosse Agarts

Barnes knocked once.

"Enter," came Coghill's weary voice.

The inspectors stepped inside. The Chief sat behind his desk, the glow of the lantern carving deep shadows into his gaunt features. Papers lay strewn across the blotter; he looked as though he had not slept in days.

"Sit," Coghill said, rubbing the bridge of his nose. "We have... matters to discuss."

Barnes and Dickman exchanged a wary glance before taking their seats.

Coghill folded his hands, hesitating. "Your report has reached the Lord Mayor."

Dickman straightened, one brow lifting. "Good. Then he understands the gravity—"

"No," Coghill interrupted sharply. "You misunderstand. He has expressed profound *distaste* for the direction of your inquiry."

Barnes's jaw clenched. "Our inquiry is supported by testimony, evidence, and three written confessions."

"Yes," Coghill replied softly. "Against men of no consequence. Victor Jenkins, Clovis, Erwin—common criminals. Their lives, in the eyes of the city's rulers, are dust. Easily swept away."

He paused. His gaze darkened.

"But Lord Horace Raynsford is another matter entirely."

A silence fell over the room that felt thick enough to choke on.

Barnes forced the words out. "We know what he has done. And we know why. His orchestration—the kidnappings... the murders... the attempt to frame his own son—"

"Enough," Coghill said, voice cracking like a whip. "You think I do not believe you? I do. God help me, I read your report twice over, hoping some detail—*any* detail—might be wrong."

Dickman leaned forward, fists curling. "Then allow us to make the arrest."

The Chief's eyes softened with something like despair.

"I cannot."

Barnes felt a cold fury ignite in his gut. "Cannot... or *will not*?"

Coghill's face twitched—pain, guilt, resignation. "The Lord Mayor has forbidden it."

Dickman's breath left him in a harsh rush. "Forbidden? On what grounds?"

"On grounds that Raynsford is a peer of the realm," Coghill replied, each word dropping like a stone. "Aristocracy does not answer to the same laws as the rest of us. Not in practice. Not in this city."

Barnes rose to his feet, pacing before the desk like a predator held back by chains.

"So that is it," he spat. "A murderer walks free because he has a title. Because his coffers are full and his connections deep. His son nearly hanged for crimes he engineered. And we must simply look away?"

Coghill looked down at his hands. "Those were the Mayor's orders. The investigation into Lord Raynsford is closed. Permanently."

Dickman slammed his palm on the desk, the lantern flame leaping in shock. "You can't expect us to stand by while that man walks the streets without consequence."

"I do not *expect* it," Coghill replied, voice suddenly raw. "I *pray* for it. Because if you do not—if you continue this pursuit—you will find yourselves stripped of your commissions. Or worse."

The room darkened further as clouds swallowed the last meagre light filtering through the window.

Barnes stopped pacing and stared into the shadowed corner of the room, jaw tight as a vise. He understood now, with awful clarity, why the city felt perpetually choked by fog.

Some fogs were not made of weather.

Some were engineered by men in high places.

He turned back to Coghill, eyes burning. "There is always one rule for the wealthy and another for everyone else."

Coghill met his gaze. "Yes. And you of all men know how dangerous it is to test that rule."

Barnes exhaled slowly—a long, simmering breath that trembled with rage.

"I always suspected," he said coldly, "that the aristocracy was a disease running through London. I see now I underestimated the infection."

Dickman put a steady hand on his partner's shoulder. "Barnes..."

But Barnes did not soften.

"There is only one thing left to do," he said, voice ringing in the dim office like a quiet vow. "Arrest Lord Horace Raynsford."

Coghill shut his eyes as if pained. "You do that," he whispered, "and it will be the end of you."

Barnes stepped closer to the desk, shadows coiling at his feet.

"Better a ruined man," he said, "than a silent one."

The lantern flickered—and for a moment, in its wavering light, Barnes looked less like a policeman and more like a revenant risen to bring judgement.

THE STATION HOUSE had settled into its grey morning hush, the kind that creeps in after a night of chaos and clings to the rafters like damp fog. The gas lamps hissed faintly along the corridor walls, their weak glow doing little to banish the gloom.

Detectives Barnes and Dickman stood in the Chief Inspector's office, the door shut firmly behind them. Coghill had dismissed them with a grave expression and a weary wave of his hand, leaving the two men alone in the dim, wood-paneled chamber that smelled of ink, pipe smoke, and rising dread.

Barnes scrubbed a hand over his face, exhaling through his teeth.

"Well," he muttered, "that was a far cry from uneventful."

Dickman let out a sigh that seemed to deflate him. "To think... Thaddeus Priest—an innocent man—nearly swung because of those two fools."

"And because of his father," Barnes added tightly. "Let us not forget *that* piece of the puzzle."

Dickman nodded grimly, lowering himself into one of the chairs. "Lord Horace Raynsford," he said the name softly, as though it fouled his mouth. "A man with influence, money, and no conscience to speak of."

Barnes paced before the window where the morning fog smeared the glass like pale fingers. "Did you hear him? Every word dripping with venom, as if his own son were no more than a pawn on a chess-board. And the gall of the man—*admitting* he orchestrated the arrest. As though the law serves at his pleasure."

Dickman's jaw worked in restrained fury. "He believes himself untouchable. Men like him always do."

Barnes turned sharply, eyes alight with resolve. "Then we shall touch him."

Dickman blinked. "Come again?"

"You heard me." Barnes planted his palms on the Chief's desk, leaning over it as though bracing himself against the weight of what must come. "If Thaddeus Priest spoke true—and I believe he did—then Lord Raynsford is complicit in conspiracy, obstruction, perjury, and God knows what else. Possibly worse."

"Hiring a murderer," Dickman murmured, a chill crawling beneath his collar.

Barnes nodded once. "Hiring Victor Jenkins. A man whose very shadow unsettles the soul."

Silence swelled for a long moment, heavy as churchyard earth.

Then Dickman straightened, bitterness sharpening his voice. "We investigate Raynsford, Barnes, and we'll be up against power, Parliament friends, old money. He will crush us if he learns of it."

Barnes gave a thin, wolfish smile. "Then he must not learn of it. Not until we have enough evidence to bring down the whole rotten edifice around him."

Dickman stared, then slowly returned the smile, though his was tinged with dread.

"By God, Barnes... you mean to challenge one of the most influential men in England."

"Aye." Barnes retrieved his notebook, flipping it open with decisive fingers. "And I'll not stand idle while he sacrifices his own son on the altar of ambition."

He snapped the book shut.

Dickman rose from his chair. "And if Raynsford tries to interfere?"

Barnes's eyes darkened, the fog-bound light catching him like a figure chiseled from stone.

"Then I swear upon my badge, *he'll learn that the law has sharper teeth than he imagines.*"

The two men exchanged a solemn nod—an unspoken pact forged in shadow. Outside, the fog thickened along Whitechapel's streets, as though the city itself were holding its breath.

They stepped out of the office together, their boots echoing down the corridor like the tolling of a distant and inevitable bell.

# EPILOGUE

A hush lay over Raynsford Manor, the kind of hush that seemed less born of quiet and more of expectation—like the house itself leaned forward to hear what would be spoken next. The storm that had battered the windows days before had long since passed, leaving the estate wrapped in a damp, heavy calm.

Judith Raynsford stood at the foot of the grand staircase, one hand lightly resting upon the banister, though her face showed no weariness. Instead, her eyes gleamed with purpose—the sharp, hard brilliance of a woman long pushed into shadows now stepping fully into the firelight.

Jackson approached cautiously, hat in hand. He had seen Judith unsettled. He had seen her anguished. But this—this composed, cold determination—unsettled *him* in ways few things ever had.

"Madam," he said carefully, "is... is His Lordship still in the study?"

"Yes," Judith replied, voice soft as velvet and twice as dark. "The laudanum should keep him quiet for another hour. He is snoring like a great boar in a mud wallow."

Jackson swallowed. "And after, Madam? What would you have done next? The detectives—well, it seems they cannot touch him. Not legally, leastwise."

Judith smiled then. Slowly. Beautifully. Terrifyingly.

"That, Jackson," she said, "is precisely what I wished to discuss with you."

She took a step closer, her expression shrouded not in madness, but in cold, crystalline clarity.

"I have been thinking," she murmured, "that perhaps Horace might benefit from a very long nap." Judith mounted the stairs and Jackson followed.

Jackson blinked in alarm. "A nap, Madam?"

"Yes." She lifted her chin, eyes glittering. "A very, *very* long nap. Years long. Decades, if possible. Long enough that he never again lifts a finger against Thaddeus. Long enough that whatever wickedness he carries in his heart has no opportunity to seep into the world."

Jackson opened his mouth, closed it, then opened it again.

"Madam... surely you do not mean—?"

"I mean," she interrupted gently, "that the man is a danger. To his son. To this household. To anyone unfortunate enough to cross his path. And if the law refuses to bind him..." Her gaze darkened. "Then *we* must."

Jackson shifted uneasily, though his loyalty held him steady. "There are... substances, Madam. Medicines one might procure from certain apothecaries. They can keep a man drowsy for days at a time. Weeks even. But for years—?"

Judith tilted her head, her voice a whisper steeped in ice.

"There must be something, Jackson. Some herb, some tonic, some tincture that makes a man... quiet."

Jackson exhaled slowly.

"There are... ways, Madam. Careful dosing. Enough to keep a man subdued, compliant, numb to the world. But it is not without risk."

Judith's lips curved—not cruelly, but with the certainty of a woman who has made peace with the cost.

"Risk is a luxury I gladly accept, if it spares my son."

She stepped past him toward the dimly lit corridor, her silhouette tall and unyielding.

"Horace Raynsford has ruled this house like a tyrant," she said softly. "But no longer. I will not allow him to harm Thaddeus again. Not in body, nor in spirit."

Jackson nodded once, solemnly. "Shall I... begin inquiries, Madam?"

"Yes," she answered. "Find what we need. Quietly. Thoroughly."

She paused at the study door, listening to the deep, senseless snoring within.

"And Jackson?"

"Yes, Madam?"

Her voice dropped to a velvet whisper.

"Let us ensure that His Lordship's sleep becomes the most peaceful—"

her eyes flashed,

"—and most permanent—gift we shall ever bestow."

Jackson bowed his head.

"As you wish, Lady Raynsford."

And in the heavy silence that followed, the house itself seemed to exhale—as though it, too, sensed the long-awaited end of Horace Raynsford's reign.

# Acknowledgments

I would like to thank my husband, Tommy Trent. He has been my greatest supporter and has encouraged me every step of the way. He has listened to me bounce around ideas, enthusiastically expound on plot points, and talk about the characters as if they are real. And he has gone along with every part of it. Thank you love, for being there for me.

# ABOUT THE AUTHOR

Photo © 2020 Dark Muse Press

Robin Trent is a novelist of Victorian fantasy and gothic mystery, weaving atmospheric tales where shadows whisper and magic lingers at the edges of the known world. With a passion for historical detail and a flair for the uncanny, Robin creates stories filled with richly drawn characters, intricate plots, and haunting emotional depth. When not crafting darkly enchanting fiction, Robin can be found exploring folklore, studying antique ephemera, or dreaming up new worlds where beauty and darkness intertwine. For more information, visit www.darkmusepress.org.

# AUTHOR'S NOTE

Thank you for spending time within these pages. If you enjoyed the story, I would be deeply grateful if you left a review on Amazon, Apple Books, Kobo, Goodreads, or at my website:

**www.darkmusepress.org**

Your words help other readers find the tale—and every review helps keep stories like this alive.

# OTHER WORKS BY ROBIN TRENT

THE GILDED FAERY CHRONICLES SERIES:
Moonshine (Book 1)

VICTORIAN GOTHIC SERIES:
Theater of Spirits (Book 1)

www.ingramcontent.com/pod-product-compliance
Lightning Source LLC
LaVergne TN
LVHW041057080826
845145LV00007B/1606

* 9 7 8 1 7 3 4 9 2 3 8 7 2 *